# A HOLLYWOOD AFFAIR

A FAKE-RELATIONSHIP CELEBRITY ROMANCE

MOLLY MIRREN

WWW.MOLLYMIRREN.COM

*For my writer friends. You are my constant inspiration.*
*I want to be you when I grow up.*

# ALSO BY MOLLY MIRREN

*To Each Her Own* (A contemporary, standalone romance)

*The B. E. Ware Trilogy: A Paranormal Romance Boxed Set*

# 1

Grant Cammish's agent was baying for blood. Without a word of greeting, Jessica Zimmerman hurled the latest issue of *People* down in front of him on the glass-top conference table. On landing, it caused a rude draft of air.

Lovely. He was in trouble again.

A small inset photo of him smirked from the magazine's cover before Jessica flipped to an article titled "Why Is Grant Cammish the Celebrity Everyone Loves to Hate?"

Ouch. That bothered him, and it took some effort not to let the two women in the room know that. They were likely already preparing damage control. He kept his face neutral, his go-to expression for anything awkward or unpleasant. Or infuriating.

"This is what we're up against," said Jessica, indicating the article with a jerk of her chin. "This"—she paused and stabbed her finger at the glossy page for emphasis—"on the heels of that one from *EW* a few weeks ago about you being a toxic bachelor."

Grant was sitting at one of the dozen or so ultramodern

—and mostly vacant—chairs surrounding the table in the spacious conference room, yet Jessica hovered over him. Her shiny black hair, which matched the chairs, was straight and cut into a severe bob that came to points next to her tight mouth. It swayed as if all one unit.

In the six years since she'd become his agent, it seemed everything about her had got pointier. Or perhaps "sharp" was a better descriptor. That was why he'd hired her: she was sharp, focused, and one hell of an agent. Good thing too, since, admittedly, Grant had never been one of her easier clients. And she was one of the few people who didn't curry favor and then rip him apart behind his back. Well, that he knew of.

She arched a razorlike dark brow—no small accomplishment, considering the amount of Botox in her forehead—but he didn't respond to her statement. He knew he was about to get an earful no matter what he might say. Better to just wait and keep mum.

Cynthia Ramirez, his PR rep, was also there, and he knew she wouldn't remain silent. As if gleaning his thoughts, she said in a deadpan tone, "Grant." She too had black hair, but it was long and pulled back into a neat bun at the nape of her neck. She also wore thin, stylish wire-rimmed glasses.

"Cynthia," he echoed in the same tone.

She shook her head in disapproval and gave him a stern stare, which, oddly enough, he found rather attractive. He'd thought more than once about asking her out, but hadn't. Better to keep things professional. He'd never want to offend her or be inappropriate.

She drew in a breath as if to say more, but Jessica beat her to it.

To his surprise, Jessica didn't launch into him about the

article. Instead she said, "I spoke with Leonard Shane a few minutes ago."

Grant had the urge to sit up straighter, but he didn't want his eagerness to show. He remained in his half-bored posture, but it took effort.

Both Jessica and Cynthia now stared at him expectantly, so he said, "I hope Leonard is well." He knew it wasn't the sort of response Jessica wanted, but something contrary in him kept him from placating her.

"Don't you look down your perfect man-nose at me and pretend indifference," Jessica snapped. "We both know you'd gnaw off your right arm for that part."

"I beg to differ," he said with languid insolence. "I'm quite partial to my right arm."

Jessica crossed her arms over her chest and leaned her hip against the table.

He'd done it now. She was going to sweat him out, make him beg her to tell him what Leonard had said.

Grant glanced at Cynthia, who was sitting across from him. She shook her head only slightly, but the message was clear: Don't trifle with Jessica. She is *not* in the mood.

"Go on, then," he said with a rolling motion of his hand. "What did he say?" Truth be told, Grant wasn't indifferent at all. He wanted that role in Shane's movie more than he'd ever wanted any role in his life.

"He who?" Jessica said with feigned ignorance.

Grant resisted the urge to shout and was extremely polite when he spoke. "Leonard Shane. What did he say?"

"His children are doing well. Beckett is in her first year of college."

"Lovely," said Grant, calling on every ounce of patience his body could produce. "Anything else?"

She waited a long beat before saying, "He's interested."

"How interested?" said Grant, fighting not to show his elation.

She scrutinized him for a second before saying, "Very."

He couldn't help the twitching of his mouth, which wanted to turn into a triumphant smile.

She held up a finger. "But..."

He should have seen that coming. "But?"

"He's leery of your superior attitude toward Americans."

"Well, I am English," Grant couldn't resist saying, although he wasn't serious in the slightest.

Now she was pointing her finger at him. "That's not funny. Aside from the problem that you're as English as Queen Elizabeth, your comment about how Americans are idiots could cost you this role."

"That comment was taken out of context. I was referring to an *article* I read. *I* didn't call Americans idiots. The article did." He loved Americans. There were some things he found ridiculous about America, but he had nothing but love for the country and people as a whole. If only they weren't so easy to *offend*.

"And the tasteless comments about how you're only into acting for the money."

That wasn't fair, either. All he'd said was the money in acting was good, and what bloke wouldn't choose first class over economy if given the choice, especially if he were over six feet tall? Anyone who said they were in it *just* for the art and craft of it was lying. And somehow that had got turned into he was a shallow arsehole who only cared about money. He'd just been honest, but apparently that made him unlikable. All he said in his defense now, though, was "I work quite hard for that money."

For the first time, Jessica's demeanor softened. "I know you do, honey. 'Hard' is an understatement." The softness disappeared when she added, "But no one cares about that. It's not fair, but people *want* you to trip and fall. They're jealous because you're too gorgeous to also be smart, extremely talented, and totally dedicated to your craft. After all, there has to be *something* flawed about you, and if people can't find something, they'll create it to even the playing field."

He could feel his neck getting hot as his ire rose. He had many flaws, actually, but lack of talent and a dedicated work ethic weren't among them. He had no social life—really, no life at all—because of his work. He put every waking hour and breath into it.

"Part of the issue," Jessica went on, "is that for every good thing you do, you undo it with your flippant comments or actions—and the fact that you never deign to make friends with any of your colleagues. You're aloof and stand-offish on set, and that doesn't win you any support. All it does is invite malicious gossip."

He pulled his shoulders back, feeling defensive. "Gossip that isn't true."

"Doesn't matter."

"Fucking hell," he muttered. He didn't show his anger often, but this was galling. He didn't have *time* to befriend any of his colleagues. What a whingeing lot they were. His only crime was keeping to himself, mainly because he was usually knackered. Five minutes to rest in his caravan instead of socializing round the craft services table was heaven, but somehow that made him Hollywood's biggest wanker.

"Facts don't matter in this industry," said Cynthia. "Spin does. You should know that by now."

He did, all too well, but it was damned unfair.

Cynthia pointed to the incriminating article on the table.

"This is just one of many that lists all your transgressions: the extremely younger women—"

"It was just one, and you know full well Lexi lied to me about her age. And even at that, she was still legal—"

"—bragging about your penis size on *Conan*—"

"Twelve years ago! I was only twenty when I said that, and I don't deny I was a tosser back then."

"—the fat-shaming of plus-size models—"

"I never said any of that! It was all complete fabrication." Well, most of it he hadn't. He might have said something to the effect that "plus size" was a euphemism for "fat," and there was no getting round it. But he'd not said "fat" was necessarily a bad thing, although yes, he could see now how one might construe he'd meant it was.

Again, he'd barely been out of his teens, a shallow idiot. He was thirty-two now. He liked to think he'd matured and grown as a man since then.

He was beginning to lose his bluster, though. The evidence kept mounting against him.

"The list goes on and on," Cynthia said. More ominously she added, "Your Q Score has fallen a couple more points."

Q Score had been invented back in the '60s to evaluate the popularity and recognition of brands, celebrities, athletes, et cetera. He didn't care about some ancient marketing firm's popularity rating of him, but it was all Cynthia could talk about.

"So what you're really saying," he said to Jessica and ignoring Cynthia's comment, "is that I don't stand a chance of portraying Captain Justice."

"Not necessarily. They are still in the very early stages of production. They haven't begun casting yet. Leo said he liked the looks of you physically, that you're on his shortlist, but that you're not exactly the poster boy for an American comic book superhero. He did say you'd make a great James Bond, though."

Great. The one role he didn't want. He could do that in his sleep. To both women he said, "How do we get me to the top of the shortlist, then?"

"Well," said Jessica, "there might be a way to repair your reputation quickly enough that your past flubs will be forgotten. Or mostly forgotten," she added dryly.

"Good. Then do it."

She and Cynthia shared a look, one that made him uneasy.

"What?" he asked warily.

Jessica assessed him with narrow eyes, as if weighing how he was going to react.

"Carry on," he said with another rolling motion of his hand. "You've already tossed it out there. What are you proposing?"

"Piper Torres."

He didn't understand and tilted an ear toward her. "Beg your pardon?"

"Start dating Piper Torres. At least until you get the Captain Justice role."

"I don't understand."

"She's America's sweetheart," said Cynthia. "An Emmy Award–winning actor. Her career took a hit, though, when she got fired from her sitcom."

Jessica snorted. "Understatement."

It *was* an understatement. Grant knew some of the story. Ms. Torres had been sacked for gaining weight, although the show reps denied that was the reason. It had caused a maelstrom from her legion of fans, but it hadn't got her her job back—or got her a job anywhere else.

Cynthia gave a smile that was both fond and sad. "Our

PR firm reps her, too. She really is a sweetheart. Very genuine and just a delightful person. Great Q Score. But, like I said, her career is going nowhere. She's pushing thirty, and if we can't give her career a shot in the arm soon, she's done for. You would be good for her."

He was about to ask how he would be good for her, but Jessica spoke before he could get it out. "I'm thinking date her three or four months, tops," she said. "Probably until you head to New Zealand for the location shoots of *Battle*. Any relationship"—she did air quotes—"with her would die a natural death because of the long-distance thing."

Grant frowned. "Forgive me if I'm being thick, but are you saying you want us to have a fake relationship?"

"Yes," said Jessica, her gaze piercing him. "That's exactly what we're saying."

"You're mad."

"Just consider it," said Jessica.

He stood and grabbed his suit jacket from the back of his chair. "Good day, ladies," he said brusquely, not in earnest at all.

Jessica grabbed his arm. "Hold on a minute. Hear us out."

He looked down at her. "No."

"Grant." It was Cynthia, in that flat *you're being a prat* tone she so often used.

But *he* wasn't the one being a prat. *They* were. "No," he said again. "Forget it."

That earned him an indignant glare and stiff shoulders from Cynthia. "Is it because she gained the weight?"

He was offended she could think him so yeasty and glared back. "No, it isn't, so kindly lower your hackles." In fact, he remembered thinking at the time that Ms. Torres had looked better with a bit more heft to her bones. And also that she was a sugary-sweet piece of fluff. She had a purse dog, for God's sake. Although he had to admit the little bugger was cute.

"Then why won't you at least hear us out?" asked Cynthia.

See again purse dog and sugary-sweet piece of fluff. He knew enough not to say that, though. "Because I don't have time to worry about someone else's tanking career."

Jessica wouldn't let go of his arm. "It's not just Piper's career that's tanking. A couple more stinkers like your last two movies, and you could be in the same boat as she is. And you know how *Battle* is. Just because you're a main character doesn't mean you won't get written off."

She was referring to his Netflix fantasy series, *Battle of Fortunes*. He'd been part of the cast since its inception five years ago. "Nonsense. Rolf is essential to the plotline."

"So was Heron, and it didn't stop them from writing him off and putting Dominick Jackson out of a job."

She had a point, but he said, "Dominick was a lazy arse, and Ezra didn't like him. Ezra likes me." Ezra Vidmar was the show's auteur director.

"Still," Jessica said with a wise expression, "you know as well as I do that there are no guarantees in this business. You're not immune to obscurity."

It irked him that she was, yet again, right. "Be that as it may, I'll take my chances." He headed for the door.

Jessica's voice rose to an imperious volume. "We're talking about *Captain Justice* here. It's going to be the biggest and most respected franchise since *Batman*."

He stopped, his hand on the long, polished brass handle of the glass conference room door. The whole office was like a department store window, all glass and modern decor that provided no privacy.

Furtive glances of the office staff toward him made him feel edgy, as if he were sat alone at the dining hall table or had been sent to the headmaster's office—a phantom feeling that made itself known on occasion, no matter how much time separated him from his boarding school days. He had to remind himself he'd done nothing wrong. In fact, he was apparently the only person here with any morals.

Cynthia's voice broke through the tension in the room. "*Captain Justice* would catapult you into the upper echelon of Hollywood's elite."

He didn't want that to matter, but it did. He wanted to be the hero for once—a hero he'd worshipped as a lad—instead of the villain. More than that, he wanted to prove he could be a box office hit. And he wanted a role his mum would be proud of—one that wasn't constantly exposing his bum.

Cynthia continued quietly, "And Piper would be the *perfect* balance to your aloofness and general doucheyness."

Grant was stung but kept his expression droll. Cynthia was usually the nice one. "Lovely," he said. "Good to know you hold me in such high esteem."

"Sorry." She pushed her glasses, which had slid a centimeter down her nose, back up. "But you know what I mean. Your *perceived* aloofness and doucheyness. Being with her will make you seem more approachable, more human."

Human? That was a new one. Besides which, he'd not been aware he was lacking in humanity.

"More *American*," Jessica interjected. "She's a down-to-earth Texas girl, and she's Latina, too, which will also give you a boost with people of color."

He wanted to roll his eyes. Americans were as obsessed with race and ethnicity as the British were with class. Not that it wasn't justified. He was all for improving things on both sides of the pond.

"She's the girl next door, the girl guys want to hang out with and the girl women want to be besties with," Cynthia extolled. "She seems accessible, unintimidating, the kind of girl you could play darts with at the neighborhood bar, maybe have a few mugs of beer with. She's funny and sweet, personable. She also has a huge, rabidly loyal fan base behind her."

He didn't want to show any interest, but he'd do just about anything to win that Captain Justice role. "And the advantage to her?"

"You have a rare kind of rapport with Ezra. You can put in a good word for her for the role of Heledd."

He laughed. "You can't be serious. Her? As Heledd?" From the few times he'd seen her on TV or in photos, the rather truncated yet spunky Piper Torres did not conjure an image of a Welsh warrior princess. She conjured the word "adorable," as in bunny rabbits and kittens.

Cynthia gave a single nod. "She's very serious. Piper wants to branch out, try something new. The role of Heledd would showcase her dramatic talents, something she never got to do when she was on the sitcom. She wants to reinvent herself into a more versatile actor. She's tired of being pigeonholed." She gave him a wry look, knowing he could relate to that.

He exhaled, unable to believe he was pondering this for even a second. But no. He wouldn't do it. "Sorry," he said, shaking his head. "I understand what you're saying, but I'm not keen on the idea of someone being coerced to date me. If you really think it will help my image, I'll find my own"—he cast about for a proper word—"companion."

Jessica's expression was derisive. "Because you've been so good at that in the past."

"I've learned from my mistakes."

"Oh, and what's that? Not to date anymore, period?"

That was closer to the truth than he wanted to admit. It was just easier not to open himself up to the possible media leaks. And the hurt.

His answer to Jessica was to open the door, making a show of leaving.

"It's your dream role, Grant. It's Captain Justice."

That stopped him in his tracks. "Bloody hell," he muttered, his back to her.

Jessica cackled in triumph. "I'll make the call to her agent."

# 2

Piper checked her appearance in the mirror of the ritzy powder room that belonged to her agent, William Das. She felt jittery, as if she'd just drunk fifteen espressos.

"I can do this. Right, Chewie?"

On hearing his name, Chewie poked his head out of the vintage converted pet carrier/Louis Vuitton handbag she'd set on the vanity—his favorite of all her handbags—and watched her with his humanlike, inquisitive dark eyes. He was a tan Brussels Griffon (mostly) that she'd rescued from a shelter. He looked exactly like Chewbacca from *Star Wars*, if Chewbacca had weighed only eight pounds and been a purse dog.

And, yes, the whole purse-dog thing was a cliché, but she didn't care. Chewie had separation anxiety and was devastated anytime Piper left him at home alone, so, as much as possible, she tried not to do that. He'd inadvertently become as much a part of her brand as her famous—or infamous, depending on how you looked at it—curvy figure.

"I mean really," she said, "it's just a job. It's just another role." She looked at Chewie and raised her eyebrows. "Piece of cake."

Chewie laid his head down on his cute little furry tan paws—now they both stuck out of the purse—and sighed as if he did *not* agree.

She couldn't blame him. As roles went, being some British snob's fake significant other was one of the more pathetic ones she'd had to play in her career. How far she'd fallen: Emmy-winning sitcom star to has-been in a little over two years. Two years might not sound like long, but in showbiz and the social media age, two years without a job or even any prospects were an eon.

No one wanted to hire an actress who'd caused a shit-storm for her employers, a PR nightmare, no matter how big her fan base. The irony? She wasn't even *that* curvy anymore. Maybe that was the problem. She wasn't a waif, but she wasn't plus-size enough, either. Producers and casting agents didn't know where to put her.

She turned sideways to check out her body's profile in the mirror. She'd lost twenty pounds but still had more to go if she wanted to get back to waifdom. Trouble was, she didn't. Life was too short to purposely starve and make herself miserable.

But she didn't want her career to be over, either.

Yes, she looked great (lack of waifdom aside). Healthy. Voluptuous. It was her go-to mantra when self-doubt tried to settle in. But she was also a realist. For one thing, she was lacking way too much in the height department to be super-model caliber, which was the type of woman Grant Cammish had been seen with in the past. Would people even buy that he would date her? Then there were the recent rumors that, since he hadn't been seen with a woman in a while, he might be into men. It seemed he had both ends of the gossip spectrum covered: womanizer and/or gay.

She just hoped for both their sakes he was a decent actor even with his pretty face, because it wasn't his acting skills people noticed on *Battle*. She'd watched that scene where he'd almost gone full frontal, and just the memory of it made her want to fan herself.

A sharp knock at the door startled Chewie, and his short, pointy ears went on high alert.

"Piper? They're here," said William in his faint Indian accent, his *r*'s soft and round, his cadence melodious. She loved that. She was a connoisseur of accents, had an ear for them, and William's was one of the most pleasing. "Their car just drove up."

Her heart started to beat faster. "Okay. Coming." She drew in a calming breath like she'd always done before a big performance and watched her boobs go up and down. That was one advantage to having curves. She had killer cleavage, and she was showing it off in a red wrap dress that minimized her waist and looked great with her brown complexion and long, dark hair.

She could do this. If Grant could get her in with Ezra Vidmar, it would be worth the little chunk of her soul this was costing her. And, after all, Grant was selling a chunk of his soul too. At least she wasn't the only one. She just hoped his reputation for being a jerk had been exaggerated. If it wasn't, the next few months would seem like an eternity.

She shoved away the icky feeling that kept gripping her insides and blew out a puff of air. Yeah. Piece of cake.

WILLIAM MOTIONED for Piper to come over to the pristine white sofa with colorful pillows where he was sitting. "Sit here," he said, patting the spot beside him. "Look as if you are completely at ease."

"I am at ease," she fibbed. Her black Sophia Webster strappy sandals with the butterflies on the high heels clicked on the polished white marble floor of the foyer as she walked across it. Once she sat on the sofa, she took Chewie out of her purse and put him on her lap.

To William's credit, he didn't blink an eye at having the dog on his flawless furniture. Then again, he knew she kept Chewie squeaky clean, and he knew Chewie had very good manners. "Of course you are at ease," William said. "And remember, you are the one who has won an Emmy, not Cammish."

She smiled. William had always stuck by her, even when she'd been at her heaviest. He'd never fat-shamed her or simply dumped her as other agents would have. He'd never stopped believing in her, even in the darkest days, when she'd stopped believing in herself. She would always love him for that alone.

The doorbell rang.

William, trim but not tall, stood and tugged at the bottom of his dapper gray suit jacket to straighten it, then went to open the door. A second later, he was gesturing for Grant Cammish and his agent, Jessica Zimmerman, to come in. Jessica sailed in first, head high, straight black bob bouncing against her chin.

Piper knew of Jessica Zimmerman. Everyone did. She was known as a shark in the talent business.

Grant, a tall white guy in his early thirties, sauntered in behind her. When he turned toward Piper, she felt a sudden swoosh deep in her belly and a surge in her heart rate.

He wasn't just gorgeous with a capital G. He was GORGEOUS in all shouty caps.

After the greetings were out of the way, William said, "After you," and, with a sweep of his arm, indicated that both Jessica and Grant should join him and Piper in the living room.

Piper pasted a pleasant smile on her face and tried not to make a complete fangirl of herself. It wasn't like she hadn't been around a hot actor before. They were a dime a dozen in LA. She'd also seen many pics of Grant, not to mention the fact that she'd been binge-watching *Battle of Fortunes* recently as research for the role she wanted on the show. In short, she should be desensitized to him.

Grant, however, was a level above. Like, he was the 102nd-floor observation deck of the Empire State Building, while all the others were the 86th. On paper, he would sound like a basic white hero: dark, almost black hair, striking light-blue eyes, perfect facial features complete with slightly clefted chin and square jaw, taller than average height, muscular build—pretty much the traits of every duke in every historical romance ever. Except that his muscles strained the fabric of his custom-made navy suit (she'd read he bought all his suits on Savile Row in London) in a way that reminded her more of a well-dressed warrior than a duke. No wonder he'd been cast as a barbaric mercenary on his show. He had *presence*, and Piper was awestruck.

Breath stolen? Check.

Pulse quickening? Check.

Uterus opening up for business? Check.

Yet once she was past these initial involuntary responses of her body, she felt oddly more at ease. He was so beautiful it was surreal. The notion they would ever date each other was laughable, and she had to refrain from rolling her eyes.

Remembering etiquette, she gently set Chewie on the sofa, then stood and held out her hand.

Grant took it lightly in his and locked eyes with her, and the faint scent of his aftershave tantalized her.

She thought for a second he might kiss the back of her hand in the old-fashioned way, and her belly swooshed again.

No kiss, though. Just a polite shake—an I'm-really-strong-and-don't-want-to-press-too-hard-and-hurt-you handshake. "A pleasure, Ms. Torres," he said in a rich, British-accented baritone that was as pristine as William's sofa. It resonated in the room, even though he'd spoken quietly. His sculpted, sensuous lips curved into a polite smile, but no warmth reached his eyes. They weren't cold either, though—just aloof.

"Likewise," Piper said. "And, please, call me Piper."

His response was a quick tightening of his mouth, and a nod before letting her hand go. He didn't reciprocate and tell her to call him Grant.

Rude, she thought, disappointed. But then she told herself to stop judging him on two seconds of interaction. She was trying not to let all the things she'd read about him influence her opinion of him.

They sat across from each other: she was back on the sofa, putting Chewie on her lap again, and Grant was across the coffee table on a sofa identical to hers. A little warmth did come into Grant's gaze when they landed on Chewie, as if her adorable dog, who was wagging his tail and sniffing the air with uncertainty at all these strangers, made Grant want to smile. That instantly made Piper feel a tad better about him.

Their agents sat down too, Jessica sitting next to Grant, William sitting next to Piper.

"Well," said Jessica in a hard-edged voice, "no use beating around the bush. Let's get down to business." She pulled a sheaf of papers out of the briefcase she'd brought with her. Looking at Piper, she said, "As William should have told you, we have a series of premieres and charity functions for you two to make appearances at together, but first you have to make it look real. To keep things as close to the truth as possible, if anyone asks, you two met here at William's house at a cocktail party. You couldn't keep your eyes off each other, yada, yada, yada."

She turned to Grant. "I think it's a good idea for you to take Piper home tonight. Try to give her a very public kiss on her doorstep. Cynthia has arranged for TMZ to receive an anonymous tip that you guys are becoming involved." To Piper she said, "You still live in that bungalow in Sunset Square, right?"

Piper raised her eyebrows.

Jessica responded with a flick of her wrist. "Don't look surprised. You're about to start dating Grant. *He's* my business, so that makes *you* my business, too."

That was annoying, but it wasn't like Piper could say anything. William had given her a dossier on Grant, too.

Grant looked bored. Apparently having his whole love life mapped out for the next few months was beneath his interest.

Jessica continued. "After you kiss—and make it look passionate—then invite him in, Piper. You two can use the time to try to get to know each other, but make sure your curtains are shut. We don't want any paparazzi photos of you two looking awkward around each other or anything less than totally enamored of one another. Hopefully they'll assume you're having sex. Got it?"

Piper nodded, although the icky feeling was rearing its

ugly head again. She reminded herself they weren't *really* going to have sex.

Grant still looked bored.

"Grant?" said Jessica. "Are you listening?"

"I am utterly spellbound."

Jessica's mouth tightened with disapproval. "Then what did I just say?"

"I'm to take Ms., er, Piper home and ravish her on the front doorstep, and then we'll go in for a pleasant chat, slash, faux shag." He said this as if he'd just received instructions on how to run the dishwasher.

Appearing satisfied they both understood their roles, Jessica added, "You should stay the night, Grant, since you live so far from each other. It will only support what we're trying to accomplish."

Grant didn't reply, but something about the set of his jaw made Piper think he didn't like any of this.

Jessica went on to outline how often they should be seen in public doing things like eating lunch and dinner out (at least twice a week), going to the grocery store (at least once a week), visiting IKEA (once or twice during the whole affair, because shopping at IKEA would make them look in touch with regular people), and posting about each other on Instagram and other social media. In short, they would lead a very cozy, typical American life as a couple—the constant stalking by the paparazzi and the attention they would draw wherever they went notwithstanding—and it would last around three or four months, until Grant left for New Zealand.

William, who'd been fairly quiet during the whole conversation because he'd already outlined the terms of the contract and nondisclosure agreement with Piper earlier, said, "I wonder what they'll call you."

"Pardon?" said Grant.

"What the media will call you."

"Oh," said Piper, "you mean like 'Bennifer' or 'Brangelina'?"

"Yes," William replied, with a mischievous gleam in his eye. "Unfortunately, your names merged together either spell 'Griper' or 'Prant' or 'Piperant.'"

A snort-laugh escaped Piper. "Sounds like a new ant species or someone who's got stomach issues."

Jessica scowled at her, but when Piper's gaze met Grant's, she was gratified to see crinkles appear at the corners of his eyes and an amused twitch of his mouth, as if he agreed that all of this was pretty weird and ridiculous. In the next instant, though, he was back to being Mr. Aloof. "I doubt we've much say in the matter," he said. "I'm sure the tabloids will call us whatever they choose."

Jessica screwed up her face in distaste. "God, I hope it's not 'Griper.' That would be a disaster."

Piper picked up Chewie and kissed his furry little head to keep from laughing again.

"Of course," Jessica went on, "it's up to you two to even garner enough interest to earn a portmanteau."

*Portmanteau?* What was that? Piper supposed it had something to do with the joining of names.

"It's nothing to make light of," Jessica told William. "If the media comes up with a nickname for them, we will have succeeded beyond our wildest dreams."

"Of course," said William, although Piper didn't think he put "couple nickname" up there on his list of priorities. He then changed the subject and went over their terms of the contract, specifically how Grant would lobby and use his good relationship with the director of *Battle of Fortunes* to try to at least get Piper an audition.

Grant flashed his perfect white teeth in a quick smile. Well, *almost* perfect. His canines were about a sixteenth of an inch too long, giving him a vague vampire vibe.

Piper supposed his canines could be considered a flaw in his otherwise flawless male beauty, but they weren't. They, along with his strong, borderline too-large nose (keyword "borderline"), kept him from being too pretty, gave his face a rugged quality.

"You do realize that I'm not a miracle worker," said Grant.

Ah, that voice. It was like a good Ethiopian coffee, percolating and complex and so smooth that...she almost missed the insult in his statement. Had he just said "miracle worker"? Seriously?

"I can only put in a good word for her," he told William, apparently not feeling the daggers she was stabbing at him with her eyes. "It's ultimately up to Ezra whom he will or won't screen test or audition."

"I don't need a *miracle*," Piper said, getting fired up. He could take his rugged qualities and shove them up his *culo*. "All I want is a chance to get my foot in the door."

Jessica flicked her wrist again. "Ezra loves Grant. If Grant asks Ezra to let you audition as a favor, you'll get your chance." She raised a brow and gave Piper the once-over. "What you do with it is up to you." By the tone of her voice, Piper gathered Jessica was as skeptical as Grant that she'd get the part.

Now more than ever Piper wanted that part, if for no other reason than to wipe those identical looks of doubt off their faces. She'd had a lot of blows to her ego in the last two years, but the one thing she didn't falter in was her belief in her acting skills. She was good, and she wanted the chance to prove it. And not just in a role playing a Latina.

"Once you start hanging out on set with Grant, that will help your case, too," said Jessica. "Use your proximity to Ezra to impress him. If you can."

*If you can.* Yet another dig Piper hadn't missed. Geez. With allies like these, who needed enemies?

"Just get her in front of him," said William. "I am sure she will dazzle Ezra just like she does anyone who has ever been around her. It is likely Grant won't even have to say anything on her behalf."

She wished. William's faith in her was touching, but she would definitely need all the influence Grant could wield. The gossip was that Ezra already had Kristen Savage in mind for the part, and Piper had to admit that Kristen would make a great Welsh warrior princess, at least in the looks department. Her last name was an apt description. Piper would bet a right rib, though, that Kristen's Welsh accent would suck.

Piper, however, had been studying how the Welsh spoke English as if it were the key to world peace. Her affinity for accents was coming in handy, and she knew she could nail it. The Welsh accent was more singsongy than a straight English one like Grant's, more lyrical.

"Okay," said Jessica, bringing Piper back to the negotiations. "I think we're almost done. Now to some matters that might be sensitive." She leaned toward the coffee table and turned her contract to the next page. "Piper, as an incentive, we'd like it in the contract that you will continue to try to lose weight, and you will *not* gain back any weight whatsoever."

Piper couldn't believe what she was hearing. "Excuse me?"

"Sorry to be blunt, but it's important. Look at him." The tip of one blade of Jessica's black bob pointed to Grant whenever she inclined her head in his direction. "He's USDA—or should I say UK—Prime. If you gain any weight back, no one will believe he would be in a relationship with you. We're already pushing it as it is, considering the type of women he's dated in the past."

Grant's expression darkened, but Piper didn't know if it was because of the way Jessica talked about him as if he were an expensive cut of beef or if he was affronted on Piper's behalf. Probably the meat part, but she hoped it was for her.

For her own self, Piper was livid. It was one thing for *her* to have such doubts, but another thing entirely for someone else to have them—and say them out loud.

"You don't have to agree to that," said William.

"Of course I don't." She stared down Jessica. "Others have tried to dictate to me what my weight should be, and it didn't turn out so well for them." She was referring to the demise of *Nine's a Crowd* shortly after she'd been fired from it. The ratings had tanked because her fans had boycotted the show, which had caused the show's sponsors to pull out.

Jessica shrugged. "Fine. It's your career."

Piper pulled her shoulders back and sat ramrod straight. "Let me be clear, Ms. Zimmerman: I like how I look, and I'll maintain a healthy weight because it's healthy, not because it's some item in a contract."

The points of Jessica's bob seemed to stiffen, as if ready for battle. Before she could respond, though, Grant said, "Cross it out, Jessica, and let's be done with this." Then he spread his arms across the back of the sofa and bent his elbow to rest his head in one hand as if weary, which caused the fabric of his jacket sleeve to strain across his biceps.

Piper couldn't help but stare in fascination at the biceps.

She wondered if he was strong enough to lift her Prius. Seriously. It might be possible.

Jessica exhaled through her nose, pressing her lips together. "Fine," she said, and viciously marked out the offending words, wielding her black pen as if it were a machete.

The rest of the contract items, which included a nondisclosure agreement, were boilerplate (if that could be said for a contract outlining a fake relationship), and soon the meeting was over. They exchanged stiff goodbyes, and then it was time for Grant to take Piper home.

Great, Piper thought wryly. Let the show begin.

# 3

Grant walked next to Piper as they headed toward his beloved car, parked at the end of her agent's long driveway. He marveled at her surefooted gait in the sky-high stiletto heels she wore—they had giant butterflies on the backs of them, for God's sake—and was enchanted by the fact that she still only came up to about his chest height. It brought out a primitive instinct in him to protect her. Her faint floral scent tantalized him, too, and he had to resist the urge to sniff the air like her dog had done earlier during the meeting.

Dogs had the way of it, didn't they? One good sniff of the arse, and you knew whether to tell someone "Hullo" or "Sod off."

Why had he agreed to this? He didn't have time for a girlfriend, and now he was meant to carve time from his mad schedule to make room for a fake one, a proper stranger. He resented it. He might as well turn in his man card and put his cock in storage if it had come to this.

Maybe in another life though, one where he wasn't being forced into it, he'd not have begrudged getting to know Piper. Her long black hair was glorious, and her inviting brown eyes were fringed by thick, incredibly long lashes. A chap could easily get lost in those eyes and not feel any urgency to find his way out again.

She had lovely curves, too, and was particularly lush in the breast department. He hoped she kept them—the curves, that was. And the breasts, too. As long as a woman was at a healthy weight, curves were a bonus, in his opinion. A woman with too many sharp angles made for a dangerous —and treacherous—bedfellow.

Speaking of, his phone rang and Amanda Cho's number flashed across his screen. Bollocks. He didn't need this right now, but he'd been trying to get her to ring him for days. He had to take it.

"Hullo," he answered. "Please give me just a moment."

He and Piper had reached his car, and he quickly opened the passenger door for her and pulled the phone away from his mouth to say, "Sorry. Need to take this."

"Sure. No prob," she said, and he carefully shut the door.

Piper was nice, too, but not as saccharine or vapid as he'd expected. He liked that she'd put Jessica in her place during the meeting. But he didn't want Piper to overhear this call, so he walked round to the back of the car and leaned against the boot.

"Amanda," he said. "Thank you for calling back." He tried not to sound sarcastic, since she'd been ghosting him.

"I don't see the point of another conversation about this," she said, forgoing any pleasantries, "since I'm ninety-nine percent sure you aren't the father, but whatever."

He clenched his jaw, striving for forbearance. "Yet that dangling one percent is of great significance to me, isn't it?"

No doubt she was rolling her eyes. "We had sex twice, Grant."

"Last I checked, it only takes once to make a baby."

"I'm sure it's Fret's. Stop calling me."

*Fret.* Grant held back a scoff at the name.

Although he and Amanda had only gone on a few dates, not even long enough for the paps to get wind of their relationship, Grant had thought she was as enamored as he when he'd had to leave her seven months ago to do a short fan convention tour for *Battle*. However, he'd returned to find she'd moved on to some rock star, the illustrious Fret, and had probably been seeing him all along while she'd also been with Grant. She'd been on the pill but swore it had somehow failed.

Grant went on doggedly, "You must have doubts, Amanda, or you'd not have told me in the first place."

"I knew you'd have questions if you saw something about the birth on social media. I knew you'd do the math. That's the only reason I called and told you at all."

Scathing anger shot through him, but he said calmly, "All I want is proof. Do a paternity test. If it's not mine, you'll never hear from me again."

"Sorry." She didn't sound sorry at all. "You'll have to wait until the baby is born."

Anger still festering, he looked up at the night sky and drew in a deep breath. "But why? I've researched it. It's easy. All you have to do—"

"I said no. Stop bugging me about it."

"But you're being unreasonable. If it's mine, I want to be there for the birth. I—"

"Oh, my God! It's not yours. You're being ridiculous."

"Ridiculous?" He kept his tone low, but he couldn't keep the acidity from his voice. "No. Ridiculous is the fact that you won't get it sorted for sure because you're hoping Fred—"

"It's *Fret*."

"—will see the child after it's born and suddenly fall in love with it, even though he's dumped you and wants no part of being a father. You're afraid a paternity test in my favor will ruin any chance—"

"Fuck you, Grant." She ended the call.

He didn't bother trying to call back. He knew she wouldn't answer.

Trembling with rage, he drew in another breath, clamped down on his inconvenient emotions, and got in the car with Piper.

---

"GREAT CAR," Piper said to Grant. "What year is it?"

"'67," he answered without looking at her. His grudging tone and the tiny muscle flexing in his (of course) chiseled jaw told her he wasn't going to say more. Not that he'd been that chatty in their meeting with the agents, but ever since that obviously tense phone call just before he'd gotten in the car, he'd gone from aloof but mostly polite to not saying a word in the fifteen minutes they'd been driving.

"Corvette Stingray, right?" The black leather bucket seats were in mint condition, as was the silver exterior, and the leather and chrome on the dash and doors looked original. The very American classic sports car wasn't what she would have pictured someone so...well...British driving.

Her dad and brothers would have drooled over it. They also wouldn't have shut up talking about it if they owned it, but Grant was taciturn. A clipped "Yes" to answer her question was all he offered.

Okay, then. She could take a hint. No conversation.

Her purse sat in her lap, and Chewie's head was sticking

out of the top. She scratched him behind his ears and then under his chin for good measure and also to give her hands something to do.

Glancing at Grant's profile, she noticed a very slight deviation in the ridge of his nose before she made herself stare forward at the road in front of them. Maybe his nose had been broken sometime in the past. It didn't detract from his absurdly handsome looks, though. In fact, she found herself looking for flaws and being charmed when she actually found one. The bump, for lack of a better word, told her that he wasn't always so debonaire, that he wasn't above roughhousing or maybe playing a rough sport every now and then. Or at least he had in the past. Of course, it could also mean someone had punched him in the face for being a douche.

She wished he didn't smell so freaking divine. His aftershave or soap or whatever he used wasn't overpowering, but the confines of the car made it more pronounced. She was getting hints of peppermint, juniper, and sandalwood. The mixture was heady, like winter and evergreens.

Despite the lack of conversation, which she blamed on the phone call and didn't take personally, he had an undeniable magnetism.

*Don't fall for him, Piper*, she warned herself. It would obviously be one-sided and embarrassing if she did. People probably fell in love with him on a daily basis, and she was sure it meant nothing to him. She would *not* be one of the unrequited masses.

The GPS on his phone alerted that her house was coming up on the right, breaking into her thoughts. The kiss was happening soon. Her nerves did a jig of anticipation, and Chewie, who must have sensed in that way dogs had that they were nearing home, wagged his tail. It thumped against the inside of the purse.

"Shall I park in front of your garage?" asked Grant. He put the emphasis on the first syllable: *GARE-raj.*

She wanted to smile. She loved and was fascinated by the differences between English English and American English, not just the slang but the differences in pronunciation and spelling too. "Yeah, that's fine," she replied.

After he'd parked, he walked around the car to open the door for her. Wow. She could count, oh, zero times a guy had done that for her before, unless it was a doorman or bouncer opening a limo door for her.

As she moved to get out, Chewie, who had momentarily burrowed back down into her purse, poked his head out.

The impersonal expression on Grant's face morphed into a half-smile. He let Chewie sniff his knuckles and then scratched him behind the ears.

Chewie let out a faint sigh of pleasure.

"What's he called?" asked Grant.

Now out of the car, Piper had to look way up at him. "Chewie."

"Offspring of Chewbacca?"

She grinned, appreciating him more and more. Most people assumed because she was Hispanic that Chewie's name was spelled "Chuy," a common Latinx nickname for Jesús. Grant was the first person to assume Chewie's name came from *Star Wars* (she was a huge fan of all of them, even the new ones). "He wishes," she replied.

Again, that half-smile.

She was filled with a ridiculous surge of delight that she'd caused it.

As if he had just remembered why they were there,

Grant's expression sobered. "Shall we?" he said with an *after you* flourish of his hand.

Her nerves gave a particularly hard kick, and she felt it in her stomach. To hide what she was feeling, she walked with her chin up, her shoulders back, and her high heels clicking at a fast pace on the brick path that led from her driveway to her front door.

A light hand on her lower back reminded her that Grant was walking beside her. He leaned down toward her, his breath a pleasant tickle in her ear, and murmured, "Slow down. Our ardor for one another won't be convincing if you're fleeing from me as if I'm Jack the Ripper."

She immediately slowed and pasted on a sweet smile. "Sorry," she said, maintaining the smile while barely moving her lips.

Once they were at the front door of her house, he bent down again and whispered, "Pretend I'm telling you something charming and funny."

His body heat so near her was more noticeable in the cool mid-September evening air. She laughed and gazed up at him, trying to look infatuated. It wasn't that hard. "Why don't you actually say something charming and funny?"

"That would require me to actually *be* charming and funny," he deadpanned.

His wry self-deprecation was surprising and made her laugh for real. "I had a nice time tonight." She said this on the off chance that a paparazzo might be able to read lips.

"As did I," he said so convincingly that if she didn't know the truth, she might believe they'd actually met in a normal way, at a real cocktail party or something—that he hadn't been morose the entire drive to her house. He *was* a decent actor.

They looked at each other for a moment, and she

wondered if he, like her, could hear an imaginary director in his head going, "Stare into one another's eyes for a few seconds before you take the plunge."

Whatever the case, he did meet her eyes with his unfathomable blue ones, and he waited the perfect amount of time before brushing a strand of hair back from her cheek.

He had taken off his suit jacket before their drive, so now he was wearing just a crisp white dress shirt unbuttoned at the collar and tucked into his slacks. She put her hands lightly on his narrow waist and felt hard, flat belly underneath the expensive fabric of his shirt and the smooth leather of his belt. Chewie hung heavily from the short straps of her purse, which were wrapped over her forearm.

As if in slow motion, Grant took his time dipping down toward her, and that clean, wintry scent of his curled around her.

A shiver of expectation rolled down her spine.

One of his hands was pressed against her back, and the other cupped her cheek. His thumb traced the edge of her jaw as he started the kiss slowly, his lips light to the point of almost tickling her. The chasteness of it was somehow more arousing than if he'd gone in guns blazing.

She wrapped her arms tighter around him, telling herself it was because they were being photographed and videoed at this very moment and she had to make it look real. It wasn't because she was enjoying it. She was just playing a role.

He deepened the kiss, his tongue seeking to open her lips, and she obliged, letting him in. He tasted faintly like mint, and his tongue glided over hers, not too aggressively but with just the right amount of firmness and swirling.

It caused a delectable sensation in her diaphragm—the one voice coaches talked about, not the birth control kind—

as if he'd pressed there and pushed a tiny bit of breath out of her. Okay. So maybe she was enjoying the kiss just a little.

He pulled her to him, and his hard body pressing against hers began to generate a friction between them, causing hot prickles along her skin. Occasionally he would suckle or nibble on her bottom lip.

She began to lose herself in it all, to just relish him and all the exquisite turmoil he was causing inside her. It had been a while since she'd been kissed like this, with passion and want, and she couldn't help but respond in kind.

Out of the corner of her eye, a camera flashed. She ignored it.

By the time it was over, her bones had all turned to rubber, and her pulse was off the charts. She smiled sultrily, and her lips felt thoroughly ravished and bee-stung. She realized that pretending to be Grant Cammish's girlfriend wasn't going to be half the chore she'd originally thought it would be. "Would you like to come in?" she said for their audience, knowing he would say yes.

He looked dazed at first, but as he came back to himself, his expression grew strangely intense, his brow furrowed. "No. I...have to go."

She frowned, then quickly remembered they were being watched and tried not to show her confusion. "What do you mean?"

"I'm... God." His jaw hardened. "It seems I'm a bit out of sorts. Enjoy the rest of your evening." Then he gave her a peck on the cheek before striding to his car as if *she* were Jack the Ripper.

WTH? Had the kiss been that bad? It hadn't seemed one-sided. It had seemed as if they were equally into it.

Apparently she'd been wrong.

Her mind racing, she was barely conscious of shutting

her front door and no longer cared if they were being watched.

Was he sorry about the kiss? The whole plan? Was he backing out?

She understood his reluctance all too well if the fake relationship was the prob. She wasn't that gung ho about it either.

So, fine. If he wanted to call it quits before they'd even really begun, fine.

She'd find another way to fix her career, another role that would showcase her acting range. Even though she wanted it badly, Heledd wasn't the only role out there. Too bad that, so far, no one was willing to give her a chance at those roles.

She shrugged off the thought and reminded herself she'd developed a tough skin over the years. She would *not* blame Grant's abrupt scrapping of the plan on herself, and she would not give up on herself, either.

Now she just had to repeat that enough times to believe it. But the ugly words that had taunted her in the media after her firing echoed in her head—that she was a lazy slug, that she had no willpower, that she'd become a bad role model. Didn't she know America had an obesity epidemic?

It was the "lazy slug" insult—courtesy of Briony Callas, a famous exercise influencer with a huge social media following—that had hurt the most, although the bad-role-model thing had been horrifying too. "Slug" conjured such a nasty vision: a grayish-brown, slimy larva of a creature that oozed along, leaving a viscous trail in its wake.

But Piper's weight gain hadn't happened because of laziness or lack of willpower. It had been stress. She'd been working her ass off, and food had become a comfort. But the cycle had been vicious: the bigger she got, the more she'd been stressed, and the more she'd wanted to eat.

By seeing an amazing dietician and a counselor, she'd found balance again. She'd learned to eat foods that would properly fuel her body. She'd learned how to lose weight without starving herself, even though it had taken twice as long and certainly hadn't been fast enough for the producers of her show. She'd stopped overeating and was learning to love her new, healthier body. She was even starting to like exercise. Kind of.

But having arguably the hottest guy in the world bolt off her doorstep when the opposite was supposed to happen? Not exactly an ego boost.

## 4

He regretted accepting Jessica's call as soon as he heard her ask, "Are you done with the shoot?"

"Er, sorry. Can't chat at the moment," he hedged.

"Call me when you're done. I'm going to text you a link to TMZ—"

"Right. I'll have a look and ring you soon," he promised, and ended the call. A text immediately came in, but he ignored it. He'd look later when he got to his caravan.

Knackered, he relaxed into the canvas chair he was sitting in, tilted his head back, and closed his eyes for a second. Even though he would still have to fit in a quick workout, he was looking forward to a few hours alone to recharge, since he wouldn't be needed until later in the evening. He'd just shot a nude love scene—always tedious and draining—and he'd spent the last two weeks doing brutal extra workouts to make his muscles bigger and more ripped. It was an unpleasant but necessary ritual he always did before nude scenes.

Derek, his personal assistant—a young wiry chap with

dark skin and a short, meticulously maintained afro—
hovered nearby. "Can I get you anything, Mr. Cammish?"

"A bed and about a year to sleep."

Derek grinned. "Sure thing, Mr. Cammish." Derek never
said no, no matter how barmy Grant's requests.

"I'm going to my caravan. Take the afternoon off. I won't
need you until this evening."

"You sure?"

"Quite."

"Thanks, Mr. Cammish."

Grant restrained a sigh and said for the hundredth time,
"Please, call me Grant."

Already walking away, Derek turned and gave him a
noncommittal thumbs-up.

A few fans had been let in and were gathered along the
roped-off perimeter of the set. For their sake, Grant forced
his face into what felt like a friendly expression. Of course, it
did seem that what he considered friendly, others often
considered snooty. So be it. He was too English and too
bloody tired to manage one of those big, toothy American-
style grins.

Today the set had been closed during actual filming
because of the nudity involved, so the onlookers must have
been let in once filming was done and everyone was clothed
—or at least robed. Normally he always tried to sign a few
autographs or take a few selfies if asked to. It never got old
and he never could really believe it, that people would want
his signature as a keepsake. He was quite humbled by it.

However, he preferred to be fully clothed—or at least
what constituted clothing for his character, Rolf—before
interacting with the public. Cynthia would be disappointed
in him for not taking advantage of the chance to work on his
image, so he mustered a wave to everyone and, to those who

expressed disappointment, his apologies as he stood up to head toward his caravan.

His costar, Francesca Gayle, the actor he'd done the scene with, had no such sartorial qualms. She'd donned a coverup that rendered her decent enough, and she was already shaking hands and taking selfies with the fans. No doubt she was also telling them in her passive-aggressive way what a toff he was. He didn't understand her blatant dislike of him.

He was always perfectly respectful and polite to her—when they weren't in character, of course. And even then, he'd once had to do a scene with her thirty times in order to make slapping her, which the script called for, look authentic. He'd been terrified of actually hitting her and hurting her because she kept moving her face too close and not turning her head properly, as actors were trained to do, to deflect the blow. It was almost as if she'd *wanted* him to slap her.

As he walked, he tightened the tie of his robe, although it was a bit late for modesty.

Sorry, Mum, he told her in his head. Yet another scene where he'd literally bared everything except his knob, which had been hidden by Francesca's thigh.

It was hard to escape these days, the graphic sex scenes, since almost every show produced for Netflix or many of the other big streaming services contained scenes where couples were shown tupping. At the rate he was going, his bum cheeks were going to be more recognizable than his face cheeks. Or else he was going to catch pneumonia.

When his contract was next up for negotiation, he intended to reduce the number of nude scenes required of him or else demand a body double. He'd surely earned enough seniority and clout now to do that.

Then again, maybe it would be a moot point. If things went well and he got Captain Justice, who knew what the future might hold? It might be time for his tenure on *Battle* to come to an end.

Thoughts of the Captain Justice role led to thoughts of Piper.

Good God, the woman could kiss. It had caught him off guard last night on her doorstep. He'd opened up to her and forgot he was supposed to be acting. He'd lost himself in it —just as he had all those months ago with Amanda.

That realization had doused him in cold anger and shut down the ardor Piper had unexpectedly ignited in him. He regretted he'd let his frustration with Amanda interfere with the PR plan and hoped Piper wasn't too put out with him. He'd strive to do better moving forward, despite his doubts about the plan's validity. He'd said as much in a short text to Jessica early this morning before shooting had begun.

He needed to keep things professional, though. No more getting blindsided by Piper's passion. "America's sweetheart" his arse. A seductress lurked beneath her girl-next-door, purse-dog-carrying exterior.

He'd felt that same intense, initial attraction with both Lexi and Amanda, and look how those affairs had turned out. He would not let himself be burned again, no matter how tempting the fire.

---

PIPER SAT on the camel-colored leather sofa next to a large window in Grant's plush trailer. Or at least the sofa looked like it was made of leather. On closer inspection, she thought it might be fake—albeit a very good fake—and she wondered if whoever had been in charge of procuring the talent trailers had been conscious of that, or if Grant had specifically requested it. Whatever the case, it was cool. She would rather work on a production that cared about animals and the earth than one that didn't.

*If* she got to work on the production. She hoped this questionable publicity stunt she was pulling with Grant wasn't all for nothing.

After last night, she'd been ready to pull the plug on it a few hours ago when she'd spoken to William, but he'd talked her into giving it another chance. Apparently the kiss alone had generated enough buzz to delight the PR machine. Whatever Grant's reasons for not staying last night, he hadn't hurt their objective—just her pride.

So now here she was, reluctantly giving it another try. She'd been assured Grant was ready to go on with the next phase, that he was wholly invested. Last night had just been a hiccup, for whatever reason.

Chewie, who was in his usual spot inside her purse, had gotten bored waiting for something to happen and fallen asleep. The little lump of fur made her smile. She would never get desensitized to how adorable he was. The cuteness just kept on coming.

The shade on the window above the sofa was down, but if she lifted one side of it, she could see out well enough. She wanted to know when Grant was heading over. She was supposed to be waiting there to "surprise" him, and it had been arranged for a photo to be taken of them in the exact moment she planted a kiss on his lips.

When she saw him walking toward the trailer in nothing but a midnight-blue terrycloth robe that reached just past his knees, emphasizing his powerful calf muscles and his sexy feet in flip-flops—yes, even his feet were sexy—her heart beat a little faster.

When he was almost to the trailer, she got up and stood in front of the door, tugging at the cute yellow minidress with the sash tied in the back that she hoped showed that she actually did have a waist. Her "girls" made it necessary to always wear something more fitted or tailored. Loose tops and empire waists made her look pregnant.

The trailer's door handle clicked an instant before Grant opened it.

Her breath stuttered for a second at the sight of him. Why did he have this effect on her every time? She'd never been so physically attracted to a colleague before.

Before he could react, she put her arms around his neck, grinned as if glad to see him, and said "Hey" in that intimate way couples in love spoke to each other. Since she was up higher in the trailer and he was still on the ground, they were pretty much at eye level.

Startlement showed in his eyes and the crinkle between his brows.

She stiffened. "You're not on board with this."

"On the contrary," he said in a quiet tone. "I'm just not sure exactly what 'this' is."

"Seriously?" she said, irritated but speaking just as quietly so they wouldn't be overheard. "I'm not doing this again."

"Doing what?"

"Forcing you to kiss me." Embarrassed, she made a move to go back into the trailer, intending to get Chewie and leave.

Grant stopped her by putting his arms around her waist, a devilish gleam in his eyes. "Don't jump to conclusions." Then he held her to him and kissed her.

Her toes immediately curled, her irritation and embar-rassment momentarily forgotten. It was a short but welcoming kiss with just a brief meeting of their tongues, but she felt tiny sparks of electricity along her skin despite her uncertainty.

After another nip of her bottom lip as a finishing touch, he pulled away and said, "Let's go inside, shall we?"

Still tingling with that strange electric feeling, she took a step back so he could enter the trailer.

As soon as he shut himself inside with her, his broad shoulders and Thor-like body (pre–*Avengers Endgame*) made the trailer seem like it was a Polly Pocket Glamping Van.

Trying to act unaffected by the kiss and the way he seemed to suck more than his fair share of air out of the room, she said, "I'm sorry. I was told you still wanted to move forward with the plan and that you knew I'd be waiting for you."

That mischief from earlier was gone, and his expression had resumed the polite, unreadable mask he used to distance himself. They were back to being work colleagues, and it was as if that sweet greeting kiss hadn't happened. "No apologies necessary, and I do want to move forward."

That made Piper feel a little better, although she half expected him to explain why he'd bailed. She didn't know him well enough to ask, though, and apparently he wasn't going to offer any more.

He moved over to a barrel-shaped swivel chair and wearily dropped down into it, then motioned for her to join him.

Just as she was sitting down on the sofa across from him, Chewie woke up and yipped from her purse. She pulled him out, and he wagged his tail when he saw Grant.

Grant spared him a small, slightly crooked smile before saying, "Jessica called earlier, but I put her off." He pronounced "Jessica" as "Jessic-er."

Piper had always found that interesting, the way Brits

sometimes said words that ended in "er" with an "ah" sound, as in "nev-ah," but with some words that ended in "a" they added an "er" sound.

Calling her back from her brain tangent, he said, "She was probably ringing to tell me what was coming next, but I've been shooting since half past seven this morning and didn't give her the chance. Care to enlighten me?"

Wow. He had balls, blowing off Jessica Zimmerman. "Well, apparently our kiss from last night is all over the internet. There's an article on TMZ about it."

"Ah. That must be what Jessica sent me." He pulled his phone from his robe pocket and began to read.

Piper petted Chewie and waited. She knew what the article said. It went on and on about how hot the kiss was and argued that either rumors of him being gay weren't true, he was bi or pansexual, or he was being an old-fashioned gentleman with Piper—the prospect of which was intriguing, given his previous toxic bachelor status.

Now that she'd met him, the possibility that he might be gay seemed farfetched. His weird freakout from their kiss last night notwithstanding, he transmitted heterosexuality like a cellphone tower. Maybe she was in denial, though, on behalf of all womankind.

Things would be better all around if he *were* gay. That would make this whole charade much easier on her—goodbye, more-than-platonic feelings that kept cropping up—although if he felt the need to be closeted in this day and age, that was sad.

At one point while reading, Grant huffed enigmatically and muttered, "Pan." His face was its normal inscrutable self, but a twitch of his mouth made her think he might be entertained by what he was reading, which didn't prove anything one way or the other about his sexuality. After another moment, he finished reading and looked up. "We were a success, it seems."

"Yes."

"So what's on next?"

Piper gave a little shrug. "Hopefully our kiss a second ago was long enough for someone to photograph it. Cynthia said she'd arrange it. She wants to keep putting evidence of our"—Piper did air quotes—"*relationship* in front of the tabloids, keep hammering them with it."

"Glad I didn't cock it up, then."

The memory of his greeting kiss still fluttered in her belly. "Excellent recovery."

"Thank you," he said with a slight, courtly dip of his perfect man-chin.

An awkward beat of silence followed, the kind of silence that happened when two people were complete strangers to one another and had nothing in common. Complete strangers who kept kissing each other. Piper searched her mind for something witty to say, but her ability to make small talk and put people at ease was, for some reason, failing her.

"Well, then," he said, standing up, "if you'll excuse me, I've got to squeeze in a workout." He looked at her expectantly.

He wanted her to leave. Awkward. "Oh. Actually, I'm supposed to stay here with you all afternoon until your next shoot."

His polite indifference slipped. "*All* afternoon?" The weariness she'd noticed earlier was back again.

"Yes."

"Brilliant," he said, although clearly it wasn't.

She'd been about to say maybe they could use the

opportunity to introduce her to Ezra, but now she felt like an intruder again. "I should just go."

He held up his hands. "No, no. Stay."

Chewie's ears twitched, and then he canted his head to one side and then another.

"I've confused your dog it seems," Grant said with that same small tilt of a smile he apparently reserved just for Chewie. He bent forward to scratch Chewie behind his ears. "Good lad. You were already staying, weren't you?"

She couldn't help but like that he was obviously a dog person. "I can go," she said. "Really. You seem pretty tired."

"I'm fine."

She was dubious. The closer she looked at his handsome face, the more she could see lines of fatigue. "Maybe you should take a nap instead."

"No rest for the wicked. But please do make yourself at home."

He didn't look wicked. He just looked like—despite his hospitable manners—the last thing he wanted to do was spend the afternoon with her.

## 5

C hewie scissored his little legs, indicating he wanted to be put down. Piper set him on the floor and admonished him, "No marking your territory. We're already on rocky ground."

He immediately went on the prowl, sniffing over every inch of Grant's trailer floor, which probably felt a mile long to Chewie's tiny body.

While Grant was changing into his workout clothes in the bedroom, Piper went over to the rack of swords hanging on the wall across from the door to the bedroom. She'd felt too weird touching his things during her earlier wait, but he *had* told her to make herself at home. She started lifting the different swords, testing them. Some had real metal blades, some were rubber replicas of the real ones, and some were cut short, as if part of them had broken off. She knew these short ones were used for scenes where CGI would be integrated to make it look like Grant's character was cutting off someone's head or whatever.

She picked up one of the smaller real ones, a saber, and slashed it through the air a couple of times. Then she picked

up the heaviest, most ornate one. It was the one his character, Rolf, always carried in a scabbard on his back.

Speaking of, there was a life-size cardboard cutout of
Rolf next to the rack, which made her want to roll her eyes.
The shirtless costume Grant wore to play Rolf bared his
broad shoulders, six-hundred-pack stomach, and narrow
waist. The leather pants of the costume left nothing to the
imagination as far as powerful thighs or the big bulge in the
crotch area between those thighs—a sword of a different
kind, she thought impishly.

The actual sword she currently held came up to her
waist, and she could barely lift it. She was about to put it
back on the rack when Grant came out of his bedroom
wearing a muscle-hugging black Under Armour T-shirt and
black and gray athletic shorts. He was still bare-footed and
still all kinds of hot.

"En garde," she said in a mock challenge, holding the
sword with both hands. She knew she looked ridiculous.
Just getting the sword to be parallel to the ground was a
mighty effort. It was a lummox compared to the light swords
she used when she fenced, and it threw her off-balance.

He pressed his lips together and then stalked over to her
and took the sword from her. "You're going to hurt yourself.
Or damage property."

"Oh, good thing you came out just in the nick of time
and saved me from myself."

He gave her a look. Then, with easy grace, handling it as
if it almost weighed nothing, he put the sword back in its
place on the rack. "This is not a toy. It's a real weapon and
could hurt someone."

She thought about telling him she knew a thing or two
about swords, but his mansplaining made her not want to
bother.

"I'm going to work out now, if you don't mind."

"In here?"

"Yes. Nothing too crazy. Just some pushups and such."

"Oh, sure. Go ahead." In fact, it would be a relief not to have to strain to make conversation with him. She sat back down on the sofa and pulled up Instagram on her phone, snapped a quick pic of Chewie sitting with a bewildered doggie tilt to his head as he watched Grant lower himself to the floor, and then posted the pic with the caption "What— or who—has piqued Chewie's interest?"

Grant started doing pushups, first the normal kind and then the freak-of-nature kind with one arm. No wonder his arms had such huge biceps and triceps.

She couldn't help but exclaim, "Wow. That's crazy-pants. How often do you work out?"

He puffed air through his lips, but otherwise he didn't look like he was straining too hard. "Two times a day"—he huffed out more air as every muscle in his body bulged— "starting at four-thirty in the morning"—huff—"and another hour or two in the afternoon or evening"—puff— "depending on my schedule. Even more"—huff—"if I've got a nude scene coming up."

Four-thirty in the morning? Yikes. "Do you do this every day?"

"Yes"—puff—"but not always the same exercises. I work different"—huff—"parts of my body."

"When does your body have the chance to recover?"

Apparently done with the pushups—he must have done around thirty reps in quick succession—he sat up and reached for an Apple AirPod case that had been lying on the nearby dinette table. While he pulled out an AirPod and stuck one in each ear, he said, "It's complicated, but I pay a trainer to make sure I don't injure myself."

"When do you have a life?"

He gave her a look that said the answer was obvious. "I don't."

"I couldn't do it."

"Obviously."

Her mouth dropped open. "You did not just say that."

He held up a palm. "I mean no offense. You're..." He paused, that little crinkle between his brows showing itself. "...lovely. But you have no idea the lengths I have to go to, and most people, like you just said, couldn't or wouldn't want to. But my physique is my brand. I've no choice but to keep as fit as possible, especially now that I'm vying for the Captain Justice role."

About all she'd comprehended of what he'd just said was that he thought she was lovely. A brightness bubbled up inside her that made her want to smile, but she fought it, mainly because she was being ridiculous. And also because there'd been that slight pause before he'd said it, as if he wasn't quite sure. "Still, it doesn't seem like it would be good for your mental health. All work and no play makes Grant a dull boy."

"It's fine." Then he told Siri to play his Daily Mix 2 on Spotify and began doing sit-ups, effectively ending the conversation.

Well, at least they'd *had* a conversation, albeit a short one, about something other than The Plan. Still, it was going to be a long three months if every time they were together it was like this.

The Bluetooth connection to his AirPods must have glitched, because all of a sudden she could hear classical music, something that almost sounded like choral or Gregorian chanting mixed with symphonic instruments, coming from the speaker on his phone.

Of course he would listen to classical music.

He stopped doing crunches and fiddled with his phone, obviously trying to reconnect the AirPods, but he wasn't having much luck.

At first she hadn't really paid attention to the music, since all classical music sounded the same to her and she wasn't really into it. But then, to her surprise, she realized it was familiar. Not Beethoven's Fifth familiar, because even *she* knew that one—but like *World of Warcraft* familiar. Her brother Julián would play the game for hours, and she must have heard that theme song a million times before she'd left home for Hollywood, although not this orchestra version of it. She wanted to laugh. "Is that the theme from *World of Warcraft*?"

Grant exhaled through his nose, and a muscle in his jaw bunched. She didn't know if he was irritated because she'd asked or because he couldn't seem to get his AirPods to reconnect. She didn't think he was going to answer, but then his gaze bounced to her and then back to his phone. "Yes. By the London Philharmonic." He'd said it so softly she'd barely heard him. He seemed almost shy about it.

Was it possible there was a smidge of geek hidden under all that haughty suaveness? Her heart melted a little at the possibility. "Really?" she said with genuine delight. "That's so cool they did something like that."

His gaze came back to her and stayed, as if he were searching for ridicule. Apparently not finding any, he said, "They did a whole album of theme songs from different video games. It's fantastic."

"Huh. I bet my brother would totally be into that."

"Your brother is a gamer?" he asked with interest.

"Yeah. It's a sickness. I mean, he's not as bad as some, but he can spend six-hour stretches on the weekends playing with other online gamers. Before I moved out here, when we were still in high school, I would sometimes have to remind him to eat.

"He still plays *World*, I think, among other things, and still needs reminding to eat. But that duty now goes to his wife, who for reasons unknown not only puts up with my brother, which is bad enough, but also ends up a gaming widow at least one evening every weekend."

Grant grinned, transforming his whole demeanor, making him seem more boyish, more carefree. "I've been known to do the same. He's lucky to have found someone who understands him."

That wasn't the answer she'd expected from him, and it made her pause. It *would* be nice to find someone who loved you just as you were and didn't try to change you. She'd always thought Hannah was kind of a pushover for not putting her foot down when it came to Julián's gaming, but now she saw Hannah's indulgence in a new light and respected her for it. After all, Hannah had known what she was getting into before she'd married him. "Yeah," said Piper. "I guess he is lucky."

Their gazes held for a moment. Another silence spread between them, but this time it was charged with something that made Piper feel acutely aware of him.

Breaking the brief connection they'd made, Grant looked down to turn his music off and set his phone aside, then took the AirPods out of his ears.

Chewie decided to investigate Grant, sniffing his bare feet and giving Grant's big toe a lick.

"Chewie, no," said Piper.

He immediately stopped, but Grant reached forward to scratch Chewie under his furry chin. "No worries. Just checking me out, yeh?" He'd said "yeah" in that shortened, clipped way that Brits said it.

Chewie sighed with contentment.

After an acceptable length of time for a chin rub, Grant pulled his hand away, and Chewie seemed to know not to push his luck.

"Well," said Grant with a quick lift of his brows, "better get back to it."

Chewie headed over and sat next to Piper's foot, watching Grant resume his sit-ups as if mesmerized.

Alrighty then. She wouldn't say she and Grant were friends now, exactly, but she felt like she'd unraveled at least part of the enigma: dashing, debonair, aloof Grant Cammish was a gamer geek.

## 6

The restaurant Le Meilleur was everything Piper had heard it was and more—white tablecloths, candles, chic modern decor in muted oranges and browns—and it was very, very intimate. In fact, it was the most romantic restaurant she'd ever been in, in addition to having just been voted one of the ten best restaurants in the world.

The dignified maître d' hadn't batted an eye when he'd seen Chewie's fuzzy brown head poking out of her purse. He'd even had one of the servers bring a bowl of water for him.

The story she and Grant had been told was that this time every effort had been made to keep the paparazzi away. Too many "tips" to the paparazzi would start to look suspicious. However, someone at the restaurant would be filming them covertly with a smartphone, not to mention any random people who might be brazen enough to photograph them without asking for permission.

Le Meilleur's clientele was extremely highbrow, though, so it was possible filming a celebrity couple would be beneath most of them. Piper figured it was more likely the secret photog would be one of the restaurant staff.

She and Grant would need to be at their most convincing all night long, because they would never know for sure when they were being watched and filmed and when they weren't. But one thing had been drilled into their heads: put on a good show.

Piper thought they'd done a stellar job so far. Grant had held her hand after he'd helped her get out of the small limo arranged by Derek, his PA, and then he'd done that proprietary hand-on-the-small-of-her-back thing that never failed to make her belly tighten pleasantly as they walked through the restaurant. Once seated, he'd also been leaning toward her to talk quietly and smile at her when she said something, and she did the same.

To any observers, it probably looked like they were enthralled with each other. The reality was far different. Instead of intimate, titillating conversation, they'd literally been talking about nothing: the weather in minute detail, the density of traffic on the various highways that ran through LA, the merits of Smart Water.

Piper thought she might actually die of boredom, and it was pushing her acting skills to their limits to keep up the captivated girlfriend pretense. But when she'd tried to steer the conversation into more personal subjects, Grant would somehow steer them into inane territory again—as he'd done whenever they'd managed to squeeze in time together during the last couple of weeks. She hadn't gotten anything of substance out of him since he'd revealed he was a gamer.

At one point this evening, he'd lifted his wineglass to take a drink of the Bordeaux he'd ordered, which made his right biceps muscle contract enough that she could see it through the tightness of his black suit jacket sleeve. It was the most exciting thing that had happened since they'd arrived.

He'd been working on the same glass of wine for nearly an hour. Piper was near the bottom of her second glass of a white French muscadet recommended by the sommelier and was feeling bolder, so as soon as Grant set his stemmed glass down, she reached out and covered his hand with hers. To any lookie-loos, it would look like a loving gesture, but in reality she did it to get his attention. His hand was warm and big, his fingers long and tapering into blunt nails. A slight thrum, like the *thwang* of a loose guitar string, coursed through her at the contact. "Grant," she said, leveling her gaze on him, "can we *please* talk about something that is actually interesting?"

He stilled. "Sorry?"

"If I hear one more thing about the various kinds of vitamin waters, I'm going to scream."

He cocked a brow. "That wouldn't be very romantic."

"No, it wouldn't."

Amusement glinted in his eyes, which were a darker blue in the dim candlelight, reassuring her she hadn't offended him. "What shall we talk about, then?"

"Us." She leaned in close and whispered, "Don't you think, after all the time we've spent together recently, we should know each other better? I mean, we should be past the small-talk phase."

His expression put up its shield, and he didn't say anything.

Great. She'd made things worse. Now he wasn't talking at all.

Something of her chagrin must have shown on her face, because he glanced away and then refocused on her, his jaw looking more chiseled than usual. "I have...difficulty."

It took her a second to realize his sentence was finished. "With...?" she prompted.

Lips pressed together, he exhaled. "I don't want to say anything...inappropriate." Then he gave a faint, self-deprecating smile that squeezed her heart. "I've a knack for saying the wrong things, and it often lands me in the soup."

Yes, she'd read some of the gaffes he'd made, but if he was wary to the point where he couldn't even *try* to have a meaningful conversation with someone, that was troubling. "Well, you don't have to worry about that with me. You can say whatever you want. I won't take offense."

He gave her the side-eye, as if he wasn't sure he should take the bait.

"Seriously. I have a thick skin. It takes a lot to offend me."

The corners of his mouth quirked. "You've just thrown down the gauntlet, you know."

She grinned. "Bring it."

He arched an eyebrow in challenge. "Where do you want to begin?"

Letting go of his hand, she sat back in her chair and slowly twirled the base of her wineglass, ignoring the twinge of disappointment her body felt at no longer touching him. "We'll start with something safe. Where are you from?"

"That *is* safe, since I'm sure you already know the answer is England."

"Well, yeah, but what part of England?"

"Didn't you get my bio from Cynthia?"

Piper rolled her eyes. "If we were normal people on a normal date, we wouldn't have seen bios of each other. Well, maybe if we'd met on a dating site. But even then, we'd probably still talk about where we're from."

"All right. I'm afraid the answer is rather boring, though. I was born and bred in London."

"That's not boring at all. Do you know, like, the queen?" she joked.

"No, but I've met her before."

Piper widened her eyes. "You're kidding. Queen Elizabeth, the actual Queen of England?"

"Yes. There's only been one for the last seventy years or so, God save her."

Excited, Piper said, "Oh, my God. I'm obsessed with *The Crown*. Have you watched it?"

His expression was one of mock affront that was adorable. "What kind of Englishman would I be if I didn't watch *The Crown*?"

"I love that show. Well, except for the third season. I thought it was kind of boring."

"Likewise."

Their eyes locked, and a buzz from connecting on a real level surged through her. Did he feel it too? Surely that faint curve to his mouth meant something. She sat up straighter, putting her palms up. "Okay. But wait. Back to the part where you said you've met Queen Elizabeth. How? Why? Give me the tea."

"Believe me, it was nothing to get your knickers in a twist over."

*Knickers!* He'd said "knickers." She loved it when British people said that.

His baritone rippled along her skin as he continued his story. "She was at a formal charity event for a mutual acquaintance, and I was presented to her there. It was only once, and only for about five seconds. I doubt she even remembers it."

Piper was skeptical. "How could she not? I mean, you're

on practically every 'sexiest man' list that exists. Trust me. She would remember you."

His gaze went to his wineglass, and he took a sip.

Piper got the feeling if Grant were capable of blushing, he'd be doing it right now.

"She's old enough to be my great-granny," he muttered, still not meeting Piper's gaze.

Wow. This was enlightening. He was being modest, and it didn't fit with his conceited image. He was probably told a million times a day in one form or another how good-looking he was, yet her mentioning it had seemed to make him self-conscious. She was becoming more and more intrigued with him by the minute.

Her appetizer arrived before she could ask him more. Nothing came for him, and the dismay she'd felt when they'd first ordered came back. They were eating in possibly the finest, most exclusive restaurant in LA, and all he'd ordered was a boring chicken entree and told them how to prepare it: no sauces, no butter. Couldn't he stray from his diet just this once?

She'd ordered oysters Rockefeller for an app and a delectable-sounding fish dish she couldn't pronounce for an entree. Both were probably swimming in butter, and her oysters had a rich herbed breading on them. Completely decadent. Grant's restraint was making her feel guilty and gluttonous.

And the chef was probably ready to kill him. She had to practically sit on her hands not to say anything, but now that she had Grant talking, she didn't want to rock the boat. After all, she wasn't his mom. But the way his gaze lingered on the oysters made her say, "You sure you don't want to try one?"

"I'm sure, but thank you."

"I feel like I'm kind of being rude."

"You're not."

Reluctantly, she let it go and moved on to another subject. "So tell me about your family. Do you have any brothers or sisters?"

His eyes instantly lit up and crinkled at the corners, which was, of course, warm-fuzzies-in-the-belly-inducing. "Yes. Five brothers."

"Five?" she said, surprised. "Wow. Is your family Catholic?"

He half-chuckled. "No. I just think my poor mum really wanted a girl, and my father was keen to have a go at it as many times as she fancied."

Piper laughed. "That was very chivalrous of him."

"Quite."

Utterly charmed by Grant now, she said, "Your 'poor mum' is right. She must be a saint."

"Oh, most definitely."

"And where do you fall in the mix?" she asked before popping another of the rich oyster concoctions in her mouth. It was so big she could hardly contain it and probably looked like a squirrel chewing it. She put a hand delicately over her mouth to try to appear more ladylike. She'd always eaten oysters on the half shell in one bite, but maybe she was supposed to be cutting these at least in half? But she didn't see any tiny knives to go with her tiny oyster fork.

"I'm number four," he answered.

Ah, so he was a middle child, the fourth of six. Maybe that was another reason he was more on the quiet side in addition to his qualms about saying the wrong thing. She knew from her own family that sometimes the middle kids got lost in the chaos of the other bossier, older kids or the more rambunctious and needier younger kids of the family.

He took another fleeting sip of his wine glass, still on his first.

She was now beginning her third. She needed to watch it, or she was going to get tipsy. Yet again she felt like a glutton compared to him. She would understand if he were going to drive them home, but they'd taken the limo, which would also be taking them to her house afterward. It wasn't like Grant needed to worry about drinking and driving. Given his strict adherence to his diet, though, she was probably lucky he was drinking wine at all.

"And what about you?" he asked. "What is your family like?"

At the thought of her own family, she smiled with nostalgia and homesickness. "I'm the oldest of four. It's me, then Julián—we're only eighteen months apart—then Raquel, then Mad."

A wrinkle appeared between Grant's brows. "Mad?"

"Short for Maddox. Don't worry. He's not loco. Well, mostly he's not."

Grant grinned.

It flashed through her like lightning, making her feel all glowy inside. She returned the grin and said, "We're a typical San Antonio family. Sunday dinners at my abuela's after mass—attendance mandatory for both if you're in town. My parents weren't poor, but having three kids to put through college was taxing on their finances. They made sure anyone who wanted to go to college went, though. Julián is a lawyer, Raquel is working as an aide for a representative from Texas in the House of Representatives in DC, and Mad is a junior at Austin College in Sherman, Texas, pre-med."

"And you're a famous actress."

"*Pfft.* I'm the black sheep of the family. Skipped college

and left San Antonio when I was eighteen for the bright lights of Hollywood. Luckily my aunt, who lived in LA at the time, was willing to take me in and look out for me, or my parents never would have gone for it." She gave a quick smile and her tone dipped toward irony. "I think my parents started to regret all those dancing and singing lessons they paid for when I was a kid. I went to a magnet high school for musical theater, too, which didn't help matters." She took a sip of wine and added, "I think they thought I would get it out of my system once I got a few rejections from auditions."

"Obviously they were wrong."

"No. They were right. I got a *lot* of rejections." Many times because she was Hispanic. Like, people had actually told her agent she was almost perfect for a role except that she was too ethnic-looking—aka too brown. And in the early days of her career, if she did get callbacks, it was for stereotypical Latina roles: thug's girlfriend, mouthy hot-headed street girl, maid.

Grant nodded and murmured in a gentle, commiserative way at her mention of rejections. Every actor could relate to that sucky, stomach-dropping moment of "Sorry, you're not good enough; better luck next time," even devastatingly hot white guys. But she'd nearly given up, almost convinced by those rejections that there wasn't a place in the industry for someone like her. Fortunately, her parents hadn't raised a quitter.

"I'm not complaining, though," she went on. "I eventually got the role on *Nine's a Crowd*, and the rest is history. I know that's more than most ever get."

She stuffed another oyster into her mouth, and the way he watched her could only be described as hungrily. Once she'd chewed it enough to be able to speak, she shielded her lips with her hand again and said, "You *sure* you don't want one? There's two left, and I need to save room for my entree."

"No, thank you."

Again, she wanted to argue but held her tongue, instead taking a sip of ice water to offset the wine. "What about you?" she asked. "Was your family supportive of your career choice?"

"Yeh, yeh. Quite so."

His answer surprised her again, given the whole Queen Elizabeth thing. "Really?" She'd pictured stuffy, aristocratic English parents grooming their sons to take care of some Downton Abbeyish estate surrounded by rolling green lawns and being horrified that one of their offspring would be so common as to want to be an actor.

"It helped I was born fourth," he mused, "and had three older brothers who had already made the family proud. My brother John is a captain in the Royal Air Force, my brother James is a successful banker, and George is working his way up the ranks of the Royal Marines. Even my younger brothers, Robin and Brandon, have done well with their furniture business." His expression grew wry. "I think by the time I arrived, all my mum told my three older brothers was, 'No bone-breaking if you tussle, and don't let him eat anything off the floor.'"

The falsetto he'd used for his mother in place of his usual masculine voice made Piper laugh, and he was smiling fondly. "Actually," he said, "my mum is great. I don't know how she put up with all the testosterone. Of course, boarding school was probably a big help. We all went aged thirteen and got out of her hair."

Piper shook her head. "I can't imagine leaving home at thirteen." And she couldn't imagine her parents allowing it, either, but she wasn't going to judge. He came from a totally different culture.

He shrugged. "I was very keen on it. It seems much more common in England than here, almost expected. I was ready to go out into the world—or the world I thought was the world at the time," he said with a crooked, self-aware smile. "My school, Bradshaw Grange, was only about two hours north of London, but it felt like the end of the earth." His expression got more solemn, and he stared at the pristine white tablecloth in front of him as if seeing something else entirely. "It was rough at first. I had to toughen up. I was a bit of a melt when I got there, didn't quite fit in. They used to call me 'Geraint the Pudgy Half-pint' because I was short and fat."

She was incredulous. "No way."

"Yes." He sat back in his chair, his broad shoulders appearing more relaxed, as if this conversation thing wasn't so bad after all. "Luckily I'd had five brothers to spar with, so I surprised more than one schoolmate who thought he would take the piss out of me. I could hold my own in a fight."

The idea that Grant had been an ugly duckling, so to speak, and bullied had her reeling. She felt for that lonely, homesick little boy he must have been. Then, remembering the rest of what he'd said, she frowned. "Who's Geraint?"

"Me. My real name is Geraint."

"That's an unusual name. Why did you change it?"

"Because it's an unusual name."

She smiled and gave a nod. "Right."

"Although not as unusual in the UK as here. No one could pronounce it here in America when they saw it on paper. I kept telling them it rhymed with 'hair pint,' but to no avail." After sipping more of his wine—*still his first glass!*

—he said, "At one audition, someone misheard and thought I'd called myself Grant, and it was just easier all the way round to go with it. My mum was appalled, though. The acting thing was all right if one must, but changing my Christian name? A travesty."

The more they talked, the more Piper liked him—and not just because every time she looked at his face, her heart skipped a beat.

He had that fond expression again, and his gaze was unfocused.

"You miss them?"

The bittersweet longing in his eyes when he looked at her sent a dart straight through her chest. "Terribly. My shooting schedule and publicity engagements only allow me to see them twice a year, if I'm lucky." He pronounced "schedule" like "shed-ule."

"Are you close to your brothers?"

"Yes. And I've not seen my brother George—he's the closest in age to me—in three years. We can't seem to get our time off to match up. He's always off on some mission somewhere whenever I get a chance to go home, and I'm always on a shoot somewhere when he gets leave." After a pause, he seemed to try to be more positive, but she could tell it was forced. "There's always Zoom or FaceTime, though, yeh?"

"Yes," she agreed. "Thank goodness for modern technology." But she knew firsthand that video chats were a temporary Band-Aid. Nothing could take the place of a bear hug from a family member. It seemed, even as an adult, Grant hadn't escaped the loneliness and homesickness he'd experienced at boarding school. "I can't imagine not seeing Julián—or any of my family, for that matter—for that long. At least if I get homesick, San Antonio is just a three-hour plane ride away. I can go home for a weekend if I want."

"You are lucky. Don't take that for granted."

"I won't." She didn't have time to say more because the server, an attractive girl wearing a white button-down shirt, black pants, and a long black waist apron that was part of her uniform, brought their entrees.

Piper's entree was gorgeous, the presentation a true work of art, but Grant's she could have cooked for him in her own kitchen—and she was not a great cook by any means. It was literally a bland baked chicken breast accompanied by steamed broccolini and cauliflower. Again, she let it go, but her inhibitions were being sorely tested, and the wine kept urging her to speak her mind.

It all came to a head when they were done with their entrees and it was time for dessert. She was leaning toward something called "Buttercake." Because it was called "Buttercake." No way it would be better than her abuela's famous Tres Leches cake, but it sounded amazing.

When she looked up to discuss it with Grant, he was watching her in a way that made a shiver ghost down her spine. Was she imagining this connection between them? Was it wishful thinking? He was so sexy, and he probably wasn't even meaning to be.

"What sounds good to you?" she asked him. "That Buttercake sounds crazy-good to me."

He frowned. "Pardon?"

"Oh. I thought—I mean, do you want to share something?" In her experience, her dates were always willing to share a dessert just to get a taste of something delectable. And this was a fancy French restaurant. It wasn't like the portions were huge. She definitely still had room for something sweet.

"Oh," said Grant. "No. I'll pass."

It was her turn to frown. "Did you even look at your dessert menu?"

"No. I don't eat sugar."

"Like, at all?"

"If I can help it, no."

She couldn't fathom it and widened her eyes. "Well, couldn't you splurge just this once? We're at one of the best new restaurants *in the world*. It's a crime not to try their dessert." And she could have pointed out that he'd sipped a glass of wine, which had sugar in it, but she didn't think that would win her any points in the argument. Besides, he was British, which was nearly the same as European, so wine probably counted more like water to him.

"No," he replied. "I can't. Sugar gets my whole body out of whack, and I have to spend days getting it sorted again. Plus, I'm constantly getting invited to eat out for one reason or another. If I 'splurged' every time I ate out, my whole workout regimen and diet would be pointless."

Okay. Maybe he had her there. She knew what he was talking about. She constantly got invited out to eat too, by friends and for business reasons, and it was almost impossible not to indulge more often than she should. But she'd been better since she'd gotten her eating under control, had adopted sort of a 70/30 rule: be good and eat right 70 percent of the time and splurge 30 percent of the time. So far that rationale had worked pretty well.

"But," she said, trying not to sound petulant, "this restaurant is special. Who knows when we might be able to get in here again? From what William told me, he, Cynthia, and Jessica all had to pull some serious strings to get us in here."

He scoffed. "What strings? Photos of us eating here will be everywhere, and this restaurant will have a million dollars' worth of free advertising by six in the evening tomorrow. *We're* doing *them* a favor. They'll want us back."

He had a point, but she didn't want to admit it. She exhaled in frustration. "Have you ever heard of orthorexia?"

"What?"

"Orthorexia. It's when someone is obsessed with eating healthy to the point that it takes over their lives. It's an eating disorder."

Grant closed his eyes for a moment as if searching for that famous—or infamous, depending on how you looked at it—restraint of his. When he opened them again, his expression was closed off in an obstinate way that told her she'd gone too far. His words were more clipped and Britishy than ever. "I don't have an eating disorder. It's called willpower. Staying fit is part of my job, and it's a full-time job. It's in my bloody contract and is essential to the role I play on the show." He leaned toward her a little, as if to drive home his meaning. "I would think you would have learned that lesson by now, since it cost you your last job because you 'splurged' a little too often."

*Lazy slug* echoed in her ears, even though he hadn't said those exact words. She swallowed a gasp and clenched her fist in her lap, trying to hide the sick feeling that balled in her stomach. The server had come back to take their dessert order. Piper smiled to maintain the two-lovebirds facade, only now she was too hurt and fuming to eat anything. "Nothing for me, thank you," she told the server and brightened her smile further to assure all was well.

Grant watched her a second, and she thought she saw a flash of regret in his eyes.

Piper held her breath, thinking he might say something to undo his doucheyness, but no. Nothing.

The server gave Grant a questioning look.

He smiled as if he hadn't just totally insulted Piper and said, "None for me either, thank you."

The server nodded and blushed, simply because Grant had looked at her and answered an inane question. "Okay," the server went on, her eyes riveted on him.

Piper realized the girl had been that way almost every time she'd come to check on them. She'd hardly given Piper two seconds of her attention, and Piper was probably more famous in the scheme of things than he was.

The server picked up their dessert menus. "Can I get you anything else? Coffee maybe?" She looked hopeful, as if she would be content just to be in Grant's presence for infinity.

He seemed oblivious and shot Piper a questioning look. "Coffee?"

"No, thanks." The smile Piper had pasted on was growing tight with the effort to maintain it. "Could we just get the check, please?"

"Of course," said the server with a little nod of her pretty head. She gifted Grant with another pretty smile to match and then left.

The silence that followed in her wake was thick and heavy.

Piper picked up Chewie, who had been lying near her feet on the fold-up mat she always carried in her pet carrier/purse, and put him carefully back into the purse.

His little head soon popped out.

Too mad to look at Grant directly, she kept her eyes on Chewie but said, "I'll be out front. I'm sure after the water Chewie drank earlier, he needs to powder his nose." More discreetly, she leaned in, still not meeting Grant's gaze, and whispered, "If you get the check, we can split it up later."

"Don't be ridiculous. I'll take care of it," he replied.

She looked at him then and noticed a muscle ticking in

his jawline. Standing up straighter and making her voice cold enough to freeze the sun, she said, "I prefer to split it." Before he could argue, she left, not remembering until she walked past other tables and heard soft murmurs that she was messing up possible photo ops, that she and Grant were supposed to be leaving together hand in hand.

Well, fuck it. She was in no mood to pretend. She just wanted this night to end. The photos "stolen" of them when they'd first entered the restaurant, plus whatever the staff had taken of them eating, would have to do.

Unfortunately, she and Grant had both been instructed again to "seal the deal." He was supposed to stay the night with her. She grimaced. It would be the most unromantic deal-sealing ever. He had definitely earned a spot on her couch. And while her couch was a chic, vintage Art Deco design she'd found at an estate sale—very old-school Hollywood—she didn't feel too guilty at the moment that it had the comfort level of a bed of nails.

## 7

Cool night air surrounded them just like the first time Grant had taken her home, and Piper was having major déjà vu.

Holding the hand that was free of her Chewie purse, Grant had just now put his forehead to hers in the perfect gesture of *I want to stay but I really can't*, and then said, "I'll see you tomorrow."

Her blood simmered. Seriously? Was he not even going to kiss her this time? Did she have cooties or something? Ugly doubts about her weight niggled at her, but she forced them out of her mind.

This wasn't how it was supposed to go at all. Yes. She and Grant had argued at the restaurant, and the limo ride over had been silent as a tomb, but they were professionals. They had a job to do, even if she felt more like punching him at the moment instead of kissing him.

She fake-smiled as if completely enamored and traced the lapel of his impeccable black suit jacket. "So you're bailing again?"

He pulled back a little and returned her fake smile. "Odd, but I find I'm not in the mood."

"You do know that we're not actually going to sleep together," she said loud enough that only he could hear. "It's just for appearances." She put a tender hand on his cheek. "No pressure on you to get it up."

He tenderly brushed a lock of her hair away from her face, his fingertips grazing her cheekbone, but there was a derisive set to his lips. "I assure you, love, that is not the problem."

She ignored the involuntary tingle his light touch had caused. "Then what is the prob—" A lightbulb suddenly went on in her head. "Oh."

"'Oh' what?"

His ditching the plan once was annoying but fairly harmless. Twice, however, was suspicious—especially since he'd agreed to it. "Grant," she said gently, "are you—I mean, if you're gay, it's okay."

He stared at her, his face dangerously bland, his broad shoulders as inert as a statue.

She put a reassuring hand on his arm and could feel the boulder that was his biceps muscle. "That's why all this makes you so uncomfortable, isn't it?"

He laser-beamed her with an intense look. "I'm not gay, Piper."

She didn't believe him. It all made sense now, and her heart went out to him. "It's okay. There's no need to hide it in this day and age. It's not that big a deal anymore. There's no use continuing with the plan if it makes you so uncomfortable."

"Bloody hell. If I were gay, I wouldn't be in the closet. Have you ever thought it might be that I just don't fancy you, that your constant nattering and wrong-headed assumptions drive me dotty?"

She recoiled in shock, and then the anger simmering from earlier turned into a full-fledged boil. "Well, if that's the case," she said with feigned civility, even though her chest was heaving, "then let me 'natter' this in terms you'll understand." She couldn't help raising her voice. "Bugger off, you bloody British wanker!" Now shaking, she stepped inside her house and tried to slam the front door in his face, but he slapped the door with his palm to stop her.

His mouth was set in a grave line. "I didn't mean any of that."

"Go," she said, pointing at the lighted street and suddenly seeing bursts of flashes coming from all directions. In the back of her mind, she knew she and Grant were blowing it, but she didn't give a single crap. When he still didn't move, she said with another exaggerated point, "Now."

He glanced at the limo still waiting at the curb. The jerk must have told the driver to wait for him. She hadn't noticed the car's lingering presence until now.

"We shouldn't leave it like this," he said.

As if on cue, a bold paparazzo jumped out from behind a hedge and yelled, "Piper! Grant! Over here!" They ignored him, but he still yelled, "Are you two breaking up?"

"Too late," she hissed in answer to Grant. Then she gave the paparazzo a regretful smile and said, "Yes. Things aren't really working out."

At the same time, Grant said over her, "No. Just having a small row."

The paparazzo looked confused but kept flashing away with his giant camera.

When Grant turned back to her, the contrition in his gaze seemed genuine.

She wasn't buying it. He was an actor, after all.

"I lost my temper," he said. "You don't natter at all. The truth is, I quite enjoy being with you."

"Whatever." His lies hurt even more than the actual insults. "Just go. We're done here."

He hung his head, palm still on the door.

But this time, when she tried, she was able to shut it before the flashing of cameras blinded her.

## 8

As Angela applied his makeup for the scene he was about to shoot, Grant fought to keep from falling asleep. The makeup chair was made of cushiony leather that cradled him like a baby, and his eyes were already closed so the makeup could be applied. It would be so easy to just let himself fall off into oblivion. Also, the soft way Angela dabbed at his cheeks was rhythmic and soothing, and he definitely needed soothing.

Last night with Piper had been a disaster, and it had been all his fault. His belly twisted. He couldn't get that stricken look on her face out of his head—the one he'd put there more than once—and wanted to kick his own arse for saying such thoughtless things to her—things he'd not even meant at all. She'd pushed his buttons, but that was no excuse. What the hell had got into him?

In all fairness, he'd warned her. But she'd got beneath the multiple layers of armor he'd encased himself in, and it had felt good to speak freely, to have a real conversation with someone again. She'd sneaked past his barriers, made him forget himself, and look where that had landed them.

He'd not checked yet, but he knew beyond all doubt there would be fallout. Their row in front of her house was probably all over bloody social media.

Suddenly the makeup caravan door banged open and hit the wall as if a gun had been fired, startling him out of his musings and causing Angela to jump and yelp—a surprising feat, considering Angela was a stocky girl with tattoo sleeves on both pale arms, piercings on various parts of her body, and black, chunky biker boots that looked like they meant business. In short, Angela seemed the type of girl who wouldn't scare easily.

A deranged Jessica barged into the caravan, and the fact that she'd appeared at the precise moment he'd been thinking about last night's debacle was uncanny. He was ninety-nine percent sure she wasn't really psychic, but instances like this made him hold on to that one percent of doubt. It had happened more than once throughout their working relationship—always at the times he was usually in some sort of trouble.

"Shit," Angela muttered, dabbing at his cheek with a clean sponge to wipe away a mistake, he presumed, and shooting a glare at Jessica.

Jessica, of course, didn't care, and her expression was wrathful. To Angela, she gave a single jerk of her head, causing her pointy black bob to swing. "Out."

Angela put a hand on her hip and huffed. "I don't think so."

Hoping to avoid what might turn out to be a brutal battle, Grant said to Jessica, "Angela has to get me ready for the next shoot in"—he glanced down at his phone—"fifteen minutes."

Jessica's tone was terse. "This won't take long." Again,

she gave that jerk of her head, telling Angela without words to leave.

"It'll have to wait," he said, not liking the way Jessica was bossing him or Angela around.

Jessica threw up a hand. "Fine. Then you can find yourself another agent." And with that, she exited the caravan, slamming its flimsy door behind her.

He knew without a doubt she meant it. "Bollocks," he muttered to himself. Bossiness aside, she was the best agent in Hollywood. He needed her way more than she needed him.

Angela unbuttoned the collar of the black barber cape that had been protecting his Rolf costume—what there was of it—and whooshed it off of him. "Go," she said with a tilt of her turquoise-haired head. "She's a bitch, but she's also the best. I know you don't want to lose her."

"Thank you," he said, as he bolted for the door. "I'll make sure my tardiness on set doesn't impact you."

She gave a wry nod.

When he got outside, he looked both directions and saw Jessica marching toward the edge of the studio grounds. Jogging to catch up to her, he was amazed she'd made it almost to the car park in such a short time. She was taking massively long strides, even in the tall heels she wore.

"Jessica!" he shouted. "Wait."

Her shoulders stiffened for a second, enough for him to know she'd heard him, but her steps never faltered. Another three jogs, though, and he'd caught her up. He gently grabbed the upper part of her arm, which caused her to spin round and give his hand an offended glower. Now that he had her stopped, he let his grip loosen into something he hoped was placating. "Forgive my rudeness. This is about last night with Piper, isn't it?"

Her chin went up in a haughty manner. "Of course it is."

He nodded. "Then let's discuss it. Please. In my caravan."

"Oh, no," she said with biting acquiescence, holding up her hands in faux surrender. "By all means, let's not make you miss your call time."

That actually was important to him, and she knew it. He wasn't like some actors, who thought the world and everyone's time revolved round them and their whims. He took pride in the fact that he never skived off and always tried to be on time and easy to work with. The thought of the crew standing round waiting for him made him tense, but he knew instinctively that if he didn't smooth things over with Jessica right now, she really would dump him. And to be fair, he had already sent two of her calls that morning to voicemail—a cardinal sin.

Not showing how much it riled him, he said, "I'll send Derek to explain to Ezra."

She relented with a single, sharp nod, and soon they were settled in his personal caravan, just the two of them—Jessica with one of Derek's fortifying Bloody Marys, complete with celery stick. He'd made it as a peace offering on Grant's behalf before heading off to tell Ezra and the crew that Grant would be late.

"What happened with Piper?" she said without preamble, the Bloody Mary having toned her wrath down a notch.

"I dazzled her with my usual charm."

"Christ," she said darkly. "Did you fight in the limo? The pictures and video from the restaurant that one of the staff took were great. You two seemed to be getting along, laughing with each other, at ease with each other. Holding hands across the table at one point, which was a nice touch, by the way. Then, by the time you walk her to the front door of her house, you're at each other's throats."

"No. It wasn't in the limo." Understatement. The atmosphere in the limo had been arctic: quiet, desolate, cold.

When he didn't elaborate, Jessica rolled her eyes. "Getting information from you is like trying to milk a piece of granite." As if speaking to a dim child, she said slowly and distinctly, "Tell me exactly what happened, Grant."

He sighed. "We were to the dessert course. I refused to order any. She criticized my eating habits."

"And?"

"It was a bit of a pot/kettle scenario, and I said as much."

Jessica's palm went to her forehead. "You didn't."

"I might have said something about her losing her role on her sitcom because of her, er, tendency to splurge."

"You didn't."

He remained silent.

"Christ," she said again.

"You do recall you're Jewish."

She raised her glass and extended her index finger toward him. "This isn't the time for your dry English humor."

It never seemed to be the time for that with her.

After taking a sip of the cocktail, she said, "So this happened at dinner?"

"Yes."

She did a single shake of her head. "Well, that's not good, but that part doesn't seem to have made it onto social media."

Again he was silent.

"How did it escalate to the brouhaha later in front of her house?"

"Tensions were high between us—not exactly conducive to an amorous production. Also, it was late, I was knackered, and if I'd stayed at her house for the night, I would have had to get up at three-thirty the next morning to make it to my training session with Jason. Thirty minutes of extra sleep may not seem like a lot to you, but to me it's everything." Perhaps he should have said that to Piper instead of insulting her. He truly was a wanker. And daft.

Jessica pointed her chin at the ceiling, then used it to trace a full arc from her left shoulder to her right. "Oh, my gawd. You refused to stay the night *again*, after we had it all explicitly planned out?"

"Yes. For the reasons I just explained. And then she inferred the real reason I didn't want to stay was because I was gay. As a result, I said some things that are regrettable." He forced a neutral expression to remain on his face, a supreme accomplishment, since Piper's assumption still rankled even now.

Jessica waved dismissively with her free hand. "Since when does that bother you? The gay rumors du jour have been making the rounds for months, and suddenly it matters now?"

She was right, and his belly twisted again as under-standing and then something close to panic dawned. He froze in his posture of nonchalance, arms spread across the back of his chair, and didn't comment.

Jessica studied him for a moment, then tilted her head and smirked. "Ah. It's because *she* thought you were gay, isn't it? You don't want *Piper* to think it."

If he'd been wearing a shirt, he would have loosened the collar.

Jessica straightened her head. "You're starting to like her for real."

He wasn't ready to fancy anyone yet. His past entanglements still wounded. Lessons learned. "She's a nice girl, but no. Don't be ridiculous." Perhaps if he denied it enough, he could convince himself.

"It's not ridiculous to like someone, especially a nice, cute, charismatic young woman like Piper Torres." Her voice softened. "It's normal."

"You're mistaken."

Jessica shot him a skeptical look. "Everyone is conjecturing why you and Piper broke up. They're blaming you, of course."

He was grateful for the change of subject and pounced on it. "Why does everyone assume *I'm* the reason for the breakup? Or that we're even broken up? Couples fight sometimes. It's normal."

"True, but *fake* couples with an agenda do not suddenly have public fights and break up in front of the paps," she admonished.

"I told the paparazzi we weren't breaking up. Just having a row."

"Well, apparently they didn't believe you. But the bigger problem is that *Piper* says you are broken up."

That settled low and heavy in his chest.

You have to fix this," Jessica said matter-of-factly. "Piper's agent called Cynthia this morning and said the deal is off. Piper wants out of the contract."

Double bollocks.

Jessica's gaze homed in on him like a guided missile. "Since dating her, already your Q Score has—or it had before last night—risen and you've gained more followers on social media, not to mention favorable blogs coming out about you and what a sweet, if unexpected, couple you and Piper make. You two have a sort of *Beauty and the Beast* vibe. And in one night you've managed to undo all the good."

He didn't know what to say to that or how to fix things, but he refused to hang his head like a naughty lad in front of the headmaster.

Jessica snorted with frustration at his lack of response. "Do you even care about your image at all?" She set her cocktail on a side table and pulled something up on her phone, then handed it to him.

It was a tweet with the hashtag #CancelGrantCammish. He began to read it, along with the comments.

What the fuck? At first he thought it was going to be some critic saying his show should be canceled, but as he read, he realized the cancel culture of the Twitterverse was calling for his head because he'd dated Crissella Faust *eleven* years ago. When he was twenty-one.

Fucking hell. He was up against it for something else totally unrelated to his row with Piper. Unbelievable.

Apparently Crissella had been idiot enough to post her unpopular, radical political views on Twitter, which had got her sacked from her current show. Now he was somehow an arsehole for having dated her, even though it was *eleven* years ago, he'd only dated her off and on over a four-month period, and he'd not exactly been dating her because of her political views. In fact, he wasn't aware she'd had any. They'd not done loads of chatting.

He handed Jessica back her phone, feeling utterly defeated and so very, very weary of it all. "I can't win for losing."

"We need to get Piper back on board. Apologize to her. Do something big and romantic. Something the paps get a tip on."

He wasn't interested in that last part about the paparazzi,

but the bit about him apologizing to Piper did strike a chord. It had occurred to him he should do so, although proper apologies to fake girlfriends weren't in his repertoire. "What do you suggest?"

"Send her a hundred flower arrangements or something like that. It has to be something over-the-top and romantic."

From what he knew of Piper, he didn't think a bunch of flowers would do the trick, but he was already on eggshells with Jessica. He supposed he should listen to her. "All right. I'll do it, but what if it doesn't work?"

"You better hope it will."

---

PIPER WAS on her way back from walking (or mostly carrying) Chewie when she stopped in her tracks. Four flower shop vans from different companies were parked in front of her house. Three guys and a woman, all dressed in various company uniforms, were standing around her front door talking. Also standing around were several paparazzi, their big cameras hanging idly around their necks as they also shot the breeze with one another.

What on earth?

The older lady who lived next door, Mrs. Jackson, was standing at her own front door in a housecoat and high-heeled slippers with fuzzy balls on top. Chewie always tried to attack them whenever she and Mrs. Jackson had neighborly chats. When she saw Piper, she said, "Hi, hon," and pointed at the florist people, a smile on her overly Botoxed face. "I told them you'd taken Chewie for a walk but that you wouldn't be gone long."

Ah. Mrs. Jackson took "Neighborhood Watch" very seriously. She knew all of Piper's comings and goings. Although

Piper wasn't sure telling perfect strangers those comings and goings was the right kind of neighborly watching.

Chewie already in her arms, she walked up her sidewalk, and the paparazzi guys started aiming their cameras. One asked, "Are the flowers from Grant?"

She usually tried to answer, because at this point in her career she needed the paps, but this time she ignored him. Instead, she went straight to the delivery people.

The lady said, "Hi, Ms. Torres. We have a hundred flower arrangements for you."

A hundred???

Immediately she knew the paparazzo had been right. These were from Grant. Probably an apology devised by his agent and/or Cynthia to smooth things over. A hundred floral arrangements were too melodramatic for reserved, refined Grant Cammish to come up with on his own. He'd probably thought it gauche in the extreme. The intriguing part was that he'd done it anyway. He wasn't the type to do what he was told. Plus, he probably wasn't gung ho to keep their fake thing going, given how her "nattering" drove him "dotty," she thought sourly.

Her first instinct was to tell the florists to take their flowers back and stick them up Grant's tight (in the most literal sense possible) ass, but America's Sweetheart wouldn't do something like that. And, really, neither would Piper. Instead, she smiled and said good-naturedly, "Wow. A *hundred*? Where am I going to put a hundred flower arrangements?" She turned and gestured to her small house with an apologetic look. She'd never seen the need for a mansion like some celebs, since she lived alone. And even this small bungalow had cost her nearly two million dollars because of the crazy real estate prices in California.

Everyone chuckled, as she'd intended.

"But are they from Grant?" yelled that same paparazzo.

She looked at him and shrugged, trying not to show the mixed bag of feelings Grant's name evoked inside her. "I don't know. You know as much as I do."

"There's a card," said the lady florist. "I'll run and get it." A minute later, she came back from one of the vans carrying a gorgeous bouquet of purple hyacinths and white peonies.

Tucked into the top of the bouquet was a small white envelope. Keeping a faint smile on her face for the cameras, Piper plucked the envelope from the flowers and opened it. The penmanship was a combo of cursive and print. It wasn't especially pretty, but it was legible and bold. A man's hand-writing. Her pulse quickened.

> *Piper,*
>
> *I realize the flowers are ridiculous, and you can probably glean they weren't my idea. Do with them as you wish.*
>
> *But whether you decide to continue seeing me or not, remember I did give fair warning that I often say the wrong thing. Now you know firsthand what I meant. Yet again, I was a complete arse. I didn't mean what I said.*
>
> *If you believe nothing else, believe that.*
>
> *Forgive me.*
>
> *—Your Bloody British Wanker*

A reluctant sniff burst from her, and compassion and sympathy spread through her chest. It was true. He *had* warned her, and she'd felt sorry for him at the time—until she'd borne the brunt of his lack of filter. It was the sincerity of this message that got to her, though. She believed him.

Besides, she *had* needled him on a subject that he was obviously sensitive about. Actually two subjects. She hadn't exactly been innocent in it all.

"Who are they from, Piper?" This time it was a different paparazzo.

For some reason, she didn't want to share this private thing with them, so she shot them a cryptic grin and said, "That's for me to know and you to find out."

Groans from the paps ensued, but none of them seemed to be too disappointed.

"Should we start unloading, Ms. Torres?" asked the lady florist. She seemed to be the one in charge.

"No." Piper carefully set Chewie on the ground, the end of his leash secure around her wrist, and then took the bouquet the lady held. "I'll take this one. Please deliver the rest to the Sunny Oaks Retirement Home. I'll pay for any extra delivery charges."

As she headed for her front door, a pap asked, "You gonna give him another chance?" Presumptuous of him, since she still hadn't even said for sure who the flowers were from.

Would she give Grant another chance? Probably. She wasn't one to hold a grudge.

From now on, though, she would be wary and guard her heart—like Abuelita guarded her Tres Leches recipe.

## 9

Piper watched Grant's lean, strong fingers scratch under Chewie's fuzzy chin. It was hypnotic. She could stare at Grant's fingers all night—except that would be weird.

She forced her gaze away, and it landed on the custom-made, sequined carrier purse she'd had made to carry Chewie around in at tonight's animal rescue charity gala. Like all the other carriers in different colors and styles she'd had made for different outfits, it had a zipper compartment in the side for lipstick, phone, credit cards—the usual essentials.

For now, though, the carrier, which matched the aqua-colored sequined evening gown she was wearing, was on the floor near her sparkly silver, strappy-heeled feet. Chewie was lying comfortably between her and Grant on the limo seat, head raised to give Grant better access, basking in the attention—which Grant seemed to lavish on him every chance he got. Chewie, at least, had figured out how to get past Grant's defenses and earn his affection.

All sides had agreed to resume the fake relationship, and

an extremely polite, cordial truce had developed. As a result, she'd been spending a lot of time in his trailer on set, since he'd been working fourteen-, sometimes even eighteen-hour days in the last couple of weeks, plus his workouts.

In private, they'd kept things superficial—never having any deeper conversations—but she'd at least helped him run lines and felt more useful this time around.

Grant still hadn't introduced her to Ezra, although she'd hung back in the wings with Derek the PA on several shoots and had also met the showrunner, Harriet, once in passing. Harriet was said to have some say on who was chosen for parts, in addition to Ezra, but Piper hadn't been able to tell if she'd made an impression or not.

Everyone on the show was putting in long, grueling days, trying to stick to the schedule they were behind on before they had to leave for New Zealand in about a month or so for on-location shoots. Every time Piper broached the subject of Ezra with Grant, he would always say it wasn't a good time, that she needed to be introduced to Ezra when he was in a good mood and not harried.

Piper was trying to be patient—after all, she didn't want to be introduced to Ezra when he was stressed out or in a bad mood—but time was running out. She wanted that part, and she wanted Grant's connection to Ezra to help her stand out among the many actresses who would audition for the part. Her talent would hopefully do the rest.

"If you don't drink your champagne," said Grant, breaking into her thoughts, "it will lose its proper chill." The low, rich timbre of his voice filled the back section of the limo and hummed hypnotically over her skin.

She was surprised he'd been the one who'd spoken, since long silences never seemed to bother him. "Mmm," she noised in acknowledgment, and tried not to succumb to that sensual awareness of him she could never shake.

He was extra-blindingly handsome tonight, with his wide shoulders filling out a classic black tuxedo jacket to consummate perfection. His bow tie accentuated his well-formed jawline and the faint cleft of his square chin, and all that black together—the bow tie, the formal jacket and pants, his short, brushed-back dark hair, even his lightly tanned white skin—contrasted with and enhanced the pale blue of his eyes. Last but not least, that minty, evergreen, chopping-pine-logs-shirtless smell of his made her head swim with yearning.

Was the universe *trying* to sabotage her heart-protection efforts? If so, it needed to stop immediately.

She glanced at the console in front of them, which held a bottle of champagne chilling in a bucket and two fluted glasses. One of the flutes, filled almost to the top, she knew was meant for her. The other one was empty.

She hadn't touched the full one because it was no fun to drink alone. Grant was abstaining because he had another nude scene tomorrow, which apparently meant his diet got stricter and his workouts even more insane. She gave him a faint, polite smile as she watched tiny bubbles float to the top of the filled glass. "I'm not really in the mood for a drink right now."

"A pity. It's Krug Brut Vintage 2003, courtesy of Cynthia."

"Mmm," she murmured again.

He looked forward for a second before refocusing on her. "Don't deprive yourself because of me," he said perceptively.

She repeated her faint smile. "No worries. I'm not," she fibbed. "Champagne goes to my head too quickly, and I don't want to arrive at the red carpet sloshed." That was not a fib.

"Ah." He gave a single nod of acceptance, and an unexpected curve of his beautiful mouth made her heart skew sideways for a second. She had to look away from him.

Ribbons of light zoomed past their darkened windows as the limo ate up the miles between them and the Beverly Hills country club where the gala was being held. Grant was now petting Chewie's back with light strokes, which was lulling Chewie to sleep. His chin now rested on his tiny little paws, and his eyelids were drooping.

"Why don't you have a dog?" she asked Grant, breaking the silence herself now.

His expression was faraway for a second before he replied, "I did have. A large Irish setter called Eileen."

"That's an appropriate name. Very Irish."

"It is. I didn't name her, though. I got her from a shelter. It didn't seem right to rename her, since she'd already got used to that one. She was an older girl, already set in her ways."

"Probably because she was a setter."

"Good one," he said, gifting her with a crooked half-smile.

Which made Piper feel clever and ridiculously light-hearted.

Humor lacing his tone, he said, "Thank you for not singing 'Come On Eileen.'"

"You're welcome," she replied regally before saying, "So, what happened to her?" Then she realized that might be a sad subject. "Oh, wait. I'm sorry. Did you have to put her down?"

"No. Nothing like that." His Adam's apple bobbed once,

as if the memory were painful anyway. "I found her a good home. Her life's beer and skittles now."

Piper deduced that meant the dog had a great life, but it was clear he still missed her. Frowning, she said, "Why did you give her away, then?"

"She wouldn't fit in my purse."

Piper gave a mild puff of amusement. "What's the real reason?"

"My schedule, mainly."

*Shed-ule*. She would never get tired of the way he said that.

"I naively thought I could bring her with me everywhere. And I could have dealt with a bit of hassle"—he leaned his head against the plush leather headrest for a second—"but asking her to lie about in my small caravan all day whilst I was shooting scenes didn't seem fair to her."

"Did she have separation anxiety? Chewie does. People think I have him with me all the time as a gimmick, but that's not it. He gets severely depressed when he's not with me. His vet suggested a doggie antidepressant, but it made him too lethargic. So I just decided to always have him with me. Makes us both happier."

Grant nodded. "Yes. She had something similar. She once chewed the fabric covering of one of the chairs in my caravan, probably out of boredom and also the fear she'd been abandoned. I walked in to find a room full of white chair stuffing."

"Uh-oh."

His mouth twisted ruefully. "It was my fault. I should have known leaving her alone stressed her." Piper didn't think he was at fault, but before she could say so, he frowned and added, "I think she'd been mistreated at some point in her life, too. Anyway, being in my caravan made her restless, but if we let her watch me work, she would often bark and bugger up the shoot."

"How long ago was this?"

"Five years ago, during the first run of filming *Battle*."

"Didn't you have an assistant who could take care of her for you?"

"My assistant before Derek wasn't a dog person. She didn't know how to handle a dog, especially a large, needy one like Eileen."

"Couldn't you have hired a new assistant?"

"Yeh, but then Madison would have been out of a job, wouldn't she?"

Wow. He'd sacrificed his beloved pet so his assistant, who didn't sound that competent, wouldn't lose her job. It was little snippets like this that Grant doled out which made Piper want to let her guard down and trust him, but that was red-alert territory. He would be so easy to fall in love with, his flawless good looks already paving the way. If that made her shallow, so be it, but it was impossible not to be attracted to him.

Of course, give him enough time, and he would probably say something to insult her. She took comfort in that, although she had to admit his behavior since his apology had been exemplary.

Jessica and/or Cynthia must have really read him the riot act. He'd been the perfect fake boyfriend in the last two weeks, even spending the night (finally) on her not-so-comfy couch a couple of times even though it messed with his perfectly timed, to-the-minute daily schedule.

And throughout this whole conversation, he hadn't stopped petting Chewie, even though Chewie was now thoroughly in doggie dreamland. Grant was clearly a dog-lover, and dog-lovers shouldn't be without dogs. "What about now that you have Derek?" pressed Piper. "He doesn't seem like anything would faze him. I'm sure he could handle it if you got a dog."

"I agree." Grant shook his head. "But it's not just my shooting schedule. It's my workout regimen, plus all the publicity events for the show and such. Any dog I adopted would be foisted on Derek much more than I could ever spend time with it. It would be Derek's dog, not mine."

The whole thing made her ache for him. What kind of life did he really have? He was arguably the most beautiful man in the world and arguably the loneliest. He couldn't even have a dog.

He grinned, flashing his near-perfect white teeth. "Are you feeling sorry for me, Ms. Torres?"

She barely heard the question because she was remembering what those canines of his felt like when nipping her bottom lip. It gave her goosebumps.

Not gonna happen, *Ms. Torres*, she admonished herself. Get that through your brain. Her teenage vampire fantasies had ended when she was...okay. Maybe it wasn't that long ago. But Grant was a thousand times hotter than Robert Pattinson and Ian Somerhalder combined, and that was a hella amount of hot.

Unaware of her Bella/Elena-ish inner dialogue, he waved his hand in front of her face. "Piper?"

She blinked and cleared her throat, *so* glad he couldn't read minds. "Yes. Just trying to think of a way to make the dog thing work for you."

"The timing isn't right," he said with finality, facing the black partition glass that separated them from the limo driver. His large hand no longer stroked Chewie's back but still rested gently on Chewie's rear end. In fact, Grant's hand easily covered most of Chewie's body. It must feel to Chewie as if someone had put a doggie-size weighted blanket on top of him.

A few more miles passed in amiable silence, and then they were in the line of limos waiting to eject their passengers in front of the red carpet, which had been spread over the front steps of the country club.

Piper gently picked Chewie up and placed him in the cushiony interior of the pet purse, then set the carrier on the seat between her and Grant. She hated to disturb Chewie. He'd been so content under Grant's protective hand.

Chewie's ID tag tinkled against his collar, and he gave his head a good shake, causing the hair of his muzzle that had been smooshed while he slept to puff back up again.

Piper was envious. How nice it would be to wake up in the morning, give her head a good shake, and be ready to go out into the world instead of spending hours straightening her curly hair with a straightening iron or spending hundreds of bucks every three months on a Brazilian blowout.

Grant's gaze drank her in, and she didn't think she was imagining the heat in it. "You look stunning, Piper. I should have said so earlier."

His words made her feel tingly and a little flushed. "Thank you." She looked him over as he had done to her, pretending that she hadn't been thirsting over him since he'd first stood at her front door, all powerful and debonair and in a hurry to pick her up for the gala. "And you look very handsome, too."

He tilted his head a little to one side. "You sure?" He lifted his chin. "No nose hairs sticking out, that sort of thing? Spinach between my teeth?" He bared them so she could see, but she knew he was teasing.

"No spinach or nose hairs, although..." She trailed off,

tilting her own head a little as she noticed his bow tie was off-kilter.

His eyebrows came together. "What's wrong?"

She pointed vaguely at his bow tie. "It's a little wonky."

Scowling some in concentration, he tried to fix it in the dim reflection of the privacy glass. Then he turned to her, brows raised, expression expectant. "Better?" he asked with that soft British *ah* sound at the end.

Somehow, he'd managed to make the bow tie more askew, and she couldn't help but giggle slightly.

One brow stayed charmingly arched. "I'll take that as a no?"

Grinning, she said, "You made it worse." Feeling suddenly shy, she motioned to the bow tie and said, "May I?"

"Please." He leaned toward her, within a couple of inches, to give her better access, but he somehow seemed to be sucking the air from her lungs in the process—while simultaneously making their section of the limo shrink and feel small.

That little flush from before had turned feverish, and it flooded her entire body now, especially when she could feel his breath stir against her nose and mouth. He had wonderful breath, kind of toothpastey, and she already knew from their past fake kisses (although was there really such a thing as a fake kiss?) that that's how he would taste. Thank God she'd remembered to pop an Altoid earlier. And brush her teeth.

Not that they were going to kiss or anything. After all, no cameras were on them.

Hoping no visible signs of how he affected her were showing, she resumed breathing and straightened the bow tie so that it looked as perfect as the rest of him. "There," she said, with a quick pat on his hard chest. "Much better."

He didn't pull away as she expected. Instead, he caught her hand and held it warmly, right up against his thumping heart, and he was staring at her lips.

Anticipation fluttered in her core, and her heart was doing a wild thumping of its own. Oh, my God, she thought. Maybe he *is* going to kiss me. For real. With no one watching us. Just because he wants to.

It would mess up her lipstick.

She would get lipstick on him.

Oh, wait. She was wearing Stila Stay All Day Liquid Lipstick. It wouldn't transfer, not even during an epic kiss. Yay!

Who cared?????

Every cell in her body begged him to kiss her. Please, please, *please*, Grant. *Kiss me!*

She might have heard a distant, paltry cry from her conscience warning her not to let it happen, but it was, well, paltry.

He met her eyes with a burning, seductive intensity. "May I?" he asked, his voice going huskier and deeper than usual.

"You may," she said, sounding as breathless as Marilyn Monroe when she'd sung "Happy Birthday" to JFK.

First, Grant's soft lips brushed over hers, tentative and exploring. It was pure heaven. But when he deepened the kiss by sealing his mouth to hers, and his tongue began to seek out hers, that heaven turned into something much hotter and naughtier. The warmth of his mouth felt amazing, his tongue gliding and flicking against hers. Her lower abdomen contracted with erotic tension.

She reached up and felt the silky short hair at the nape of his neck.

He put his arms around her, pulling her closer but still careful of Chewie's carrier—which just made Piper want him more.

A little moan escaped her, and she felt like her soul might be leaving her body. If Grant's kiss killed her, she couldn't think of a better way to go.

Suddenly, she heard the limo door next to him burst open, and she could see a million camera flashes intruding through her closed eyelids.

The floating sensation, the euphoria of it all, came crashing down in an instant.

"It's Grant Cammish and Piper Torres!" one of the paparazzi yelled, clearly delighted to have caught them kissing.

She and Grant immediately separated, and his mouth molded into the confident, red-carpet smirk she'd seen in a million photographs of him as he squinted at the blinding flashes. He got out of the limo and then held out a hand to Piper, who had scooted over to his side, Chewie hanging from her forearm by the handles of his carrier.

Still a little dazed from the kiss, she took Grant's sturdy hand.

He made eye contact with her for a brief second, that confident smirk still in place.

A sinister possibility occurred to her that made her stomach fall. Had he realized they were close to the red carpet and would be exposed when he'd initiated the kiss? Had he done it for the cameras? Had it meant nothing to him?

She wanted to believe he hadn't known, that he'd done it out of pure attraction to her, that he'd felt at least a little of the raw electricity she'd felt. But nasty doubt invaded just the same.

Whatever the truth was, she had a role to play. So she pasted on her most glamorous smile, let her fingertips remain in the snugness of his hand, and exited the limo as gracefully as she could in the long sheath evening dress with the revealing split up one side. She was grateful for Grant's support as she found her balance on her sky-high Blahnik heels.

And when someone shouted, "How does he kiss, Ms. Torres?" she pressed her lips together in a coy smirk of her own and said, "I don't kiss and tell."

## 10

H e'd somehow cocked things up again. And what had she meant by her cool "*I don't kiss and tell*"?

Now he wondered if the kiss had been bad. He'd been just as curious as the paparazzo what her answer would be and disappointed at her enigmatic response. He'd never got complaints about his kisses before, but what if he'd lost his touch?

He'd certainly had no criticisms from *his* perspective. As always with Piper, she'd been arousing and passionate, and he had the primal urge to plant another smacker on her lips at this very moment, right in front of everyone, just to redeem himself. He took a deep breath and then exhaled slowly to help keep himself leashed.

He watched her chatting to the group of people she'd ditched him for, all of them dressed in formal gowns or tuxes and laughing at something witty she'd probably said. He was unsure whether they were her friends or just acquaintances she knew for various reasons.

This charity event had attracted not only entertainment insiders but also wealthy animal lovers and those who did the "dirty" work, the actual care of the animals. But no matter their vocation, everyone who spent five minutes with Piper felt like she was their best friend.

Him, not so much. He'd been asked for several selfies and signed several autographs for strangers, but none of the people who should be his friends, like his five fellow actors present here from *Battle*, had made any effort to speak to him. He supposed he couldn't fault them too much for that, since he'd not approached them either. But what was the point? They would smile and act phony to his face, then probably make snide remarks behind his back once he walked away. At least, that had been the way of it in the past.

He was ready to get on with things. The banquet portion of the evening should start soon, and he was more than ready. All he wanted was for the evening to end and a bed. *And Piper beneath his body.*

Good God, he needed to quit having thoughts like that. She was a colleague, nothing more. Besides, he would be leaving for New Zealand, and it didn't make sense to start something with her, even if she were willing.

He watched her take a sip of champagne, the beverage she'd refused earlier in the limo, and admired the graceful column of her neck and the plumpness of her lips. He'd fallen asleep in the limo on the way to collect her at her house, but one look at her when she'd opened her front door had jolted every atom in his body awake. Her petite yet curvy body could only be described as luscious. The aquamarine evening confection she wore had tastefully covered most of her body, but the gauzelike, sequined fabric had molded to every one of her delectable curves in a way that didn't leave much to the imagination. Nothing inde-cent, but the ample cleavage of the *very* ample globes of her bosom—and the one bare leg exposed by a slit in the dress and elongated by the heels she wore—had quite stolen his breath.

She'd parted her silky black hair in the middle and pinned it up in a style that reminded him of a flamenco dancer's, and the color of her dress contrasted with and highlighted her brown complexion, accentuating her skin's luminous effervescence.

*Ample globes? Luminous effervescence?* Where had those come from? Bugger. She was turning him into a ruddy poet.

He'd thought things were going well in the limo. She'd seemed a bit pensive but more genuine and amiable instead of the impeccably polite, yet distant persona she'd adopted round him since their row.

His attraction to her, plus the fact that he'd been absurdly tired, had made him feel reckless and unguarded, perhaps a bit out of his head.

He'd thought they'd been enjoying each other, and she *had* given him permission to kiss her in a come-hither voice that had nearly driven him mad with lust. But once someone had opened the limo door and the snappers had begun photographing them, she'd grown distant again and hadn't seemed to give him a second thought once they'd entered the fray of the gala. Perhaps she now regretted the kiss, but it seemed like more than that. Whatever he'd done, though, he was mystified as to what it could be.

So he found himself standing alone, as usual, having already done polite small talk with the people he knew, including Jessica, who was probably flitting about, schmoozing when necessary as part of her job.

It didn't bother him, really. He was content to watch Piper in her element, unselfconscious and radiant. She was a people person. He was not.

Marjorie Ng, the head of the animal rescue organization,

walked up on a small stage where the band was set up, distracting him from his enjoyable perusal of Piper. The conversation began to die down as other people noticed. "Ladies and gentlemen," said Margorie, her voice carrying over the PA speakers throughout the country club's ballroom, "dinner is served. Please join me in the dining room for the banquet and awards ceremony."

That was his cue to walk over and stand next to Piper so he could escort her. Once he arrived, the women in her group either gave him lascivious once-overs or stared at him with slightly dazed eyes. Depending on how each female reacted, her male partner's demeanor became either cautious or hostile.

Piper looked at them with a bemused expression on her face, as if she weren't sure what had happened, why the conversation had suddenly died.

He ignored the various undesirable reactions he'd evoked and offered her his arm. "Shall we?"

Recovering herself, she smiled up at him with a delight and pride that seemed so believable it gave him a pang of regret that it wasn't. Placing her hand on his arm, she said, "Of course. But, Grant, let me introduce you to a few people first."

He tried to keep his expression open and approachable, shaking hands where appropriate, but to no avail. When she made the introductions, the result was the one he always got. Whatever each person's reaction had been at first, now everyone just seemed wary, except for a few of the women who gave him openly admiring, flirty looks, ignoring the fact that his girlfriend—or the woman perceived as his girlfriend—was standing next to him.

Yes, at age sixteen, when he'd shot up in height and his body fat had got distributed more proportionately, the fact that girls had suddenly stopped rolling their eyes at him and started batting their eyelashes instead had been a relief to a shy lad like him, had made interacting with the opposite sex much easier. And wanker that he was back then, he'd taken advantage of it, broken a few hearts, even had a bout with a stalker in his twenties.

But now, the way women openly flirted with him had driven away more than one of his brief, real girlfriends in the past. Never mind that he'd never cheated on someone he was dating. The fact that women—and some men— threw themselves at him without regard to whether he had a partner or not was apparently taken as a sure sign that he would inevitably cheat, however unfair the assumption. His past girlfriends had never been willing to give him the benefit of the doubt.

He couldn't fathom it, the unwanted attention he got and the animosity that sometimes came with it. Jessica said it was because he was handsome to the point of being a threat to other men, while he was simply irresistible to women. They either forgot their own names on meeting him or immediately tried to find a way into his trousers.

He thought Jessica's theory was rubbish, mainly because he'd never made friends easily, looks or not. Whatever the reason, whether it was that he naturally repelled people or that his alleged good looks were intimidating, it was getting old.

"What was that all about?" asked Piper as they began heading toward the dining room.

He knew what she meant, but he said, "Sorry?"

She looked back at some of the people over her shoulder. "They were so rude. Half of them turned up their noses when you arrived, and half of them clearly wanted to boink you. They were so flagrant about it, and I was standing *right there*."

"Ah, yes. Just my usual penchant for being a buzzkill. I've quite the talent for it." He was wryly resigned to it and half expected Piper to make some quip about it to tease him.

Instead, she bristled and pursed her mouth as if she disagreed, as if she were disgruntled on his behalf. "You were totally nice." Her brows drew together, and her upper lip stiffened. "And the way those *putas* were devouring you right in front of me!"

"*Putas*?" he repeated, amused. "Would your mother approve of such language?" He didn't speak Spanish, but he'd lived in California long enough to have gleaned a few words of the more colorful Spanish vernacular. He knew *puta* was not a compliment.

She huffed, expression still fierce, and her shoulders did a sort of indignant roll. "No, but my abuela would if she knew some skank was trying to move in on my man. I should kick their asses."

He fought to keep a straight face, knowing she'd not appreciate it if he laughed. But most of those women had been several inches taller than she, and the visual he got of her kicking them in the arse with her stilettos was both funny and captivating. He bent down and said in her ear, "Your vigorous defense of me is very kind, but the paps and gossips might think your expression of displeasure is aimed at me."

She gifted him instantly with that dazzling smile of hers, the one that always seemed to put him and everyone else in its vicinity at ease, and he knew in that instant why people said a smile could light up a room.

"That's better," he said, straightening, but not before inhaling the scent of her, something feminine and addictive.

It made him feel as if he had drunk a couple of pints of Guinness, even though he'd not taken a drop.

Maintaining the smile, she said, "But I still want to kick their asses. The men, too." She shook her head as if it were all so ludicrous. "It was like being in a pasture full of bulls. Like, you could literally *see* the testosterone levels rising and the realization that a new bull had come to impregnate the herd."

A laugh escaped him. "Interesting analogy. And your passion to protect what's yours is truly stirring." He bent down to her ear again and said sotto voce, "But you do remember we're not really dating, yeh?"

Her smile turned brittle.

At once, he wondered what in God's name had made him say that. He reckoned he'd meant to be droll, but the exact reverse had happened.

"Yes," she said, looking away from him, "but the point is, *they* don't know that."

He cursed himself for being a prat but didn't know how to unsay what he'd said.

She hardly spoke to him after that or through dinner, which was a draining, boring affair for him. Piper was on his left, chatting animatedly to the dinner partner to her left. On Grant's right sat a man near Grant's age who'd hardly said two words to him, even after Grant had made a valiant effort to engage him in conversation.

It was a relief when someone started clinking a spoon against a glass to get everyone's attention, and he noticed that Marjorie was at the podium. The lights dimmed in the chandeliers, and a spotlight shone on her. She went through her speech, giving a history of the organization, talking about its purpose, and mentioning various people she wanted to thank. It was a worthy organization, one Grant had gladly supported with an anonymous donation.

Unfortunately, her droning started to make his eyelids droop. He knew it was rude, but he rested his elbow on the table, chin in hand, hoping no one would notice in the darkness if he shut his eyes for just a second.

The next thing he knew, Piper was jarring him awake. It probably hadn't been more than a minute or so, but he really had no idea how long he'd dozed.

Everyone was clapping and staring at him, and now the blinding spotlight was on him.

Piper seemed to recognize he had no clue what had happened, so she whispered in his ear, "You're Donor of the Year. Go up and get your award."

He stiffened. Bloody hell. He was going to kill Jessica and Cynthia.

## 11

Piper couldn't believe that, first of all, these bitches were dumb enough to gossip about someone without checking the toilet stalls first. (Her abuela would call gossips like this *chismosas*.) Second, they were skewering Grant for winning an award for being charitable. Unbelievable.

"It's probably some publicity stunt or something," said Chismosa #1.

Ha, thought Piper. Close, but no cigar, at least not for this.

Piper had finished her business and had been about to leave her stall when she'd heard the two women walk into the restroom talking about Grant. She knew she should have made herself known, but she couldn't resist hearing what they had to say. So here she was, standing as still as she could so they wouldn't detect her.

"And did you see how haughty he was, so reluctant about going up to the podium?" said Chismosa #2, the nasal one. "Piper Torres practically had to shove him out of his seat to get him to move."

"That's pretty much what he's like on set, too," said Chismosa #1. "He's such an asshole. Never deigns to speak to any of us, except for Ezra, of course."

That was true, the part about urging him to go up to the podium—Piper had actually had to wake Grant up—but she'd seen the look on his face before he'd composed himself. First it had been befuddled surprise. Winning the Donor of the Year award had completely blindsided him. Second, he'd been about to face-plant into what was left of his fish entree. If she hadn't woken him, he totally would have. He'd had to blink several times to orient himself and shake off his bewilderment.

Then, when Piper whispered to him that he'd won, his jaw had hardened and his nostrils had flared before he donned that indecipherable, slightly insolent expression that masked whatever he was really feeling.

She'd been both surprised and proud of him for winning the award. She'd sensed that he loved animals, but to be top donor for an organization of this size with such famous and wealthy donors, he must have given a huge sum. She'd had no idea he was *that* into animals or that he'd even donated, for that matter. She'd thought they were attending the event to be seen together—as they had several others—and for no other reason. Grant had never mentioned a thing about being a supporter of the charity.

But the glimpse of his rock-hard jaw before he'd gone up to the podium had told her he wasn't happy to be recognized in such a way. It was as if he were mad that he'd been outed, and maybe he was. She'd been around him long enough to know he was intensely private—fake relationship for the paparazzi notwithstanding—so maybe the people who ran the fundraising part of the rescue had made a mistake. Or maybe he'd wanted to remain anonymous, but they'd honored him anyway. She could understand their need to worship him in whatever form they could, she thought wryly.

Whatever the reason, though, his short, curt thank-you after he'd received the award and lack of a speech afterward had not been a crowd-pleaser. It had, however, perpetuated the image of him as snooty and bored of the whole thing, as if it were all beneath him.

It didn't matter that he'd just won an award for doing a good deed. How easily people forgot the good things and held onto the bad.

Chismosa #1 snorted. "And Piper Torres. What the hell? That is a seriously odd couple."

"I *knoooow*," Nasal Chismosa replied. "She's cute, I guess, but doucheyness aside, *he* looks like a Greek god. He could have any woman he wants."

"He knows it, too. Believe me."

"I can't believe he's with *her*," said Nasal. "She's not as fat as she was, but she's not what anyone would call skinny, either, at least not by industry standards."

"I bet he practically has to bend in half or crouch down on his knees in order to kiss her, she's so freaking short."

Piper had to put her hand over her mouth to keep a gasp of outrage from escaping.

Nasal laughed. "Unless she's wearing those sky-high heels. You have to give her credit. She has great taste in shoes. Do you think they're Choos?"

"No. Blahniks. I saw the same ones on the Bergdorf website." Going back to the subject of Grant, Chismosa #1 mused, "Maybe she's his beard. Maybe those rumors he's gay are true. He certainly spends a lot of time in his trailer with his assistant, Derek."

"Oh, God," said Nasal. "I hope that's not true."

"Why? You think you stand a chance with him?"

Nasal snorted. "If that has-been Piper Torres has a chance with him, surely *I* would."

They both snickered.

Their cruel words were like bricks slamming into Piper's chest. It hurt, and she felt her eyes get watery. But she'd rather die than mess up her mascara—or let these two vultures know how much they'd gotten to her.

Pulling her shoulders back and raising her chin, she exited the stall as if she were Meryl Streep and coolly walked over to a free sink to wash her hands. She liked the way the five-inch heels of her Blahniks clicked on the marble floor, echoing loudly in the sudden cavelike silence of the opulent restroom, giving her much-needed height and badassness.

The two white, blond, emaciated bitches also standing at the vanity shared an *oh, shit* look.

Piper recognized them now. Chismosa #1 was an actress from *Battle*, one with a minor role. Piper couldn't remember her name. The nasal one was Elizabeth Ruth, a beautiful up-and-coming actor who'd been part of the group Piper had introduced Grant to. Now that Piper was seeing her, she couldn't believe she hadn't recognized that nasal voice. It had been annoying, but other than that, Piper had thought she was nice when they'd talked earlier.

"Ladies?" said Piper cordially.

They stared at her, faces red underneath their makeup, clearly speechless.

Piper reached over and got a thick, disposable guest towel from the nearest tray, dried her hands, then threw it away. As she walked past them toward the door, she held her head high and gave them both a look that would have turned them to stone if she'd been Medusa. As she was about to open the door, she looked over her shoulder toward them and said, "You sure Grant is the asshole?" She zeroed in on the one who worked on *Battle*. "Because you might want to rethink who the asshole is here."

Then she looked at Elizabeth, the one who'd been talking about trying to get her claws into Grant. "As for you, *mamas*," she said, using the common Mexican endearment with matter-of-fact disdain, "he's taken."

They watched her go, mouths slack, not saying a word— probably knowing any sort of apology would have fallen flat, if they'd even had the decency to attempt one.

Once she was back out in the ballroom, where everyone had gone to dance once the banquet had ended, it was as if she had Grant-dar. Her eyes immediately found him standing near the bar holding a glass of wine he probably wasn't going to drink in one hand and her very sparkly pet carrier with Chewie poking his furry head out in his other.

The image of them together was adorable, and the contrast of the girlie purse in such a masculine hand had the reverse effect of emphasizing everything about Grant that was all man: the set of his broad shoulders that shouted capability and a smidge of arrogance, as if there was nothing he couldn't handle; the fact that he thought nothing of holding Chewie for her because he was comfortable in his own skin, in his own sexuality. (Her brothers, on the other hand, would have looked at the pet carrier as if it contained the plague.)

He commanded the room like a giant sequoia tree, while everyone else was a pine.

Piper saw yet another gorgeous predatory woman heading straight for him, a sight as menacing as a shark's dorsal fin cutting through ocean water.

"Oh, hell no," Piper muttered to herself. She pulled her

shoulders back to make herself appear as tall and confident as possible and headed toward him. She was going to get to him before that heifer, and she was going to prove to every one of these jackals that Grant Cammish was *not* out of her league.

She rummaged through her mental bag of acting techniques and tried hard to make herself believe it. Fake it till you make it, she told herself. You are the most desirable woman in this room, and don't you forget it.

When Piper reached Grant a few seconds before the other woman, whose face fell when she realized she'd been outrun, Piper took the full red wineglass from his hand and set it at the end of the nearby bar with other discarded empty drink glasses and wine stems.

He looked blithely surprised. "I just got that."

"Yeah, well, we both know you have no intention of actually drinking it."

He cocked a brow. "Do we?"

"We do." She took his hand and got the usual spurt of endorphins its warmth and strength always stirred in her. "Come dance with me."

"What about Chewie?"

"We'll give him to my friend Tara." She indicated a table not far away where her friend Tara sat with a few others, watching people dance.

Tara, who was nearly eight months pregnant, was happy to watch Chewie instead of dancing—as Piper knew she would be—and was already taking him out of the pet carrier to cuddle him before Grant and Piper had even walked away.

The band was playing a Muzak-sounding version of an Ed Sheeran song, and Grant pulled her to him, one hand on her waist and the other holding her hand up near their chests.

Their closeness and that compelling junipery scent of him caused a flare of heat to curl around her stomach.

He studied her for a moment. "Is there anyone you don't know?"

"Um"—she pretended to think about it—"no."

He smiled.

It tickled her insides. *Híjole.* It was like he was a king, and winning his favor was a boon of the highest order.

She could feel the hardness of everything where their bodies touched (like his chest, not another part of his anatomy that had the potential to grow hard but wasn't at the moment because he wasn't fourteen). "Nice dance moves," she said, trying to keep her brain working properly and out of the drooling zone, more than for the sake of conversation.

"Thank you, but I'd hardly call this swaying we're doing real dancing," he said without doucheyness.

She raised her eyebrows. "Oh? Would you like to break out some more complicated moves, maybe start doing the Macarena?"

"Good God, no," he deadpanned, sounding extremely droll and English. "But I do know a few waltzes and Boulangeries."

"Really?"

He nodded. "Had to learn them for my role in *Pride and Prudishness.*" He gave her a cagey wink. "Surely you saw that masterpiece of cinematic triumph."

"Oh, of course," she said in a tone that conveyed she'd never seen it.

He laughed, his eyes crinkling at the corners. "Not surprising you've never heard of it. It was a massive flop in theaters, a modern take on *Pride and Prejudice* that was quite silly and, unfortunately, borderline pornographic. Needless to say, it didn't make my career, but I did learn a new skill from it."

"Oh?" she said archly.

Deliberately misinterpreting her innuendo, he said, "Oh, yes. One never knows when a Boulanger might come in handy." He said the name of the dance with a French accent, like *boo-lawn-zhay*, and his French was just as sexy as his English.

She wondered what exactly a Boulanger was and tried not to think about the more porny skills he might have learned, mainly because she knew she would never be the beneficiary of them. She racked her brain, trying to remember if he'd had any love scenes on *Battle* with that *puta* in the bathroom. Probably. He'd had love scenes with just about every actress on the show. Why did that rankle her so much? It was his *job*, as was his fake courtship of Piper herself.

It made her feel jaded. It used to be one of the things she loved about acting and Hollywood, the fact that nothing was real, that everything was make-believe, that anything was possible, but suddenly it just seemed...sad.

He ducked his head down to look into her eyes. "Was it something I said?"

"Oh, no. Just—" She cleared her throat and tried to smile. "Just checked out for a minute."

A slow nod of his head told her that he didn't know what to make of her sudden change in mood, that he was uncertain.

"Really. It's not you. I think I'm just getting tired. You know. Long day being Grant Cammish's girlfriend," she teased.

He glanced toward the ceiling in an *oh, please* gesture. "Right. The role of a lifetime."

"No," she said airily. "That would be *you* playing Piper Torres's boyfriend."

"Of course." He turned his head to give her his profile while still managing to whisk her around the dance floor. "How's it all working? Am I exuding humanity?"

She frowned, not understanding. "What?"

He gazed at her directly again, the allure of his light eyes causing a sudden lilt in her chest. "Jessica and Cynthia say dating you makes me more human. What do you think?"

That was so ridiculous that she couldn't give him a straight answer. "Well, you've definitely got the 'man' part down. Jury is still out on the 'hu' part."

He grinned at full wattage, tilting his head back a little. It was so boyish, so real, so thoroughly disarming. And she loved it that he seemed to know she was ribbing him, that he clearly wasn't taking offense. She was discovering he had a sense of humor after all.

How could anyone ever think he wasn't human? Maybe the trick was just to treat him like one instead of like some unattainable idol or a commodity. "You're actually a decent guy, if maybe a little too reserved sometimes. You're hard to get to know."

He sobered, and his eyes strayed from her for a second. "I suppose you're right about that." He'd said it so quietly she'd almost missed it.

The way he'd agreed with her—as if he knew she was right but wasn't sure how to change it—made her heart constrict a little. "You didn't seem too happy you were Donor of the Year. Why? It's a worthy cause. Why wouldn't you want people to know you support it?"

"It's none of their business. And I don't want people to

think I did it just as a vulgar show of wealth or a publicity stunt."

A valid concern, considering one of the bathroom bitches had said almost the same thing earlier.

His stoic mask fell into place—she could literally see it happen, that moment he turned from the real Grant into the stiff-upper-lipped, closed-off Brit—and she knew it meant he was hiding his emotions and he didn't want to talk about it anymore.

She wasn't going to let him off so easily. She wanted the real Grant back. "Was there a mistake?" she prodded. "Were they not supposed to give you the award or something?"

He watched her for a moment, then sighed. "I made the donation anonymously, but someone somewhere—probably someone who handled the accounting of the organization—must have seen the name on the credit card I used or something. Since I had apparently donated the most money for the year"—he broke eye contact for a second, as if a little embarrassed by that—"they contacted my people, meaning Cynthia, who then contacted Jessica, to see if I might change my mind and accept an award for it." A muscle ticked in his jaw. "I told them both no and thought I'd heard the last of it until tonight."

Piper was irked on his behalf. "So they totally ignored your wishes and told the charity to give you the award?"

"That's the most likely scenario."

"And you had no idea you were going to be recognized tonight until they called you up to the podium." How shitty of Jessica and Cynthia to do that to him, however much good they thought winning the award might do for his image—especially since he wasn't exactly known for saying the right things on the fly.

"No idea," he confirmed. "And the topper is that a perfectly good kip was interrupted."

She snorted and grinned. "Ah. No wonder you were grouchy."

"Precisely," he said, his gaze sparking with amusement and showing signs the real Grant was for sure coming back.

The first song ended, and a slow, romantic one came on. She reached up and wrapped her arms around his neck, craning to look up at him—and tried not to think about what the bathroom bitches had said about her height. He only had to bow a little so she could reach, so there.

She felt his hands go around her waist and had a moment of self-consciousness, afraid he might feel her less-than-flat *panza*, but soon got over it. It wasn't like she needed to impress him. He would never be anything more than a friend, and it struck her that that's what they might be becoming. Slowly but surely, they were getting to know each other—and like each other.

As if to reiterate that, he was earnest when he said, "I've quite enjoyed this evening with you, Ms. Torres." Then he had to stifle a yawn with his hand before putting it around her waist again.

"Yeah. I can see that."

He looked sheepish. "Sorry."

He didn't need to apologize. Aside from the obvious yawn, he practically personified exhaustion. She might have to prop his eyelids open with toothpicks if they stayed much longer.

"I did mean what I said, though," he said. "It has been my pleasure to be your escort."

His words went straight to her bone marrow, nearly killing her with their simple kindness. "Thank you," she said, her throat feeling a little lumpy. "It's been a pleasure to be escorted by you."

He nodded and then stifled another yawn.

As much as she would have loved to stay in his arms, she decided it was time to end his torture. "I think we've been good little actors tonight. Pictures have been taken. Intimacy has been displayed. I think we can safely leave now, if you want."

"Only if you're truly ready. We can stay if you're still enjoying yourself." He gave her another earnest look, and she was touched that he was willing to sacrifice more of his evening if she wasn't ready to go, when all he probably really wanted to do was face-plant on his bed.

She got lost in his gravitational pull for a second, that pesky unwanted attraction to him pooling in her core. *I would enjoy myself anywhere you are*, she almost said. She stiffened, thanking God she hadn't said that out loud. "Nope. Let's grab Chewie and go. I'm ready."

The relief he wasn't able to hide when he heard her say that spoke volumes.

Soon they were taking the limo back to his house—a first for their "relationship." He'd crashed at her house a couple of times, but she'd never stayed at his until tonight. An overnight bag with a change of clothes and a few other interesting items had been delivered to his house earlier in the day, courtesy of a courier, since her house and Grant's were almost an hour's drive apart—and that was when it wasn't rush hour.

She was supposed to stay the night in one of the guest rooms and then hang out with Grant by his pool after his morning shoot tomorrow, which was the only thing scheduled for him workwise. Shocker. They were letting him have a half day of downtime. On a Saturday. So nice of them. And a pap would be taking telephoto lens shots of them from some rooftop somewhere to make sure their leisurely afternoon was documented. And on Sunday they were scheduled to take a domestic trip to IKEA, which would also be documented, since Grant was also off on Sunday. Poor guy. Now that he was "dating" her, he would never have a day off from acting.

She, on the other hand, had a great gig. All she did was sit around and try to look cute and besotted with Grant. If he weren't so gorgeous to look at—and if it weren't for that annoying gravitational pull thing—it would be the most boring job ever.

He still hadn't introduced her to Ezra, citing the same old excuses, but that was going to change. He was too tired for her to bring it up tonight—he'd fallen asleep already now that they were in the limo on their way to his house— but tomorrow she was putting her foot down.

She suspected he was delaying her intro to Ezra for another reason besides busy schedules: Grant didn't think she stood a chance of getting the role.

She smiled to herself as she watched him sleep. She had a plan, and after tomorrow, he would think differently.

## 12

P iper sat near the fabulous infinity-edge pool in the back of Grant's large-but-not-ostentatious, super-modern-style house. It sat on a cliff on Laguna Beach, not too far as the crow flies from the studio where his show was filmed. Why hadn't they been hanging out here instead of her place all along? This was paradise.

AirPods in her ears, she was listening to the latest daily mix playlist on Spotify. Grant probably had an awesome stereo system and speakers out here somewhere, but she had no idea how to connect to it. She was worse than Abuelita when it came to technical stuff.

Chewie was napping beneath her chaise on an extra folded towel she'd put down for him.

The house had clearly been professionally decorated inside and out with tasteful contemporary furniture, mostly in neutral colors like black and white, but a few pops of color were scattered strategically throughout to add drama and interest. Grant had some very cool modern art, and she wondered if he had collected it or if his designer had.

Grant's house was way different from her more boho historic bungalow, but she liked it. It fit his urbane image to a T. It was a fully grown, successful male's house.

It also had some Euro touches that one might expect from a pseudo-European English bachelor, like a stainless-steel electric teakettle and about a thousand boxes of tea, mostly English Breakfast and Darjeeling, in one of the cupboards. He also had a French press, which she had absolutely no idea how to use. Thankfully, no YouTube instruction was required because there'd also been a Nespresso coffeemaker, and she'd made herself a divine cappuccino to go with her breakfast.

No sugary pastries in Grant's pantry, although there had been about nine different kinds of body-builder-looking protein powder. Steering clear of that, she'd settled on peanut butter toast with sliced apple and cinnamon on top and had patted herself on the back for her healthy yet satisfying concoction. That was one benefit of hanging out with Grant: it had been much easier to stick to a healthy diet for herself, even though she still thought his was over-the-top. She might have even lost a few pounds. She hadn't weighed lately, but her clothes felt looser, and she was feeling good about herself in the cute bathing suit she wore.

Nowadays she preferred a tank suit, which consisted of a tank top with thin, removable straps and a mix-and-match microskort bottom. The top showed off the girls but still had enough support and wasn't too granny. Both pieces were made of fabric ready for the pool or ocean. It looked good on her, and it covered enough of her that she didn't have to bother with a coverup if she wanted to get up and walk around. It was like a sport outfit she could also swim in.

Sometimes she switched the skirt out for boy shorts, but

the skirt made her feel more girlie. And she did *not* want Grant to think of her as just one of the guys.

The pool's chic curvy tanning chairs sat on a tanning shelf in the water, but Piper sat in a cushiony chaise farther back under the shade of an aqua-blue umbrella. The house was on a cliff that overlooked the ocean, and a constant breeze blew, making the unusually hot, early November day balmy and comfortable.

She took a sip of the sparkling Evian she'd found in the little outdoor fridge. She liked that it was in a glass bottle— not only classy but also better for the environment—but decided that if she was going to be at Grant's house more often, she was going to have to stock it with Topo Chico, which tasted way better. Of course, she might be biased since she was from Texas, where the Mexican mineral water known for its purity and superior fizziness had been popular for a decade. Since Coca-Cola had bought it a few years ago, though, it was everywhere now.

She'd been tempted to make herself a cocktail from Grant's well-stocked bar, but it wasn't quite noon yet. She didn't want to drink alone, and she didn't want him to think she was a lush. (Although that ship might have already sailed, considering the many times she'd drunk in front of him while he'd either just watched or drunk one glass to her three.)

She hadn't seen him yet today. He'd been long gone for his workout and then the *Battle* shoot before she'd woken at nine. God only knew what crazy hour he'd gotten up to leave, but definitely before the crack of dawn.

When she'd explored his house out of boredom earlier (no snooping, just admiring the decor), she'd found the home gym Derek had mentioned to her once when they were hanging out, and she wondered why Grant's trainer,

Jason, didn't come to him instead of the other way around. She smiled with satisfaction when she saw the fencing equipment hanging on one wall just as Derek had described.

Grant had literally stumbled up the stairs to his bedroom as soon as they'd walked in the front door last night, he'd been so tired, so she'd stayed up with Chewie and watched a rom-com on Netflix. The irony wasn't lost on her that those following their "budding romance" on social media would probably assume she and Grant had done the "Netflix-and-chill" thing at some point by now. At least they were half right.

Her favorite song came on, and she closed her eyes and let the breeze and the glorious day lull her into a meditative doze. So when someone lifted the sunglasses off her face, she kept her eyes closed and said, "I really hope you're not a burglar."

"I could say the same about you," said a deep, beautifully accented voice that heated her in a way that had nothing to do with the weather. "You've made yourself at home, I see."

It was then she remembered she'd never put away her breakfast dishes from this morning. She'd fully intended to but had been distracted by the self-tour she'd taken of his house. She didn't know for sure that's what he was referring to, but oops.

His house was immaculate—like it was waiting to be in an *Architectural Digest* spread and no one actually lived there.

She opened her eyes, squinting a little, to see his eyes smiling down on her. They shone like blue diamonds in the bright sun.

There he went, stealing her breath again. And if he was

talking about the dirty dishes, he didn't seem to be perturbed by it.

His dark hair was disheveled by the wind and probably also from the shoot. She wondered which lucky girl he'd done the love scene with and ignored the way her insides twisted from what she could no longer deny was jealousy. She was starting to get used to it. "I *have* made myself at home. You coming to join me?"

That question was really a formality. They were supposed to spend at least a couple of hours "canoodling" by the pool so the invisible photographer out there, wherever he was, could get some good "forbidden" shots of them. But Grant hadn't exactly been known to follow the plan to the letter, so there was always a moment where she wondered if he was going to bail on her.

He handed her sunglasses back and crouched down to pet Chewie, which made his powerful thighs stretch the denim of his jeans. "I think I'll have a shower first," he said, straightening back to a stand, "but then I'll be out to join you."

"Why take a shower? Aren't you going to get in the pool?"

"Yeh, yeh," he said, then made a face. "But I'm minging a bit."

"You're what?"

He gave her a crooked half-smile. "Bit sweaty and smelly from the set. Probably best I don't get in the pool yet."

She snorted. "If you were my brother Julián, you wouldn't care. To him, shower, pool, same thing."

He laughed. "I've got a brother or two who would probably think the same. I like to think I'm more civilized, though." Then, contradicting himself, he grabbed her Evian off the side table next to her chaise and chugged about half of it without asking, his Adam's apple bobbing in his smooth, muscular throat.

"Would you like a sip of my water, Grant?" she asked as though he hadn't already helped himself.

"Yes. Kind of you to offer." He drank the rest of it, burped suavely (which she hadn't known was possible), then thunked it back down on the table as if it had been a shot of whiskey. "Be back in a tick."

She watched him stride back into the house, his tantalizing butt, accentuated by his low-slung jeans, commanding most of her attention.

While he was in the shower, she went into the kitchen and cleaned up her dishes. Chewie had followed her, and the little metal ID tag on his collar jingled, letting her know where he was so she wouldn't step on him.

As she was finishing up, Grant came in wearing a plain gray T-shirt that complemented his eyes and black swim trunks. Not the banana-hammock Speedo kind, thank God. She'd seen enough of those on various trips to Europe to last her a lifetime. Grant's were the good old American-style board shorts, and when combined with the just-showered scent of him and his wet hair looking raven black, they were more than enough to make her heart go pitter-patter.

And his hair was curly! Not Napoleon Dynamite curly, but hot-foreign-soccer-player curly. She'd seen it a little wavy a few times, but usually it was straight. She'd never seen it *au naturel* before. It was adorbs. And had she mentioned hot?

"Wow," she said, joking, "your hair is as curly as mine when I don't straighten it. If we had kids together, we'd never get a brush through their hair."

His gaze sharpened on her, and she was instantly

embarrassed. "I mean, not that we'd ever have kids together."

He didn't respond, just stood there for a second until saying in a neutral tone, "Right."

Why, oh why, had she said that? She scooped Chewie up and nuzzled the top of his head with her chin to give herself something to do and to hide her embarrassment.

Grant went to the wide Subzero fridge and opened the door. His handsome face was instantly spotlighted by the fridge's golden light, and the muscles of his back flexed against his T-shirt as he held the door open. Then he reached in and pulled out a bottle of Guinness, which caused more muscle-under-T-shirt flexion along with some bulging biceps action. "Fancy a pint?" he asked, his expressive dark brows raised in polite inquiry. "Or wine? Cocktail, perhaps?"

He was so effortlessly refined, even when he was being casual. She felt like she'd just been offered a drink by James Bond. She weighed whether she should go for the beer, which was what she really wanted, or a cocktail, which would be girlier and the more expected choice. The beer would also make her feel more bloated. But screw it. Guinness was usually a bit too dark and bitter for her, but a good hearty beer sounded good to her right now. Besides, she hadn't had lunch. The Guinness would tide her over. "Pint, please."

He nodded with a slight curve of his mouth. "Excellent choice." He got down two pint glasses—Guinness ones with the harp logo—from a cabinet.

This amused her. God forbid he drink Guinness out of anything other than a proper Guinness glass.

Once he had a dark, frothing pint in each hand, he said, "Shall we?" and gestured with his chin across the open-concept kitchen and living room toward the sliding patio doors that led out to the pool.

"Sure. Show must go on, right?"

His gaze flattened, as if wearied by the thought. "Right."

She wished she hadn't reminded him.

## 13

The mention of kids had thrown him for a loop. At first he'd thought Piper knew something about his ongoing matter with Amanda, but it seemed her remark had been just a casual musing and not a reference to the possibility of his impending fatherhood or lack thereof.

He smiled to himself at her remark about curly-headed children. He couldn't deny that, for a split second at least, the thought of her being the mother of his future children had been quite a pleasant notion.

As for the matter of his impending fatherhood, the suspense was gutting him. The baby would be born toward the end of this month. He just hoped Amanda didn't drag her heels about getting the paternity test after the baby came. He wanted to be there for its birth, whether it was his or not, but she'd gone home to New York to be with her family for the big event. He was stuck in California filming *Battle*, so there was no way he would be able to get to her in time to witness the birth, unless he took the week off before she was due and just hung round near her—which she'd made clear she didn't want.

Treading water in the deep end of the pool, he watched Piper now as she slowly got in, getting used to the slightly chilly water gradually by having just her feet and ankles in the water on the tanning shelf. She should just jump in like he had. Much faster to get acclimated that way.

Not that he wasn't enjoying a leisurely perusal of her. Like the evening gown she'd worn last night, her aqua-and-black tank top and black...skirt? shorts? both? covered her adequately, but the voluptuous shape of her body was still outlined as if the bathing suit were a second skin. And her nipples had responded instantly when she'd first stepped into the water, hardening to enticing pebbles and nearly driving him mad with the need to flick his thumb over one of them and kiss the other.

Speaking of children, Chewie had resumed his position on his towel in the shade under Piper's chaise. If the way she babied him was any indication of her mothering skills, she would be excellent. Her compassion and patience would serve her well.

And why did Grant carry on thinking about mother-hood, especially connected to Piper? The Guinness must be going to his head.

He and Piper had each had three by now—not enough to be pissed, but definitely enough to lower inhibitions, get a nice buzz going, and apparently cause one to have barmy thoughts. He was impressed at her capacity to handle her alcohol. He'd been with loads of women who were legless after one drink, which was annoying. Propping up his dates all night wasn't his idea of fun.

"This pool is crazy cold," said Piper, thankfully distracting him from his thoughts on domesticity and bad dates. "Don't you have a heater or something?"

"Heater?" He scoffed. "In the UK, this would be bathwater."

She looked dubious. "If I get hypothermia, please let the doctors at Cedars know what happened."

He laughed. "Just get in. It's like ripping off a plaster."

"Yet again, I have no idea what you're talking about."

"Band-Aid," he supplied.

"Oh, right," she said with a wry glance to the sky and a fetching smile.

Which in turn made him want to smile back like an idiot. He didn't, but he wanted to. He'd noticed she made him want to laugh and smile in excessive amounts, which was bad. Jailbait Lexi had had the same effect on him at times. It was good to remember that.

"Okay," Piper said solemnly, and drew in a dramatic breath, as if she were about to undertake some life-threatening task. "Here goes."

Again, he held in a smile.

She glided into the water using her arms to propel her, sucking in breaths and squeaking, "Oh, my God. This is really effing cold!"

He met her at the spot where her feet could no longer touch the bottom and took her hand. "Here. Perhaps if we... frolic some together, you'll get warmed up."

She half-snorted, mirth in her gaze. "Frolic? Did Jessica use that word?"

A mirthful snort managed to make its way out of him, too. "She did."

For some reason, that made them both snicker like school children. Trying to act serious again but feeling the loosening effects of the Guinness, he said, "I think the first step to proper frolicking is to put your arms around my neck."

She pretended to contemplate that, her eloquent brows coming together. "Like this?" she asked, as she reached up and wrapped her arms around him.

"Yes. Excellent technique."

She dipped her chin to one side in a courtly manner and smiled. "Thank you."

He could still touch bottom and stand, so treading water wasn't necessary. He put his arms round her waist and felt an instant sizzle between them despite the chilly water.

It wasn't unlike dancing with her last night, except they had more clothes on then. Now the only thing between their bodies was the water that could easily be displaced. He liked having her in his arms, the solidity of her, the knowledge that he was supporting her, even though she was buoyed by the water too. And he could smell her hair, which she'd not got wet yet—that flowery, herbal, womanly scent that always went to his head. Her hair was in a ponytail, but he could see now that it did have the potential to curl, if the little spiral tendrils at the nape of her neck were any indication.

He had the urge to give her a good dunking to get it thoroughly wet but thought better of it. He wouldn't put it past her to kick him in the crown jewels for such an offense.

"Do you think they're watching?" she asked in a low tone.

He didn't have to ask who "they" were, of course. She meant the snappers. It would be impossible for anyone to hear them, but he matched her low tone anyway. "Likely."

"Hmm... So William used the word 'canoodle.'" There was a devilish twinkle in her eye. "Do you think that's the same as frolicking?"

"No," he said with mock authority, knowing they were in agreement that both words were ridiculous, that this whole scenario was ridiculous. "Huge difference between frolicking and canoodling. Didn't they teach you anything in Texas?"

She laughed, and it captivated him.

She was so bloody tempting. He wanted to do much more with her than canoodle. "Frolicking involves more flitting about. Canoodling is.... Er, perhaps I should kiss your neck. That is the first step to proper canoodling, of course."

"Glad at least one of us is an expert," she said with a grin.

"Yes. Quite lucky, that."

She tilted her head to one side as if to make it easier for him. "Okay. I'm ready."

Good God. All that expanse of lovely neck exposed for his pleasure. He felt as if he'd won the lottery. He began at the spot just below her ear where her jaw met her throat and took his time making his way toward her collarbone, giving her little nips and licks all along the way and enjoying the taste of salt mixed with a bit of chlorine on her skin.

She gasped at a particularly enthusiastic nip, and then suddenly her legs were wrapped round his waist.

Well, then. He paused in his sampling of her to inform her that might be a bad idea. He was already perilously close to an erection, which would be terribly unprofessional of him.

But he forgot what he was about when she gave him a sultry look that would tempt the devoutest of monks and said, "My turn."

She began at a similar spot on his person, that spot below his ear, and her nibbles combined with little swirls of her tongue sorely tried his erection-suppressing capabilities. When she reached his collarbone and slid her tongue and hot breath all along it, his own breath hitched.

He began to recite the eleven tenets of his boarding school, Bradshaw Grange, in Latin in his head—something he did on set during the filming of love scenes in order not to embarrass himself. Any thoughts to do with Bradshaw Grange would do the trick to get rid of his stiffies, but he usually didn't have to employ the tactic until much further into the scene, when the actual faux tupping started.

Odd, that. When he'd been a randy twenty-year-old, a love scene with just about any girl with a fanny had him fighting a hard-on. As he got on in age, though, he'd become more discerning. However, if he'd not had so much self-restraint practice on *Battle*, Piper would have already caused a proper stonker.

What in the bloody hell was the matter with him? Was it because he felt comfortable with her, that she put him at ease? Or maybe it was because the last time he'd been with a woman was with Amanda, which seemed like eons ago. Or there was the Guinness. Whatever the reason, he was going to have to put a stop to it.

He put his hands on Piper's cheeks, intending to gently tell her he needed a breather. But her scorching brown gaze sent a trail of kerosene straight into him and then struck a match. The next thing he knew, he was kissing her—hard—and she was opening up to him, the innate passion in her making itself known.

Those glorious breasts of hers pressed against his bare chest, and he pulled her tighter to him. He wanted to remove her top so he could feel her skin on his, but somewhere in the back of his mind was the awareness that they were being watched and photographed. If he ever were fortunate enough to see her naked breasts, they would be for his eyes only.

He couldn't get enough of her, and he loved the way her

tongue dueled with his in a sensual manner that made his pulse hammer. It was as if they were trying to devour each other, and he finally lost control. He frantically began reciting the tenets again in his head, but his cock was having none of it and began to harden.

Panting, he broke away from her, freeing himself from her arms and legs and swimming a few feet away from her, then raking a hand through his wet hair.

Piper was panting too and was now treading water with a bewildered, sort of dazed expression.

"Well," he said with too much cheer, "that should do the trick."

She seemed to be speechless, but now a small frown was forming on her face.

He scratched his cheek with his index finger, trying to regain his self-control but suddenly feeling as if he were giving a speech to the House of Lords in his underpants. With a stiffy. Drawing in a deep breath and exhaling, he said, "I think that can be classified as proper canoodling, don't you?"

She cleared her throat. "Um, yeah." Slight pause. "Yeah," she said, looking down instead of at him. Then the frown changed into what he recognized as her sunny, everyone-loves-Piper smile, and she was more certain when she met his gaze again. "Yeah. Probably totally did the trick. Yeah."

His breathing was still erratic, and he swallowed. Glancing at the black waterproof sport watch on his wrist—and knowing if he checked, it would tell him he'd just burned about a million calories in that one kiss—he said, "Time for an afternoon run. Care to join me?"

She looked at him like he was a nutter. "You're kidding, right?"

"No. Absolutely serious." In fact, he was desperate to run off some of his lust before his balls exploded.

"Um, you do realize your legs are about fifteen feet longer than mine. It would be like running a marathon for me, while it would be like a leisurely stroll for you—that is, if you don't get bored and just leave me behind to choke on your dust."

He laughed, not only because she was funny but also because he was relieved that the awkwardness and passion between them—and his stonker—was dissipating. "I promise, no dust-choking."

Her mouth curved, and she tilted her head as though thinking something sly. "I have a better idea. Let's have a sword fight."

That took him aback. "Sorry?"

"A sword fight. I noticed you have some fencing swords in your home gym." She swam backward toward the edge of the pool to get out. "Which, by the way," she said, glancing over her shoulder at him before turning to step onto the deck, "why don't you train here instead of going to Jason's gym?"

"His is bigger and has better equipment."

"That's what she said."

Grant gave her a wry look from beneath his brows. "Love, really."

"Sorry. Low-hanging fruit." She grinned.

He returned it. She was so fetching in that moment that he wanted to pull her back into the pool with him for another snog, but he resisted. Barely. "Also," he went on pointedly, "we film promo workout videos for his gym there. Good publicity for both of us."

"Mmm." She grabbed the towel from the chaise she'd

been sitting on earlier and began to dry off. "So do you want to have a friendly bout?"

He lowered his chin and regarded her from under his eyebrows, doubtful. "I think you're more pissed than I thought you were."

"If you mean miffed, then you'll be happy to know you have not said anything today to piss me off."

"Wonders never cease, do they?"

She smiled, biting her bottom lip a little bit. "If you mean tipsy, I promise I'm of perfectly sound mind. I can hold my alcohol."

"I've noticed."

She made a face. "I'm not sure if that's good or bad."

"Oh, it's good. Believe me." He swam over to the side closest to her chaise and rested his forearms on the coping of the pool. "Do you fence?"

She shrugged. "I've had a few lessons."

He was skeptical. "I've been fencing for years, since I started working on *Battle*. I don't think it would be a fair fight."

"Tell you what. Let's have a bout, and if I win, you will *finally* introduce me to Ezra on Monday. Which," she chided, "is long overdue, by the way."

He pushed away from the side of the pool and floated on his back, trying to hide his guilt. He knew he'd not been holding up his end of things. She *had* been good for his image—and Jessica said Leonard Shane was returning her calls again—but Grant had yet to get Piper an introduction to Ezra. Mainly because he didn't want to see her disappointed or hurt.

He must have conveyed that somehow because she narrowed her eyes. "You don't think I stand a chance for the Heledd part, do you? That's why you keep putting it off."

"Perhaps having a go at a different role might make more sense," he hedged. "Really, I think Ezra already has someone in mind for Heledd."

"You mean someone not Latina," she said, her voice dry as sand. "Someone like Kristen Savage. But let me point out that Catherine Zeta-Jones played a Latina in *The Mask of Zorro*, and she's Welsh. So why can't I do the opposite?"

"Fair point."

"And did you know a large part of the Welsh population is dark-haired, dark-eyed, and darker-skinned?" Before he could answer that, she said, "Besides, Kristen might look like everyone's misinformed idea of what a Welsh warrior princess would look like, but she can't act her way out of a paper bag, let alone do a Welsh accent."

Amused, he started treading water again and arched his brows. "And you can?"

She began to recite the poem *Do Not Go Gentle into That Good Night* by the Welsh poet Dylan Thomas in a Welsh accent that would have impressed Thomas himself.

For certain Grant was impressed. Most Americans wouldn't be able to distinguish between the more singsongy Welsh accent and an English one. To be honest, he doubted most Americans could even point Wales out on a map. It was just part of Prince Charles' title to them. Yet Piper was getting it bang on. She occasionally put too much roll in her *r*'s, but it was subtle and would be easy to correct.

She was loads better than most American actors, who couldn't even do a proper *English* accent, let alone any *regions* of the UK. Most of the English accents he heard Americans do were quite atrocious. In fact, although *Battle* was an American-produced series, most of the actors hired to be on it were from the UK or Europe for that very reason, since for some reason Americans thought fantasy characters all spoke with British accents. And also because British actors were less pompous and were willing to do grunt work that some American actors thought was beneath them.

Piper, apparently, was an anomaly, and something that felt quite like pride in her welled inside him. But the fact that she could do an accent and could probably act too didn't mean she had the right physique for the role. He knew Ezra had someone tall and Amazonish like Kristen in mind, someone who emitted badassery. Piper would have to be really bloody impressive to change Ezra's mind, and her diminutive physique and spunky demeanor, despite her assertion she could pass as Welsh, simply did not scream "warrior princess." It screamed "protect me, kiss me silly, motorboat your face between my sizeable breasts."

When she finished the dramatic poem, she said in a triumphant tone, "Well?"

Still envisioning the motorboating, it took him a second to reply, "Not bad."

She grinned. "It was awesome, and you know it." She raised a brow. "What about you? Let me hear your American accent, Captain Justice."

He obliged her, reciting the lines he'd once done for a venereal disease drug commercial when he'd first come to America.

Her eyes grew large as saucers, and then she threw her head back and laughed bigger than he'd ever seen her. "Oh, my God. I remember that commercial. That *was* you!"

"Some of my best work."

That got her laughing again.

He felt his lips twitch.

"Not bad," she conceded, once her laughter had abated. "So, back to the fencing. We on?"

"No. I don't fancy kicking your arse in a sword fight."

"Afraid you might lose?"

"Hardly."

"Chicken."

The image of her barely able to wield his prop sword in his caravan came to mind. The sword had been almost as big as she was.

As if reading his mind, she said, "During my tour of your house, I saw foils in your gym that I can handle just fine. Are they electrified?"

"Tour of my house?"

She shrugged again. "I was bored. It's a gorgeous house. I hope you don't mind."

"I don't."

"I didn't snoop."

"I wasn't bothered you did."

"Cool."

"If I've not been clear, I want you to make yourself at home here."

"Thank you," she said with a nod. "But I'd feel even more at home if we fenced."

A surprised laugh escaped him.

"Are your foils electrified?" she repeated, her eyes sparkling with cheek.

"No. They're not wired and have dummy tips." He'd not used them in a while, but when he had first started working on *Battle*, he'd wanted fencing practice outside of what the show required, so he'd hired a fencing coach to come to his home. They had practiced with the saber, of course, but also with the foil and épée because he'd wanted to know how to fence with all types of swords. After a year of extra practice in addition to the coaching and fencing choreography he was taught on set, he'd got quite proficient. At least, he'd been told that his swordplay on the show was convincing.

"Dummy tips," she echoed. "Good. No worries that I'll scar any parts of that pretty body of yours."

He rolled his eyes but found her sudden hubris both unexpected and amusing. And it did sound as if she knew the basics of fencing.

"Come on," she urged. "It'll be just for fun. We'll keep score on the honor system, acknowledge each hit with a 'touché.' If nothing else," she said with that same impish glint, "it'll be a good workout."

He stifled another eye roll at her tease about the workout. "I don't have a proper uniform for you. Nothing I've got will fit you."

"I already thought of that. I packed my own. I have everything I need."

"Full uniform?"

"Full uniform."

He lifted his brows, growing suspicious. "And how would you have known to pack your own if you only just saw my gym today?"

She grinned. "Derek might or might not have told me about your home gym and what was in it."

"Is that so?"

"'Tis," she said in a perfect imitation of Grant's own accent. Switching back to her American, she said, "Meet you in the gym in ten minutes."

And that was how, soon afterward, he found himself in an epic fencing battle with Piper. She was small but quick as a viper and made him feel like a bumbling oaf. Granted, his forte was with the saber, but still, he shouldn't be getting trounced this badly.

He couldn't see her features because of the screened fencing mask she wore, but he could very well imagine the ruthless expression that must be on her face. The phrase "take no prisoners" came to mind. He was beginning to think she might have been a swashbuckling pirate in another life. Or possibly Errol Flynn.

Her pretty calves were defined by her white fencing socks and white knee breeches, and he was distracted for a fraction of a second admiring them. He found it hard to concentrate while sparring with her. It wasn't just her incredible speed but also the economy and sureness of her movements. In short, she was immensely athletic and talented, and he found it quite attractive—as well as astonishing. Looks could indeed be deceiving.

Lightning quick, she took advantage of the target area he'd inadvertently left open and lunged forward, thrusting the tip of her foil to his heart. It bent, as was proper, on impact.

"Touché," he said in defeat for the thousandth time. In fencing, the fencer who was hit had to acknowledge the hit.

"That's fifteen," she said. "You're dead. Again." She sounded both breathless and triumphant.

Each bout lasted about nine minutes, and this was their third bout. In all three bouts, he'd only scored ten points. Total. It had been quite the drubbing.

The only satisfaction he'd got out of it was that he was not as out of breath as she was. Raising his sword arm and his other arm so that his entire torso was exposed to attack, he said, "I yield."

A muffled laugh came from behind her mask. "You're not a knight in the Middle Ages."

"I know. I just want to make sure you know I'm done."

"Great bout, then," she said, and saluted him with her sword.

He did the same.

They both pulled off their masks, and her long, slightly

sweat-dampened dark hair spilled out around her shoulders in stark contrast with the white jacket as if she were in a shampoo advert. He'd been turned on throughout the whole match, but the sight of her hair, combined with the exhilaration of fencing with her, had him wanting to do something rash. He tossed his mask to the side and grabbed the front of her lamé, the outer vest worn over the jacket in foil to delineate the target area, and pulled her to him until their faces were just inches apart. "'A few lessons' my arse. You weren't exactly forthcoming, were you, Ms. Torres?"

Her gaze dropped to his mouth before regarding him with cocky challenge. "The fact that I brought my own uniform should have been your first clue."

"Touché."

She shot him an arch smile, completely unapologetic. "I could have had a fencing scholarship to the University of the Incarnate Word in San Antonio, but I turned it down. Bright lights. Hollywood. You know the rest."

"I bet your mum and dad loved that."

"Oh, yes. They were thrilled," she said, meeting his eyes head-on with both irony and good humor.

There was something very alluring—very sexy—about so much confidence in such a small, compact package. "I want to kiss you again," he said on impulse.

Her chin went up. "Do it."

He needn't be told twice. He locked his mouth onto hers, and a second later her mask and both their foils clattered onto the floor, neither of them having a care that the hilts might get bent. Her hands at the nape of his neck, one still wearing its fencing glove, pulled him down toward her, and he wrapped his arms round her, loving the feel of her body molding to his.

He must have kissed a hundred women over the course

of his career and dating life, but nothing had felt this... desperate, not even with Lexi or Amanda, not ever. It was intoxicating. It was disturbing. It made his heart race as if he were about to jump out of a plane. And all his hard work of earlier fighting his erection? Flown out the window. He was hard as a battering ram.

Just having his tongue in her mouth wasn't enough anymore. "I want to take you upstairs to my bedroom."

"Do it," she said again without hesitation, her lips dark red and swollen, her gaze smoldering.

"You're sure?"

"I'm sure."

Before she could change her mind, he swept her up in his arms like some scene from a romance novel and dashed through the living room past Chewie, who was content lying on Grant's sofa watching DOGTV.

Chewie gave an ear twitch to indicate he'd seen them but had no interest in following.

"I can walk, you know," said Piper, a rather self-conscious smile playing about her lips that did strange things to his heart. "I know I'm probably heavy."

He gave her his best *Don't be mental* scoff and didn't feel the need to dignify that with a worded response. She was about as heavy as a load of laundry.

Once they were in his room, he set her on the bed as carefully as his urgency would let him, then fought to get off the thousands of pieces of gear he wore, throwing each piece behind him, not having a care where they landed.

Piper did the same, also throwing each piece of her uniform about the room. By the time they were mostly done, it looked as if the honey-colored bamboo hardwood floor had just gained a new, if somewhat spartan in places, white carpet. Doffing the second of his long white socks, he turned to her.

Her brown eyes grew large, her mouth slightly agape as she took in his nudity. "In the immortal words of Emma Stone in *Crazy, Stupid, Love,* it's like you've been Photoshopped."

He was unable to respond because seeing her nude, seeing her amber-hued breasts with their lovely brownish pink areolae fully revealed, had turned him into an imbecile. He closed the distance between himself and her, and finally—*finally*—her bare breasts were there waiting, his for the taking.

She grabbed his wrists and placed his hands on top of them, giving him permission to do what he ached so badly to do.

He caressed and then squeezed them, and they were that perfect combination of soft and firm that made him groan. He ran his thumbs over her nipples, doing that thing he'd dreamt about for weeks.

Her response was to take his engorged cock in her small hand, stroke it, and then squeeze his balls.

Desire shot through him like a bullet. "Good God. I'm going to combust," he croaked.

Leaning into him, she licked one of his own nipples and whispered as she continued to swirl little circles on his pec, "Then we'd better get started."

He groaned again. Yes, they'd better. But if he let her continue what she was doing, he was going to come too soon, and that wouldn't do at all. He put his hands on her shoulders and kissed her neck before saying, "Love, turn around for me."

"But—"

"Trust me."

She turned slowly to face the bed, her bare back now against his chest and belly, and he rewarded her with a kiss behind her ear and a light pinch of her nipples for obeying him.

She gasped with pleasure, and that, along with the feel of her curvy hips and buttocks against his cock and thighs, made him shudder with need. He wanted to bend her over and take her right there, but he wasn't a heathen.

He would make sure she was more than ready first.

## 14

———

She could still see his magnificent body burned into her retinas as she faced away from him, eyes closed. Why had the sight of him made her reel like it had? She'd seen him in the nude before. It was hard to watch an episode of *Battle* without at least seeing him with his shirt off.

But seeing him buck naked in the flesh, in person, had been almost more than she could handle. Every muscle in his body was sculpted beyond belief, and his...well. She could say with legit authority now that Grant's penis was just as perfect and large as the rest of him.

She should feel self-conscious. He was a paragon of fitness and virility, all corrugated and firm. She was short and soft. Somehow, though, the way he was worshipping her body now, every kiss on her neck, every exquisite kneading of a breast or twist of a nipple, every minute movement of his erect penis against her back just above her buttocks, made her feel like she was his equal. She was very much his seductress, even as he was her seducer.

Beating him at fencing had helped. It had been such a

rush to hold her own against someone as skilled—and as tall—as he was. It had made her bolder than she normally would have been, made her feel dynamic and confident.

Now his lips on the back of her neck felt divine. She liked that he had a thing for her neck. Maybe he was a little bit vampire after all.

He gently nudged her shoulders, indicating he wanted her to lie on her stomach.

Holy crap. Was he an ass guy? She didn't know if she was comfortable with that, but the way Grant was licking each bump of her upper spine made her decide to cross that bridge when she came to it. No sense putting the cart before the donkey, as her abuela always said.

And okay. No more thoughts of Abuelita right now.

She did as he asked, lying on her stomach, feeling both vulnerable and provocative.

He licked and flicked his tongue all down her back, and his fingers were everywhere all at once.

Her skin tingled and tightened all over.

When he reached the area just above her buttocks, he paused. "Your arse is the loveliest I've ever seen."

Okay. It wasn't exactly a sonnet by Shakespeare, but it still made her feel…proud. After all, he'd seen a lot of ladies' "arses" to compare hers to. She had no doubts about that.

The breeze of his breath in her ear tantalized when he murmured, "Your skin is like satin. You make me so hard, Piper, and I'm going to make sure you're good and ready for me."

It wasn't the skin compliment that had her lady parts pulsating. It was the intimacy of his mouth so close to her ear, the low, thundery rumble of his voice, the fact that this demigod of a man wanted *her*, was rapt on giving *her* pleasure.

He licked the crease where her buttock met her thigh and she tensed with awareness, especially since his talented tongue was getting near that place that was now swelling with wet anticipation. Then he nipped her butt cheek with his teeth.

She yelped. He was bringing her to the brink just by touching and kissing—and now gently biting—every inch of her, but it was beginning to become torture. She wanted more, but all she was able to articulate was a high-pitched "unnh."

In the back of her mind was the worry he would think she was boring in bed, that she wasn't considerate of his own pleasure. She moistened her bottom lip and tried to form words. "I'm going to turn over." She pushed herself up with one arm so she could see him over her shoulder. "Let me take care of you, too."

His eyes had gone an inky indigo with purpose, his handsome face intense with the importance of his task. "Trust me, you are," he said on a pained little laugh. "This is driving me beyond pleasure into madness. Lie back down." He rubbed his erect, steely penis along the back of her thigh, and she got the message.

His sexy baritone was back in her ear again. "I want you to be ready for me because—"

She gasped, interrupting him, and bucked because two of his long fingers had suddenly slid into her slit and found that oh-so-important spot inside her, getting her closer to the edge she so desperately wanted to topple over.

"—I'm going to fuck you, Piper," he went on, "harder than you've ever been fucked before."

By now, those were about the only words that would have penetrated the fog of lust in her brain. She'd never had a guy talk dirty to her before, and it was a shock, especially in that proper English accent of his. She hadn't thought she would like dirty talk, that it would be demeaning to her. She was wrong. Coming from him, it sounded devilishly civil and was a huge turn-on. "Please," she said, suddenly at the point to where she might die if he didn't give her relief from the sweet restlessness that kept building and building within her.

"I want you to be ready."

"I'm ready!" she shouted, pleading.

"But *how* ready, Piper?" Again, he was talking into her ear, his voice a sultry warning. "Ready enough for me to take you from behind? Or would you prefer the front?"

She couldn't think. At this point, both options were equally enticing, as long as he was talking about the vaj. It was driving her wild that this man the rest of the world thought of as detached and cold could be so commanding and wicked in bed. This wasn't a man with no feeling. This was a man who was playful and attentive and passionate.

She must have taken too long to decide, because he flipped her over onto her back with one deft move as if she weighed nothing, his insane biceps bulging with each flex and movement of his arms. "Never mind," he said, his lips brushing over her lips. "I want to taste your cries of pleasure when I make you come."

Okay. Sounded good to her.

His fingers were back inside her again, resuming their work with the addition of his thumb massaging her clit, and he was quickly bringing her to that precipice yet again. She'd never been so ready for a man in her life. Not that there'd been that many—two—and neither of them had ever made her anticipate having their cock inside her like Grant was. In fact, one of them had never even brought her to orgasm. But if Grant kept this up, she was going to come before he ever got inside her.

His other hand kneaded her breast, making her nipple peak and pucker, and then his hot mouth was on her other one, sucking. She hadn't thought things could get any better, but she'd been wrong. Arching her back, she moaned.

He muffled it by using his mouth to cover hers, giving her one of those toe-curling kisses that always managed to spark something inside her, even when they were doing it for the cameras.

But she didn't want to go there now. No cameras were on them. That was enough for her. None of this felt fake, but then what *was* this?

Never mind. They'd figure out the aftermath...when it was the aftermath.

His tongue thrust against hers, and that unfulfilled need in her crescendoed to dangerous levels.

She broke their kiss out of desperation and grabbed his dick, stroking it and reaching a little lower to squeeze his balls.

He grimaced and threw his head back. "Oh, God."

"I want you inside me, Grant. Now."

"Your wish...," he said as he groped for a condom packet that had magically appeared on the nightstand, "...et cetera." In two seconds, he had the packet ripped open and the condom on, and then his gaze captured hers, the wicked rough-talker from before gone and an earnest gentleman in his place. "Last chance to back out."

"I'd rather die."

"Can't have that, can we?"

She reached up and pulled his dark head down to her for another searing kiss, and that was all it took.

He pushed inside her, *finally* fulfilling and stretching

that gaping need inside her. She was so ready for him and so enamored of the man himself that stars exploded inside her the moment he entered her.

He became all of her five senses: the muscles of his back undulating under her fingers and palms; the breadth of his shoulders and chest filling her vision and then their gazes fixated on each other; the evergreen-juniper essence of him plus something a bit muskier from their fencing bout that filled her nose; the taste of his skin when she kissed and sucked on his broad shoulder as he bowed his head over her; the primitive, guttural sounds he made as he both came to his climax and brought her to heights she hadn't thought possible.

The waves of ecstasy kept bursting within her every time he buried himself deeper and deeper. She loved not only the orgasm but also the connection to him.

When they were both thoroughly satisfied, he gave her one last tender kiss in denouement, then eased out of her and rolled off onto his back. After a minute or two, his frantic breathing and hers began to return to normal. He clasped her hand in his, then held it over his chest, sending another jolt of melty warmth through her debauched, pampered, and sated body.

Even though it was the middle of the afternoon, they both fell into a postcoital doze. She woke first and rolled onto her side, noting that he must have covered them both with the top sheet at some point while she napped.

Still on his back, he looked sort of innocent when he slept, his usually expressive dark eyebrows relaxed and still. She could study his face a million times and never want to look away.

She had the urge to trace the cleft of his chin, to run her finger over the perfect ridges of his strong cheekbones and the hollows beneath, but she didn't want to risk waking him.

She let her gaze travel from his face to the thick column of his throat and down to his pecs. Okay. Maybe she didn't care if she woke him after all.

Memories of licking the firm contours of his pecs and the light matting of hair on them that had tickled her upper lip made her unable to resist lightly running her finger over the area again. His chest hair actually went lower, lightly dusting the moguls of his abs and the part of his man V that was not covered by the top sheet. It matched the wiry hair on his arms, and it surprised her that the feel of it turned her on.

He didn't have *too* much hair. He wasn't hirsute like an early caveman. And it wasn't in weird places like on his shoulders or his back, but it was different from the perfectly smooth torsos of her past boyfriends who got manscaped on a regular basis. Grant's "untamed" manscape shouted, *I am all man, not a Ken doll.*

Eyes still closed, he responded with a sleepy mumble.

She smiled, loving the hoarse vibration that seemed to come from his chest. "Good afternoon," she said.

One eye opened and found her, and a languid smile made his mouth go lopsided. "Not good. Stupendous," he corrected before closing his eye again. The smile remained, and she liked the cocky satisfaction she saw in it.

"How come you have so much chest hair?" she asked idly. "Why does *Battle* let you get away with that?"

"I'm a villain."

"Huh?"

"Rolf is a blackguard. I think only the heroes have to get waxed."

That made her snicker.

He looked at her full-on, humor still evident in the tiny crinkles in the corners of his eyes. "Have you not noticed?" he asked.

"No. I guess you're the first villain I've slept with."

"Ah. I hope it lived up to expectations."

She gave him an appreciative look. "Oh, yes. Only villains for me from now on."

"Good," he said, arching his brow. "Because I'll not be letting anyone near my pelt with wax."

She giggled at his use of the word "pelt" and said, "I don't blame you. It's torture on my legs." And other parts he might have noticed but, like his, were now also modestly covered. So were her boobs.

He was polite enough not to mention the unmentionable parts. What he did say was, "Bloody right it's torture. Bad business, all that waxing. In fact, a bit of chest hair is acceptable these days. Completely smooth is no longer mod."

"Hmm. I wouldn't know. It's been a while since I paid attention to that stuff."

"Well, I wouldn't think current manscaping fashion would be on your radar, you being a lady."

"I mean, since I was close enough to a guy to notice that sort of thing."

"Ah." He was staring at the ceiling now.

She waited for him to say more or to ask her about her past love life. When he didn't, she worried she'd said too much.

She gave one last feather-light undulation of her fingers over the dark smattering of hair on his stomach, watched his abs contract at the touch, and then rolled onto her back, joining him in his inspection of the ceiling.

She thought about how long it had been since she'd had

sex. Over a year. She couldn't believe it, that so much time had passed. And now she'd had sex with *Grant* of all people. It wasn't part of their contract.

Now the silence between them was growing awkward.

She didn't know how to handle this. Did it mean something fundamental had changed between them? It had to be significant that what had just happened had happened with no cameras around, right? (Not that it would have happened at all if someone had been filming. Her entire family would freak if she was ever in a porno.)

She'd never gotten carried away like this with any guy before, had never experienced the kind of clothes-ripping-off-passion that had been between her and Grant. It might not mean anything to him, but it meant something to her.

Her stomach dropped at the thought. Damn her stupid heart. She was starting to have feelings for *him*—for his sense of humor, for how easy he was to banter with, for his love of animals, for his politeness to a fault, for his surprising humility and his nerdy shyness when it came to his love of gaming. It wasn't just his looks. In fact, she took way more delight in discovering these other things about him than she did the usual thrill she got every time she saw his face. She'd never stood a chance of not falling for him, had she?

His continued silence was already damning enough. It wasn't like he was suddenly declaring his love for her or telling her he'd felt something too, something earth-moving like she had.

"Welp," she said, popping up like a jack-in-the-box, "this was fun." She got out of bed and started gathering her clothes, slipping on the fencing pants and jacket just so she would be decent enough to go to the guest bedroom where all her stuff was.

"Piper—"

"I think we can both agree," she said, picking up what she was pretty sure was one of her white socks, "that we just got carried away." She didn't want to hear the let's-just-be-friends speech from him. It would hurt too much. So she was going to beat him to the punch. "We're both consenting adults. Like I said, we got carried away, were buzzing from the Guinness." That was a lie. By the time they'd finished fencing, she'd been sober as a judge and was sure Grant had been, too. "It was fun but probably shouldn't happen again. End of story."

She glanced at him and saw that his unreadable mask was in place. "Let's not make a big deal of it," she said. When he didn't say anything, she added, "You good with that?"

"Of course," he clipped out in his crisp accent. "No need to make a massive thing of it."

"Right. Things don't need to get awkward."

"No."

"We can go back to being friends."

"Of course. Friends."

She could feel his eyes on her as she picked up the last pieces of her fencing gear. Hiding the piercing ache inside her, she tried to sound teasing. "What we *will* make a big deal out of is that I beat you at fencing not once but three times. Fair and square," she teased.

Still with the unreadable face.

She chalked it up to wounded male pride. Okay. If he was going to be a spoiled sport, fine. She dropped the teasing tone and said more seriously, "You owe me a meeting with Ezra."

"Of course."

"On Monday."

"I'll see what I can do."

She shot him a chiding look.

"Don't worry," he said, suddenly getting out of bed and walking unabashed across the room in all his nude glory, big shoulders back, ass cheeks so tight she could have used them to crack pecan shells. He opened the door to the adjoining bathroom and said over his shoulder, "You'll get your meeting." Then he disappeared into the bathroom, shutting the door with a click. A second later, she heard the shower turn on.

She stood there for a second, not sure what to think. Either she'd said something wrong or, now that they'd had sex, he was just done with her. Both options were unsettling.

Since she'd only said out loud what she knew he was thinking, she was inclined to think it was the latter. After all, he was a man, one who had a reputation for womanizing— although she hadn't seen anything in the past few weeks to corroborate that. Until, apparently, now.

She tried to put a positive spin on it. At least she'd broken her year-long dry spell with a bang (figuratively and literally) by having spectacular sex with the hottest man in the world. The bad news: she was pretty sure it would never happen again.

## 15

H e should have been in a good mood. He had a full day off, a rarity these days in the rush to get all the studio scenes shot before the production moved to New Zealand for the location shoots. But it wasn't really a day off, was it?

It was torture.

As mandated by the PR machine, he was at IKEA having to touch Piper and hold hands with her as they perused items in the giant home goods store. As always, she played her part impeccably well. She was the sweet, doting girlfriend who looked up at him with adoring eyes. After her postcoital comment yesterday about their sex just being casual, a mistake basically, he realized just how good an actor she actually was.

Before she'd declared that they'd just got carried away and that it shouldn't happen again, it had been on the tip of his tongue to tell her...*something*. He'd been trying to work it out in his brain, how to not cock things up for once and say the right thing. He'd not wanted to say anything to turn her off, as he famously had a knack for doing.

Her casual dismissal of what had happened between them had hurt more than he wanted to admit. And then she'd bloody friend-zoned him.

Getting into his "role" today as Piper's boyfriend had been near impossible. It was quite difficult to act as if you were in love with a girl, but were faking it, but in reality were insanely attracted to her, but didn't want her to know how pathetic it was you really liked her since she obviously didn't feel the same. Every time they touched, he remembered their epic—for him, anyway—shag yesterday, and he was sick to death of reciting the eleven tenets of Bradshaw Grange in his head in order not to react to the slightest brush of her hand against his.

He hated the inane conversation they kept having, too. He didn't bloody care what a Grundtal was and didn't bloody want one, but Piper seemed to think it necessary for his guest bathroom.

He longed for this endless shopping trip in this endless maze of a store to be over, for people to stop surreptitiously taking pictures and videos of them or more blatantly asking them for selfies, and for Piper to finally go back to her house and stop torturing him with her sexy body and the distance she'd firmly wedged back in place between them.

On the upside, the steamy photos of them in his pool yesterday had already leaked, and now they had a portmanteau, much to Cynthia's and the agents' delight. "Torrish" was the winner, a combination of their last names instead of their first names. He supposed it made all the trouble worthwhile, the positive publicity his image sorely needed and was receiving. After all, he thought cynically, they "made such a cute couple." Apparently Americans loved cute couples. But he looked forward to the day it would all finally end.

He had the dark realization that the people closest to him were all paid to be in his life: Derek, Jessica, Cynthia, Jason. He didn't want Piper as another "friend" who was only in his life because she had to be. He wanted more from her. More fool he.

———

"COME ON, JUST ONE MORE," urged Jason. "You can do it."

Grant wanted to roll his eyes, but they were making another video to post on Jason's YouTube channel, so he had to act like the three-way shoulder raises he was doing with twenty-pound free weights weren't making his shoulders and arms burn as if his muscles had been dipped in acid. In a sense, he guessed they had been—the lactic acid his body was producing.

Another reason to remain stoic: a few other gym addicts had braved the early hour to work out, and he didn't want to look weak in front of them. The last thing he needed was Leonard Shane seeing a video of him looking less than heroic.

"One more," Jason said again.

Jason was as muscular as Grant, and Grant knew he worked out as hard as Grant did at some point in the day, but the fact that Jason was strolling about right now, arms folded across his chest, telling Grant what to do—not a drop of perspiration on him—made Grant want to punch him.

"Ohp, I lied. Give me one more, Grant," he said with his veneered white teeth showing, as if he were clever and was doing something no one else had ever thought of.

Grant clenched his jaw. Every trainer he'd ever worked with had always done that, made out like he was almost done and then squeezed more out of him. It was effective, he supposed. But now when Jason kept saying "just one more," all it did was get on Grant's nerves. *Just tell me how many bloody reps and get on with it, for fuck's sake.*

"Aaannd, *good job*," said Jason, giving Grant a hearty "bro" pat on the back.

Grant wanted to lie supine on the floor, such was his relief the workout was finally over, but instead he pretended as if Jason hadn't worked him to the brink of shattering and that all was well.

So when Jason faced the video camera he'd set up on a tripod, Grant stood next to him, weights at rest down by his sides. He kept a pleasant, closed-mouth smile on his face while Jason finished up the video with final thoughts and comments about healthy eating and safe workouts.

Grant wished he could go home and go back to bed, but that was a pipe dream. It was Monday morning. He was due on set in an hour for hair and makeup and another grueling, long day. Most of the scenes slated were action scenes, too, which meant even more physical exertion. He wasn't chuffed at the thought.

Something else he wasn't chuffed about? Introducing Piper to Ezra. The mercurial director wasn't known for his tact, and Grant didn't want to see her hopes crushed if Ezra took one look at her and laughed, as if it were a great joke that Grant was suggesting her for the role of Heledd.

Yes, Grant had a good rapport with Ezra, which was a rare thing, and Ezra had on occasion listened to Grant's suggestions on various matters. But that didn't mean Grant had any control over the man's manners or lack thereof. Grant took heart in the fact that Ezra knew Grant was dating Piper and had actually teased him about it the other day, so maybe the fact that Piper was Grant's partner was enough to protect her from Ezra's possible scorn.

Once Jason was done with his comments and signed off, Grant put the weights back on their rack and sat on a nearby bench, where a small towel was waiting for him. He was sweating loads, and it felt good to close his eyes and rub the towel over his face and sweat-soaked hair.

Jason was putting some of the other weights and resistance bands they'd used back in their places and was banging on about some actor, which he had a bad habit of doing during their workouts. It was why Grant never told him anything personal. Jason gossiped as much as TMZ. The clanging of the weights drowned out the name of the actor, and Grant didn't care enough to ask Jason to repeat the name.

In fact, Grant tuned Jason out completely because he knew all too well what rubbish most gossip was. Instead, he was going over some of the lines he would need to know today in his head, testing himself to see if he still remembered what he'd stayed up last night memorizing. He would have a chance to go over them again during hair and makeup, but he wanted them to be second nature, to not have to think about them.

"Right?" asked Jason, looking directly at Grant with expectation.

Grant still didn't know who the subject of Jason's soliloquy was, but he'd broken Grant's concentration and caught his attention.

"I mean, seriously," Jason carried on, apparently not requiring an actual response, "she could use a professional trainer. I'm surprised she doesn't have one. I'm sure she could afford it. She's lost some weight, but I could help her do it so much faster and efficiently. I mean, she's a cute girl, but she could still stand to lose a few—at least if she wants to get anywhere in this business."

"Mmm-hmm," Grant responded absently, hoping to concentrate on his lines again and not have to truly engage.

Alas, it was not to be. Jason kept up with his droning. "I mean, everyone wants to have a great body, but no one wants to put in the work—the sweat, the strict diet, the *pain*. It takes discipline."

Discipline? That was putting it mildly. Self-flagellation, more like. It was ironic, the fact that everyone admired Grant's physique but scorned the copious amounts of time and sacrifice it took to sustain it. "No," he said, feeling bitter about that fact. "You can't be lazy. You can't be a slug."

Still talking as he went over to the camera, Jason added, "I think it's great you're dating her, though. Shows you've got *depth*, dude, that looks aren't the only thing that's important to you."

Grant froze in the process of rubbing sweat off his neck. "Sorry? Wait. Are you speaking of Piper?"

"Yeah. For, like, the past five minutes. Did you somehow miss that crucial part of the convo?"

"Apparently," Grant ground out in a hard voice, a visceral anger bringing him back to life. "Because if I'd been listening closely, I would have told you that there's nothing wrong with Piper's body and that I find her whole person to be quite beautiful. She's healthy and doesn't need to change a thing." He meant that. Unbidden images of her naked, of her soft skin beneath his fingers and the fresh scent of her filling his head—that lovely, sexy smile of hers—all flickered across his mind, making him both randy and morose that he wouldn't be seeing her in such a state again.

Jason held up his hands in surrender. "Hey, man. I'm not dissing your woman. She seems like a sweetheart." He fiddled with the camera again. "I mean, to each his own, right? Like I said, you've got depth. If you're into some curves, there's nothing wrong with that. But I'm just saying she's not your usual tall-thin-and-gorgeous supermodel, you know? Not that every dude in America hasn't dreamed of having a cool, fun girl like Piper who is low-maintenance, you know? Someone whose shit you don't have to put up with because she's so fucking hot."

Grant rested his head in his hands, the towel dropping to the floor. If he weren't so bloody tired, he *would* punch Jason on principle alone. Jason was a decent bloke for the most part and an excellent trainer, but he was also immature and too focused on looks. Of course, considering the industry he was in, Grant supposed it was to be expected. "Then perhaps you should try it sometime."

Jason's forehead furrowed under a hank of blond hair that had fallen down. "What's that?"

"Depth."

Finally, Jason stopped talking.

## 16

Piper sat next to Ezra Vidmar, totally freaking out. He was a portly yet imposing white man, his hair gray and long and pulled back in a ponytail. He had a deep booming voice and the kind of face that gave the impression it rarely smiled. He also had black eyes that could probably turn into fireplace pokers and skewer a person if they were unlucky enough to get on his bad side.

True to his word, Grant had finally introduced her to him very early this morning and told Ezra he thought she would make an excellent Heledd.

Ezra had not seemed too enamored of the idea, but he hadn't laughed in her face either, which she sensed Grant feared would happen. Mainly because, with a worried crease between his brows, he had told her just before meeting Ezra, "Don't take it personally if he laughs when I suggest you play Heledd. He's not known for tact and can be a twat."

Not being laughed at by Ezra had been a definite plus, along with the fact that Grant had been worried for her feelings, even though she knew not to read too much into it.

The biggest plus, however, had been when Ezra patted Chewie's furry head, which was sticking out of her purse, and asked Piper to come sit next to him when they began filming the first action sequence of the morning—hence her current freak-out. Judging by the raised brows she was getting from the crew and the unfriendly looks from some of the cast, this was *not* something they saw often, if ever.

It was true Grant was one of the few actors on the show Ezra seemed to actually like, probably because Grant worked his ass off day in and day out, took direction like every director's dream, and (contrary to what everyone said about him) did not act like he was God's gift to the craft of acting. He never complained, worked hard, and was humble. Some of the other actors on the show, like that ho-bag she'd overheard in the country club restroom, should try following Grant's example instead of being jealous and deriding him.

The scenes they would be filming today would be a lot of hand-to-hand combat, sword fighting, and a scene where Grant would have to run through a medieval-style gauntlet —a double line of male actors costumed in various outfits of leather and furs, facing each other and armed with clubs, axes, or other weapons, who would strike at Grant when he ran between them. The gauntlet scene would be filmed first, and Piper could feel a thrill surge through her at being on a set again. She'd watched Grant from afar a few times in the past few weeks, but nothing beat sitting right next to the director in the thick of it all.

This set closely resembled a medieval European village street, except for the curlicue-like flourishes in some of the buildings' architecture and the elf ears, among other "creature" prosthetics, on some of the actors that gave it a fantasy flair. And, of course, the "village" was surrounded by dozens of crew, cameras, lights, microphones, booms, cables, and various people running around with tablets and headphones on their heads. Also, the village had no sky, just the ceiling of the large warehouselike studio they were in. It would seem chaotic to an outsider, but Piper knew it was a controlled chaos and felt right at home.

Ezra occasionally explained to her what was being set up between barking orders to his crew. She sensed she wasn't supposed to speak unless spoken to, but sometimes she forgot in her enthusiasm and asked him questions, which earned her funny looks from him. After all, she was just a peon he'd deigned to let near him because of her connection to Grant.

Oddly enough, though, she didn't feel too intimidated by Ezra and got the feeling that he would respect her more if she didn't totally kiss his ass like some of the other syco-phants around him. Also, it wasn't like she was a nobody. She *had* won an Emmy for her role on the sitcom. Most people in the industry at least knew who she was, even an auteur director who thought he was Orson Welles reincar-nated. And it had to be a good sign that he actually answered her questions, right?

Grant, along with the actors who would make up the gauntlet and the set choreographers, were going over last-minute moves, making sure Grant knew where each swing of a weapon would be coming from and when to dodge. Ezra said they'd been practicing the gauntlet for two weeks and that everyone's roles in the scene were second nature by now.

"And the weapons aren't real, right?" asked Piper. Most prop weapons were made of foam or rubber and were painted to look amazingly authentic.

"All are fake except the last one, the club," Ezra said

absently. To one of the cameramen, he shouted, "Where's my grip for camera 2? I need him to raise it an inch and a half on its dolly."

The cameraman nodded and went off to find the grip.

"What's the last one made of?" asked Piper.

"Last what?" Ezra asked absently, looking down at his copy of the script that was in his lap.

"The last weapon."

He stopped making notes on the script and studied her.

It made her feel self-conscious, but she didn't let it show.

"It's maple," he finally answered. "We have several of them. Paul, the actor who will be swinging it in a top-to-bottom motion, will splinter it on the ground for dramatic effect once Grant dodges it and gets free. We had enough of them made for twenty takes, most of which will be close-ups." The number of takes he wanted to do didn't surprise her. It was one of the hardest, most tedious things about acting, having to do the same scene over and over with fresh, genuine emotion each time so the director could film the scene with different lighting angles and camera positions, among other things.

She didn't like that a wooden club would be used. "Why maple and not balsa?" Balsa wood was what was normally used for breakaway furniture and weapons.

"We needed something with more heft, something more realistic since it will be in a close-up. It doesn't really matter, since it won't come into contact with any actors. And the wood has been scored in each club so it will crack and break apart on impact when it hits the ground."

Uneasiness must have shown on her face, because Ezra chuckled and said, "Don't worry, Pepper."

She refrained from rolling her eyes and said, "It's Piper," with a congenial smile to show she hadn't taken offense.

Although she kind of had. Really? She'd been dating Grant for over a month now, and Ezra still didn't know her name? True, they'd never been officially introduced until this morning, but she'd practically been glued to Grant's side for weeks. Surely someone had told Ezra who she was at some point. She had a feeling he did know and was just being a dick. Plus, not to be a diva, but she was Piper freaking Torres.

He went on as if he hadn't heard her. "We won't let anything happen to that pretty boyfriend of yours. Plus, Grant's a pro and quick as lightning. He won't let Paul get near him with that thing."

And he was right. Everything went like clockwork, each movement choreographed to perfection. Grant's character was supposed to receive a few "blows" and "slices" from the foam and rubber weapons for realism, but for the most part his character escaped any real harm during each take, which lasted about three minutes.

Grant's athletic grace alone was impressive. His tall, muscular body dodged, jumped, whirled, and deflected as if he were a dancer. His reactions to the few "blows" he received were so real that she wondered if they might have actually hurt, although logically she knew they couldn't have.

After the tenth take, though, he seemed to be slowing down and was more winded. Even though each take was short, it was like running hurdles at a track meet and took a lot of stamina.

Should she suggest Ezra give him a break? It was one thing to ask questions and another thing altogether to tell a director who was known as a control freak what to do. And it wasn't like Grant didn't get *any* break. It took around ten minutes, sometimes less, sometimes more, each time to reset the scene, so he had small respites.

But the way he sank into the canvas chair that had been allotted to him and seemed a bit dazed as the hair and makeup people fixed any smudges, wiped away sweat, and fixed any hairs out of place made Piper think he needed a longer break. It was also nearing lunchtime. He needed food, especially with all the physical exertion. He was getting another workout after the one he'd already had this morning with Jason.

It was too much, but all of Grant's days were pretty similar to this. No wonder he never wanted to hang out with other cast members. Couldn't they see that it wasn't personal, that Ezra worked him like a mule?

She'd heard from Derek that some of the other stars of the show actually had it written into their contracts that Ezra could only ask them to work twelve-hour days, max. Apparently their agents actually cared about their clients' health and well-being and knew the workaholic reputation Ezra had. He would film twenty-four hours a day if it were humanly possible. For that matter, so would Grant, so maybe Jessica had tried to get him to go for an hours rider in his contract and he'd refused.

Whatever the truth was, after the seventeenth take, it was obvious that Grant was running out of gas, that his reaction times were getting slower, and Piper couldn't keep quiet any longer. They'd been at it almost four hours, and she had to close her eyes every time he got to the end of the gauntlet and Paul held the club high over Grant's head as if to crush him.

"Mr. Vidmar?" she said respectfully, even though he'd told her when he first met her to call him Ezra. (She didn't think he'd been sincere.) "I think Grant is slowing down a bit. Do you think a break and some food might make him more energetic?"

"Bah," he said with a wave of his hand.

Yes, he'd actually said "bah."

He leaned forward in his chair. "Nonsense! Look at the guy. He's in incredible shape. He could run a marathon without breaking a sweat."

She wanted to point out that the makeup person was wiping sweat off Grant's face as they spoke, but she thought better of it. Instead, trying to be as reverent and tactful as possible, she said, "Still, I'm kind of concerned. He's not as indestructible as he appears."

She was jarred to realize how significant it was that she knew that was true. She was getting to know Grant intimately—not intimate like the amazing sex they'd had—but learning his habits, his moods, how to read him. All this despite keeping each other at arm's length again. He hadn't said anything about their "afternoon delight"—they'd proceeded as if it hadn't happened—and she figured she'd been right to assume it hadn't meant anything to him. She was glad she hadn't let on that it had meant anything to her.

Ezra turned the full wrath of his piercing, beady gaze on her, bringing her back to the moment. "He doesn't need a break. I know what I'm fucking doing. He'll be fine." The *Your novelty has worn off and you are to be seen and not heard* part of the exchange didn't need to be said. It hung heavy in the air as he turned and called for everyone to get in place for the next take.

Not used to being spoken to that way, she stiffened with anger. Keep your mouth shut, she told herself. Do not blow this. You've dealt with plenty of asshole directors. What's one more?

At least they could only do three more takes, because

that's how many clubs were left. So far each club had splintered, as it was supposed to, every time Paul, a huge hulk of a guy, brought it crashing down to the cobblestone street after barely missing Grant's head.

When someone yelled, "Places, everyone! Quiet on the set," Grant got up from his chair with a little less spring in his step, but it wasn't like he was slogging around by any means. He was still an absurd example of Herculean male prowess: shredded abs and arms exposed because he was shirtless, brawny thighs and legs accentuated by tight brown leather pants tucked into tall black boots, longsword sheathed in a scabbard along his back. He was a badass warrior who could literally (or his character, Rolf, could anyway) slay dragons, among other mythical creatures.

Too bad Rolf was such a worm in the *Battle of Fortunes* world. His dastardly deeds were legendary among fans.

Ezra yelled, "Action!" and the controlled mayhem began again, cameras rolling. The gauntlet was rather long, but Grant commenced ducking and dodging each swing of an ax or swirl of a mace again like a pro and didn't seem to miss a beat—just as he'd done in the other seventeen takes before this one. He was almost to the end now, and she tensed, her fingers clenching the wooden armrests of the classic-style canvas director's chair she sat in.

What was wrong with her? If it had been her out there, she would have scoffed if someone was concerned about her or told her to be careful. But the possibility that Grant might get hurt was an entirely different animal. Dread balled in her stomach, and she felt like crossing herself, even though she didn't normally do that unless she was going to mass with her family back in Texas.

It's all foam and rubber, she kept reminding herself, and tried to keep from adding, *Except for the last one.*

And then it was over. He'd made it again. Thank God.

Chewie's head was inside her purse, but she took the risk of waking him from his nap to scratch his head and whispered into the purse, "He made it. Just three more takes to go."

Chewie's response was a doggie sigh.

The last few takes went by fairly quickly, and soon enough, after yet more lighting and camera adjustments, Grant was making his last trip down the gauntlet. Piper was relieved. Surely he wouldn't get hurt on the last take after doing it what seemed like a million times.

She was wrong, of course.

In the end, Grant was a half a second too slow and missed a dodge he'd remembered to do nineteen times before. Paul's club came down and splintered like it had nineteen times before, this time not on the cobblestones but on Grant's head.

Grant dropped like a bag of wet sand, thudding face-forward onto the fake street.

———

## 17

Everything was surreal in that first hour after Grant was rushed to Cedars-Sinai Medical Center, the go-to hospital of Hollywood's elite.

When he'd first been hit, Piper had shot up out of her chair as if she'd been ejected and run toward him.

Paul, the guy who'd accidentally done the hitting, knelt over Grant, his hands hovering as if he wanted to touch Grant but didn't know if he should, an expression of horror on his face.

Piper basically did the same when she reached Grant: she knelt and wanted to touch him but was afraid that might somehow make things worse.

"He was just there all of a sudden," said Paul, distraught and looking as if he were near tears. "I didn't have time to pull back." He shook his head. "I'm so sorry. I'm so, so sorry."

"Grant?" she said, trying to keep calm. "Grant, can you hear me?"

As she was saying this, the set doctor, who had been on standby, reached them.

Grant didn't respond to Piper's questions. He was out cold. He had fallen face-forward onto his stomach, and his head was turned to one side, his dark, straight lashes resting on the cheek that was visible, his mouth slightly slack. Blood seeped steadily from a wound on the crown of his head, matting his dark hair.

The sight of it made Piper woozy, but she reminded herself that head wounds always bled a lot, that they sometimes looked worse than they actually were. She hoped that was the case now, although the fact that he was unconscious put her on the verge of panic.

Both of his arms were sprawled out beside him, and it didn't look as if he'd even tried to break his fall. It was like his lights went out before he'd even hit the ground.

The doctor, an older guy with short white hair and metal-framed glasses, said, "Stand back, please." He had a medic bag with him and quickly put on some blue disposable gloves, then pulled out some gauze and pressed it to Grant's head to stanch the wound.

Piper and the others surrounding Grant, including Ezra, did as he asked and cleared the space around Grant, but Piper could still see everything that was going on. She felt someone come up next to her and put his arm around her. It was Grant's assistant, Derek. She hugged him, his tall, wiry body a comforting shelter as they all waited and watched the doctor examine Grant.

To her weak-kneed relief, Grant began to respond to the doctor's attempts to wake him. He groaned, and his eyes flickered open.

"Grant," said the doctor, "can you hear me?"

He grimaced, then closed his eyes.

"Grant? Do you know where you are?"

"Course I do," he said groggily. He pushed up onto his arms a little, then grimaced again and mumbled, "Fuck."

"Easy," said the doctor.

Swallowing hard, Grant lay back down again on his stomach.

"Grant, do you know where you are?"

After a second he answered, "*Battle* set."

"Good."

This time, instead of trying to sit, Grant rolled slowly onto his back, blinking his eyes several times.

The doctor held up three fingers. "How many fingers do you see?"

Grant focused for a moment, then answered, "Three."

"What city are we in?"

"Los Angeles." He pronounced "Angeles" the British way, *An-je-leez*.

"What day is it?"

"A bloody long one, but they all are." His mouth quirked in a half-smile that was both wan and glib at the same time.

Piper grinned, knowing he wasn't confused. He was joking. That had to be a good sign, right?

The doctor looked up, his demeanor no-nonsense. "He seems cognizant, for the most part, but it concerns me that he was out at least a minute. Let's get the medics in here with a stretcher. He needs to be taken to the ER. I can continue the assessment on the way."

Most film sets contracted both a set doctor and an ambulance unit to be on standby for things like this. Piper had never been more grateful for that fact than right now.

"Not necessary," Grant said in a thick voice. "I'm fine." When he gingerly sat up with the doctor's help, though, he turned the color of a tomatillo.

"It's just a precaution," said the doctor, again pressing the gauze to the wound on Grant's head.

With a scowl, Grant said a little drunkenly, "Bugger off." He tried to bat away the doctor's arm but missed his mark.

"Just trying to stop the bleeding," the doctor said matter-of-factly. "This will need stitches."

That made Grant turn a little greener, and when the medics helped him up, had someone take away the sword still in its scabbard on his back, and moved him onto the stretcher, he was silent.

Piper was glad he seemed coherent and had moved mostly under his own steam. It was so surreal, seeing him dressed like Rolf—a big, burly warrior from a fantasy world —but lying on such a stark, very real-world piece of medical equipment. Make-believe and reality had collided, and it was jarring. She walked forward and took his hand, giving it a squeeze. "Hey. I'll see you at the hospital."

"Overkill," he grumbled with half a wince. He had what looked like the beginnings of a bruise on his cheekbone where his face had hit the pavement.

"Maybe," she humored him, though it seemed like the effort just to get on the gurney had taxed him. "But better safe than sorry."

He grunted. "Your hand is trembling."

"You scared the shit out of me."

He closed his eyes. "It's just a little knock. I've had worse."

"You were freaking *unconscious*."

His lids opened and he met her gaze, as if something in her tone had caught his attention.

Maybe it was the fact that, even to her own ears, her voice had sounded weird, a tad too vehement. It was a charged moment, one that made her lungs feel constricted inside her chest, and she couldn't resist giving him a short but fierce kiss on the lips. Then she gripped the wide leather strap crossing his chest that had held his scabbard on, could feel his warm, very-much-alive skin beneath her knuckles. "Don't ever do that again," she said hoarsely.

He seemed sort of taken aback and searched her face, but before any more could be said, the medics loaded him onto the ambulance. That was a good thing, since she was acting as if she really was his girlfriend and as if she really had just experienced the scare of her life. Even now, her hands still shook and her entire body felt strangely numb—except for her lips.

Once the ambulance was out of sight, she grabbed Chewie and let Derek drive her to the hospital. When they were in the hospital's VIP waiting room, along with Ezra and Harriet, the set doctor walked in about thirty minutes after they'd arrived.

Everyone stood and converged on him, including Ezra, who had his hands in his jeans pockets and his shoulders slumped, the humblest Piper had seen him so far. "Alan," he asked the doctor, "how is he?"

Alan took off his glasses and rubbed the front of the lenses on his red polo shirt with his practice's logo on it, then put them back on again. Just as he was about to answer, Jessica and Cynthia burst into the room.

"Oh, my gawd!" shouted Jessica dramatically. "How is he? What happened?" She glowered at Ezra and jabbed her finger at him, the points of her black bob also aiming at him and echoing her index finger. "This is *your* fault. You push him too hard. Something like this was bound to happen." She looked wildly around at the rest of the people in the room. "What happened? Did he collapse from exhaustion?"

Piper was surprised no one had told her the details.

Then again, they might have tried. Jessica didn't seem to be in much of a state for listening.

Cynthia seemed much calmer. "Jessica, give them a chance to tell us what's going on."

"Well, somebody better!" She glared at Ezra again. "If you've done permanent damage to my client, we will sue the pants off you and the producers!"

Ezra crossed his arms, glaring right back at her. "None of this is anyone's fault. Accidents happen."

Piper disagreed and knew Jessica had hit close to the truth.

Cynthia put a hand on her arm. "Jessica, let the doctor talk."

Jessica scoffed angrily. "Well?"

Alan cleared his throat, not looking too thrilled to have to deal with the angry whirlwind that had just entered the room. Nevertheless, in a clear, quiet voice that cut through the chaos, he said, "I'm Dr. Alan Heywood, the doctor who was on set today."

"And?" barked Jessica.

She was being a beast, but Piper saw her behavior for what it was: worry. The woman was a shark, but she was losing it over Grant. Piper gained a new respect for her in that moment.

"Grant was able to answer all my questions in the ambulance and was coherent, if a bit dazed," said Dr. Heywood.

"Coherent?" repeated Jessica. "Would somebody please tell me exactly what happened to him? All I was told was that he was rushed to the hospital."

Harriet spoke up. "He's trying to, Jessica, if you'd just be quiet and listen."

Jessica narrowed her eyes. "Don't you tell me what to do. We'll sue your ass, too."

Again Cynthia put a hand on Jessica's arm. "We can worry about that later. Right now, let's listen to the doctor."

Jessica's chin began to tremble. She put her fingertips to her lips, then nodded.

Once he had the floor again, Dr. Heywood said, "As I was saying, Grant answered my assessment questions satisfactorily both at the scene and in the ambulance, which is a good sign. As you can imagine, though, his head hurts."

Understatement. Piper *could* imagine—the visual of that club coming down on him kept replaying in her mind—and the thought of him in pain made the contents of her stomach congeal.

She could see Jessica still didn't understand exactly what had happened and was about to erupt again, so in order to avoid another tirade, Piper said, "Excuse me for interrupting, Doctor." To Jessica, she said, "One of the cast members accidentally hit Grant on the head with a wooden club. Knocked him out."

"Oh, my gawd," Jessica drew out. Her face flushed and she sent a blistering look Harriet and Ezra's way that could have peeled off the top layer of their skin. To the doctor, she said, "Is he going to be okay?"

"I believe so."

Everyone looked relieved.

"He is, however, showing definite signs of a concussion. They took him for a CT scan just to make sure there aren't any nasty surprises we can't see. I've turned him over to the very capable hospital staff here, and I'm sure the doctor on his case will come talk to you as soon as he gets the results of the scan back."

Jessica sat down, as if her legs would no longer support her. "What about the press? Do they know?"

"The paparazzi hasn't shown up yet," said Harriet.

They all knew, though, that it would be just a matter of time. It was one thing to court the paparazzi when you needed them, but they were like bloodhounds. They could scent a story you didn't want them to find and spread it to the world when it was most inconvenient or embarrassing.

"I want him listed under an alias," said Jessica.

"Already been done," answered the doctor.

"Good. He doesn't need to be harassed by the media or fans right now. I also want security as a precaution."

"Won't be necessary," said Dr. Heywood. "I'm sure he will be allowed to go home—"

"Home?" Jessica gave a shake of her head and huffed. "I don't think so."

"As long as his scan is good and he has someone who can stay with him, standard of care does not warrant an overnight observation." He looked at Piper when he said this, as did everyone else.

Oh, right. She was his girlfriend, his very public girlfriend. She wondered if Grant would rather have Derek stay with him, since he'd actually known Derek longer, but realized that suggestion would sound strange to Dr. Heywood and everyone else who wasn't in on their fake relationship. "I'll stay with him," said Piper.

"Of course you will," said Jessica, popping up from her chair and taking Piper's hands, giving them a meaningful squeeze. "Thank *God* he has *you*." Then she pierced the doctor with a haughty look. "But we're not taking any chances. He's staying the night. Remember Natasha Richardson? Fell and hit her head during a ski lesson, and two days later she was gone. No. He's staying."

This felt so weird. It was one thing to do a few publicity events together and a few PDAs at IKEA or a restaurant, but shit was getting real. She shouldn't be here. She was nobody to Grant, which made her realize they needed to contact his family before they heard what had happened from TMZ or some other tabloid. "We need to call his family," she said. "We need his phone. He'll probably want it later anyway."

Derek said, "It's in his trailer. I'll go back to the studio and get it."

"Thank you. That would be great."

He didn't waste any more time on goodbyes and nearly steamrolled over a nurse who was entering the waiting room.

"Oh, sorry!" he said with a quick, are-you-okay grab of her shoulders before heading toward the elevator.

The nurse seemed startled for a moment but recovered and homed in on Piper. "Ms. Torres?"

"Yes?"

The nurse was pretty, a tall, lithe woman with dark skin and a delicate oval face. She also had a faint, soothing, musical accent that reminded Piper of someone from maybe Nigeria or Ethiopia. Piper instantly liked her. "He's asking for you," said the nurse. "You can go back and see him if you like."

"Thank you. Yes, of course." He was asking for her?

The nurse eyed Chewie hanging from Piper's arm and pressed her lips together as if she were about to protest his presence.

"I'll take him," said Cynthia.

That was good, since Piper was still hung up on the fact that Grant had asked for her. "Thank you," she said, handing Chewie off to Cynthia. Chewie liked her and would be okay with her for a few minutes.

"I'm coming too," said Jessica.

Irritation flashed through Piper, but she didn't argue. After all, Jessica had known Grant much longer than Piper and had more cred with him than Piper did. Although, she thought with satisfaction, he hadn't asked for Jessica, had he? The elation Piper felt from that was way bigger than it should have been.

The nurse led them to one of the rooms off the ER area. The room had a large sliding glass door and window. A curtain had been pulled across the glass for privacy, so they couldn't see Grant until they entered the room.

He was lying with his eyes closed on a hospital bed with large white wheels, looking pale, his dark hair matted and wet at the crown of his head where they must have dealt with his wound. At least they hadn't shaved it. He opened his eyes when he heard them enter and blinked a few times.

Piper's heart lurched at the sight of him. Despite his current state, he was still the most beautiful man she'd ever seen, and she felt overly emotional all of a sudden, a huge lump forming in her throat. He could have died today.

The head of the bed was raised enough that he was almost sitting, and he'd been given a hospital gown to put on over his Rolf costume, or lack of it. His muscular legs, still clad in the leather pants, were at odds with the gray gown printed with little navy diamonds. His boots had been taken off and were sitting near the bed, but he was still wearing black socks.

"Hey," said Piper, instinctively going over and kissing him on the forehead. She was doing a lot of kissing, but she justified it by telling herself she would have done the same if it were one of her brothers. Although *ew*, not on the lips, as she'd done with Grant earlier. "How are you feeling?"

"Fine."

Piper was skeptical. There was tension around his eyes, as if he had a headache.

To underscore that, he absently rubbed his temple. "I'm keen to get out of here, but they won't release me until the CT scan comes back." He looked at the nurse. "What's taking so bloody long?"

She smiled serenely, apparently used to impatient patients. "Sometimes it takes a while, two or three hours."

"Bugger."

"It doesn't matter anyway," said Jessica. "You're staying the night."

"What? The doctor said that wouldn't be necessary."

"I don't care. *I'm* saying it. You're staying the night."

He started to roll his eyes, then winced mid-roll. "Don't be ridiculous."

Jessica bristled. "I'm not. Remember Natasha Richardson? Enough said."

"I'm not Natasha Richardson."

"You were knocked out cold. Poor Natasha didn't even lose consciousness, but then two days later she died of an epidural hematoma."

He frowned. "You're quite versed on a matter that happened ages ago."

"It was a big deal at the time." She shook her head. "I'll never forget it. Such a shame. Poor Liam was devastated. And her boys." She groaned with what seemed like genuine anguish, as if she knew Liam Neeson and his family personally. She probably did. "Just *such* a tragedy."

"Be that as it may, I'm not staying here." Grant scooted toward the edge of the bed and started to stand, then swayed.

Alarmed, Piper grabbed his waist, and he leaned on her

shoulders more heavily than she would have liked. "What are you doing?" she chided.

The nurse hurried over and helped Piper get him back onto the bed.

"Just a head rush," he murmured. He was sitting on the side of the bed now, head in his hands.

"I think you just made my point for me," said Jessica. To the nurse, she said, "Is that normal?"

"It's to be expected," said the nurse. "Dizziness is common with a concussion."

"I'm all right," said Grant. "I just got up too fast."

Piper was starting to think Jessica was right about insisting he stay the night. "What if I hadn't been standing here?" Piper asked him.

Jessica beat him to the reply. "He would have face-planted, that's what." She pointed at Grant. "You're staying the night." Then she ordered the nurse, "Get me his doctor. I want to talk to him."

"He'll be back soon with the CT scan results."

Piper noticed for the first time that the nurse's name, Nyala, was written on a dry-erase board hanging on the wall. Even with Jessica at her bossiest, Nyala remained unperturbed, which Piper admired.

"Jessica," said Grant, adding that extra British *er* on the end of her name, "you're overreacting. I'm not staying."

Jessica did something surprising: she walked over and gently took Grant's face in her hands, looking into his eyes. It was a motherly gesture.

A wrinkle formed between his eyebrows, and his expression said he was wondering if Jessica had been the one hit on the head instead of him.

Voice soft for once, she said, "Humor me, darling. You

are important to me. Stay so that I'll be able to sleep tonight knowing you're in good hands."

Piper's heart warmed. Jessica truly did care about him.

Grant just sat there, apparently dumbfounded by Jessica's rare show of affection.

"You can sleep as much as you want," coaxed Jessica, brows arched.

Those were the magic words, because he muttered with resignation, "Bloody hell."

## 18

S oon Grant's CT scan came back clear. However, his symptoms indicated he did have a concussion (no surprise there), and, mostly due to Jessica's badgering, he was admitted to the hospital for overnight observation.

Piper was relieved. Although she could have been the one to wake Grant every two hours to assess him and make sure his symptoms weren't worsening at home, she felt better that trained nurses would be doing it instead. Still, she was staying the night too. It just didn't seem right to leave Grant in the hospital all alone, even though he'd insisted he would be fine. Besides, Grant's room was like an apartment. One half was a contemporary-style living room with a sleeper sofa, and the other contained the patient's bed, the overbed table, and other hospital stuff. The living room could be partitioned off from the patient's part with a hard, accordionlike plastic curtain.

Grant's doctor on staff at Cedars had laid down the law to everyone, even to Ezra: Grant needed lots of rest for the next few days and not a lot of stimulation—and that included well-meaning visitors. He was to keep TV, video games, reading—basically anything that required thinking —to a minimum. No working out for at least five days (which wouldn't be a problem for a normal human, but Grant wasn't normal). When he did resume workouts, he was supposed to keep them light.

He might have a persistent headache for the next few days. He could keep taking acetaminophen, but nothing with ibuprofen or aspirin in it because they might increase the risk of bleeding (yikes).

No work (Ezra had not been happy). A week off was highly recommended, but definitely no work for the next few days, depending on how Grant felt. And if he did go back, it could only be part time and couldn't involve anything strenuous. He was supposed to ease back into it and not push himself too hard. And if any activity he did caused a headache, dizziness, blurred vision, or nausea, he needed to stop doing it immediately.

Piper had decided she might as well go all the way and stay with Grant at his house for the next week. If she didn't, he'd be up at four-thirty in the morning first chance he got working out with Jason, doctor's orders be damned. But Piper was going to make sure he took care of himself. He would *not* be overdoing it on Nurse Piper's watch.

She was sitting on the sofa now next to Chewie, who was watching DOGTV.

Grant was asleep. Despite being disgruntled about staying the night, he had fallen asleep soon after he'd gotten settled in his bed. They'd been told that was normal with a concussion, the urge to sleep, but Piper suspected Grant's exhaustion was a factor too.

A light knock on his door made her jump up to answer it before whoever it was woke him. She opened the door to find Ezra, Harriet, Jessica, and Cynthia standing in the hall. Piper silently motioned for them to stay there and stepped out, shutting the door behind her.

"I want to see Grant," said Ezra.

"He's sleeping."

Ezra looked at his watch. "It'll only take a second, and then he can go right back to sleep."

Seriously? He did not just say that. He loomed over all of them, but Piper didn't feel cowed by him, even though she, as the shortest person there—especially wearing sneakers and not heels—had to look way up at him. She shook her head. "No way. Not for the rest of today. He needs to rest and isn't supposed to have visitors."

"I'm not a visitor. I'm his boss. Harriet and I need to discuss adjusting the shooting schedule with him for the next few weeks, figure out what scenes he can and can't do."

Jessica looked furious. "I told you to leave him alone."

"And I told you this can't wait," Ezra shot at her. "My time is valuable."

"You arrogant ass."

"You bitch."

Jessica threw her arms up in the air. "Unbelievable." Then she showed him her phone. "See this? I've got our lawyer on speed dial."

"Don't threaten me."

"Don't harass my client, who now has a traumatic brain injury because of your negligence."

"Stop being melodramatic. It's a simple concussion."

Jessica got in his face. "A concussion *is* a traumatic brain injury. Google it!"

Before the argument could escalate more, Piper said calmly but firmly, "Regardless of the terminology, it can wait until tomorrow, Ezra."

He jerked his gaze toward her as if he'd forgotten she was there, his face thunderous.

Harriet and Cynthia both widened their eyes.

"And Grant's not supposed to do anything strenuous for at least a week," Piper continued, stretching the recommended "few" days to seven. Go big or go home, she thought to herself. Even if the concussion weren't an issue, Grant needed a freaking break, and Thanksgiving was coming up anyway. "He doesn't need to be reading scripts or memorizing lines or anything else that requires concentration unless he feels up to it." She looked at both Harriet and Ezra pointedly. "Not even love scenes or anything else with his shirt off. He shouldn't stress his body with the diet and workouts he does for those." The doctor hadn't specifically said that part about the love scenes, but Piper justified it as common sense.

Ezra was about to speak, but she added, "And even if it's just a dialogue scene, he shouldn't do a million takes. Really, you should give him at least the next two weeks off just to be sure he's okay."

Ezra's complexion darkened to a maroon shade. "Two weeks!"

"Keep your voice down. Do *not* wake him up right now." Piper meant business, and she shot him a warning look that backed it up. She might not be very tall, but she had a strong backbone.

"Are you crazy? Two weeks will kill our schedule. We're already behind. We'll have to delay the location shoot in New Zealand!"

"Again, keep your voice down. Besides, next week is Thanksgiving. He should be getting at least a couple of days off for that anyway. Why not give him a little more?"

A derisive snort came from Jessica.

"What?" Piper asked her cautiously.

"He wasn't going to take Thanksgiving off," Jessica replied.

"Why not?"

"He's British," said Ezra, obviously put out that he was even having to explain this to her. "They don't celebrate Thanksgiving."

She was appalled. "But what about the rest of your cast and crew?"

"They all had a choice. They could take time off or stay and work for the extra holiday pay. Most of the crew chose to stay and make the extra money. It was their choice. I'm not breaking any Guild rules."

Incredulous, Piper looked at Harriet to confirm this, but Harriet had crossed her arms and was studying a speck of dust or something on one of her shoes.

Extra pay my ass, thought Piper. Anyone who didn't want to get on Ezra's bad side would probably sign on to work the holiday whether they needed the extra pay or not, except for some of the other diva actors on the show. She was starting to rethink whether she wanted to work for Ezra so badly after all. No role was worth the bullshit he was dishing out.

Of course, some might say that's why she was having such a hard time finding another job. Her history with *Nine's* had labeled her a troublemaker. That wasn't true at all—she hadn't been a troublemaker—but it *was* true that she was no longer willing to sell her soul for a role.

Except for faking a relationship with someone. Cue the inward cringe. Ignoring it, she pulled her shoulders back and said to Ezra, "I'll have Grant call you tomorrow if he feels up to it."

"Not good enough," he blustered. "Millions of dollars

are riding on the fact that this production stays on schedule. I need to assess for myself and talk to Grant." He moved as if to go around Piper and barge into Grant's room.

*Oh, uh-uh.* She stepped in his way and shoved at his chest, which was spongy compared to Grant's crazy-hard one. She planted her legs wider to give herself more stability against him, since he was almost twice her size.

He glanced down at her palms on his chest as if he were having a hard time believing she had the nerve. "Get out of my way," he said with menace. "You have no authority here. You're not related to him by blood, and fucking him doesn't count. You won't last. None of them ever do."

Ouch. That barb went deep, piercing her to the core—and he had just cemented the fact that he was a douchebag deluxe. "You don't have any authority here either," she countered, her words steady and made of iron. "You heard his doctor. What part of 'Keep visitors to a minimum' and 'He needs plenty of rest and no stress' did you not comprehend?"

Instead of blowing up like she expected, Ezra halted and regarded her with those calculating black eyes of his for a long moment. "It won't take long. I just want to see him for myself."

She met his gaze with determination, resolute he was not getting past her. She'd taken a self-defense class before. It had only been one class, but still. She was prepared to kick him in the cojones if she had to. She'd learned that much. "Sorry. You should assume he won't be back for two weeks and adjust your shooting schedule accordingly."

Again, he stared at her as if taking her measure. "He's a workaholic. He'll never agree to that."

"He won't have a choice." She had no idea if she could back up her claims, but Ezra didn't need to know that.

"Especially," she added with pointed suggestion, "if you don't give him anything to come back to until he's better. We all know he missed that mark because he was worn out."

"We know nothing of the sort."

She eyed him dubiously.

"If you want the Heledd role," he growled, "this is not the way to get it."

Her heart sank down into her stomach like an anchor, but pride wouldn't let her show it. "Whatever. I won't put the well-being of the man I love on the line for a role, no matter how much I would like a chance at it."

Ezra glared down at her. "Suit yourself." Then he stalked toward the elevators without another word, and Harriet followed him.

Once they were gone, Jessica practically cackled with glee. "Loved it! Brilliant performance, Piper! You're a fierce little thing when you want to be."

Cynthia was smiling brightly in apparent agreement.

Adopting a terrible Texas accent, Jessica mimicked Piper: "'I won't put the well-being of the man I love on the line for a role.' A little over-the-top, but still convincing."

That annoyed Piper. A, she hadn't been performing (well, maybe "love" had been laying it on a bit thick, but she did have...strong feelings for Grant), and, B, she didn't have an accent. She'd lost any vestiges of her already minimal Texas accent soon after moving to California.

"I'm glad you're still on board," said Jessica, lowering her voice, "but it does mean you'll have to stay with Grant for at least the next few days in order to make things look legit. It will be a great PR boon once the tabloids get hold of it. Are you okay with that, staying with Grant at his house? That kind of ups the stakes as far as what you signed on for."

"I know. It's okay." Good PR or not, Grant needed her. That was all that really mattered.

Jessica's sudden shrewd expression made Piper self-conscious.

"And you may be doing it for nothing," said Cynthia. Her voice grew sympathetic. "While it was noble, standing up to Ezra didn't help your chances for Heledd. You'll be lucky if he even lets you audition for it now."

Piper's insides squeezed painfully, even though Cynthia hadn't said anything Piper didn't already know. Still, the sense of failure was crushing. She wanted to be alone to process it, to figure out a plan B. She could try apologizing, but for what? She hadn't done anything wrong. It went against every fiber of her being to pander to that jackass. *He* should apologize to *her*.

"Let me point out, though," said Jessica, more businesslike, "that Grant upheld his end of the contract. He got your foot in the door with Ezra. The fact that you just ruined your chance is not Grant's fault."

Okay. The piling on was getting old. "I know that," Piper ground out.

"Good." Jessica's voice was almost a whisper. "Then you're still on board for the duration of the contract? You *are* good for his image. His Q Score has jumped several points in the last few weeks. 'Torrish' is America's adorable new 'it' couple. The public sees a softer side of him when he's with you."

At least one side of the plan was working. Piper wouldn't mess up things for Grant just because she'd probably blown it with Ezra. If being seen with her helped his image and got him the Captain Justice role, she wouldn't end their contract. She ignored the niggling possibility that she might be doing it for more than just the contract. "Yeah. I'm in for the duration."

Jessica patted her arm. "Good girl. You truly are a sweetheart."

Yep. That was Piper, always a sweetheart—but apparently not a warrior princess.

## 19

As expected, a nurse came in every two hours to wake Grant and ask him questions to assess how his brain was functioning. He was sometimes a little disoriented at first, but Piper thought part of that could have been waking from a deep sleep in a strange place. He would answer the questions satisfactorily and then immediately go back to sleep.

The nurse said his reactions were normal and encouraging, that he wasn't showing any signs of anything unexpected. He wasn't running a fever, but he had been nauseated a couple of times and had thrown up once—a normal thing, apparently, after sustaining a concussion.

Piper was exhausted. She hadn't slept through any of the necessary intrusions because she'd always wanted to see how Grant would react and if he was still okay. She hadn't been able to fall asleep after the last wake-up session nearly two hours ago, so she'd just been lying there on the sofa bed waiting for the night nurse, Yvette, to come in again. She should be coming in any minute. It was almost five in the morning, almost time for the day to start. For some people at least.

On a normal day, Grant would have already been up and on the way to work out with his trainer. Piper couldn't fathom it. His schedule was insane. On one of her normal days, she wouldn't have opened her eyelids for another two hours at least. Of course, things were different when she was working. Like Grant, she wasn't a diva and didn't expect the crew or other cast members to wait on her whims. Her parents had instilled a good work ethic in her, and she took pride in being on time and acting professionally.

Failure, no matter how unfair it was, settled like a hot stone in her belly at the memory of her clash with Ezra. She wouldn't be working as soon as she'd hoped. All this fake-girlfriend stuff with Grant, plus the fact that she'd put her heart in serious peril, had been for nothing. She wondered what scheme Cynthia and William would come up with next to try to jump-start her career—or whether they would even bother. Maybe she was a lost cause now. Maybe she needed to face the possibility that her career was over.

That made her sinuses sting and her throat narrow—both signs of oncoming eye-water leakage. She swallowed hard to keep it at bay.

No. Ezra hadn't said outright he wouldn't consider her for the part. There was still hope. Not much, but some was better than none. Maybe he would realize he'd been a jerk and still give her a chance.

But if he didn't, she would find another role, would keep fighting to do what she loved. If worse came to worst, she would rep that shampoo company that had recently contacted William. It was a brand she'd never heard of, but she did know that a big part of their sales came from QVC and HSN.

Ugh. It was hard to stay positive when selling stuff on a home shopping network was her best option.

Chewie slept down by her feet under the covers of the sofa bed, and she tried to concentrate on him instead of her disheartening career situation. When she'd first rescued him, it had made her nervous when he burrowed under the covers like that, afraid that he might suffocate so deep under the thick linens. But she'd decided he must have special doggie gills that allowed him to breathe easily. He'd always seemed perfectly happy either down by her feet or curled up in the bend of her legs behind her knees, although sometimes if she shifted positions and interrupted his cuddling, he would growl in irritation.

Yvette knocked softly on the door, and Piper called in a low voice for her to come in. It really didn't matter if they woke Grant, though, since Yvette was about to wake him on purpose anyway.

Piper, who was still dressed in her clothes from yesterday, sat up but stayed sitting on the edge of the sofa bed to watch Yvette do her thing. Yvette was thin and petite, brown-skinned like Piper, and reminded Piper of her sister Raquel, except Yvette was much older, like in her forties. And nicer.

Instantly Piper could hear her abuela in her head admonishing her for thinking something snide about her younger sister. Blood was thicker than water and all that. But Raquel was such a snob now that she was living in DC, all involved in politics even though she barely made enough salary to pay rent working as a personal staff member for Representative Amez.

Chewie scooched his way up the bed and poked his fuzzy head out from under the covers.

Piper smiled at his disheveled appearance. One side of his muzzle was smooshed down as if he'd been lying on it.

He put his head on his paws and looked up at her under his brows with puppy-dog eyes, as if patiently waiting to see what came next, the whites of his eyes glowing in the smidgeon of night light that filtered in through the blinds of the window above the sofa. He was such a good dog. She scratched him between the ears and smoothed his fur back with a couple of strokes, earning a soft snort of contentment from him.

Yvette switched on the low ambient lighting around Grant's bed and gently woke him by nudging his shoulder and then squeezing his hand. His fingers were long with hard angles, so masculine compared to Yvette's small hand, his white skin tanned but lighter than Yvette's. Piper wished she were the one touching him.

Stop it, Piper, she thought to herself, and scrubbed her face with her hands. She was so tired that her Grant defenses were weaker than usual.

His lids opened slowly.

The way his dark lashes fluttered and then revealed his eyes—a dark, inky color in the dim, bluish light—caused Piper's heart to somersault. And now she was getting turned on because his *blinking* was sexy. She was hopeless.

"Good morning," Yvette said. She was obviously as American as apple pie, but there was a faint Spanish-sounding rhythm in the way she spoke that made Piper nostalgic for some of her friends and family in San Antonio. "Let's do this one more time," Yvette said apologetically. "Can you tell me your name?"

He squinted at her, his brow furrowing, the bruise that had begun yesterday visible on his cheek just above the black stubble on his jaw. "Erm..." The furrow got deeper, as if thinking hurt. "...Geraint Gerard Nigel Cammish." He'd said it clearly, if sleepily, and very Britishy.

Piper had never heard his full name before but wasn't surprised he had four names. And "Nigel"? God. Again, so freaking British. It was moments like this that she had serious doubts he was really a contender for the Captain Justice role. Maybe their relationship farce was a fool's errand on both sides. Then again, she'd heard him speak with an American accent that day at the pool, and he'd done it perfectly. He'd shed his Britishness like a cloak. She smiled to herself at the thought of the VD commercial.

He'd always just answered "Grant Cammish" before when the nurses questioned him, and Piper wanted to laugh when she saw Yvette's face screwed up in a comical expression of alarm. She looked to Piper for help.

"His real name is Geraint," Piper explained. "I think he just told you his entire name."

"Course I did," Grant replied irritably. He grimaced and started to reach for the stapled wound at the crown of his head.

"Uh-uh," said Yvette, gently grabbing his wrist and pulling it back down. "Try not to touch your head, *mijo*. You don't want to introduce germs, and it won't feel too great, either."

He sighed and turned his head so he could see Piper better. "You're still here."

"Yep."

His gaze held hers—causing another heart somersault—before Yvette distracted him with the rest of the questions she had to ask him and the temperature-taking ritual. "How does your head feel?" she asked.

"Oddly enough, as if it were bludgeoned with a club," he said with feeble but devilish sarcasm.

Her smile was sympathetic. "I know," she said, patting

that elegantly rugged guy-hand of his again. "I have some Tylenol for you."

One brow lifted, and he half-squinted at her. "Perhaps something more bracing would be in order."

"Oh, it's supercharged Tylenol, I promise you. But we have to be careful not to give you anything that will cause bleeding or blood clots."

"Mmm." He closed his eyes.

Once Yvette had given him the Tylenol and explained that the doctor would be doing his rounds at seven, around the same time a breakfast tray would be coming—and that Grant would hopefully be discharged soon afterward—they found themselves alone again. This time he didn't go back to sleep, though.

"Piper?" he said in a gruff voice.

"Yes?"

"Come closer."

"Oh." She was still sitting on the sofa bed but rose and went over to him. "What do you need?"

"To thank you for staying," he said quietly, taking her hand and idly rubbing his thumb over the back of it. His gaze was on their hands, but then he lifted his eyes to hers. "It wasn't necessary, but good of you just the same."

His humble gratitude caused a flare of affection inside her chest, and the motion of his thumb had an electric effect on her skin. "Of course," she said, trying to sound nonchalant, trying not to let him see how even the smallest scraps of tenderness from him affected her. "No need to thank me." She gave him a quick smile and teased, "Any fake girlfriend would have done the same."

One side of his mouth quirked wryly. "Right." His expression went to his default unreadable one, and he changed the subject. "Where's Chewie?"

"On the sofa bed."

"Better bring him over here," he said, his eyelids falling shut. "He won't like being away from you."

She was pretty sure Chewie was okay with only being about five feet away from her, especially since he could see and hear her, but whatever. She was touched that Grant was thinking about him.

When she brought Chewie over and set him on the bed next to Grant's hand, Chewie promptly licked his fingertips. Grant scratched him under the chin in return, and one corner of Grant's mouth rose in a tired, lopsided smile.

"I'm probably not supposed to be letting him on your bed," said Piper.

"Oh, he's quite rabid. Better watch him."

She smiled at her small, fuzzy, curled-up dog, who looked utterly at peace. All that was missing was a cozy fire in a fireplace to complete the picture. "Yep. I can barely restrain him."

Grant repeated that lopsided smile, which caused even more heart gymnastics in Piper. Chewie seemed to soothe him, and Grant's eyelids began to grow heavy before suddenly popping open. "My mum. My family. I need to ring them straight away. Where's my phone?"

"No worries. I called them yesterday while you napped, before the story broke, and explained everything. They know you're okay."

He seemed to sink farther into his pillow with relief. "Thank you. Has it been bad? The stories?"

"No. Twitter was full of concern and well wishes. Cynthia said even your haters were either silent or sort of sympathetic."

He snorted. "How kind. How's Paul? He must be bricking it."

"Bricking it?"

"If only you Americans would learn the Queen's English."

She grinned.

"Worried," he clarified. "Felt bad he struck me."

"Oh. Yeah. He was totally distraught and is extremely sorry."

"Poor chap. Wasn't his fault, was it?"

She knew he wasn't asking.

"I zigged when I should have zagged. That's the right of it."

She was impressed he was owning it instead of making excuses. "You were exhausted. You've been burning the midnight oil too much. You were at the end of your rope, burning the candle at both ends."

"Sorry. I need another cliché to understand your point."

She searched her tired brain. "Your Energizer Bunny ran out of batteries."

"Hmm," he said with a slow, owlish blink. "It's called the Duracell Bunny in Europe."

She looked up to the dusky ceiling, pursed her lips, and responded dryly, "Of course it is." More serious, she tried to keep the anger from her voice when she said, "Ezra should have given you a break."

Grant perked up a little. "Please tell me you did *not* say that to him."

"I plead the Fifth."

"Is that a reference to your silly Constitution?"

"Revolutionary War still hurts, doesn't it?"

"Ungrateful Yanks."

She snickered.

He grew serious again. "What did you say to him?"

"Nothing. Everything's fine," she answered, because she

didn't want to rehash her argument with Ezra right now. Grant was watching her closely, so she made sure her face didn't reveal anything.

He still didn't appear entirely convinced when he said, "I should ring my parents. I expect they're still worried, even though you called them."

"Sure," said Piper, glad he wasn't pressing her on the Ezra thing. She grabbed Grant's phone, which had been charging on the seat of a chair by the wall, and handed it to him. "Will they be awake?"

"They're eight hours ahead. It's half past one in the afternoon there," he said absently as he tapped at his phone.

"Oh, right." She pulled the chair over and plopped down in it, her lack of sleep catching up with her and causing a wave of fatigue.

Soon he was video chatting with his parents, and he seemed happier than Piper had ever seen before. The dulcet yet chipper English accents of his parents were a pleasure to listen to, and Piper could feel herself getting drowsy, only to be poked back to wakefulness by Grant's laughter.

She wasn't really listening to Grant's conversation—something about his dad teasing him that his head was hard and his mom clucking over his bruised cheek—because Piper was mesmerized by him, by his animated way of speaking to his parents despite his injury. He looked so happy, so accessible and affable. It was hard to believe this version of Grant was the same stuck-up guy everyone knew and vilified. She could have stared all day at this version of Grant.

Oh, who was she kidding? She could stare at the stuck-up version of him all day, too.

"Piper?" asked Grant.

"Hmm?" she said, still thirsting for him in an almost trancelike state.

"My mum and dad would like to say hullo."

"Oh." She stood and leaned over Grant's bed a little, her head next to his in order to get in the video frame, trying to ignore the fact that he still smelled hot-guy good, even after not showering since yesterday morning. He also had some sort of antibiotic ointment on the back of his head where his stitches were. His essence was still there, though, and his pheromones were like chocolate. She got a jolt of happiness just being near him and had the overwhelming urge to snuggle with him.

Before she could drum up the nerve to do it, he took the decision out of her hands by scooting over to make room for her, then put his arm around her to pull her onto the bed.

He was so warm, so sturdy, his arm around her a comforting weight. His shoulder was the perfect place to rest her weary head. So she did, and it was bliss.

His parents smiled back when they saw her join in. "Piper! Hullo, dear," said his mom.

"Hi, Mrs. Cammish."

"Oh, pish," she said with a dismissive wave. "Call me Susan, please. And call him," she jerked her thumb at her husband, "Richard. No need for formality, is there?" she said with a little chuckle.

Both parents appeared much more jovial this morning than when she'd spoken to them right after Grant was settled in his room yesterday. They'd been so obviously worried about him, but apparently seeing him talking and smiling had done wonders to alleviate their concerns.

Piper could see a resemblance to Grant in both of them, of course, but Grant had his mother's light-blue eyes and her mouth. His hair color was more like his father's, although his father's was more gray than black now. Both of his parents were attractive and distinguished-looking, but neither had the overwhelming, awe-inspiring beauty their son did.

As Piper spoke with them, she was struck by how ordinary they seemed. That wasn't a bad thing at all, of course. But maybe a tiny portion of her subconscious *had* wondered if Grant had been forged on Mount Olympus. It was good to know that he came from a normal human gene pool, albeit one that had come together to produce a one-in-a-billion specimen of a man.

And his parents were so freaking *nice*. She knew they didn't have actual nobility titles, but she'd gotten the impression from things Grant had said that they were definitely part of England's upper crust. They had royal connections, after all. She'd thought they would be reserved like Grant and imperious, but they couldn't have been more cordial. In fact, Piper thought they would get along well with her parents. Not that they would ever meet them, but still.

"Love, you're looking knackered," Susan said to Grant. "We'd better let you rest."

"I'm all right," he answered, although Piper could tell he was getting tired now that the strong acetaminophen had kicked in and his head probably wasn't hurting as bad. He might get another hour of sleep in before the doctor and the breakfast tray showed up. Maybe Piper would, too.

His mother shot him a *You can't fool your mother* look before saying to Piper, "Take good care of him. Don't let him get shirty with you."

"Mum—"

"And don't get shirty with me either, Geraint Cammish.

You'll be out there running round in that leather loincloth of yours tomorrow—"

"It's a far cry from being a loincloth," he protested.

"—filming God knows what of your dangly bits, I might add, if someone doesn't stop you."

Piper pressed her lips together, holding in her amusement.

There was a gleam in Susan's eye when she said, "You're lucky to have such a lovely girl like Piper. Let her take care of you and, above all, *rest*."

"Of course," he said, sounding...shirty.

Susan arched a skeptical brow in the same way Grant always did, while Richard, who seemed content to let Susan do most of the talking, sat there with a placid expression.

"I *will*," Grant reiterated.

That seemed to satisfy Susan, and she smiled. "All right, then, love. We'll ring off for now. Oh, and, Piper, I hope you know that if you fancy coming home with Geraint for the Christmas holiday, we'd be absolutely delighted to have you."

"Oh, wow. Thank you." Piper was touched by the invitation but also felt guilty about it. When she'd signed on to be Grant's fake girlfriend, she hadn't thought it through far enough. It was one thing to hoodwink the public and the paparazzi, a nameless mass of strangers who constantly tried to invade the privacy of celebrities and judge them based on shoddy social media. It was another thing totally to lie to friends and family, and it gave her an icky, watery feeling inside. She glanced at Grant, whose jaw had gone rigid, before she replied, "Um, we haven't even talked about Christmas yet, though. And I'd have to talk to my own family about it. It's a big deal for us, for my parents and grandmother especially, and I'm not sure how they would take me not showing up."

"Oh, it is for us, too!" Susan exclaimed with joy. "We've quite the gathering. I completely understand. Anyway, food for thought. Just wanted you to know you'd be welcome. We'd really love to meet you in person. It's a little over a month away, you know. Time to make plans and purchase flights, isn't it?" She did that same not-a-question echo thing in her sentences that Grant sometimes did.

Grant's mouth was in a tight line.

Piper's own guilt and discomfort ratcheted up a notch.

After they'd all said their goodbyes, snuggling was no longer necessary and made Piper feel self-conscious, so she used Grant's phone as an excuse to get up. She set it back on the nightstand and plugged it back into its charger.

"They like you," he said.

"I like them too."

"You sound as if that's unexpected."

She gave a muted smile. "It is. I thought they'd be more like you."

He snorted out a vague chuckle, but it quickly died. "I hate lying to them."

"Me too."

## 20

G rant was going mad from boredom. It had been four days since the bludgeoning, as he liked to call it and which Piper did *not* like to call it. She just referred to it as his "injury," as if recalling the incident made her feel a bit ill. It was apparently too soon to be glib or light about it.

He'd not seen the footage of it yet, so, aside from the effects of the concussion, it was surreal to him. After all, he'd never seen the blow coming. One moment he'd been awake and thinking about what was for lunch; the next it was lights out and then waking up with a doctor having a go at his head.

He supposed if he'd seen his injury the way Piper had, he would think differently about it. As it was, he just found the whole thing acutely embarrassing. After all, it had been his fault. Paul had done nothing wrong.

He'd come to see Grant two days after Grant had got home from hospital, and the huge man had broken down into tears that had made Grant quite uncomfortable. Grant had explained that he didn't hold Paul at fault, but Paul had been inconsolable.

Grant had made a call to Harriet minutes after Paul's visit and asked her if she could get the prop department to make, at Grant's expense, one more replica of the club Paul had hit him with.

It had been an easy request to fulfill, and the club had been delivered to Paul with a note that read, "Paul, please enjoy this as a token of my appreciation. Someone finally knocked some sense into me." And in case Paul had not got that Grant was joking, as people frequently did not, he'd also added, "In all seriousness, please don't beat yourself up —especially not with this gift, haha. I'll be quite bothered if you carry on feeling bad about it. Regards, Grant."

It was possibly the longest note he'd ever written to anyone, aside from occasional letters to his mum when he'd been in school and his apology to Piper.

Speaking of, she had turned into quite the martinet, but he found he didn't mind. She hardly even let him bend over to pick something up. Granted, there was that one time he'd felt lightheaded after picking up a sock, but that was just after he'd got home Tuesday. Other dizzy spells and head rushes had occasionally assailed him, but it was now Friday and he was definitely mending.

Still, he wasn't allowed TV or anything with flashing lights, including video games—a travesty, since when in the last five years had he unlimited time to game? Even his phone and tablet time had been limited. The doctor had said they might bring on concussion symptoms, like headaches.

On that point, the doctor had been spot-on. Grant had had a dull, persistent headache that was manageable with

Tylenol but did—although he'd never admit it to Piper—get worse if he tried to concentrate on anything for very long.

It hadn't been as awkward or strange having her about as he'd thought it would be. It was as if she'd always been in his life, like they were a married couple who did the daily dance of mundane life together well.

Good God. *The daily dance of life.* There he went, waxing poetic like a proper fool. She often had that effect on him.

Whatever her feelings—or lack thereof—for him romantically, it was clear she'd been quite worried about him and wouldn't even entertain the idea of leaving him to fend for himself. And although he was perfectly capable of looking after himself now, it was nice that she genuinely cared.

It was nice to have a friend—a real one, as it turned out, after all.

Yes, their friendship had started out as a business arrangement, albeit a strange one, but he was sure it went beyond that now, despite previous doubts. Because caring for an invalid wasn't part of their contract, was it? She didn't have to help him, but she'd done it anyway. No cameras were about which required a performance, so he'd come to the only rational conclusion: she wasn't performing.

It made him feel cozy in corners of his heart he hadn't known existed before, so he'd not protested too loudly when she'd insisted on staying. He'd also not made much of a fuss when she'd barred him from video games, because he'd not wanted to do anything to annoy her or make her want to leave. He would rather live without the gaming than without her.

A disturbing thought he didn't want to dwell on.

They were sitting now on the terrace of the back garden in the shade drinking Topo Chico, which Piper had got him hooked on. Chewie was in his spot under her chaise, having a kip on a folded towel.

Piper had provided Grant with extra-dark sunglasses she'd found somewhere that reminded him of what pensioners wore after cataract surgery. The glasses weren't the height of fashion, but they did allow him to enjoy the terrace. Bright light gave him a spike of pain in his head (another thing he'd never admit to Piper but that she'd figured out anyway), so he supposed the things were a necessary evil.

He could imagine the comments that trolls on social media would make if any paps got pictures of him wearing them, although he couldn't be bothered by it. It would distress Cynthia more than it would him. He didn't care what anyone thought of his fashion choices, but Jessica and Cynthia said he had to maintain the urbane image of his brand, or he could kiss goodbye certain lucrative designer modeling contracts he'd landed in recent years to supplement his acting income and also to keep him visible when *Battle* was between runs.

He and Piper were under an overhanging balcony, so he didn't think they could be seen by any paparazzi. It was the pool that put them in the visible zone, and they were steering clear of that today. No canoodling or frolicking permitted, unfortunately. And he sensed that mandate hadn't come from the doctor.

Piper had just rung off after chatting to her mother. The conversation had mostly been one-sided, with lots of "uh-huhs" on Piper's end, but there had been no mistaking that her mother had been telling her all the whatnots for their family's big Thanksgiving and who would be coming.

The "Oh, I'm so sorry I'll be missing Courtney and her new baby!" he'd overheard Piper say gave him a visceral reaction for two reasons. One, Amanda had given birth to a baby boy on the day of the bludgeoning. She'd finally deigned to call Grant yesterday and tell him—after he'd seen it on her Instagram feed and left her a voicemail threatening a lawsuit (which he had no idea would be valid or not) if she didn't call him back immediately. Lovely way to learn you might have a son.

Grant had pored over the picture of the newborn, trying to find a resemblance to himself, but he couldn't make out much but a surprisingly thick thatch of black hair on the baby's head. That told Grant nothing, since Amanda also had black hair.

He'd immediately had Derek get him a drugstore paternity test, done the cheek swab, and overnighted it to Amanda. She'd promised to personally take the test to a lab in New York today.

Piper didn't know about any of it. It wasn't that Grant didn't trust her or thought she would be angry. It was just that this was a part of his past before he'd ever met her and didn't involve her. Also, just thinking about it caused his blood pressure to spike and made his head hurt. He didn't feel like having a lengthy conversation about it.

So the word "baby" set him on edge, reminding him that he might have a son and all the responsibility that would entail—but it also made him hopeful that he might have a son and all the *joy* that would entail. They would receive the results of the paternity test in three to five days. Until then, he would try not to go off his trolley from the waiting.

The second reason for his visceral reaction was guilt. Family was obviously important to Piper, as his was to him, and he hated the thought she was missing a family holiday because of him. "You should go to Texas for Thanksgiving," he told her. "I'll be fine."

She gave him a baleful eye as she set her sparkling water down. "I don't trust you."

"I promise I won't cheat on you with someone else, love," he said with mock sincerity.

She rolled her eyes. "I meant I don't trust you to stick to doctor's orders."

"It's been five days. I feel fine."

"Right. That's why this morning I had to listen at your door while you showered in case you face-planted."

"Terrible overreaction."

"You got dizzy when you got up from your bed and almost squished me."

She had him there. If she'd not shoved him back onto the bed, he would have taken her down with him—but no need to admit it. "Just a one-off head rush. And I still think my shower would have been more therapeutic if you'd joined me," he said with a lascivious waggle of his eyebrows he knew she wouldn't take seriously—if she could even see his eyebrows under the massive sunglasses.

"You wish." Her lovely bronze complexion, however, now bloomed with two spots of subtle red on her cheeks. Perhaps she'd not been unaffected by his shower comment after all.

He didn't know what had come over him, why he'd flirted with her that way at the time of the shower or now, but once he'd said it, her showering with him had seemed like a brilliant idea. Even though she'd been sleeping in the guest room, she'd been tempting him day and night since she'd been staying with him. Perhaps his injury *had* addled his brain, made him less inhibited.

Actually, there was no doubt it had. He found it hard to concentrate on anything for very long without triggering a headache, among other issues, and holding back his attraction to her had, at times, taken more effort than he'd felt like putting forth. It had to be his injury that made him keep wanting to touch her soft skin—and getting her in the shower with him was one of his most prominent fantasies, which he had loads of since he couldn't do anything else to entertain his brain.

Listening to audiobooks had been his only respite, but he kept falling asleep while listening to them—or had until she'd figured out from the books on his shelves that he fancied the fantasy genre and had found a new fantasy series for him to listen to. He managed to stay awake a bit longer for those.

She'd not taken him up on the shower offer, of course. Instead, she'd stood outside his bathroom door listening to him wash and use the loo. Not exactly what he'd had in mind.

But back to the problem at hand. He knew that both she and her family were disappointed she wasn't going home for the turkey-gorging holiday, and he wasn't going to be the reason she didn't get to see them. "Again, it was merely a head rush and certainly not serious enough to deprive your family of your presence."

"It's fine," she said in a voice with a little too much cheer in it, meaning but failing to hide her obvious disappointment. "They totally understand. I can make Thanksgiving dinner for us here." Uncertainty passed over her features even as she said it.

He held in a smile. "I would assume it is quite the under-taking. You sure you're up for it?"

"Yeah. Uh-huh." She was nodding too much.

Having learnt recently that her cooking skills were rudi-mentary at best, he was skeptical but didn't say so. A first, to be honest. Maybe he was learning some tact after all.

Instead, he said, "Whilst I'm sure it would be quite tasty, I must politely refuse. Go to your family. If I need anything, I can always call Derek."

She huffed. "Yeah, right. Unless you've face-planted on the floor and hurt yourself." Before he could protest, she added, "Besides, I'm not leaving you to spend Thanksgiving alone."

"You forget I'm English. We don't do Thanksgiving. I can't be alone on a holiday that's not a holiday to me." That wasn't the whole truth. He'd always wanted to observe a real American Thanksgiving just to see what it was like, but he wasn't about to tell her that. Or that he'd lived in America for almost ten years, yet no one had ever seen fit to invite him.

She shook her head. "Well, it's a holiday to me, a big one, and I can't in good conscience celebrate it without you."

A tender dart burrowed itself into his chest, leaving him speechless for a moment. Again, traumatic brain injury.

Once he'd composed himself mentally, another solution presented itself, one he never would have considered in a million years if he'd been in his right mind. He wasn't one to impose himself on anyone, but the head injury spoke for him. It was the only explanation for why the following words made their way out of his mouth: "I could go with you."

She stared at him as if he'd suddenly appeared before her riding a zebra with a pink saddle.

He felt like a berk. "Neverm—"

"I would take you with me in a heartbeat," she said, "but you're not supposed to fly."

His pulse quickened. Maybe she wasn't so averse to the idea after all, and it made something uncoil inside him that he'd not even known was tight. "I'm right as rain. A short flight isn't going to affect me."

She looked wary. "It's three hours."

"As I said, short flight." That was nothing compared to a flight to London.

She shook her head. "Doctor said it could exacerbate your symptoms."

"I'm much improved."

"Dizzy spell," she reminded.

"Head rush," he insisted.

"I don't think we should risk it."

He looked at her over the top of his sunglasses, resisting the urge to squint. The light wasn't that bad, really. He suspected his sensitivity was due more to shielding his eyes for several days rather than from his injury. "The doctor said flying was fine. It just might exacerbate my symptoms if I get overstimulated. Key prefix there being 'over-.'"

"Hmph. Flying is stressful enough even without a head injury. I hate it."

"I love it. Get to catch up on movies, drink cocktails, sleep. Especially if we fly first class."

"I never sleep on flights, no matter how much they pamper me."

"Good thing you've not recently been bludgeoned, then."

This time her "hmph" was silent, more of just an expulsion of breath.

"We wouldn't have to fly out for a couple more days," he pointed out. "I'm certain I'll be more than ready by then." As soon as he said it, a surge of excitement he'd not felt in—well, he didn't even know—flowed through him. "We've got the time. I still can't believe Ezra gave me two full weeks off."

She didn't acknowledge the last part of his statement

and glanced away a second before looking at him squarely again. "I don't think we should risk getting hassled by fans or the paps. That could cause you stress."

He resisted telling her to stop coddling him and maintained a neutral expression. "I'll hire a private aeroplane, then."

"That would be horrible for the environment."

"We won't make a habit of it, will we?"

She did half an eye roll. "It would also be obscenely expensive."

"I'm rich."

She responded with a begrudging *You're incorrigible* laugh that was quite charming, then crossed her arms and stared pensively straight ahead. He could almost see the gears turning in her head, despite her outward protests. "I could split the cost with you."

He would never allow that, but he kept mum, getting the feeling she would talk herself into this if he stayed quiet. He almost had her.

In one last volley, she said, "What about your staples? You're supposed to get them out on Tuesday."

And good God, he couldn't wait. Even after his shower, he still had a slight manky feeling where his scalp was concerned because she always dabbed antibiotic ointment on his cut once his hair dried. The staples holding the cut together also itched like the effing devil. He had to stop himself a hundred times a day from touching them. He'd made that mistake once on the first day after the accident, and it wasn't one he wanted to repeat.

Still, he didn't have to get the stitches removed in LA, did he? "They don't have doctors in San Antonio?" he challenged.

She let out a defeated sigh. "Yes, they do."

"So it's settled."

"I guess so." She grew stern. "But only if your doctor says it's okay."

Grant wasn't worried about that, but he gave a single nod of agreement. "Of course."

"Then I guess we'd better charter a plane."

Elation shot through him, and he grinned.

Which, to his surprise, caused subtle spots of color on Piper's cheeks for the second time that day.

## 21

Their flight had been uneventful. As he'd predicted, he'd slept for most of it and felt fine upon landing. Piper, on the other hand, had been refreshingly wide-eyed when she'd first entered the small cabin and taken in the luxurious appointments the four-passenger jet had to offer: creamy leather seats and lacquered wooden trim, plush furry blankets to cover up with, fully stocked refreshment bar with snacks and beverages of all kinds, and Wi-Fi. Her awe was infectious, and he found himself really appreciating his surroundings through her eyes. It amused him that she could still manage to be impressed after her years in the business and all the luxury and pampering that came with fame.

That was one of the things he liked about her: fame didn't seem to have gone to her head. She was very practical and down-to-earth, all things considered. For someone who carried a purse dog, she was really quite frugal. While her clothing was always flattering and fashionable, her house was modest, and she drove a Prius, for God's sake. The car enthusiast in him shuddered, although he did have to concede her car was much better for the environment than his beloved classic Corvette.

Her frugality had kicked in when they'd arrived at the airport. Instead of allowing the jet company to arrange a private car for them, she'd insisted they take a Lyft. (She'd laughed when he'd asked about taking a train, which were apparently nonexistent in San Antonio.) Aside from the fact that she'd deemed the private car a ridiculous and unnecessary extra expense, she'd explained that arriving in her neighborhood in a limo would have been embarrassing and called too much attention to them, like she was putting on airs. Never mind they'd just flown in a private jet.

If she knew how much he'd paid, she would have been horrified. Good thing he never intended for her to find out, no matter how much she kept asking him what her share of the flight was.

As they'd walked round to the rideshare area, they'd both been wearing hats and sunglasses, and a few days' growth of beard helped disguise Grant a bit—although Chewie hanging from the purse on Piper's arm was a beacon that practically shouted who they were. Grant had insisted on exchanging the cataract sunglasses for his Hugo Boss ones before they left LA because he'd not wanted to appear weak or like a bloody pensioner to Piper's family, especially to her father and brothers. Why he cared what her family thought was another thing that required more thought than he was willing to dwell on.

Piper and he had surprisingly not made too much of a stir as they'd made their way to the curb with their baggage and waited for their Lyft driver. They'd garnered several points, stares, and smiles, but no one had accosted them. Piper had explained that most San Antonians were, A, not used to seeing that many celebrities in town except for

Spurs basketball players, and, B, were mostly too polite to bother asking for an autograph, even when they did recognize someone.

Their Lyft driver, Ruben, once he'd pulled up to the curb, had done a double-take when he saw whose baggage he was loading into the boot of his car, but then he'd just grinned and said, "Welcome back to San Antonio, Ms. Torres." To Grant, he'd said, "Welcome, Mr. Cammish," and that had been that.

They were now in the Lyft heading to her parents' house. Grant was surprised to learn that the airport was surrounded by the city and only a fifteen-minute car ride from the downtown area of San Antonio, which was apparently where her parents lived. Piper was pointing out a few landmarks along the motorway, like the Pearl Brewery shopping area and the civic stadium known as the Alamodome.

She'd said they wouldn't be driving by the actual Alamo but that her parents' house was only a twenty-minute walk from it.

"Lovely," he'd replied, having only a vague notion that the Alamo had something to do with the American Wild West. He was going to have to Google it when he had a moment alone because it was apparently very important to the city. He'd noticed "Alamo" was in the name of many of the businesses they passed. He had the feeling Piper would be disappointed to learn he didn't know what it was.

He wondered if he would finally see someone wearing a cowboy hat there. So far he'd not seen a single Texan wearing one. He'd seen a few wearing cowboy boots, though.

A song came on Ruben's radio that had loads of accordion music along with a man who sounded anguished singing in Spanish.

Grant asked, "Is that some sort of Latin polka station?"

Piper met Ruben's gaze in the rearview mirror, and they both looked on the verge of smiling. "It's Tejano music," she said.

"Tejano?"

"Yeah. It's a blend of Mexican vocal traditions and German and Czech polkas and waltzes. It's really popular in Texas."

"Really? I've never thought Texas a coveted destination for Germans and Czechs."

"Oh, back in the 1800s, tons of them immigrated here. There's a huge Czech and German influence you can still see today, especially in certain areas of San Antonio and surrounding towns like Fredericksburg. The King William Historic District in San Antonio, where my parents live, was settled by German merchants—at least where the big mansions are. My parents' house is not a mansion, though. It's one of the normal houses in the neighborhood."

"Interesting."

"It is. I love it. The houses are all these small, quaint, hundred-year-old Victorian houses or Craftsman houses—I think Brits call them Arts and Crafts—that are so cute. Well, and then there's what everyone unofficially calls King William Proper, where all the big mansions are and where they hold the King William Fair during Fiesta in April. Fiesta is sort of San Antonio's version of Mardi Gras.

"The area is becoming popular again—all of Southtown and the downtown areas are—and a lot of the houses are being restored. I love that people are saving them and not tearing them down. They're very strict about what you can do to the outside of the houses, though—like, the city is. Because the area has official historic designation. You have to get a permit for *everything*, even if you just want to paint it.

"Anyway," she went on, "I don't think my parents will ever be finished with their house. My dad is such a perfectionist. I think he's rebuilt the back deck, like, a hundred times. He keeps wanting to refinish the hardwood floors in the house, too, but they would have to move everything out of the house and my mom is like, 'No way, José.' Which is funny because his middle name really is José. He goes by his first name, though, Frank. It's short for Francisco."

Grant grinned, charmed by how animated and excited she was, hardly even taking a breath when she spoke about her neighborhood and her home. He also found it delightful that a hundred-year-old house was awe-inspiring to her, as if something built a hundred years ago were old.

In England, something built *eight* hundred years ago was considered old. Something that was a hundred years old was barely broken in.

When another rapid-fire accordion song came on, she said, "So what do you think of the Tejano?" Her alluring brown eyes were expectant.

Ruben was glancing at him too, in the rearview.

Grant felt put on the spot. He wasn't partial to accordions, no matter what genre of music they happened to be in. So how to answer without being an arse and insulting her and the driver? He was apt to do it no matter what he said, if past instances were any indication, so he reluctantly told the truth. "I can't say I'm too keen on it, to be honest."

To his relief, she laughed, and so did Ruben. "Me either," she said. "My abuela loves it, but I'm not that into it." To the driver, she said, "Sorry, Ruben."

"Ah, it's okay. It's an acquired taste," he replied.

"I did like Selena," said Piper, "but she had a lot of songs that didn't really sound Tejano—especially her later stuff."

"Sorry, who?"

Ruben exclaimed, "What? Dude! You don't know who Selena is?" He shook his head.

Piper rolled her eyes and said good-naturedly, "Seriously?"

"Can't say I've had the pleasure."

"She was from Corpus—"

"Corpus?"

"Corpus Christi. It's on the Gulf Coast about two and a half hours south of San Antonio." Her eyes got big. "Ooh. We should go down there while we're here."

"Yeah," cut in Ruben. "It's pretty nice this time of year. The water doesn't look like chocolate milk."

Blandly, Grant said, "Sounds lovely."

Piper smiled. "Sometimes the seaweed is really bad and turns the water brown, but usually around October things clear up and the water is nice."

"Yeah," said Ruben. "I actually like Port Aransas better, though."

"Me, too." To Grant, she explained, "It's a small town across the causeway from Corpus, on Mustang Island. Anyway," she continued, "now that you know more about the birthplace of Selena—"

"And Eva Longoria," Ruben cut in again.

"Oh, yeah. I forgot she was from there, too. *Anyway*," she said again, clearly hoping the peanut gallery would let her finish, "Selena was one of the most famous Tejano singers of all time. She broke through to the mainstream charts."

None of that rang a bell. "I must confess I don't think Tejano has a large following in England," he said.

She shook her head in mild disappointment, but he

knew she was teasing him. "But *Selena* the movie was a huge hit. It was released internationally and dubbed in over twenty languages."

"When was this?"

"Late '90s, I think? I didn't see it until later, when I was older."

"The only woman on my radar around that time was my mum—"

Piper smiled.

"—so I doubt I would have fancied a movie about a woman Tejano singer. Now, if the Teenage Mutant Hero Turtles had been in it, I might have given it a go."

Her smile morphed into laughter.

Ruben's expression said, *Huh?*

"Ninja," said Piper.

"Sorry?"

"It's Ninja Turtles."

"Really? They were called Hero Turtles in the UK."

"That's lame," said Ruben.

Grant didn't take offense. He had to agree that "Hero" was indeed lame compared to "Ninja."

"Why 'Hero'?" asked Piper.

Grant half-shrugged. "Can't say. Perhaps 'Ninja' was too violent?"

She shook her head with good humor. "You Brits are so weird. But okay. You get a hall pass, then, on *Selena*." She cast him a smile that was both enticing and faintly diabolical. "But guess what we're watching this week."

"Sorry." He pointed to his skull. "Head injury. Not allowed to watch movies."

She waved a hand. "We'll saturate you with Tylenol. You'll be fine."

He laughed. "Oh, now that you want me to watch *Selena*, I'm suddenly mended?"

"It can be your first test to see if your brain can handle it," she said with a saucy wink.

To Ruben, she said, "You got any Selena?"

"You really have to ask?" he said with mock affront, then quickly had a woman crooning on the stereo that Grant assumed was Selena.

Piper started singing with the song in a voice that was quite lovely despite her not being serious. It was quite rich and resonant, her musical theater training evident. "*I could fall in looooove with you...*" She'd closed her eyes and was really into it, then froze.

Grant had been lulled by it, but when the lyrics she'd sung sank in at about the same time their meaning must have for her, she abruptly stopped. Grant looked out his window, mainly because his obviously still-addled brain had been thinking it would be nice if Piper *could* fall in love with him.

Ruben seemed oblivious to the sudden awkwardness and was humming along to the song that was still playing.

Piper cleared her throat. "You never heard that one?" she said as if no fraught seconds had passed between them. Before giving Grant a chance to answer, she said, "Also, Jennifer Lopez played Selena. It was J-Lo's big break."

"What happened to her, to Selena? I'm assuming she must have met a bad end, since you speak of her in the past tense."

"Oh," said Piper, putting her hand to her heart in sincere sadness. "It was so terrible. She was a role model for Mexicans and Mexican Americans everywhere, especially girls, but the crazy manager of her fan club and boutiques, Yolanda Saldívar, shot and killed her."

"Such a waste," said Ruben, shaking his head and suddenly looking angry.

"Yes," said Piper, her expression similar to Ruben's. "Any Latinx person worth their salt hates her with a passion."

Strangely, Grant's heart ached at Piper's distress, and he too was angered that Selena's life had been cut short.

As an afterthought, Piper, more subdued, added, "My mother used to sing her songs to me when she was putting me to bed."

They didn't speak after that. Even Ruben was quiet. Piper was probably musing about her family and the Selena tragedy while Grant was content to admire her profile—her straight, pert nose, her glossy black hair pulled back in a ponytail, her cashmere-soft skin.

And before he knew it, they were pulling up in front of Piper's family home.

---

## 22

Piper's pulse quickened when Ruben pulled up in front of her parents' modest, two-story Queen Anne Victorian house with its yellow exterior, white trim, and dramatic black front door. The colors had reminded her and her siblings of a bumblebee when they were kids, so they'd always called it the beehive.

The house was one of the few on the street that had a driveway, albeit one that would fit two cars at the most, parked one in front of the other. Most of the houses in the area were built in the era before cars were invented, and none in this part of the King William Historic District were large enough to warrant carriage houses either. Several of the mansions in the "rich" part of King William did have carriage houses, most of which had been turned into garages, but those houses were worth millions.

It dawned on her that she could actually now afford one of those houses. Weird. They'd always seemed unattainable while she'd been growing up. She'd never really gotten used to being rich and famous. She mostly felt like the same person, except when the paparazzi were invading her life or someone asked for her autograph. Or when trolls on social media—like Briony Callas—were calling her a fat, lazy slug.

And there came the gut-punch those words still had the power to make her feel. Not that she would ever admit that to anyone.

Her parents' house only had three bedrooms: one for her parents, one she'd shared with Raquel as a child, and one that Julián and Maddox had shared. Of course, Julián was married now and had a house not too far away, so he wouldn't be staying overnight for the holiday, but Raquel, who lived in DC, would be occupying her and Piper's old room during her visit.

Parking had always been a problem in the neighborhood, since most people were forced to park on the street. Sometimes the cars were so thick on both sides that the middle of the street almost got too narrow to drive down, especially during holidays. Julián's Tesla and Mad's classic muscle car were both parked in front of the house, so she asked Ruben to double-park on the street long enough to let her and Grant out and to get their luggage.

Despite the parking issues, her parents were lucky. Their backyard was big enough to fit a guesthouse, also known as the *casita*, in the back, which they'd built while she was a teenager. However, it could only be accessed by going through the main house. It had no street access, which was why they had made the bottom of it a man cave for her dad instead of a garage.

Piper had been relieved—and surprised—when her mother told her she and Grant could stay in the *casita* in the one-bedroom apartment above the man cave. They hadn't offered that arrangement the one other time Piper had brought a boyfriend home for a holiday. Abuelita usually lived in the apartment, but while Grant and Piper were visiting, Abuelita was going to sleep below on the man cave's daybed sofa, which was actually pretty comfy but only fit one person.

Of course, staying in the same room, the same *bed*, with Grant was going to be a hell of the sweetest kind. He stood next to her now, tall and excruciatingly handsome, carrying both his suitcase and hers.

She said to him, "I can carry my own suitcase, you know." Or she could roll it. "You shouldn't overexert yourself. I know mine weighs a ton."

He shot her a quelling *Don't be daft* look, which made her want to smile.

The healing bruise on his cheekbone, his strong-featured profile—complete with the dark scruff of a beard he'd grown in the last couple of days and a jawline that might get her pregnant if she stared at it too long—were dashing and rakish. Holding the heavy bags caused his large biceps and ropy forearms to flex and undulate under the snug fabric of his rolled-up, light-blue cotton sleeves. And if all that weren't enough, since he hadn't been able to dry his hair because of his wound, his dark hair had been perpetually curly and wavy in a way that had constantly tempted her to run her fingers through it.

Although she would rather Grant hadn't been cold-cocked, she couldn't deny that playing Nurse Piper had been much easier than she'd thought. He'd been a surprisingly good patient, and it had brought them closer as friends. They'd gotten along remarkably well, which only made her like him more and made it harder to keep her feelings in check.

Sometimes she wished she could carry a sword around and point it at him whenever he was being particularly funny or charming and bulldozing his way through the fortress she'd tried to build around her heart. During the last few days, she'd realized that fortress was pretty much made out of Styrofoam.

She wondered how he and her family would mix: he the couth English blue blood, her family proud Mexican American to the core and decidedly *not* blue-blooded, even though their roots went further back in Texas history than the roots of most white people she knew. What if he and her family were like oil and water?

Then again, why did she care? It wasn't like he would be her "boyfriend" for much longer. Rumor had it that he should be finding something out about the Captain Justice role soon. Meanwhile, she'd probably already blown her reason for fake-dating him, so their contract would be coming to an end. Funny how she'd neglected to tell him what had happened with Ezra, but she didn't see the point. Grant still needed her, even if she no longer needed him.

But anyway, even if her family hated him or he them, it wouldn't matter in the long run.

That scenario would actually be for the best. It was better they didn't get attached to him, since there was no way anything but friendship would ever develop between him and Piper. Still, a part of her wanted Grant and her fam to like each other because she wanted the people she loved —or who at least meant something to her, in Grant's case— to get along. It was as simple as that.

As she and Grant walked up the short sidewalk toward the front door, her burly brothers burst out of it, distracting her from her worries. Her parents Trisha and Frank, Abuelita, and Raquel followed close behind.

"*Mija*, why didn't you let us come get you?" scolded her mother before enveloping Piper in a bear hug.

"I didn't want to put you guys out."

Mom made a *That's ridiculous* noise.

Piper forgot Grant for a moment in her jubilance to hug the rest of her family, whom she hadn't seen since Father's Day back in June. With all the squeals of delight and laughter—plus the loving, tight hugs she got from everyone except Raquel, whose embrace was tepid—it probably seemed to Grant they hadn't seen each other in twenty years instead of five months.

Her mother took Chewie out of Piper's pet-carrier purse and let him lick her face. "Here's my baby," she said in a silly voice. "My *nieto*. Oh, Grandma has missed you."

Chewie's tail was wagging furiously, causing his entire rear end to wriggle. He basically became Mom's dog—she actually called him her grandson—when he was visiting her. She spoiled him like crazy with doggie treats and never put him down. He was either cradled in her arms or in her lap practically the whole time.

Remembering Grant, Piper turned away from her family to find him.

He was watching them with a grin on his face that was blindingly beautiful and joyous, as if he were living vicariously through her and enjoying the reunion.

Her heart skipped a beat, and her lungs felt as if all the air within a mile around the house had been stolen for a split second.

She motioned for him to step forward, and he set their bags down and began shaking hands with everyone.

No one in her family was very tall—Mad was the tallest, at five foot ten—and she noticed Grant somehow seemed to make himself seem less imposing by courteously bending toward everyone as he was introduced, especially when talking to her tiny, round abuela, who simpered and flirted with him as if she were eighteen instead of eighty.

Piper beamed, proud of him even though he wasn't really hers.

It seemed her fears that they wouldn't like him had been unfounded. He had them all wrapped around his finger about two seconds after they met him—even her dad and brothers. He was being the real Grant around them, the friendly, outgoing, unruly-haired Grant, not the debonair-yet-taciturn, straight-haired Grant.

His demeanor was still very British and extremely polite, but that couldn't be helped: you could take the man out of Britain, but not the Britain out of the man. He was being himself, though, the same way he'd been while talking with his own parents, and it made Piper's heart swell with gratitude.

It was the perfect homecoming until Raquel, the last to greet Grant, slunk up to him and batted her eyes as if she'd just met him in a bar, ignoring the fact that his girlfriend—her *own* sister—was standing *right next to him*. Piper was sort of used to this by now, the way women reacted to him, but it hurt that Raquel would do this, even if they hadn't been that close in recent years. There was a sister code, and Raquel had just taken a sledgehammer to it. It didn't help that Raquel was a beautiful little twig: small and petite, with big Bambi eyes and a bow-shaped mouth. She looked the way Piper used to look before gaining weight.

Grant withdrew his hand politely from Raquel's and put his arm around Piper's shoulders, then planted a possessive yet tender kiss on her temple, clearly showing where his allegiance lay.

And yep, all the normal reactions happened: stomach flipped, heartbeat skipped (again), body flushed with heat—and another chunk of her fortress crumbled at his feet.

"Whose '71 Camaro is that?" asked Grant.

Mad's face lit up like a bottle rocket. "Mine."

"That is absolutely banging," said Grant with the fervor of a true car enthusiast.

From the look of uncertainty on Mad's face, he wasn't sure if "banging" had been an insult or not.

Grant's admiration was more apparent, though, when he said, "Mind if I have a look?"

"No," said Mad with proud-car-owner delight and practically fell over himself to show Grant the car, immediately popping its hood for engine inspection. He told Grant how he'd found the car sitting up on blocks and spent a year and a fortune fixing it up. It was now worth way more than he'd paid for it, even though he still had a few more things he wanted to do to get it into mint condition.

After that, all the men were discussing the merits of the V8's horsepower in a car language Piper had heard them speak all her life but never really cared to understand. Her dad and brothers loved classic cars—any kind of car, really —and the fact that Grant had one of the best ever made (because of course his '67 Stingray came up in the conversation) and could talk shop meant he was instantly all right in their book. Never mind that he was a famous actor. They couldn't have cared less about that.

Then again, they were kind of used to meeting famous people whenever they visited her in LA, since Piper had been in the industry for ten years. They'd become desensitized.

The women, however, were more in awe of Grant, drooling over *him* as he bent over the car's engine, his delectable ass accentuated by his lightly faded jeans, and Abuelita seemed mesmerized.

"Abuelita?" said Piper in a low tone, "are you staring at Grant's butt?

She shrugged. "Art can be found in unexpected places, *mija*." Then she patted Piper's cheek.

Mom's shoulders shook with a silent laugh.

Raquel stood there with her arms folded, eyes also on Grant. "He is a work of art. Wonder what he's doing with Piper."

"Raquel Brianne!" their mother snapped in admonishment.

Raquel's snide words ripped into Piper like thorns, and she didn't know how to respond. Ever since she'd left for California, Raquel had been different toward her. It was as if she'd been angry at Piper for leaving her behind, which was dumb. Piper was five years older than Raquel. Of course Piper would have had to leave her at some point. She'd been a legal adult when Raquel had still been in middle school. Piper had just chalked it up to the hormonal ups and downs of Raquel being thirteen.

But now that Raquel had Washington, DC, all up in her ass, she was an outright snob and a bitch, and Piper was getting fed up. "What's your problem, Raquel?"

"What?" she said, feigning innocence. "Oh, sorry. That was rude of me." To Mom and Abuelita, who were both scowling at her, she said, "Sorry. But it came from a good place." She looked at Piper, pity in her eyes. "I'm just worried about you. I know you've lost weight"—she eyed Piper up and down—"but you obviously still haven't met your goal. I worry about all the sugar you eat. I don't want you to get diabetes."

Hot anger tore through Piper, her palm itching to connect with Raquel's face. She knew Raquel's concern over her eating habits was all bullshit, and besides, Raquel had no way of knowing what or how much Piper ate, let alone how much sugar. Furthermore, it was none of her fucking business. Piper opened her mouth and was about to let Raquel know where she could shove her "concern" but was stopped by her mother's hand.

Mom squeezed Piper's upper arm and said, "I mixed up a batch of margaritas. Let's all go have some on the back deck."

Raquel shook her head. "Is that a good idea, Mom?" Then she mouthed "sugar" while inclining her head toward Piper.

Again Piper was about to let her have it, but again her mother stopped her with a firm hand. "Enough, Raquel," she said in a way that conveyed Raquel would be in deep shit if she kept it up. And no one wanted to be in deep shit with Mom.

Abuelita piped up and said to Raquel, "At least Piper doesn't look like she's got one of those eating disorders. You're too skinny." Then she gave Piper another pat on the cheek. "*Eres muy hermosa, mija*. Don't listen to her."

Piper kissed Abuelita on the cheek for calling her beautiful. "Thank you."

Raquel just rolled her eyes.

Trying to cool her anger, Piper took in a deep breath and gave Raquel one last scathing glare, barely keeping herself from punching her sister in one of her tiny, pert boobs. But this wasn't over. At some point during this visit, she was going to have a talk with her sister and find out what the hell her problem was.

With a huge effort, Piper smiled, put an arm around her mother's shoulders, and hugged her. "A margarita sounds like heaven." Late November in San Antonio could either be perfectly sunny and in the low-to-mid-seventies, or it could be freezing. Luckily, today was the former, and it was perfect weather for sitting on the back deck and hanging out.

"Indeed," Grant agreed, coming up behind them as they went through the front door, her brothers and dad in tow. Grant was carrying their bags again.

Piper hoped he hadn't heard Raquel's snide remarks. No matter how much Piper told herself she was healthy now and looked good, it was scary how easily well-placed barbs could put a dent in her self-esteem. She didn't want Grant reminded of how big she'd once been, even though the whole world knew she'd gotten fired because of it.

Trying to forget it, she said to her mother as they walked through the living room, "He's never had one before."

"Not true," he said. "I live in California. I've had loads of margaritas."

"Just set the bags over here for now," her mom told him, pointing to a nearby wall.

Grant obeyed.

"But you haven't had one of my *mom's* margaritas," Piper corrected him.

"Ah," he said. "Then I look forward to the pleasure."

"Oh," her mother whispered into Piper's ear, her hand going to her chest. "The way he talks. I'll never get enough of it."

Piper grinned, knowing Grant could probably hear them but admiring that he kept his expression neutral. "I know, right?"

Raquel tried to squeeze herself in next to Grant, but much to Piper's satisfaction, Abuelita beat her to it and took his arm so he could escort her to the back deck. He had to bend down some to one side to accommodate Abuelita's diminutive height.

"You know, of course," Abuelita said to him airily, "Trisha got the margarita recipe from me."

I   t was late afternoon, and Piper was sitting outside on the shaded back deck of her parents' house, sipping coffee with the women of her family, including her cousin Courtney and Courtney's sweet two-month-old boy, Baby George, aka Baby G, who was getting fussy. Even though he was about to cry, he was precious in his blue Dallas Cowboys T-shirt, miniature jeans, and soft leather Adidas baby booties.

Courtney was a single mom. Her husband, Big George, a sergeant in the army, had been killed nine months ago in a freak accident unrelated to combat, before Courtney had even known she was pregnant. To her credit, though, she'd kept it together and was handling the newborn like a pro, although the bags under her eyes attested to the fact that Baby G was a night owl.

It broke Piper's heart every time she thought about what Courtney, who was Piper's same age, must have gone through and was still going through, dealing with such a tragic loss. Today, though, Courtney seemed to be enjoying being with family and had laughed a lot.

Thank God Courtney had her mother and older sister, Ashley, to help her with the baby. They were also present, along with Courtney's dad—known as Uncle Mike to Piper —who was now in the house, probably napping or watching football with the rest of the guys, including Grant.

Piper smiled inwardly at how Grant had seemed to enjoy everything about her family's very traditional Thanksgiving feast. She was glad she'd asked him to come.

He hadn't even appeared concerned about what he was eating at all. He'd had at least one helping—sometimes two —of everything, including slivers of each of the two pies and, of course, a piece of Abuelita's famous Tres Leches cake. Piper had been surprised: with what their immediate family had cooked plus what Courtney's bunch had contributed, they'd had enough food to feed a herd of cattle. But Grant had been a trouper and had gorged himself as much as the rest of them, as was required for a respectable Thanksgiving.

It was cute how he'd tried to fit in, like trying to learn the bajillion rules of American football and which team he should be rooting for (the Cowboys, of course), among other things. And he took it in stride when her brothers had ribbed him for mistakes like calling the football field the "pitch."

Inevitably, of course, a few other things had set him apart: the fact that he'd looked fine with a capital F in a navy long-sleeved shirt, his beard shaved off and his handsome face fully visible again; his well-bred yet foreign manners (like the way he held his fork in his left hand and his knife in his right to cut and eat his turkey, instead of switching them out like most Americans do); and, last but not least, the ever-present, cultured English accent. Every time he spoke, his words always stood out from everyone else's. His voice commanded as much attention in their dining room as Captain Picard's did on the Starship Enterprise.

His white skin among all her mostly brown-skinned family (Hannah, Julián's wife, was also white) also set him apart, but that was the one difference no one seemed to pay any attention to, either on his part or her family's.

They had eaten around one o'clock, and it was nearing four now. All the dishes had been washed and put away and the leftovers divvied up. While Piper enjoyed the whole Thanksgiving ritual, this was her favorite part of the day: reconnecting with everyone in a laidback way and basking in the dappled late-afternoon sun filtered through the tall pecan trees, a pleasant fall breeze blowing, while sipping coffee to ward off the effects of the nap-inducing tryptophan from the turkey.

"I think he's getting hungry again," said Courtney, jostling Baby G to comfort him before discreetly opening her shirt and letting him latch on to her breast. She put a light blanket over her shoulder to shield her exposed boob to everyone while the baby nursed. Not that anyone would have minded if she hadn't covered up. After all, breast-feeding a baby was one of the most natural, beautiful things in life.

"Oh, my God," said Ashley. "When Grant held Baby George for you, Courtney, I think my ovaries went into mass production."

Everyone laughed.

Earlier that day, during the meal, Courtney had been contending with Baby G, who had protested when she'd tried to put him in his bouncer. She was trying to hold the baby and cut a bite of turkey at the same time—a task she really needed four hands for.

Grant, who'd finished his first round of food and was

sitting to Courtney's right, said, "Shall I hold him for you? So you can eat?"

Piper, who was to Grant's right, was glad he'd offered. She'd been about to do the same, even though she hadn't finished eating yet.

Courtney, who had seemed a little self-conscious and shy when she'd found herself sitting next to Grant at the beginning of the meal, looked at him with awe. "Seriously?"

"Yeh, yeh. I'd be happy to."

Courtney carefully cradled Baby G's head and round, diapered bottom and then handed him to Grant.

He held the infant in his muscled arms like a pro, smiling down into Baby G's dusky gray eyes. "Hullo, mate."

He and the baby seemed enthralled with each other, and when Baby G didn't start crying, Courtney relaxed and resumed eating, a small smile playing across her lips.

Another one bites the dust, thought Piper. Courtney was now the latest female to fall prey to Grant's unintentional charm, which was much more potent than his or anyone else's deliberate, self-aware charm.

The picture Grant and the baby made was so adorable and impressive that Abuelita said, "*Dios mío*," and fanned herself with a napkin.

Piper's dad rolled his eyes, but the other guys went back to their conversation about the upcoming football game, not clueing in on what was happening.

Clearly Grant had misunderstood Abuelita's reaction, because he raised his brows in reassurance and said to her, "Don't worry. I've loads of nieces and nephews. I've held an infant before." He had no clue that he'd just melted the hearts of every female there.

Abuelita smiled at him indulgently. "I'm not worried, *mijo*. Not at all."

Grant smiled and held his finger to Baby G's little waving palm.

Baby G gripped Grant's long finger with his tiny baby fist in that way babies like to do. "Oh, you're a strong lad, aren't you?" said Grant, clearly delighted and fascinated by the baby.

Piper could imagine what kind of father he would be, but then had to look away. The scene suddenly made her chest constrict. It would probably happen someday, but he wouldn't be the father of any of *her* babies. Their contract was drawing to a close soon, and that would be that.

"I've got something he could hold," said Raquel with innuendo, yet again breaking the sister code and bringing Piper and probably all the other women in the backyard back to the present.

"Damn, girl," said Ashley, who was never one to keep quiet about anything. "What does that even mean? He's your sister's boyfriend. Stop thirsting after him. It's embarrassing."

Piper was grateful Ashley was on her side, but she could fight her own battles. "It's okay. She's just one of many. Women throw themselves at him all the time. He never pays them much attention."

Raquel bristled. "Maybe those rumors are true that he's gay, then. Maybe you're his beard."

Piper was so sick of people saying that. "Maybe you should shut up, Raquel."

Trying to defuse the situation, Courtney's mother, Olivia —"Tía" to Piper—said, "Maybe he's ready for a good girl." She was sitting next to Piper and put a hand on Piper's knee, which was covered by the jeans Piper was wearing, and leaned toward her. "Maybe he's ready for a *wife*."

"That's true," Courtney said quietly. "Maybe he's ready

for a family. It's obvious he likes kids, the way he was so comfortable with Baby G."

They were all silent for a second, all remembering Big George and how Courtney would have to go on without him, that George himself had never gotten to hold Baby G.

She exhaled as if exasperated. "Would y'all stop? Not everything I say is related to George. Big George, I mean. Not everything I say has to have a sad connotation." Valiant words, but she swallowed hard and her eyes welled for a second before her gaze went to Piper. "Are you and Grant getting serious? Have you talked marriage?"

That sick, guilty feeling Piper got whenever she was about to lie regarding her relationship with Grant crept into her stomach.

Fortunately, she was saved from having to do so by another one of Raquel's snide remarks. "Everyone is so provincial here in San Antonio. All you ever think about is getting married and having babies. Hispanic women can do more than that, you know. I'm so glad I got out of this small town."

Voice dripping with irony, Ashley said, "Yeah. San Antonio is so small. Like, it only has about 2.3 million people. Total backwater."

Raquel waved a hand. "I wouldn't expect you to know what I mean."

"Right. Nothing but us Mexicans here," Ashley said in an exaggerated Mexican accent. "Too clueless to know about culture or sophistication." Then she grew serious, her tone biting. "But at least we're not a bunch of bitches and snobs."

Raquel looked ready to retort, but Tía said, "Girls, that's enough."

No more was said, but glowers were exchanged.

Piper couldn't believe how full of herself Raquel had

become. She'd known it was bad, but not *this* bad. She'd tried to talk to Raquel alone yesterday to see if she could get to the bottom of why she was so rude toward Piper, but Raquel had just blown her off and looked at her with that faintly piteous look she'd had when she'd been giving Piper a hard time about her weight.

Piper had wisely left the room before she really did punch Raquel in the tit. She couldn't believe she'd even had that urge—and had it more than once—on this visit. She'd never hit anyone in her entire life (except for swats to her brothers when they were kids, but that was just play and didn't count). But Raquel was definitely in the running to be Piper's first victim. Especially if she didn't stop flirting with Grant every chance she got.

It sucked. She would like to be closer to her sister, but she'd reached out and been rebuffed. As far as she was concerned, it was up to Raquel now to decide whether she wanted Piper in her life or not. Until then, Piper had decided to take the high road and ignore all of Raquel's spiteful little jabs as much as she could. Raquel certainly wasn't making that easy, though.

Raquel and Ashley glared at each other for another second, and then Raquel stood up from the table. "I'm getting cold." With a smirk toward Piper, she said, "I guess I don't have enough meat on my bones to insulate me, unlike some of us."

"Thanks," said Courtney sarcastically, because she still hadn't lost her baby weight and was a plump, beautiful new mother.

The smirk on Raquel's face faltered as everyone there scowled at her. Courtney and Piper weren't the only women there who were of the curvier variety. Poor Abuelita was almost as round as she was tall.

*High road, high road*, Piper chanted to herself. *Don't rise to the bait. Don't give her the pleasure.*

Raquel lifted her chin haughtily and said, "I think I'll go see how the guys are doing," not offering anyone an apology.

Piper stiffened. If Raquel thought she was going to seek out Grant, she had another think coming. Screw the high road.

She was saved from having to take preventative action when the back door to the house opened and Grant came out looking hunky and breathtaking and...not right. Piper knew instantly that something was wrong. Her mind went immediately to his concussion.

His expression was grim, the muscles in his jaw bunching, the tendons in his neck prominent as if he were straining to hide either a strong emotion or pain.

Piper's heart rate picked up. She was about to jump up and see to him when he held up a palm to stop her. "No worries. Pardon me, ladies." He flashed a closed-mouth, half-hearted smile. "The tryptophan must be having a go at me. I think I'll have a kip."

They'd had a big discussion during the meal about whether tryptophan—which someone had said was a hormone in turkey (and which Raquel corrected and said was an amino acid)—really made people sleepy after eating it or not. Raquel, on whose authority Piper had no idea, had said it really had more to do with overeating carbs than with the actual tryptophan, since all proteins had tryptophan and it wasn't like you got sleepy every time you ate a steak.

Someone had of course Googled it and found that Raquel was annoyingly right. The carbs in the desserts did have more to do with making everyone sleepy than the turkey did.

So the fact that Raquel rolled her eyes when Grant said the tryptophan had made him sleepy, knowing he'd probably said it just to irritate her, gave Piper a juvenile sense of satisfaction. However, she still didn't like the look of him.

It must have shown on her face because he said directly to her, "I'm fine. Just a bit knackered. Please continue to enjoy your afternoon." Not giving her a chance to protest, he headed toward the *casita* and disappeared inside it.

No one commented until every last delicious vestige of him was out of sight. Then Mom, who was scratching Chewie between his ears as he lay in her lap, jerked her head toward the *casita*. "Piper, go."

Piper didn't need any such urging. She was already getting up from her seat.

# 24

His head was killing him. Today had been a long day, with the cooking (of which he'd played a small part by peeling potatoes for mashing) and festivities starting fairly early in the morning and lasting until now, a quarter of four. It was the longest he'd gone without a kip since his injury, plus all the screen time from watching American football and yelling at the telly with the men of Piper's family—which had been a lot like being with his own brothers.

He might have overdone it. He'd thought himself mended for the most part, but his body was letting him know otherwise.

Oh, and, also, the baby wasn't his.

He'd just received the call from Amanda, who had known the results of the paternity test since yesterday but had been so busy with the baby and Thanksgiving activities with her family that she "just hadn't had a minute to call him until just now."

Perhaps the fact that he wanted to pulverize a wall had

something to do with his headache too, since his boiling blood was a geyser about to jet out of his skull.

But aside from Amanda being a callous, thoughtless git for making him wait for the news, he told himself he'd be mental not to be relieved. A baby would have complicated things. For one, custody would have been difficult with Amanda living on the opposite coast, especially given that he spent a significant part of the year filming in New Zealand. And he highly doubted he and Amanda had the same ideas on child-rearing.

It was all for the best.

He slammed his eyelids shut, trying to block out the image of holding Courtney's baby earlier. He'd liked the feathery yet solid weight of the infant in his arms and the way the baby had gripped his finger with surprising strength. The baby had tugged on Grant's heart in the same way that holding his infant nieces and nephews had done.

No matter what he tried to tell himself, he *wanted* that. Badly. A family of his own.

Idiot. Just because he found himself homesick from time to time was no reason to make a baby. He should count himself lucky he'd dodged a bullet.

He was lying down on the bed in the upstairs of the *casita*, and he put his forearm over his eyes to prevent his head from splitting open. The bed was quite large, a king size, but not large enough to keep his cock from stiffening whenever Piper had inadvertently rolled into him or flung an arm over some part of his body during their strictly platonic nights sleeping together.

Unfortunately, she always managed to find her way back to her side of the bed before he could ever develop the nerve to take action. So he'd lain awake at least an hour or two every night since they'd been in Texas, fighting his lust for her.

Not shockingly, it only took about three minutes for the muse herself to now enter the room. He should have known she would follow him, even though he'd told her not to. He found it both irritating and...not.

He didn't move, his forearm still pressing into his eye sockets.

"You have a headache," she stated, sympathy in her voice.

He made a noise somewhere between a grunt and a "hmm."

"Why didn't you tell me?"

"I'm not an invalid. I can take care of myself. Go back to your family."

"Oh, so you took some Tylenol then?" Her arch tone said the question was a formality.

His answer was to grind his teeth.

"Didn't think so."

He exhaled, exasperated and not wanting to admit that he'd not medicated himself but instead was suffering and wallowing in his own self-pity.

After a moment, he heard her rummaging around amongst her million toiletries in the bath they shared and then a brief rush of water from the tap. He'd brought his own Tylenol, of course, but apparently she'd packed some as backup, because she was soon back at his side. All the floral and herbal scents that commingled to make her essence tantalized him, even though he couldn't see her.

"Here you go," she said softly.

He put his arm down. The creamy white walls of the room reflected the afternoon sunlight coming in through the room's lone window, and the shards of light poking at his headache caused him to squint up at her. She was holding out a small glass tumbler and, on her other palm, two extra-strength Tylenols.

Just thinking of the effort it was going to take to sit up caused him to sigh, but he wasn't *that* bad off, was he? So he pushed himself up into a half-sitting position, relying on his elbow for support, and took first the pills and then the tumbler from her.

The glass had been rinsed, but it still tasted faintly of toothpaste. Far from repulsing him, it felt very domestic and intimate that he'd just drunk from the glass she used when doing the mundane task of brushing her teeth. (He wasn't the sort to use a tumbler after brushing. He drank directly from the tap like a heathen, so there wasn't one for him.) "Thank you," he said, handing the empty tumbler back to her and letting himself fall back down onto the bed.

She set the cup on the nightstand and sat next to him on the bed. "You overdid it today." She looked guilty, her brown eyes full of concern.

"Don't be ridiculous." He didn't want her to feel guilty.

Her pretty mouth curved with fond skepticism, telling him it was silly to deny it.

He liked that she never took him too seriously, that she saw the humor in most situations and saw beyond the walls he put up. "Well, maybe a bit," he admitted. He closed his eyes again for a second, feeling the effects of the headache but also feeling emotionally drained.

Shrewd as ever, Piper studied him more closely. "Something else is wrong."

"Not at all. I'm fine."

"No," she said, shaking her head. "Does your stomach hurt or something? Are you feeling nauseated? Crap. We shouldn't have let you eat so much rich food. Your body probably doesn't know what happened to it. It's probably gone into toxic overload."

He watched for signs she was mocking him in that indulgent-but-snarky manner she had sometimes regarding his workouts and diet, but he could see she was serious. "I'm not nauseated." He *had* eaten enough for ten men, but that wasn't the problem. "It's nothing the Tylenol won't mend."

She sat down next to him on the edge of the bed. "I can tell there's something else."

He raised his eyebrows. "Oh? Clairvoyant, are you?"

His hand was lying on his chest, and she took it in hers.

The pressure and affection of the contact caused his insides to do an odd swivel.

"No, but you're being straight-haired Grant again."

Mirth plumed inside him despite his broody state. "As opposed to?"

"Curly-haired Grant."

"And the difference between the two?"

Her smile reminded him of the Mona Lisa's and was just as enigmatic. "Straight-haired Grant is aloof and distant, although he is still insanely attractive and charming in a sort of unattainable way that both turns people off and, conversely, entices them against their will."

Again his brows went up. That was quite the description.

"Curly-haired Grant," she went on, "has a tenth of the emotional barriers of straight-haired Grant and is affable and approachable. He's a gamer and likes to read fantasy books—a bona fide nerd who would shock a lot of people—but that's only scratching the surface of who he really is. He's real."

*He's real.*

Why did that statement harpoon his heart so? He had to clear his throat of the emotion. "And I suppose you prefer the curly-haired Grant?" His breath paused as he waited for her answer. Was it possible someone finally fancied the awkward lad he'd never quite got rid of from his school days, that lonely boy who'd been desperate for a single friend?

But he was to be disappointed. Her enigmatic smile deepened and, if he wasn't mistaken, grew sadder. She glanced away for a second before pinning him with those long-lashed eyes. "Tell me what's wrong."

He wanted to beg her for the answer to his question, but dignity wouldn't allow him. He didn't want her to know how pathetically he longed for the answer.

"Grant," she deadpanned, saying his name as both an encouragement and an admonishment.

He was tempted to tell her the whole unsavory tale of Amanda, but confiding his deepest disappointments and failures wasn't something he could cope with just now. Too much danger of it making the tabloids, for one thing. It seemed the walls always had ears, no matter how much he trusted someone.

A heavy sigh from Piper told him she was disappointed in his diffidence. "Okay, then," she said, using her hands to push on her thighs as she stood. "I'll let you rest. Text if you need anything."

He didn't want her to leave and grabbed her hand before she could get too far away. "It's really quite laughable," he found himself saying before his fear of laying himself bare could catch up with his mouth.

"What is?"

He tugged on her hand. "Close the blinds and lie down with me, and I'll tell you the whole sordid tale."

Her brow furrowed, but she did as he asked. They were soon mirroring each other, lying on their sides, face to face, one arm under their pillows, other arm bent at the elbow and out in front of them, hands a fraction of an inch apart but not touching. He felt as if she were the moon and he the earth, orbiting one another yet doomed to stay separate. Damned poetry.

The room was now bathed in a soothing, grayish-blue glow from the waning afternoon sun that leaked in around the sides of the window covering. It was easier on his eyes and therefore his head.

"How's your wound?" she asked.

He let one corner of his mouth lift. "Just a trifling scratch. Hardly deserves to be called a wound. 'Wound' sounds as if I were injured in a battle."

"That 'trifling scratch' had to have eleven staples to close it."

"Which I'm quite grateful to have out." He'd had them removed at a clinic yesterday. He'd also been allowed to use normal shampoo for the first time this morning, and he felt a thousand times cleaner. The baby shampoo she'd insisted he use for the past week hadn't really cut it, not to mention the fact that he'd smelled a lot like Baby George.

"So it's not hurting?"

"No." Not unless he touched it, but it was getting better.

"Good."

They stared at each other for a moment, he waiting for her to prod him into telling his story, her probably waiting for him to do it on his own.

Her impatience won out. "I'm ready for the sordid tale."

"Right." He drew in a fortifying breath. "Have you heard of a model called Amanda Cho?"

"Yeah. Isn't she the face of Naomi Cosmetics?"

"Was."

"Okay?"

"Well, about nine months ago, give or take, I had a brief, er, liaison with her."

It could have been his imagination, but he thought Piper had blanched a bit. "Nine months ago?" she repeated wanly.

"Yes. I can see you know where this is going. She had a baby boy the day I was bludgeoned."

It was telling that Piper didn't give him a hard time for saying "bludgeoned." Instead, expression strangely blank, she said, "And it's yours?"

"No. As far as I know, the little bundle of joy is some rock star's. She got the results of the paternity test yesterday, although she didn't see fit to let me know until just a few minutes ago."

He saw relief on Piper's face—relief *he* should be feeling.

Her brows knitted together. "Then I don't get it. What's the problem?"

"There's not one, is there?"

"Wait," she said, frowning. "Why did she wait until today to tell you the test results? You must have been on pins and needles."

"Quite."

"So? What was her deal?"

"She cherished making me squirm, I suppose. Probably did the same to the other bloke."

"She sounds like a real sweetheart."

He didn't answer. He didn't trust himself not to let loose the torrent of vulgar words he could use to describe Amanda.

"Sounds like you're lucky that you won't have an unbreakable connection to her for the rest of your life."

"Yes."

"How did you keep it out of the tabloids?"

He shrugged as much as he could while lying down.

"She was nearly sure the baby was the rock star's, and I think she was in love with him. She didn't want it made public I could be the father. She didn't want the rock star to see a reminder of me every time he went on social media. I didn't want my privacy breached, so we both worked hard to keep the paps from learning of it."

She searched his face. "You don't seem that relieved about it all."

Ah, Piper. Perceptive as ever. He closed his eyes, his emotions all over the place.

A sharp inhale of breath was his clue she'd figured things out. Her voice was filled with what sounded like wonder. "You wanted the baby to be yours, didn't you?"

He gave the answer that was expected. "No. Don't be daft."

She put her hand on top of his, a simple gesture that made his chaotic emotions even more confusing. "Yes," she said evenly, "you did."

"Nonsense. A child would have been a major disruption to my life. To my career."

When she didn't say anything, he opened his eyes and was surprised to see tears welling in hers, her gaze tender. He could feel that tenderness along his skin, a sweet torment.

"Oh, Grant." So much was conveyed in those two words. It was as if she'd seen into his soul, could see that lonely void in him he'd hoped to fill with a son or daughter. He didn't want or need her pity, but he didn't think that was what she was giving him.

He'd never had someone understand him on such a personal and basic level before, and he had the over-whelming urge to kiss her. He stared at her sensual, beautiful mouth and then moved closer to her so that their noses were almost touching. Lightly, he brushed his lips over hers. "Forgive me," he said, those emotions inside him now bucking and whirling and making him sound gravelly.

He knew she didn't want this from him. She'd made it clear they were meant to be only friends, but...head injury and all that. Hopefully she'd cut him some slack.

She didn't resist, but also didn't react. She seemed frozen, and he saw it as a challenge, cad that he was.

Taking it slow so that she could stop him at any moment if she chose, he let the touch of his lips become a bit firmer and ran the tip of his tongue along the seam of her mouth. Her lips had a suggestion of the sugar-laced coffee she'd been drinking earlier. He'd learnt while dating her that she preferred her coffee to taste as little like coffee as possible— a travesty, although the best option in certain circumstances, since what passed for coffee in the US was sometimes hideous.

In this case, however, he yearned to taste more of it, more of her. He wasn't going to push too hard, though. A warning in the back of his mind about #MeToo had him cautious but desperate enough to try anyway.

She opened her mouth enough for him to slip his tongue inside, but he didn't invade just yet. Instead, he met the tip of her tongue with his, a gesture of trust and greeting between two people still circling each other, still wary. When she didn't throw him out, he grew bolder and suckled her plump lower lip.

She made a sound that he hoped he wasn't misinterpreting as pleasure and then gripped his hand, which he took as further encouragement.

He slid his tongue deeper inside her mouth this time, learning all of its contours and feeling his cock harden. He eased his hand from hers and pulled her body closer to his, then ran his hand up to her shiny dark hair and released the clip that had been holding it in a loose bun.

He knew she went to great lengths with a high-powered flatiron to wrangle her curly hair into submission, and he ran his fingers through the thick strands to loosen it more, the ribbony texture of it cascading through his fingers and making him throb with need.

After thoroughly ravishing her lower lip, he delved with his tongue deeper into her mouth.

At first she responded with a fervor that matched his, but then she pulled away, panting. To add insult to injury, she also put her palm on his chest and pushed to create some distance between them. "I can't do this. I'm sorry."

Guilt gave his gullet a hard twist, and he grimaced and lowered his eyes. "Right. Sorry. Should have asked. I—"

"No, no. It's not that."

He surveyed her face, not comprehending. "Then what is it?"

Her gaze was penetrating. "I prefer both."

He still didn't understand. "What?"

"You wanted to know which Grant I like better. The truth is, I prefer both." Her eyes flickered down to his chest, but not with the usual relish he'd noticed in the past, which she thought she hid from him. His chest got stared at loads by both women and men, which gave him unusual insight into what it must be like for women with large breasts—although not for exactly the same reason. He did *not* have man-boobs. He didn't think she was even really seeing his pecs now, though, especially when she murmured, "I'm just like all the rest."

"All the rest what?"

"The millions of women who can't resist you." Her eyes came back to his face, their dark-brown depths burning now. "I like everything about you, all forms. I would even like you if you smelled like swamp water and had a beer belly."

An incredulous half-laugh escaped him. He couldn't believe what he was hearing.

"It's not funny."

"No," he agreed. "It's fantastic."

"No, it's not." She broke eye contact with him again, her eyelids almost closing.

"Why not?"

She didn't answer.

"Piper," he said, nudging her chin upward with his finger. "Tell me why it's not."

Her expression was one of utter despair.

It slayed him.

"Because it's not fake for me anymore. If we kiss, it means something to me. I can't... I don't..."

His heart started to drum like mad.

Misery etched her face, and she glanced away. "I know it's not the same for you, and that's okay. You don't owe me anything. I know it was never supposed to turn into anything more. But I can't do casual with you because..." She paused, as if shoring herself up for her next words. "...I don't want you to break my heart."

A giant fist squeezed his belly, and his heart, still beating madly, expanded so that it was cutting off air to his windpipe. But who needed air when happiness of the purest kind was suddenly careering through one's veins? It was the perfect cure for his headache.

It was suddenly imperative that his mouth be fused with hers. He surged toward her and, hand on the back of her head, urged her to meet him. She didn't resist, to his great relief, and he kissed her with a hunger and possession he could no longer control. When he'd thoroughly plundered her mouth, he drew back enough to speak, his mouth still so very close to hers, his voice ragged. "I was never acting with you. I don't want you to break my heart, either."

She stilled as if stunned. "Wait. What?"

"I don't want you to break my heart, either. You've the power to obliterate it, you know."

"I do?"

The emphatic "Yes" he gave her was almost savage. He tried to resume kissing her, but she stayed him again with a hand to his chest.

"But," she said breathily, "I thought last time didn't mean anything to you. You know, when we had sex?"

Women. Must it be thrashed out now when their feelings could be shown in much more pleasurable ways? He began nibbling along her jawline, then made his way down to her throat. A little "oh" escaped her that stoked the fire inside him. He really, really loved the gorgeous column of her neck.

"You were so...indifferent afterward," she said, a hitch in her breath.

Even though every cell in his body protested, he paused to address her comment. Drawing back a little to look at her, he said, "*I* was indifferent? You're the one who friend-zoned me. Did you think I was going to make a fool of myself and declare my feelings after you'd told me you'd just got carried away, that it was a mistake, that it wouldn't happen again?"

"Are you telling me *you* didn't feel that way?"

He frowned. "No. I didn't at all. I'd have thought the fact that I whisked you up in my arms and carried you up the stairs to my bedroom to make love with you was indicative of my feelings."

"But I figured you did that kind of stuff all the time."

For the love of... A craggy laugh escaped him. "No. I can assure you I don't."

"Really?"

He rolled his eyes. "No."

"What about the kiss in the limo?"

"What about it?" he asked, flummoxed.

"Was it real?"

He huffed, the memory of it exacerbating his already amorous mood. "About as bloody real as it gets."

"I thought maybe—" She waved her hand. "Never mind."

He grabbed her hand and held it. "You thought what?"

"The timing was so perfect with the opening of the door..."

He widened his eyes. "Good God. Did you think I did it for the paps?"

Her sheepish expression was his answer.

No wonder she'd been more distant after they'd alighted from the limo. It all clicked into place. He let go of her hand and brushed his thumb over her delicate cheekbone, making sure to capture her gaze. "Piper, I did it because I wanted to kiss you and for no other reason."

"Oh, my God," she said. "We've been so stupid."

He arched a brow. "Well, one of us has." He let his tone imply it wasn't he.

She exhaled a rueful sniff.

"Why did you keep pushing me away?"

"Because I didn't think I stood a chance with you."

Again, he frowned. "Why on bloody earth not?"

"Because you're a freaking Greek god, and I'm not."

A slight coldness settled in his stomach. He didn't like where this was leading.

She scoffed. "Do I have to spell it out for you?"

"Apparently."

"You are the most beautiful man alive. I'm just ordinary." Before he could protest, she held up her hand. "I'm not saying I'm ugly or anything. I know I have my charms—"

He snorted at that understatement and said dryly, "A few, yes."

"—but, I mean, I could still stand to lose a few pounds, and—"

This made him borderline angry, and he interrupted her with a laserlike intensity. "Let me be clear: you are anything but ordinary, Piper Torres. You are *extra*ordinary in every sense of the word, and despite what you've read or heard about me, I don't shag anyone who's willing, man or woman."

He reached out and brushed a strand of hair behind her ear, then caressed her downy cheek again with his thumb. "I don't know how you've missed it, but I'm quite enamored of you and have been for some time."

"Well, you're not exactly easy to read."

"Pot, kettle, et cetera."

"Yeah, right. I wear my emotions on my sleeve."

"I beg to differ. You're an excellent actress, because until this moment, I thought you were only interested in friendship."

She studied him as if trying to discern if he were being true. "But," she said with doubt, "I don't fit your normal type. I'm not a model, and I'm not petite and thin like Raquel, either."

He tightened his mouth in dismay at the mention of her handsy sister. "Sorry, but your sister is a bit of a cunt."

Her eyes rounded like saucers, and then she laughed, exposing her lovely straight teeth. "Oh, my God. I can't believe you just used that word."

Not bothered that he'd shocked her and glad he'd made her laugh, he said, "You Americans. Such prudes."

Eyes still big, laughter fading to a smile, she said, "No. I know that word isn't as offensive in Britain, but if you use it in front of Abuelita or my mom, they seriously might have heart attacks."

He thought her mother and gran were made of sterner stuff, but he decided to allay her fear. "I know I can be tact-less," he said, "but I do have enough sense not to use that language in front of your family—especially your mum and gran."

"Just making sure," she said with the ghost of a mischie-vous smile.

They didn't say anything for a moment, just watched each other. The joy and exuberance he felt from her revela-tion were reflected back at him in her gaze.

Hoping they could now get to the good bits, he said, "Now that we've established a mutual..."—he cast about for the correct word, not wanting to alarm her with just how utterly consuming his ardor was—"...attachment to each other, do you think we could—"

Piper's answer was to grab him as he'd done to her earlier and pull him to her, then kiss him as if the future existence of the planet depended on it. Perhaps the moon and the earth were meant to be together after all.

And from there, things only got much, *much* better.

---

EVERY INCH of Piper's body had been thoroughly kissed, licked, and/or nibbled, and a satisfied languor stole over her.

She and Grant had come full circle (after experimenting with several interesting positions during their lovemaking) and were now lying on their sides again, facing each other, both their gazes heavy-lidded and self-satisfied in the knowledge they'd brought each other to unimagined heights of pleasure.

The only difference now was that they were both naked, and she didn't feel self-conscious at all. The way Grant had worshipped her body had dispelled any residual qualms she'd had about his attraction to her. She'd never felt more beautiful.

He liked her. For real. She couldn't believe it. Then again, the way he was looking at her now, a small smile playing on his sinful lips, made her want to believe it.

She was just going to take each minute as they came, not look too far ahead, not hope for more. Just being with him was enough. He was worth the risk to her heart.

She traced her finger down the bump in his otherwise perfect nose, then let her hand fall away.

He watched her in a way that made her shiver and want to smile at the same time.

"What happened?" she asked, obviously referring to his nose. "Did you break it?

"*I* didn't break it. Another lad did me the favor."

She winced. "What happened?"

"First year at Bradshaw Grange, my boarding school. Remember I told you I wasn't exactly the most popular chap?"

"Yeah." She did remember now that he'd reminded her. After spending so much time with the nearly flawless man he'd become—at least in the looks department—it had been easy to forget he'd been pudgy and bullied as a kid.

"Well," he went on, "my father tired of me ringing them and whingeing about this one bully in particular, so he told me I wasn't allowed to come home at all, not even on holiday, until I punched the—his words—little bastard in the face. So I did." Grant's mouth twisted sardonically. "And the little bastard punched back."

"Who won?"

His expression was the picture of male smugness and satisfaction. "I did, of course. Broken nose notwithstanding."

She grinned. "Of course."

"That was the first time it was broken. I broke it another time playing rugby."

She could picture him playing rugby. He certainly had the right body type for it.

"I probably should have tried to get it fixed, considering the industry I'm in, but I couldn't be bothered."

She shook her head, hindered a bit by her pillow. "I'm glad you didn't. It gives you character. And at least there's one part of you that's not perfect."

His mouth quirked with self-deprecation. "There's a lot of me that's not perfect."

"Not from my point of view," she countered.

He copied her earlier movement by tracing her nose with his finger. "Likewise."

Her heart completely melted. Like, into a puddle of wine —the richest, most velvety Cabernet.

Then he punctuated his comment with a sweet kiss that was pretty much all either of them could muster, after the way they'd just spent the afternoon and evening.

She had no idea what time it was. The sun was gone, but she didn't have the energy to look at her phone, which was hidden somewhere among their clothing strewn all over the hardwood floor.

It was suddenly hard to keep her eyes open, and she blinked slowly.

Without saying anything, Grant pulled the top sheet and

comforter up over them, then coaxed her into lying with her back to his chest so they could spoon.

She loved being surrounded by his big, hard body and fell asleep in about two seconds, secure in the knowledge that she was falling in love with Grant and thrilled by the strong possibility that—did she dare to think it?—he was falling in love with her too.

## 25

Apparently it had been early yesterday evening when Piper and Grant had fallen asleep, because she woke up at the ungodly hour of five o'clock on Black Friday morning all bright-eyed and bushy-tailed. She was also still naked. Next to a naked Grant Cammish.

It boggled the mind.

At some point in the night they'd changed positions and were no longer spooning. She was facing him now but still close enough to feel his body heat. She was tempted to snuggle up to him, to run her fingertips over his hard pec muscles, but he was in a deep sleep and she didn't have the heart to wake him. He was still healing from his head injury and probably needed the rest, especially since he'd had a long, tumultuous day yesterday—which had, of course, ended with phenomenal sex that had required a lot of stamina, to put it mildly.

Elation surged through her, and she let a huge grin spread across her face. It might never go away. She might have this goofy, besotted grin on her face for the rest of her life.

Unable to go back to sleep, she eased out of bed and tiptoed over to her suitcase, which she'd left open on a bench under the window. The chilly predawn air raised goosebumps on her skin, and she quickly found what constituted her winter pajamas, which also doubled as loungewear.

It wasn't the most fashionable of outfits. She only wore it when sleeping or when no one was going to see her vegging around the house: black Spurs T-shirt, baggy gray zipper hoodie, generic gray athletic pants that were comfy if not the most flattering to her figure, and old running shoes that she'd found in her old closet in the main house yesterday. After finger-combing her long hair, she grabbed the clip from yesterday that had somehow found its way onto her nightstand and twisted her hair up into it without even looking in a mirror.

She didn't even brush her teeth. She would get a breath mint from her purse, which was in the main house. She would be eating breakfast and drinking coffee soon, so she didn't see the point of brushing and possibly waking up Grant in the process.

Maybe she shouldn't let him see her looking so ratty, but he wasn't showing signs of stirring. And, oddly enough, she didn't think he would care that she wasn't all glammed out. He would probably appreciate more that she felt comfortable enough to be herself around him, warts and all.

Her gaze went to him again, and a silent, wistful sigh escaped her. The pale-blue sheets and comforter only covered him from his narrow waist down, and the sight of his broad chest and insane abs made her core clench with a flash of desire. His unruly, curly black hair fell every which way onto his pillow, making him enticingly disheveled. His hair had grown out a little, since he'd been due for a haircut when he got injured, and since then it hadn't been possible. Afraid she might accidentally hurt the cut on his scalp, which had to still be tender, she hadn't had the chance to run her fingers through his hair yet.

All in good time, she told herself. She and Grant had plenty of time to get to know each other better and indulge in silly yet necessary urges like running their fingers through each other's hair.

Unable to resist, she crawled across the bed and gave him a peck on the mouth, feeling a bit of his morning stubble tickle the outer edge of her lips. He smiled without opening his eyes, made a cute indistinct noise of acknowledgment, and burrowed deeper into his pillow. Since he hadn't been allowed to work out with his trainer, he would sometimes sleep in all the way until *seven*. It was unheard-of. Scandalous.

She pulled the covers up to his shoulders so he wouldn't get cold. He didn't stir again.

Tiptoeing down the stairs and through the man cave's living room, she slipped out the door without waking Abuelita. Piper wanted to get the keys to her mom's car, which were always hung on a hook inside the kitchen door of the main house, so she could go to Mi Tierra Cafe y Panadería, a Tex-Mex restaurant and bakery. It had been an institution in San Antonio for, like, as long as Abuelita had, and Piper wanted to get breakfast tacos and Mexican pastries for everyone. The restaurant was open twenty-four hours a day, so it would be open even at this ludicrously early hour.

When she walked out of the *casita*, she was relieved to see a light on in the main house's kitchen that lit her way in the predawn darkness. Of course her dad would already be up. He'd gotten up around four-thirty or five every single morning since she could remember. Unlike Grant, though, it wasn't to work out. Her dad owned a construction company, and he'd always used his extra time in the mornings to review what was going on in the company's various projects and do his books. He didn't trust anyone else with the task.

She walked across the deck and tapped on the old back door's windowpane.

Dad looked up, and instant pleasure at seeing her lit up his features. He got up and let her in, then gave her a big bear hug. "Good morning, sweetheart."

She could feel the rumbling timbre of his voice vibrate through her and smiled, loving his familiar Old Spice scent and the safety of his embrace. "Good morning."

When they separated, she grabbed the keys off the hook and spoke in a low voice. "I'm going to Mi Tierra to get some breakfast tacos and *pandulce*."

"Mmm," he enthused. "I didn't think I'd ever want to eat again after yesterday, but I could do with one of their guava *campechanas*."

"Oh," said Piper, rolling her eyes in ecstasy, "that sounds soooo good." *Campechanas* were flaky, glazed turnovers filled with various kinds of fruit that were pure decadence.

Glancing at the hook with the car keys, she said, "I was going to take Mom's car, if that's okay."

Dimples appeared in his cheeks when he grinned. "Grab the keys. I'll go with you."

A few minutes later they were on their way to Mi Tierra, which was only about an eight-minute drive from her parents' house. In the rearview mirror, although a ways back, the headlights of a car cut through the darkness.

It made Piper wary. "I think someone might be following us," she said to her dad.

He turned around and looked out the rear window. "At this hour?"

"Yes. That car has been behind us since I pulled away from the house. I've been watching."

Paparazzi usually didn't harass her when she visited San Antonio, and her hometown did not have its own version of the annoying but necessary nuisances. There just wasn't enough celebrity activity in the city to keep the paps employed or to draw them from New York or LA.

In fact, she could pretty much forget her fame and be herself whenever she came home, because most San Antonians respected her privacy. She could go shopping or out to dinner and not get hassled for the most part, except for the occasional fan who would politely ask for a selfie. Even then, like if she were at a restaurant, they would usually wait until she was done eating.

Of course, several LA paparazzi had made the trip and staked out her parents' house when she'd been fired from her sitcom. When they'd figured out Piper wasn't coming home to be comforted by her family, though, it hadn't taken them long to give up and head back to their lairs in LA— where they had then dogged her every step when she was forced to venture out of her house.

The mystery car followed her and her dad until they pulled into the Mi Tierra parking lot, then kept going.

Dad said, "It's gone. Maybe it was just someone else in the neighborhood going to one of those early Black Friday sales."

She was skeptical. "There aren't any stores near Mi Tierra—at least not the Christmas-shopping kind. More for the tourists."

"The Rivercenter mall's not too far."

"Yeah, but they went the wrong direction for that."

He shrugged. "Then I don't know, but they're gone now."

Maybe she was just being paranoid. Yes, she and Grant had been in the media a lot lately thanks to their PR people, but she didn't think the paps would travel all the way to San Antonio just for a few cutesy Thanksgiving pics of her and Grant being lovey-dovey—which, by the way, they wouldn't have to fake anymore.

The thought both thrilled and relieved her. And she wouldn't be lying to her family anymore, either. Or Grant's. Maybe she and Grant would even tell them all the whole story someday if things worked out. Hopefully they would laugh it off and not be angry or disappointed they'd been lied to.

It only took about twenty minutes to pick out all the pastries she and her dad wanted and get the breakfast tacos they ordered. She had two big boxes of pastries, and her dad had a small sack full of mini salsa containers along with a large sack full of various types of tacos—chorizo and egg was her favorite—that were all wrapped in foil. She knew from many years of experience the tacos would still be warm by the time they got back to the house. Her mouth watered just thinking about it.

She and Dad were almost to the car when a camera flash temporarily blinded her.

She blinked her eyes to try to clear her vision while, at the same time, her stomach instantly sank to her toes. She knew without a doubt she'd been right about that car following them. Even worse, in her ratty loungewear, she looked like she'd just crawled out from under a rock.

A split second later, someone yelled, "Piper, have you seen the latest video of Grant on the *Glitz Report*'s Twitter or Instagram feeds?"

Ignoring the question, she said, "Let's go," in a low,

urgent voice to her dad, keeping her head down. She didn't know what video they were talking about, and she had a feeling she didn't want to know.

Dad gave a quick nod and didn't even look in the direction of the voice. He didn't have to be told what was going on. This wasn't his first rodeo with the paparazzi.

Instinctively she knew not to engage. The PR people and agents hadn't planned this. For one thing, they would have given Piper a heads-up. Second, Grant wasn't with her, so what reason would the photogs have to be taking pictures of just her? Of course, they might have assumed her dad was Grant until they'd seen him just now.

It was only two guys about five feet away. They wouldn't stop her and Dad from leaving. She could tell by their demeanors that they weren't the aggressive type, that they would be content to harass her from a respectable distance.

She'd already gotten the key fob out of her purse before she'd picked up the pastry boxes, and she mashed the unlock button, then quickly set the boxes in the back seat. Dad had gotten his door open and was getting into the passenger seat while still juggling the sacks in his hands.

Just as she was about to slam her driver's door shut, one of the paps walked tentatively closer, his phone screen facing outward and held out as if he wanted her to see it. So much for him not being the aggressive type. "Come on, Piper. We're representing the *Glitz Report*, and we have a video we think you'll want to see. The story's going to officially break this morning in the magazine, even though teasers went out on social media late last night."

She shook her head and shut her car door.

The guy came and knocked on her window anyway, showing her a video of Grant in workout gear wiping his face with a towel.

She started the car.

The guy knocked again and shouted, "What do you think of Grant saying you're lazy and a slug?"

She froze for just a second, not wanting to believe it even as a sick feeling seeped into her belly. These paps wouldn't have traveled all this way for nothing, and he was trying to show her the proof. She just wasn't letting him.

Another camera flash from his partner captured the current expression on her face, which probably matched the roiling of her stomach.

"It's going to come out, Piper." He sounded almost apologetic, as if it wasn't his fault a video was about to be released that was going to hurt Piper beyond belief, if what he'd said about Grant was legit. "This is your chance to tell your side of it. You have an obligation to your fans. Everyone knows the 'lazy slug' thing pushed your buttons after you got fired. You and Briony Callas had a pretty public feud."

Piper wouldn't call it a feud. She'd never engaged with Briony personally. However, plenty of her fans had.

The *Glitz Report* was one of the most popular entertainment tabloids in the country—as big as or bigger than TMZ —with a huge readership both online and in newsstand sales and subscriptions. If the "slug" thing was being dug up again, everyone and their dog was going to see it. The thought that Grant might somehow be involved would make it a million times worse.

"Get away from my car," was the only warning she gave the pap before putting it in gear and backing—probably too fast—out of her spot, then pulling out in front of another car and cutting them off as she entered the street. The other car didn't honk at her, although they would have been justified. But this was San Antonio. If someone honked at you, they weren't from around here.

Traffic was light, so she stepped on the gas, trying to get away from the paps before they had a chance to get in their car and follow her. Of course, they would probably just go back to her parents' house anyway, but she at least wanted to get there first so she could run inside without having to deal with them again or having her picture taken again. She needed to see whatever this video was and figure out how to handle the fallout with her PR team's help, figure out what her answers to questions would be before facing the paparazzi again.

To her relief, she and Dad did make it back to the house before the *Glitz Report* people and rushed inside with the food before anyone messed with her again.

When she and Dad walked into the kitchen, Abuelita and Mom were sitting at the small breakfast table having coffee, Chewie in his usual spot on her mom's lap. He usually still slept with Piper at night, even though her mom was his go-to lap during the day. But since Piper and Grant had been no-shows for the rest of the afternoon and evening yesterday, Chewie, Piper assumed, had slept with her parents. Probably on the bed with them instead of his usual bed in his purse/pet carrier, where he normally felt the safest.

It was almost six now. Maddox and Raquel would probably sleep for another few hours, and Julián and Hannah probably wouldn't get here until later, either. Piper was glad. If Grant had said something derogatory about her weight in the video, she didn't want the first time she watched it to be in front of everyone, especially Raquel. She didn't want to watch it in front of Abuelita or her parents, either, but she might as well get it over with. They would see it anyway, if what that paparazzo had said was true.

The expressions on her and Dad's faces must have been

dire, because Abuelita and her mother both frowned with concern.

"*Mija*, what's wrong?" asked Abuelita as she set out a few tacos and then got up to turn the oven to a low temperature to keep the rest warm for later.

Piper shook her head. "I'm not sure."

Abuelita sat down at the table again, and both she and Mom looked to Dad for an answer.

Casting an uneasy glance toward Piper, he said, "Paparazzi hassled us at the bakery."

Mom tilted her head in dismay and pursed her lips. "Oh, no."

Abuelita muttered a curse word in Spanish under her breath.

"Something about a video," said Dad.

Now the same uneasiness on her dad's face was also on Abuelita's and Mom's.

Piper was already searching for the *Glitz Report*'s Twitter feed and soon found it. The tweet above the attached video said, "*TGR* exclusive: Grant Cammish calls girlfriend Piper Torres 'lazy slug' in workout video with celebrity trainer @JasonMcMuscle." Feeling numb, Piper clicked on the video link.

It was mostly Jason talking at first. Grant sat on a bench drying his face and his sweaty, curly black hair with a towel. Even though she had a pretty good inkling her heart was about to be smashed to smithereens, the stupid organ still leapt at the sight of him. His body was even more sculpted than his trainer's.

Jason was putting away weights, talking to Grant as he did so.

*"You should put in a good word for me with Piper," said Jason. Grant didn't respond. His head was bowed, his face buried in*

*the towel. The clanging of weights by others in the gym was a distant noise in the background.*

*"She would listen to you."*

*Grant was still hunched over.*

*"Right?" Jason prompted.*

*Finally, Grant pulled the towel down and looked at Jason, his expression unreadable.*

*"I mean, seriously, she could use a professional trainer. I'm surprised she doesn't have one. I'm sure she could afford it. She's lost some weight, but I could help her do it so much faster and efficiently. I mean, she's a cute girl, but she could still stand to lose a few—at least if she wants to get anywhere in this business."*

*"Mm-hm," Grant said absently.*

That deceptively simple response tore into Piper, shredding her insides with monstrous claws.

*"I mean," Jason went on, "everyone wants to have a great body, but no one wants to put in the work—the sweat, the strict diet, the pain. It takes discipline."*

*Grant seemed to come alive at that and spoke with intensity. "No. You can't be lazy. You can't be a slug."*

Piper couldn't help but gasp when she heard those words, possibly the most demoralizing words he could have ever chosen in reference to her. He *had* to have heard how people had used that to describe her and make fun of her. He *had* to know the history. Everyone on the planet did. He *had* to know how much they would hurt. Yet he'd tossed them out as if they were no big deal, as if not caring that he'd just reopened a very nasty old wound of hers.

*Jason walked toward the camera. "I think it's great you're dating her, though. Shows you've got depth, dude, that looks aren't the only thing that's important to you."*

It ended there, with Jason commending Grant for basically taking her on as a charity case.

Rage enveloped her, scorching and brutal, roasting her face and body. She welcomed it. She'd much rather feel this than the crushing hurt and betrayal she knew was to come.

"Now, *mija*," said Abuelita, "let's think this through. Maybe this trainer guy edited the video to make Grant look bad or something. I just can't believe Grant would knowingly say such things about you."

Piper shook her head. "No, Abuelita. Those words..." She shook her head again. "Those specific words. If he'd just called me fat, that would be one thing, but to use the words that *puta* Briony Callas called me were specific to me. He had to know what he was saying." Her throat closed, and it was suddenly hard to speak. "Yet he said them anyway. There's no way that was edited." It burned, this anger. She hadn't blown her top outwardly yet, but she was about to.

"But, *mija*," said Abuelita. "I've seen how he looks at you. Trust me, he's attracted to you, and why wouldn't he be? You're a beautiful girl, and I'm not saying that because I'm your grandmother. He can't keep his eyes off you. I think there's more to this story. Give him a chance to explain. Maybe it was taken out of context."

"You're just taking up for him because he's blinded you with his looks just like he does every woman on the planet."

"No—"

"Don't fall for it, Abuelita. He's like a chocolate Easter bunny: tempting shell on the outside, hollow on the inside."

"There's more to him than that," Abuelita said stubbornly.

Piper's parents hadn't said anything, as if they were processing it all and hadn't made a judgment yet.

"It's over. I'm flying to LA the next flight I can get out. I don't want to attract more paparazzi here to you guys."

"Don't you worry about that," said Dad. "We can handle those *pendejos*."

She appreciated his willingness to deal with the media, but she wasn't going to put them through that. She would tell Grant to get out as quickly as possible too. Not that he'd want to hang out with her family once she was gone. They wouldn't want him around either—well, maybe Abuelita would. And Raquel. But her brothers and parents would probably make things very uncomfortable for him.

"I need to get with William and Cynthia, figure out how to handle this." It helped that her mind was racing now, that she had to come up with a plan. It helped her table her rage and hurt for the moment.

"I'm going to pack," she said, and didn't wait for anyone in the room to protest before she walked out the back door and headed toward the *casita*.

She had to get out of here, away from San Antonio—as far away from Grant Cammish as she could, at least until he made it back to LA. And thank God LA was a huge city. First, though, she had a video to show him.

He awoke when the door downstairs slammed. He reached for Piper, but her side of the bed was empty. Ah, yes. He had a vague memory of her kissing him on the lips before she'd got up earlier.

Footsteps trudging up the stairs that lead to the first floor (or second floor, as Americans called it) where he lay abed reminded him more of the giant in *Jack and the Beanstalk* than Piper. *Fee, fie, foe, fum.* He'd not have thought she could make such noise with such a diminutive body.

He smiled to himself. She was normally quite graceful. His sword fight with her came to mind. God, those calves of hers, among other assets, had been exquisite, her speed quick and potentially deadly. And now the morning wood he'd awoken with was turning into a proper Vlad. He hoped Piper would soon help him remedy the situation.

He turned onto his back, rested his hands behind his head, and waited for her to come in, find him awake, and ravish him—or, rather, they could ravish each other like they had yesterday. It had been so...well, there were no words. Suffice it to say, the proper amount of pleasure had been achieved on both sides. As bed partners went, she was his perfect match.

She was his perfect match in other ways, too. He was glad they'd finally opened up to one another. She was everything he fancied in a woman: smart, beautiful, charming, funny, into family. He wondered if she'd want loads of children. He hoped so, but it wasn't a deal breaker. He would settle for two or three.

The alarm bells that usually went off when he had these sorts of domestic thoughts were silent, and he thought with satisfaction that it was about time.

Yes. If she wanted to take things slowly, get to know one another better than they already had in the last two and a half months, he was okay with that. He had no problem proving to her that he was different, that he wasn't his bloody brand.

All he wanted was a soulmate and a family of his own. His gut told him Piper wanted the same and that he'd finally found his person.

In the next second, she burst through the door doing an excellent portrayal of what he imagined Heledd, Welsh warrior princess, would be like if she were *massively* pissed off.

He had no idea what was wrong, but it was clear something had upset her. And from the way her gaze was skewering him, he had the feeling he was the culprit. He racked his brain for something he might have done or said but couldn't remember anything. Of recent times, at least.

She stared at him a moment, her nostrils flaring. He could see her breathing, which caused her lovely full breasts to rise and fall.

Sitting up, he said, "What's wrong, love?"

"Check your phone," she said, eyeing the apparently offensive object lying to his right on the nightstand. "I just texted you a link."

He'd not heard the notification. Or maybe he had. Maybe it was what had awoken him instead of the door. Warily, he reached for his phone and clicked on the link. It was a video, and as soon as it began, his heart dropped like a telly he'd once seen thrown from the top of a building on, well, a TV show.

The video was the conversation he'd had with Jason. The one where he'd agreed with Jason about people having no right to whinge about being fat if they were lazy in the exercise and diet department. The conversation he'd not been paying attention to at first. The one he'd not known was about Piper. The one where he'd not fucking realized until now that Jason, his trusted trainer and friend, would use against him.

The part of the conversation that had gone on well after this video ended, the one where Grant had defended Piper and made sure Jason knew how attractive he found her, wasn't there. Only the parts that made him look like a complete prick.

When he looked up and met her eyes, the pain and betrayal he saw there finished off his heart. It was now lying in a million pieces on the tarmac next to that smashed-up telly. "I can explain this."

She went over to her suitcase and began refolding the clothing in it. "Don't bother."

"This isn't the whole conversation. I defended you. I told him how attractive I find you. And I didn't—" He cut himself off with a growl of frustration, raking a hand through his hair and aggravating the sore spot on his scalp. He knew how implausible this was all going to sound to her, but he had to try.

Her back was turned to him, her movements feverish as she packed her things.

His morning wood unfortunately no longer a problem, he got up, quickly slipped on the black cotton boxers that were lying on the floor, and went to her, putting his hands on her shoulders.

She tensed, then shook him off. "Don't."

"Piper, look at me."

She ignored him.

"Bloody hell." Desperate to make her hear him, he touched her shoulders again, then turned her round to face him before she could think to react. "Listen to me," he said, looking down into her eyes and holding her attention captive. "I was only half listening to Jason in the beginning, plus all the clanging of weights made it hard to hear. He prattles on about people all the time. I always ignore him. It wasn't until later, *after* the part of the video you saw, that I even realized he was speaking of you. I swear to you that I was angry once I knew he was referring to you. I *never* would have said those things about you. I swear to you. I was just talking in general terms."

"Really? So you're saying using the words 'lazy' and 'slug' weren't about me?" Her voice was saturated with skepticism.

That took him off guard. "No. Of course not. They just popped into my head."

"Oh, really? So the fact that Briony Callas basically made those words a catchphrase about me on social media had nothing to do with what you said?"

He frowned, trying to remember what she was talking

about. "I never paid attention to any of that. Before I met you, you were hardly on my radar."

"Gee, thanks."

"Well, did you pay attention to what went on with me or my career before we met?"

"Some," she said, but there wasn't a lot of conviction behind it. "I knew the basics." Her chin lifted a bit, as if more certain. "I knew some of the gaffes you'd made in interviews. Like, for instance, dissing on plus-size models."

He rolled his eyes. "Lovely. We're bringing that ancient history up, are we?"

"It suddenly seems extremely relevant," she said pointedly.

Bollocks. He again held her gaze. "Piper, I swear to you I barely know who Briony Callas is. I only know her name because Jason has mentioned her once or twice. I've never once looked at her social media and certainly never paid attention to what she said about you. And as for the model comments, I was a knob back then. I shouldn't be held to something I said when I was a young fuckwit."

"So you're telling me you just pulled the words 'lazy' and 'slug' randomly out of thin air, and that you didn't know Jason was talking about me?"

God, when she put it that way, he really did sound guilty, but he hoped truth would win in the end. "Yes."

She eyed him dubiously. "You'll forgive me if I think you're full of shit."

Clearly he was not winning, but he had to carry on trying. "I was exhausted. It was after my workout, and Jason had just worked my arse off. You know how hard I work, how strict I am, the discipline I have. People admire my physique but scorn me for the time and sacrifice it takes to maintain it." He cringed inwardly, knowing he sounded exactly like vain, muscle-headed Jason in that moment. Still, he kept on, hoping she would somehow understand. "It makes me bitter, the unfairness of it. Being fit doesn't happen by magic. That's what you saw in that video. I was speaking in general terms, not about any particular person—especially, for fuck's sake, not you."

The ire in her expression didn't change.

He wasn't getting through to her. "Piper, how can you doubt me? You know how videos can be manipulated, how things can get taken out of context, especially by the vultures. There's more to that video that he cut off. I can't be certain, but I think the camera was still on when I praised you and defended you. There's no telling how much Jason made off this edited version of the video—much more than he would have if he'd sold them the whole thing in its entirety, I can assure you. My defense of you wouldn't have been nearly as interesting as my supposed insult of you is."

Tears welled in her brown eyes, and she quickly wiped them away before they could slide down her cheeks. "I want to believe you."

"Then do so." He cupped her face in his hands. "Remember what I said about you having the power to obliterate my heart?"

She didn't respond, just watched him, still wary.

"If you believe this drivel over me, that's exactly what will happen. I'm asking you after everything we've shared in the past few hours—in the past few months—to believe *me* and not *him*."

She seemed to waver for a moment but then tugged on his wrists, pulling his hands away. "I'm sorry. I saw it with my own eyes. Yeah, maybe there's more to it, but even if the video was edited or whatever, you're *right there* saying those words, right after he was so clearly talking about me. How could you not know? Even if you didn't hear my actual name, the context of it is clearly about me. People made fun of me with those exact words you said, Grant, and they did it for over a year. Again, how could you not have known?"

He inhaled deeply, trying to cleanse the sick feeling inside him, and went through his defenses again. "As I said, I was only half listening. I always tune him out when he natters. I was going over lines in my head. I wasn't listening to a word he uttered until he commanded my attention. There were weights clanging all around me, which made it hard to hear. Neither you nor Briony Callas has a monopoly on the terms 'lazy' or 'slug' when referring to issues of fitness or lack thereof, and you're not the only people to have used them thus." Unable to keep the frustration from his voice, he said, "Will any of those do?"

"No."

"Christ. I didn't hear your name, and I've never thought of those words relating to you ever!" Instantly he wished he'd not shouted that.

Anguish contorted her face, and her voice was wobbly when she spoke. "But you did just that in that video."

A lump the size of the western United States choked him hard. His voice went raw with regret. "I would never knowingly say them about you. I swear to you I didn't know they'd been used to malign you. They just bloody popped into my head—possibly the most unfortunate coincidence in the history of man. And, again, *I didn't know he was talking about you*."

She shook her head and turned back to her suitcase, but not before he saw a new batch of tears she didn't bother to wipe away.

Fuck. He couldn't take this. It was hurting him more than it was her, even though she would never believe that:

the injustice of it, the betrayal by someone he trusted (and paid loads of bloody money to every month), the fact that the woman he cared about so much was hurting, the irony that it didn't have to be so if she would just believe him. Believe *in* him.

"Let's work through this," he pleaded.

"No. I'm taking a nine o'clock flight back to LA."

Now panic added itself to the stew of emotions scalding his insides. "No. Don't. That's the worst thing you could do."

Her voice was stronger now. She seemed to have mastered her feelings. "I need to get away from here, from you."

Good God, how wrenching that was.

"Plus," she added, "I don't want to bring a shitstorm of paparazzi down on my family."

He muttered another curse. That hadn't yet occurred to him, that her family would be harassed. Not that he'd had time to digest the ramifications of all this. He was utterly gobsmacked.

"You need to leave, too."

"Of course."

"Aside from the paparazzi issue, my family won't want you around."

Of course they wouldn't. They would probably hate him now. It was another strip skinned off his hide. He'd not felt so at home with anyone in so long, but Piper's family had almost felt like a surrogate for his. Now he was losing them along with her.

"The sooner we can both get out of here, the better," she said in a flat tone.

"At least fly back with me on the private jet. I'll see if I can get our departure moved to today."

"No."

"I've still got the head injury," he said, jabbing a finger at his head. It was playing dirty, since he'd felt more than fine this morning, but desperate measures and all that. "I shouldn't travel alone."

She paused in her packing, holding a cream-colored sweater in her hand, one he remembered her looking particularly luscious in. "You're doing fine," she said cautiously. "Just sleep the whole way like you did coming here. Plus, you'll have the pilot. You won't be alone."

"You forget I had a massive headache just last night."

The almost imperceptible guilt that flashed across her features gave him a frisson of hope, but it didn't last. Her features went back to that combined look of indifference and steel he knew hid a wealth of emotion—probably mostly anger at him—just underneath the surface. "Take some Tylenol. It seemed to do wonders for you last night." Her words dripped mockery like an ice cream cone in summer.

He ran his hands through his hair again, this time not caring when he touched his wound. The pain of it was nothing compared to what was happening to his heart right now. "That's it? You've been coddling me for the last week and a half, but now it's 'Take a bloody Tylenol and Bob's your uncle'?"

"My uncle's name is Mike."

He bit back another curse. She knew what he meant and was being deliberately obtuse.

She wadded up the sweater, along with a bra, underpants, and a pair of jeans that she'd grabbed, and pressed them against her chest. "I'm going to take a shower."

"This isn't over, Piper."

Almost to the door of the loo now, she said over her shoulder. "It is. I was stupid to think it would work. We go together like oil and water. Or chalk and cheese, in your language."

"Funny," he said, with sarcastic lightness. "I would have said tea and biscuits. Or, considering our location, tortilla crisps and salsa."

She exhaled through her nose and turned to fully face him once again, the clothing still clutched to her chest. "It's chips. Tortilla *chips*. And it's not just about the video."

"Then what else is it about?"

"It's about me being me," she said. With her chin, she indicated her body, which was thoroughly hidden underneath the layer of baggy leisure wear she wore. Her eyes ranged over him, reminding him that, except for his boxers, he was all but naked. "And you're...you."

"I see. So perhaps the video is just an excuse for you to end things before they've really got started."

"What's that supposed to mean?"

"It means *you* are the one who has issues with your body, not I."

"Whatever."

Not exactly a denial. He walked closer to her, filling up her personal space so she would be forced to listen to him. "Let's get real, shall we?" He was probably about to make things worse, but since when had that ever stopped him? "I think you've this daft notion that we're not equals or something, that eventually I will tire of 'pity fucks'—your thoughts, not mine—"

Face ruddy red and gaze incandescent, she said in a ragged voice, "I have never thought you were pity fucking me."

"Haven't you? Remember, I'm me and you're you. I'm a Roman gladiator or some such rubbish, while you're just ordinary, correct? So either you believe I'll rut with anyone who has an orifice in their nether regions, or I've just been doing you a favor by deigning to shag you."

"You're an asshole."

"I believe the tabloids have already beat you to that sentiment many times over. Now, let's get back to it, shall we?" He moved in closer so that they were sharing the same air, the same heat mingling between their bodies, and willed her to believe him with every fiber of his being. "Let's be clear once and for all: I am madly attracted to you *just as you are*. I don't want you to lose a few more pounds. I do not, for the love of God, think you are lazy or a slug."

"You sure about that? You're the one who pointed out at our first dinner how I splurge-eat too much."

"No. Not what I said exactly. You just took that out of context. I would expect better from you."

She looked as if she wanted to argue.

He didn't let her and pressed on. "I don't want you to lose *any* pounds. I find it ludicrous that anyone would even suggest it to you." He stroked her rosy cheek—albeit rosy with rancor—and said softly, "How many ways do I have to tell you I don't want anyone else? I don't want some bony supermodel, nor do I want a wispy yet bitchy shrew like your sister."

"The video indicates otherwise."

"Bugger the video. Believing it and not me just gives you grounds for your self-fulfilling prophecy, doesn't it? That we never stood a chance. And you've just been handed a reason on a silver platter, haven't you?"

Her face was almost wistful, but she sounded defeated when she said, "I saw you say it, Grant. I can't get past that. Maybe with time..." She shook her head. "I don't know. I need to think." With that, she retreated into the bathroom and slammed the door shut with her foot, literally shutting him out.

Hot fury and a jagged helplessness blasted through him. "Fuck!" he yelled at the top of his lungs, just barely refraining from kicking the door.

Of course, that did nothing to persuade her to open it.

## 27

G rant's life was a complete balls-up, and it was all to do with that bloody video Jason had released.

Now Grant could add "fat-shamer" to his list of real and/or perceived transgressions. Anything he'd ever said that could be remotely connected to such a sentiment had been dredged up. He was now universally hated by women the world over—and Piper's fan base was particularly rabid over his inadvertent insult to her.

His Q Score had plummeted.

The Captain Justice role was now out of the question. Not surprisingly, he'd been offered the movie's villain role instead. Jessica had encouraged him to take it. The money had been good. But he would essentially be playing the same character he played on *Battle*, except that the villain in *Captain Justice* was more diabolically insane in that way comic book characters tended to be more over-the-top. But even the fact that this character would be fully clothed throughout the whole film held no temptation. Grant wanted no part of it.

He got out of his car and was tempted to slam the door

out of anger but refrained. It wasn't the Corvette's fault that Piper had sent him packing (literally) or that his career was going in the opposite direction from what he wanted. No, that fault belonged to Jason, and he was about to show Jason what a proper villain looked like.

He caught sight of his reflection in the car window and didn't recognize himself. Holy hell. When was the last time he'd showered? He honestly couldn't remember.

He'd been living in a fog since coming home from a short Christmas holiday with his family in London, sans Piper of course. His mum had been disappointed but had accepted the excuse he'd given, that Piper had felt she needed to spend it with her family, since her grandmother was getting on in age.

Ha. What a piece of fiction that was. Abuelita would probably outlive them all. At least *she* was still speaking to him. She'd been texting with him on a fairly regular basis, the feisty old dear, encouraging him not to give up on Piper.

He told his family to ignore the tabloids and the stories that his relationship with Piper was in trouble. No one had questioned him, really, since none of them had any love for the media and how it had maligned him over the years.

Why he'd not just told them the truth, he wasn't sure. He supposed he didn't want them to think badly of Piper for not believing him.

He looked up to the sky. Judging by the position of the sun, it was still morning. He barely even noticed the passing of time anymore.

Oh, well. Morning was as good a time as any to settle a score.

The paps, who of course had followed him to Jason's gym, were shouting questions at him that he had no intention of answering. They were also snapping pictures of him

—pictures that would further solidify his villainous reputation when they were posted.

He did look rather maniacal with his unkempt beard, messy hair, and wrinkled hoodie—the one he'd slept in last night when he'd passed out from the scotch he'd drunk. He'd got proper pissed, and his bloodshot eyes and the bags under them attested to his hangover. His head pounded almost as much as it had when he'd awoken in hospital from his bludgeoning.

Ignoring the snappers still shouting at him, he stalked toward the front entrance of the gym with a singular purpose: to kick Jason Nagel's arse.

What would he gain from it? Nothing good, probably, except for a primal satisfaction that the bastard got what was coming to him.

Grant knew his actions might, at worst, get him arrested for assault. Or Jason would probably sue him. Or both.

But he couldn't bring himself to care any more about those possibilities than he cared that he'd not showered in days. There was a hollow place in his chest where his heart was supposed to be, and it was filling up day by day with a blackness he couldn't fight.

And really, why should he? No matter what he did, no matter how hard he tried to say and do the right things, his good intentions always somehow got sabotaged. Admittedly, it was often from his own mouth, but not this time. This time he was innocent. It was why he'd not issued an apology on social media—which had, of course, outraged people even more.

But they could all sod off. He didn't owe anyone anything. This time it was all Jason, and Jason was going to pay for his lies.

Despite Grant's stance on apologizing, he *had* made one

exception and apologized to Piper in several forms—email, text, voicemails—but to no avail. It gutted him she wouldn't accept his explanation, but he did understand how much that video had hurt her. And he had to admit that if he didn't know with a hundred percent certainty he was innocent in all this—apart from the disastrous fluke of actually saying the words "lazy" and "slug"—he might be hard pressed to believe it too. The evidence was difficult to refute.

He'd tried to be patient. He'd tried to give her time to do all the dreaded ruddy thinking she needed to do but still kept letting her know he'd not given up, that he was there when she was ready to talk—that is, until Christmas Day. She'd given a polite-but-detached, obligatory response to his "Happy Christmas" text. That had been it. She'd given him nothing else and had effectively crushed what was left of his waning hope. If the "magic" of Christmas couldn't bring them back together... Well, straw, camel's back, et cetera.

Perhaps his complete absence and silence would make her heart grow fonder. Or else she'd forget him entirely.

That possibility slammed into his solar plexus like a wooden post—and fueled his fury toward Jason.

When he entered the gym, he immediately spotted Jason flirting hard with a beautiful girl in a tight, cropped tank top and yoga pants that Grant knew wasn't Jason's girlfriend.

When Jason saw Grant, he had a smile on his face as if he were going to greet him as usual, but then the smile faded, either because he remembered his betrayal or because Grant probably looked murderous. At least he hoped he did. It was certainly how he felt.

He strode toward Jason and took great satisfaction when Jason held up his hands and stumbled back, almost tripping over a weight bench that he skirted at the last second.

"You lied," said Grant, almost on him now.

Jason shook his head, still holding up his palms. "I didn't lie. Everything on that video is exactly as it happened."

"There was more. You lied by omission."

"Someone record this," said Jason, his gaze casting about the room. "Is anyone getting this?"

"Where's the rest of the video?" Grant growled.

"What rest? There's nothing else." Jason had nowhere to go now, but he kept searching for an escape route.

Grant bared his teeth, cold rage coursing through him. His balled fists at his sides begged him to put them to good use. "You've ruined my life, you lying little twat. You've cost me the only thing that meant anything to me." He grabbed Jason by the front of his shirt. "Tell the truth, or you'll regret you didn't."

Jason looked directly at the rather slight guy who had taken him up on his request that someone film what was happening. "Are you getting this?" asked Jason. "He's threatening me."

"Yeah," said the camera-phone guy. "I'm getting it."

To Grant, Jason said, "If you hurt me, I'll sue you. I'll own you."

Grant tilted his head, for a second darkly amused by Jason's threat. Then he thought about Jason's betrayal and how desolate it felt to have someone you thought was a friend fuck you over so thoroughly. "I trusted you."

"It was nothing personal, man," said Jason. "It's just the business."

Grant let a bitter, rusty-hinge laugh escape. Jason had unbelievable gall. He'd give him that. "Yeh. The business. You're bloody right about that." Show business had never been uglier than in this moment.

He let go of Jason's shirt, and the sudden lack of support caused Jason to fall back against a nearby wall behind him.

Grant turned and walked a couple of steps as if to leave in order to give Jason a false sense of relief, but he had no intention of letting Jason off so easy. Without warning, he turned and punched Jason in the jaw with a right hook that was quite brutal, if he did say so himself. Perhaps it might be considered fighting dirty, but he'd learned back in his school days that when one fought with honor, one usually got one's arse handed to him.

Several of the people scattered about the gym gasped with an "Ooh!" of what sounded like wincing admiration.

Jason looked dazed as he sank to the floor.

Grant had a small qualm he might have broken the man's jaw, but that black hollowness inside him wouldn't let him muster any real remorse. "It was nothing personal, mate," he said, looking down at Jason while throwing his words back at him. "It's just...you're a fucking wanker."

Again, various noises and exclamations of surprise and "Oohs" came from the gym patrons.

As Grant walked away, he heard Jason spit what was probably blood and then slur, "Thanks, man. You just made me another million."

Ah, so jaw not broken then. Without turning back to look at him, he gave Jason the American version of the finger instead of the traditional two-fingered way Brits did it because he wanted to make sure Jason understood.

Then he swaggered toward the exit like someone who didn't have anything to lose. So what if he got charged with battery? So what if he got sued? At least justice had bloody well been served.

## 28

A little over four weeks after the release of the video, Piper was still pretty much a prisoner in her own home. In one stupid video, Grant had obliterated all her hard work to get her career back on track. Well, the video plus those horrible pictures taken of her outside Mi Tierra.

She didn't want to face the paparazzi who were camped outside her house, still begging her for comments. Cynthia had told her to get out there dressed to the nines, turn on the charm, and confidently answer their questions. More importantly, it was time to confirm her relationship with Grant was over (as if that wasn't already readily apparent).

Actually, it wasn't. Not to Piper. Until four days ago, Grant had called, texted, and even emailed her several times over the last month, but she'd never responded—well, except for that perfunctory "Merry Christmas" she hadn't been able to resist responding to him. She'd needed more time to figure things out, but she had to admit his persistence sometimes made her desperately want to forgive and forget.

But it didn't help that anytime she looked on social media—or any media, for that matter—the pics of her all decked out in ratty loungewear and coming out of Mi Tierra with two large boxes of pastries were all she saw. Talk of how she'd let herself go again, how her career was on a downward spiral, had reached a fever pitch. She'd gotten a lot of support from her fans, but the trolls coming out of the woodwork hadn't let her off easy. The jokes about the two pastry boxes had been brutal. The fashion bloggers had also had a field day picking apart her less-than-figure-flattering outfit and her lack of makeup, saying she looked like a ragged housewife who'd hadn't slept in three years.

And of course there were the never-ending replays of the lazy-slug video and all the chatter about it. That *puta* Briony Callas had weighed in by saying, "Who could blame Grant for simply speaking the truth?"

It must have been a slow news month, because nothing seemed to be knocking that freaking video out of the lime-light. Well, not until the video of Grant punching Jason yesterday had come out.

Thanks, Grant. The paparazzi staking out her front lawn had almost given up until he'd done that.

He'd already been shouldering the fat-shaming fallout, but the jaw-punching video had added fuel to the fire. All of Cynthia and Jessica's hard work, the fake relationship, it had all been for nothing. He was being skewered on social media, absolutely and universally maligned. It made Piper cringe, despite her confused feelings where he was concerned.

She'd been shocked by—and, okay, a little turned on by —his scruffy, roguish appearance in the jaw-punching video. She might or might not have watched it several times. He hadn't looked like the Grant she knew. He'd looked like a wrathful Zeus about to open a can of whup-ass on all the annoying mortals on earth—a Zeus who, by the way, was in dire need of a shower and shave, which wasn't like urbane Grant Cammish at all.

He could now add "violent bully" to the list of disparaging adjectives his haters on social media called him.

What had he been thinking? Last she'd heard, before she'd stopped looking at entertainment news and social media yesterday altogether, was that Grant had been arrested.

The thought of him in a jail cell made her feel nauseated. Her instinct was to defend him, to stand by him—to bail him out, even. But then his words from the lazy-slug video kept going round and round in her head in his condescending English accent: *"You cahn't be lazy. You cahn't be a slug."*

She'd heard them so often lately from others, she'd almost become desensitized. Almost. It was hearing it from *him* she couldn't seem to handle.

She sighed. Maybe if she hadn't been so thin at the beginning of her career, it wouldn't be such a big deal now that she would never get back to that size zero again. But so many people wanted to see that "makeover" success story that she was never going to give them, and they scorned her for not delivering it.

Or maybe it was more that social media gave everyone a voice—even those who would never be happy or satisfied with anything, those who just loved to hate on someone or some thing because it made them feel superior. It made those with pathetic, lonely lives feel important.

That was why she'd decided to be done with it. She didn't want the toxicity in her life anymore. Cynthia and William would probably say that was career suicide, but if they did, then they could start doing her social media posts. Or urge her to hire an assistant again to do them. Or dump her.

She'd be devastated if they did that. William would tell her she'd chosen to be famous, to be a public figure, so get over it. Building her brand was part of the job, so quit sabotaging her career.

Maybe sabotaging was her thing, though. Maybe Grant had been right. Was she sabotaging things with him before they could really get going because she was afraid? Was it her own hang-ups keeping her from forgiving him or believing him? She talked big about learning to love her body, but those niggling doubts she'd tried to bury kept digging their way out like little moles. A part of her just couldn't accept that he could truly find her attractive, even if the lazy-slug video had never come into play.

And his words on that video were so incriminating. On *video*. It always came back to that, didn't it? No matter how much Grant swore it hadn't been about her.

So here she was, moping around her house, keeping Postmates in business for food and grocery deliveries and decidedly *not* exercising despite all her protests that she wasn't lazy, that she led a healthy lifestyle.

"Argh!" she groaned, sitting on the couch and yanking at her messy hair. She hadn't straightened it in days, and it looked like a snarl of river weeds.

What should she do? Her pride said one thing, and her heart said another. So far, despite Cynthia's advice, she hadn't officially ended the agreement, and Grant didn't want to, if his voicemails and texts were to be believed.

Of course, his desperation to get her to talk to him might stem from the fact that he could kiss the Captain Justice role goodbye unless he could patch things up with her and somehow redeem himself.

That was the problem with everything in Hollywood: you never knew what was real, and you never knew anyone's true motives.

Another complication: time was running out. Grant was leaving for New Zealand tonight, even though he hadn't been scheduled to leave until next week. His departure had been moved up a week because of the Jason thing. According to Cynthia, the powers that be had all decided it was better to get Grant the heck out of Dodge before he got himself into any more hot water.

So if Piper was going to forgive him, it was do-or-die time. The ball was in her court, and not hearing from him since Christmas was making that painfully clear. If she did nothing, he would be gone from her life tonight.

It was the coward's way out, but maybe it would be easier for both of them. Only problem? The thought of leaving things as they were had misery and despair playing a vicious tug-of-war with her heart.

Someone knocked on her door, a different kind of knock than the occasional too-persistent paparazzo tried.

Her heart leapt, thinking maybe it was Grant. Maybe he'd come to speak to her one last time, and maybe this time she would listen.

Chewie, however, who'd been lying next to her on the sofa, remained stoic. He wasn't interested in whoever was at the door, which made her heart fall. If it were Grant, Chewie would sense it and would be wagging his tail and jumping off the sofa to greet him.

She paused the TV show she'd been streaming but not really watching and got up from the couch. She had a split-second thought that she looked like Medusa after a bender. Probably better it wasn't Grant after all.

As she neared the door, she heard a familiar female voice yell, "Hurry up, Piper. I'm being mobbed by *pendejos*."

"Raquel?" Piper asked, frowning.

"Yes." *Bam, bam, bam.* "Open up."

Piper sighed. This was weird, her sister showing up out of the blue, and the last thing she needed right now was Raquel's snark and gloating.

"Please," said Raquel.

Was that contrition Piper heard in her sister's voice? Surely she'd misheard. And what the hell was Raquel doing in LA? Of course, the only way to find out was to open the door, so she did.

Once it was open, Raquel stepped inside and jerked the door closed, shutting out the suddenly reawakened paps and their shouty questions outside.

"Oh, my God," Raquel said with a shake of her head. "You really need Jennifer Aniston and Brad Pitt to get back together or something like that to divert their attention. I can't believe they still give a shit about you and Grant."

"Thanks, Raquel. So great to see you, too."

For once, Raquel looked abashed. "Sorry. I just mean"— she turned her head toward the door and the melee beyond it—"that must really suck."

"It does." Piper had no right to complain, though, since she'd been complicit in creating it.

Raquel met Piper's gaze, and Piper waited for her to make a move. Piper had the urge to hug Raquel, despite how awful she'd been at Thanksgiving (Raquel hadn't come home for Christmas, which had been a relief), but Piper was afraid of being rebuffed again.

Raquel looked Piper up and down, lips pursed in disapproval. "Whatever you do, do *not* let them see you looking like this."

Tears instantly welled in Piper's eyes. She couldn't take Raquel's disdain right now, not on top of everything else. She shook her head. "Raquel—"

Before she could say, *Get the hell out of my house*, Raquel enveloped her in a tight hug. A real hug with real affection, not one of the tepid ones. "I didn't mean that the way it sounded," said Raquel next to Piper's ear. "I just mean they will crucify you even further if they see you like this."

Piper couldn't speak, but she knew Raquel was right. She nodded her head and clung even tighter, desperate for someone to hold onto, even if it was a sister she didn't get along with.

After several moments, Raquel finally pulled back enough to look at Piper. "Do you have any coffee?"

"Nespresso maker is in the kitchen. We can make macchiatos."

Raquel rolled her eyes, but it was good-natured. "Of course we can. I'm surprised you don't have a Jura."

Did Raquel not know her at all? She would never pay thousands of dollars for a coffeemaker, no matter how awesome it was. "I'm not that pretentious." Shoes and handbags, of course, were a different story. A girl had to keep up her image.

Raquel smiled wryly. "I am."

Was that self-deprecation coming from her little sister? Piper gave a tentative laugh.

This time, Raquel's smile was the genuine one that Piper hadn't seen for a very long time. Raquel put her arm around Piper's shoulders and said, "Come on. We need to talk."

They made surprisingly snide-free small talk while Piper made the coffees, and when Piper was sitting across from

Raquel at the small dinette table in her kitchen, she was ready to get to the bottom of why her sister had flown clear across the entire country to see her. "So spill. What are you doing here?"

Raquel shrugged. "I missed my big sister."

"Yeah, right. I can't believe you said that with a straight face. What's the real reason?"

"Abuelita and Mom made me."

Ah, so they'd given up on talking to Piper directly and had somehow talked Raquel into coming all the way out to LA to try her hand at persuading Piper. Abuelita in particular had lobbied hard for Piper to forgive Grant. He could do no wrong in her eyes.

Raquel took a deep breath, then exhaled, her tone wry again. "As you know, I'm always broke, so they bought my ticket out here. They said you were too sad at Christmas because of the shitstorm that video started and I should have been there to support you. They said I needed to start acting like a sister to you and stop being such a cunt."

Piper spit her mouthful of macchiato onto the table, then quickly wiped it up with a napkin. "What?"

Raquel laughed.

"They did not!"

"They did. Well, actually, it was Abuelita who said the C-word. Apparently she's been texting with Grant."

Ah, that explained why Abuelita kept taking up for him. Piper's heart did a funny tilt at the thought of Grant being nice to Abuelita (and apparently teaching her bad words), even though Piper hadn't given him any reason to. Of course, it could just be a different tack to try to get Piper to talk to him, but she didn't want to believe that.

"They also told me to make you come to your senses and start talking to Grant again," said Raquel.

"I wish it was that simple," she said glumly.

Raquel shook her head. "You can be so stubborn."

"He stirred up all that 'lazy slug' crap again, Raquel. I'm just supposed to forget about it, even though I saw him saying it on that video with my own two eyes?"

"Yes."

"Right," Piper said sarcastically. "I don't think so. And by the way, I know you didn't come out here just because Mom and Abuelita want Grant and me back together, so what gives?"

Raquel was dubious. "Have you met Mom and Abuelita?"

Piper just stared at Raquel and waited.

"Okay. Fine. I thought you might be hurting from all of this, and I wanted to be here for you."

"Sorry. Who are you, and what have you done with my sister?"

Raquel looked offended. "It's true."

Maybe it was, but Piper knew there was still more to it. "You've hated me for years, and suddenly you've had a change of heart?"

"I've never hated you."

Piper arched her eyebrows to convey, *You could have fooled me.*

Another minute stretched between them and then Raquel caved. "Okay." She pressed her lips together before saying, "I had a come-to-Jesus talk with Mom, and she made me see that I've basically been pissed at you for abandoning me when I was thirteen, at a time when I practically worshipped the ground you walked on."

Piper furrowed her brow. "But I didn't abandon you. I was eighteen, finally old enough to leave home and follow my dreams. I wish I could have taken you with me to California, but you were too young."

"It didn't feel that way. It was like you couldn't wait to leave me, and then you never looked back. You never even noticed those nights I cried myself to sleep after Aunt Gabby agreed to let you stay with her in LA. Then you got the sitcom, and suddenly you were everyone in America's sister and/or friend except mine. You didn't have time for me anymore, even when you came home to visit."

Piper should have realized this and was mad at herself for not seeing it. She'd thought DC was the problem, that living there had turned Raquel into a snob. She took Raquel's hand. "I am so sorry. I never in a million years would have wanted to make you feel that way."

An almost imperceptible wobble was visible in Raquel's chin, but she quickly composed herself, and then some of her trademark snark was back in her voice. "And then, on top of that, you got rich and famous, and I can barely afford to buy cereal. DC is so freaking expensive. My job might sound swank and important, but it doesn't pay shit." She smiled crookedly and then sipped her coffee. "So there you have it: I was pathetic and jealous. End of story. And I flirted with your famous, stupid-hot boyfriend, which is even worse. And he never flirted back, by the way. He was totally into you." More softly, she added, "I'm sorry I broke the sister code."

Piper appreciated that, and her heart felt a little lighter. She sighed. "Thanks for that, but don't be too sorry."

"What do you mean?"

"It was all an act, all the lovey-dovey stuff."

Raquel gave her the side-eye. "What are you talking about?"

"It was, literally, an act." Since they were getting everything out in the open, it was time for Piper to confess, too. "He was never my boyfriend. It was a publicity stunt put together by our agents and PR people."

Raquel looked shocked. "Shut up."

"Welcome to Hollywood." Piper stared at her coffee cup, both embarrassed and sad. "So you really don't have that much to be jealous of. My fake relationship is over, and my career is probably taking its last dying gasps. Not to mention I lied to my entire family, which I know was really shitty."

Raquel looked delighted. "Well, nobody's perfect."

"Thanks," Piper said dryly.

"It's just that I used to think you were. It's a revelation to learn you're human like the rest of us."

Piper snorted and felt her chest tighten. It wasn't too long ago she'd learned the same thing about Grant.

Raquel's expression turned skeptical. "I don't believe Grant was acting, though. There's no way what I saw between the two of you was fake."

"It's our jobs. It's what we do for a living. We know how to be convincing."

"Oh, really? So you're going to tell me you spent the whole afternoon and evening of Thanksgiving up in the *casita* with him running lines?"

Piper could feel her face blush. "He had a headache. I was just making sure he was okay."

Raquel gave her a skeptical look. "Mm-hm. Right. And it took you twelve hours to give him a Tylenol."

Knowing she was busted, Piper laughed.

"Girl, everyone in the family knew what y'all were up to. Probably even Baby G."

Piper put her forehead in her hands. "Oh, God. That's so embarrassing."

"And you know how else I know it was real between the two of you?"

Piper looked up. "How?"

"Because if your relationship had been fake, there's no way you'd be this pissed off at him. Yeah, you might have been for a few days, but then you would have turned on the diva and shown the world he was dirt beneath your Louboutins. Instead"—she gave Piper the once-over again—"you're holed up here looking like someone who's had their heart broken." She pointed her finger at her sister. "If I called *Merriam-Webster's* right now, they'd totally put your picture in the dictionary under 'brokenhearted.' And they would put Grant's picture right next to yours."

"Whatever."

"Uh, hello? I don't think he punched Jason McMuscle's lights out just because he was bored. And he did *not* look like himself. He basically looked like the guy version of you."

"All right, already. I get it. I look like crap."

"I can say it because I'm your sister, and I love you. And that's another thing I'm jealous of, by the way."

"What is?"

"That you're beautiful—when you're not wallowing, anyway. Sorry about all the fat innuendos and sugar references. Green-eyed monster talking. Can you forgive me for being such a bitch?"

"Done." Piper smiled. "I'm glad at least one thing has been set right in my world."

Raquel returned the smile. "Thanks for forgiving me so easily."

"I love you, little sister. It's a no-brainer."

With a telling look, Raquel said, "Don't you think you owe Grant the same courtesy?"

"That's different."

Raquel glanced at the ceiling as if looking for divine help. "There's more to the story. I'm telling you, he's been proven guilty with shoddy evidence. I just know it."

"How do you 'just know it'?"

"Because Abuelita said so." Her eyes were sparkling.

Piper smiled and shook her head. God, how she loved her family.

Growing more serious, Raquel said, "Give him another chance, Piper."

Piper wanted to so badly.

"I know he said the 'lazy slug' thing, blah, blah, blah, but you just admitted not everything in Hollywood is as it seems. Maybe that video isn't, either.

Piper couldn't argue with that, and things suddenly seemed so clear. She *knew* Grant. The real one. "Oh, my God. I've been so stupid."

"*Aaaannd*, my work here is done."

Piper's pulse started to thump. Widening her eyes, she gripped Raquel's hand again and said, "I should do this in person, but he's leaving later today for New Zealand."

"Then do it. He deserves to see it on your face that you believe him. And he deserves an apology."

"But he lives in Laguna Beach." Piper looked down at herself. "And I *do* look hideous. How am I going to get dressed and drive clear across the city in time to catch him before he leaves? It's the beginning of rush hour in LA. I'm so screwed."

Raquel scooted back from the table and stood. "No worries, chica. Your fairy godsister is here." She yanked Piper up, and they rushed toward the bedroom, Piper already throwing off clothing as they made their way down the hallway.

Chewie was barking at their heels. He didn't understand what was happening, but he knew it was something big.

And later, as Piper sat in her car on the 5 at a complete standstill, she wished her fairy godsister could fix the fact that she was in the worst traffic jam she'd ever been in since she'd moved to LA—and that was saying a lot.

## 29

G rant was standing out in his back garden—
"backyard" in American—looking over the cliff
where the ocean waves crashed far below. It was
evening, the sun already gone, but landscape lighting strategically placed on the cliff wall illuminated the private beach
below, and the garden and pool were lit with tasteful
ambient blue and white lights that gave everything an ethe-
real, peaceful glow.

He inhaled, breathing in the faint saltiness of the breezy
air. He could smell the sea even this high up.

He'd been vindicated, but it didn't feel like much of a
victory. The newest video—the *complete* video—had come
to light three hours ago, but still nothing from Piper. Not
that he wanted to hear from her because she'd seen it.

Barmy bloke that he was, he still wanted her to trust him
and believe him without the proof of his innocence that the
full video showed. He wanted her to have *faith* in him. For
once, he wanted someone to believe what *he* said and not
the bloody tabloids.

But it appeared that, even with the complete video

published, she didn't care. He'd have thought she would have reached out by now, since he knew Cynthia had told her about his changed travel plans, but no. All he'd got was radio silence. She had to have seen the video or at least heard about it. Surely someone would have called her or the snappers would have shouted questions at her about it. It was all over the place since it had been released. News traveled at the speed of light in these times of social media.

Perhaps she was having a hard time admitting she'd been wrong. That didn't seem like Piper, though. He would have thought she'd be bigger than that.

Perhaps she'd just decided to have done with him, that he was more trouble than he was worth. He couldn't exactly argue on that point.

Punching Jason had definitely landed Grant in more trouble than he'd already been in. It had only taken Jason's solicitor twenty-four hours to file a civil suit for the assault, and the police had come knocking on Grant's door only about an hour after Grant had served his justice (he preferred that turn of phrase to "battery of Jason Nagel"). He'd had to post a colossal amount of bail and had not got home from the clink until about noon today. Because he was bound for New Zealand—Derek was packing for him right now—the judge had made sure he had enough monetary motivation to come back for the adjudication of the matter.

Jessica had said not to worry. It would be taken care of in that mysterious way bad things seemed to be taken care of for Hollywood celebrities. Cynthia, however, had been beside herself when his arrest photos had quickly made it online, followed by the decidedly-not-on-brand mugshot that had been leaked and was now ubiquitous on the web.

But now that he'd been exonerated of insulting America's sweetheart/his "girlfriend"—and now that most agreed

Jason had got what was coming to him—Grant supposed things were looking up.

The corner of his mouth lifted in a half-hearted smile, which was more than he'd been able to accomplish since Piper had left him at her parents' house. Grant's solicitor wasn't quite as quick as Jason's, but Jason would soon be getting his notice that he was being countersued for defamation. The *Glitz Report* would also be served notice for their part in it all. Grant didn't care how much money he spent on legal fees or how much time it took in court. All he cared about was that Jason and that dodgy tabloid paid for what they'd done.

Grant had sent Jason's girlfriend Erica—correction, now ex-girlfriend—a hundred red roses as a thank-you. Apparently the lovely girl had found out Jason was cheating on her and, for revenge, had somehow got hold of the entire, proper "lazy slug" video and sold it to TMZ, the *Glitz Report*'s biggest rival. The part where Grant had made it clear he'd not known Jason was referring to Piper and the part where Grant had defended her and said how attractive he found her were all there for the world to see.

Grant hoped Erica had got paid twice as much for the truth as Jason had for the lie.

Jessica said this was just the beginning, that if Cynthia worked her magic and spun things correctly, Grant would end up being a wrongly accused victim instead of an arsehole. They didn't need Piper anymore. Cynthia could repair his damaged reputation without her.

It was nice Cynthia didn't need Piper anymore. Too bad the torture device currently beating in his chest still did.

How ironic that the very moment he knew he'd lost Piper was the moment he'd realized he was in love with her —utterly besotted, in fact. Then again, he'd fancied himself in love before, and he'd been wrong. Trouble was, none of those times before had ever been as excruciating as this.

But every cloud had a silver lining, or some such drivel. He'd finally taken a hot shower and shaved. He'd washed off days of heartsickness, hangover, and jail-cell scum, and he would never take being clean for granted ever again. He'd even dried his unbiddable hair into some semblance of order and put on a decent suit.

"Hey, jailbird," said a quiet feminine voice behind him.

The aforementioned torture device nearly stumbled out of his chest and over the cliff. Good thing his rib cage prevented it. He was hesitant to turn around, wondering if he'd imagined her voice.

She came to stand next to him, resting her arms on the top of the tempered glass railing that kept them from plunging to their deaths but didn't obstruct the view. She clasped her hands loosely together, just as he was doing. "When did you get sprung?"

If things were normal between them, he would be amused at her bluntness. Not wanting her to know just how much her presence affected him, how her presence had immediately put his emotions into a tailspin, he answered as if spending the night in jail were no big deal. "Noon. Lovely accommodations, although I can't quite recommend it."

She didn't seem horrified by his delinquency or his stay in the clink. Instead, she said, "Jason got what he deserved."

Ah. So she had heard the whole story, and she'd finally come. It made Grant feel jaded.

"I'm sorry you had to stay the night in jail. I hope you're not in too much trouble."

He shrugged. "Jessica's getting it sorted, and the charge

was entered in as simple battery, which is a misdemeanor. She says I'll get 'celebrity justice.'"

Piper gave a wry snort, as if that didn't surprise her. "It hasn't helped your image, though. It's taken a major beating. I'm so sorry for that."

Now that all the facts had come to light, it was odd she'd not noticed his image was on its way to redemption. He might have remarked upon it, but her scent wafted toward him, instantly making him yearn for her and muddling his thoughts for a moment. It felt like eons since he'd seen her.

Still, he was cautious. He didn't consider himself a petty man, but she'd hurt him. He didn't want to chat about his image or his legal problems anymore, so he changed the subject. "How did you get in here?"

"Rang the doorbell."

"Ah. Derek." So much for all the security measures that had been ramped up since all this had started. Of course, it wasn't like Piper was a paparazzo.

"Derek," she confirmed.

Since Derek had been witness to Grant's pity party with the scotch and probably a few incoherent mutterings about Piper, he'd probably thought letting her in might help.

"Don't be mad at him. I know he probably wasn't supposed to."

"I'm not angry with him."

"Good."

She wore a stylish, puffy black jacket and jeans. Her golden-brown skin was limned by the full moon and the landscaping lights, and her long dark hair, more wavy than usual, was down and blowing every which way in the strong, cold wind. A strand caught near the corner of her mouth, but he resisted both the urge to brush the silky strand away and to kiss her. Instead, he focused again on the tumultuous waves down below.

He could see out of the corner of his eye that she brushed the errant strand away herself. "If you'd answered the door, would you have let me in?"

"I don't know," he answered honestly.

She looked down, something like dismay in her expression.

Noticing she was missing her ever-present arm accessory, he said, "Where's Chewie?"

"I was in a hurry, so I left him at my house with Raquel."

That was surprising. "Your sister Raquel?"

"Yeah. Long story, not important right now." She exhaled a whoosh of air that was contrite. "What is important is that I'm sorry, Grant, for not believing you."

So he was right. She'd seen it, the full video, and only because of that was she now deigning to speak to him. "Ah," he said with more lightness than he felt. "You must be here about the video."

She frowned. "Well, yeah."

He waited for her apology.

"Oh, Grant. I'm really, really sorry."

Now that he'd heard it, he was mostly ambivalent.

He met her gaze and was struck again by how truly beautiful she was. Too bad it was so bloody hard to convince *her* of it. "Well, better late than never."

"I should have listened to Abuelita."

He quirked his mouth at that. Abuelita had been the only person who'd believed in him when all this started— apart from his own family, who were thousands of miles away in London. And they were obligated to be on his side. Abuelita was not. "Yes. Your gran is very wise. You should have listened to her. Or here's a thought: you could have listened to me."

Piper looked so earnest. "I know. You're so right, and I'm sorry it took me so long to come around. All I can say is that it was sort of like reliving the whole getting fired from *Nine's a Crowd* all over again. It brought back a lot of bad feelings I thought I'd put behind me."

"Understandable." But her words didn't alleviate the angry tightness beginning to take hold of his body. If she'd just given him the chance, he could have shown her in a hundred other ways how he felt about her. But she had not.

Instead, she'd made him wait, each minute of not hearing from her a special kind of torture. It had been just as bad—or worse, actually—than waiting to hear whether he was the father of Amanda's child. Not as long in terms of time, but, then again, the passing of time could be relative.

Again she was contrite. "You have every right to be pissed."

"Charitable of you, but I'm quite sober."

"You know what I mean. You have every right to be angry with me. Can you forgive me?"

"Of course."

She eyed him skeptically. "I'm not getting the forgiveness vibe from you, despite what you're saying."

"Tell me again why you came today."

"I realized you were innocent and I'd been a douche-canoe for ghosting you."

He raised a brow at her word choice. "But it took seeing the video to make you come round," he said, making absolutely sure.

Again her delicate brows came together in a frown. "Well, actually, Raquel helped me come to the realization I'd been stupid. But yeah, the video, too."

Interesting she was giving Raquel some of the credit. "Well," he said with polite dismissal, "I should be helping Derek with the packing and a few other last-minute what-nots. Thank you for the apology. Take care."

"That's it? You're just leaving?"

"Yes. What more is there to say?" And with that he left her standing at the rail alone, his heart having turned to marble. He could accept her apology, but he couldn't be with someone who would believe just about anyone else's word but his.

## 30

"**B**loody hell," Piper muttered under her breath, borrowing Grant's favorite epithet. She'd sensed she wasn't getting anywhere with him, despite his polite acceptance of her apology, and the fact that he was now walking away from her across his vast patio proved she was right.

Panicked, she ran after him, shouting, "Grant, wait!" When he didn't stop, she begged, "*Please.*"

He stopped, his back ramrod straight, the expansive shoulders beneath his gray suit jacket as stiff as a soldier's at attention. The wind picked up one side of the lower split in the back of his jacket, making it flap in the wind, but that was the only part of him that moved.

She maneuvered so that she was in front of him, feeling out of breath from nerves and desperation more than the fact that she'd just sprinted across the pool deck and patio.

Was he going to travel all the way to New Zealand in that freaking suit? Then again, maybe because of how off-brand he'd been for the last week, plus the hits to his reputation, he had to be totally on-brand today to be seen at the airport:

sophisticated custom suit with crisp white shirt, black tie, and the hint of a white pocket square peeking out from the breast pocket of his jacket. In addition to his impeccable attire, his black, wind-tousled (straight) hair and the remote expression on his handsome face effectively separated him from mere mortals like her.

She placed a palm on his chest, which felt like a brick wall. Grasping for anything to keep him from leaving, she said, "I heard about the Captain Justice role. I'm sorry."

"Wasn't meant to be."

"Still, I know it sucks."

"I really must go, Piper. I'm leaving in less than an hour for the airport."

"Please don't," she said in a near-whisper.

"Take care," he said again, stepping around her and walking toward the sliding electric patio door.

"Look, I know shutting you out was wrong, but I've apologized for that."

He kept walking.

Frustrated, she yelled, "Why won't you accept my apology?"

He stopped and looked over his shoulder. "Why wouldn't you accept mine?"

Ouch. He had a very good point. "I just needed time."

He faced her fully, the muscle contracting in his jaw the only thing marring the perfection of it. Then he said in a clear, raw voice, "It took you an eternity, and you're only here now because of the video."

The walls of her chest suddenly seemed to close in on her heart. "Oh." Not the most eloquent response, but she could feel his pain, how she'd hurt him, although she didn't really understand his comment about the video. "I guess..." Her voice came out odd, and she had to clear her throat. "I guess I wasn't much better than Amanda, was I, in the stringing-you-along department."

A slight tilt of his head and a bob of his Adam's apple was the only indication he agreed, but she knew she was right.

She began to feel shaky, and it wasn't from the cold. "Again, I'm so sorry, Grant. I wish I could go back and change things."

He stood motionless for a couple of beats, and then, all of a sudden, he stalked back over to her, his mouth a thin, hard line, his striking blue eyes glinting with silvery intensity in the light coming from the patio's overhang. "I thought you were different. I thought you *knew* me. I thought you would believe me, have faith in me. I *needed* you to believe in me."

Her eyes filled, and he shimmered before her. She could barely speak without losing it, but the words needed to be said. "It wasn't you I didn't believe in," she choked out. "It was me."

He looked away, that muscle in his jaw from earlier working overtime now.

Hoping she was finally getting through to him, she kept talking. Babbling, actually. "You're right. I should have completely ignored that video instead of getting mad at you. And it shouldn't have taken seeing you looking so ragey and punching Jason—and talking to Raquel, even though sometimes just talking things out helps—to make me realize my own insecurities were the problem. I mean, what you said to Jason, that he lied by omission—I know you probably took up for me, that he probably left something like that out. I mean, you even told me you did—take up for me, I mean—but I didn't listen."

Grant was studying her strangely now, perplexed lines in his brow.

She kept up the babbling, afraid if she stopped he would walk away from her forever. "I mean, knowing you, it was probably something scathing, your defense of me. Especially delivered in that pithy English accent of yours. Or British. Or whatever you usually call it. I mean, we Americans use 'English' and 'British' interchangeably, but I know the difference. Like, someone who's Welsh is still British but not English, right? I guess yours is really a London accent, right? Because I know there's all these different regions within the UK with all different—"

He held up his index finger to silence her. "Just to be clear, when you say 'video,' to which video are you referring?"

Now *she* was perplexed. "Well, I mean, there's the original one where I thought you said I was lazy and a slug, and then the one of you punching Jason."

"Just to be certain, you've not seen a third video, one that came out today?" His demeanor had changed. He seemed less hostile but still cautious.

Was he kidding? "What third video?" she asked. "Don't tell me there's another one." She rubbed her forehead with her fingers. Just the thought of another scandalous freaking video was exhausting. "I really, really can't—"

"Are you telling me you've not seen it nor even heard about it?" he demanded.

"A third one? No. I haven't seen it, and I don't think I want to."

His features morphed into wonder. "How is that possible?"

"I've been off-grid all day. I was sick of the toxic bullshit, so I turned off my phone. And then Raquel came over. And then I headed here."

"Extraordinary. You didn't even turn it on in your car to listen to music?"

"Well, yeah. I mean, I got stuck on the 5 trying to get here. It was rush hour, so it was like a freaking parking lot. I listened to Spotify, but you know I always have my phone on Do Not Disturb when I'm driving, so I didn't get any calls."

"And you didn't check it when you got here?"

She huffed. "No. I had other things on my mind, like groveling to you."

"I can't believe you've not seen it."

Feeling like stomping her foot but not doing so because she wasn't a three-year-old, she said with a very Mexican gesture of frustration, "*Por el amor de Dios*, Grant. What's the big deal about this third video?"

When he took a step toward her, a fierce look on his face, she felt like a bunny rabbit about to get eaten by a really badass coyote.

She stood her ground, although her pulse pounded.

Framing her face with his hands, he fused his lips with hers. His hot tongue was sinful, passionate, and deferential all at once as it raided her mouth.

Surprise, relief, and a bit of confusion warred with the instant feeling that her body was trying to hug itself—and him—from the inside out. She became greedy, wrapping her arms around his neck and pulling him closer, inhaling the peppery, wintry scent of him, which gave her an instant high.

Her other senses were filled with him too: her fingers touching the hair at the nape of his neck and the stiff collar of his expensive shirt, the thumping of his heart in her ears (or maybe that was her own heart thumping), the familiar

Aquafresh taste of him. Even his occasional puffs of breath on her face filled her with desire and delight.

She didn't know what she'd said to deserve this, but she wasn't going to look a gift horse in the mouth.

To her great disappointment, the kiss eventually came to an end. They were both breathing heavily.

Unable to go cold turkey, she brushed her mouth against his and lightly nipped his bottom lip, then smiled. "So, I'm really hoping that was an 'I forgive you' kiss."

One of his hands slid onto the back of her neck, and the thumb of his other hand traced her mouth. Then he pressed his forehead against hers, and she could hear the smile in his voice when he said, "That was a 'You believed me after all' kiss."

She still didn't understand. "Oh?"

He pulled back a little to look at her. "It bloody well took you long enough." Little crinkles in the corners of his eyes took the sting from his words.

"Okay," she said with uncertainty, still not under-standing exactly where he was coming from.

He released her but then took her hand in his large one and tugged her toward the outdoor dinette table under-neath the overhang. "Have a seat."

She obeyed.

Before he sat, he pulled his phone from an inner pocket of his suit jacket, then undid the jacket's top button with his elegant long fingers. After he was seated, he pulled up something on his screen and then handed it to her. "Press play."

She could tell it was the beginning of that stupid video, the cause of all their troubles—the one she'd seen a thou-sand times. "Why do you want me to watch this again?"

His expression was unyielding. "Press play. This one

came out on TMZ about three hours ago, about the same time you got stuck on the 5."

"I'd rather you just kissed me again."

His mouth lifted in the sexiest half-smile she'd ever seen.

Her insides contracted deliciously.

"I promise you, I will." He nodded toward his phone. "But watch this video first."

Okay. Whatever. She would humor him, although she wasn't particularly excited about watching something that had caused her so much pain and humiliation. She pressed play and began to watch, keeping her face carefully neutral when the parts that hurt came on. But when she came to the end of the video, it didn't end. It kept going after the part where Grant froze in the process of rubbing sweat off his neck.

*Grant's expression went from fatigue to incredulous outrage. "Sorry? Wait. Are you speaking of Piper?"*

*"Yeah. For, like, the past five minutes. Did you somehow miss that crucial part of the convo?"*

*"Apparently," Grant said in a hard voice. His shoulders came back, a scary intensity replacing the fatigue. "Because if I'd been listening closely, I would have told you that there's nothing wrong with Piper's body and that I find her whole person to be quite beautiful. She's healthy and doesn't need to change a thing."*

A *whoosh* of some wild emotion—gratitude, maybe? No. Love. It was love that stole Piper's breath in that moment and made her tremble. She covered her mouth with her hand, barely containing the tidal wave of feelings that were trying desperately to escape her.

*Jason held up his hands in surrender. "Hey, man. I'm not dissing your woman. She seems like a sweetheart." Jason moved out of the frame and went behind the camera, but he could still be heard.* "I mean, to each his own, right? Like I said, you've got depth. If you're into some curves, there's nothing wrong with that. But I'm just saying she's not your usual tall-thin-and-gorgeous supermodel, you know? Not that every dude in America hasn't dreamed of having a cool, fun girl like Piper who is low-maintenance, you know? Someone whose shit you don't have to put up with because she's so fucking hot."

A noise of indignation slipped out from Piper. "*Pendejo*," she muttered. She glanced up at Grant, who looked like he would like to punch Jason all over again.

*Grant rested his head in his hands as if to reset himself and tap into that legendary self-control and stiff upper lip he was known for. Letting the towel drop to the floor, he looked up at Jason. "Then perhaps you should try it sometime."*

"What's that?"

"Depth."

And *that* was the real ending of the video.

She scrolled down to the comments, more to compose herself than because she actually cared to read them. Most of them skewered Jason and were sympathetic to Grant. Already the catchphrase "Try it sometime: depth" was being used and hashtagged.

This might very well end Jason's career. She normally wouldn't wish that on anyone, but Jason pretty much deserved whatever he got.

As she met Grant's gaze, regret and shame now mixed with the overwhelming love she'd felt earlier. She said again, "Oh, my God. I'm really, really sorry."

He exhaled, as if relieved, and gave a short nod.

"I hope you'll let me make it up to you."

"Don't worry. I've plenty of ideas on how you can."

She grinned but then grew serious. "Thank you for forgiving me."

"Thank you for forgiving me. *Before* you saw this video."

And then she truly understood. "You needed me to believe you not because of this," she said, indicating what she'd just watched on his phone. "You needed me to believe you because hearing the truth coming from you should have been enough."

"Yes."

Her heart sank. "But I didn't. I mean, it took me so long." Guilt closed off her throat, and her next words were like needles being pulled out of her. "I don't deserve your forgiveness."

"Don't be ridiculous." He took her hand and urged her to come over and sit on his lap. "I'm no saint, as we and most of the world know. Don't think of it again. It's water under the bridge."

Her heart filled with love, and she had to let some of it out. Otherwise it might overflow into her chest and kill her or something equally dire. She hadn't wanted to be the first to say the L-word, hadn't wanted to be the one in the relationship who was more into it than he was, but maybe he needed to hear it. "Don't freak out, okay? I'm going to say something, but you don't have to react. You don't even have to say anything. You can pretend—"

"I love you, Piper."

"—you didn't hear it if—" Once her brain had processed what he'd just said, it jammed. She stared at him, wondering if she'd heard him right.

His eyes were suddenly hooded and fixated on her mouth. Or maybe it was her neck—that vampire in him coming out again.

Sparks shot through her veins. When she could finally speak, she said, "Um, did you just say—I mean, I probably misheard, but it sounded like—"

"I love you." He kissed that special place behind her jaw, just below her ear. "I love you." His voice was a whispery growl that was incredibly provocative. Then he kissed her again, this time a little lower. "I...love...you."

Okay. Much as this was firing up all her engines, it was also monumental. She took his face in her hands to stop him and peered deeply into his eyes, searching for any doubts.

He gazed resolutely back. "In case I wasn't clear, I'm in love with you."

She beamed at him, literally feeling as if her entire body was filled with sunshine. "I'm in love with you too, Geraint Gerard Nigel Cammish."

He threw his head back and laughed, and the joyous sound of it would feed her soul for the rest of her life.

## 31

They'd been on the South Island of New Zealand for four months. Piper had fallen in love with the country: its stunning scenery, its friendly and extremely polite people, its green-lipped mussels. Piper could have stayed there forever if it weren't for her family back in Texas. And also Chewie. She'd had to leave him with her parents while she was in New Zealand because she didn't have the heart to make him go through the routine ten-day quarantine New Zealand had always required of any animals entering the country. Thank God she had her mom. She was about the only person Chewie would accept as a surrogate for Piper.

There was also her career. Being in New Zealand wasn't exactly the best thing for it, but it wasn't like she was getting any calls for any acting gigs anyway. Even the Home Shopping Network thing was off the table now.

Of course, being in love with Grant—and him loving her back—helped to take most of the sting out of that.

She did want to find something worthwhile to do with her life, though, other than being Grant Cammish's significant other. Maybe she would become like Audrey Hepburn and leave Hollywood behind for a life of charity work. Grant had his animal charity thing. She just needed to figure out what she was passionate about. Then again, animals were always a good start.

Maybe it would be fighting to end world hunger. Or maybe she would start a foundation for homeless and down-on-their-luck actors—of which, sadly, there were many. The entertainment industry was a vicious, unsympathetic business.

She did realize how lucky she'd been, even if her career was now over. At least she'd made enough money to be set for life, which was no small thing. Grant had made it more than clear that he would indulge her every whim, but she didn't like the idea of being totally dependent on him. Not that she didn't trust him. She did.

His old toxic-bachelor, love-'em-and-leave-'em reputation was laughable to her now. All he'd ever wanted was to settle down. Well, maybe not when he'd been in his early twenties. But he did now, and if someone had studied him closely for the last seven or eight years—especially if you studied his social media posts—it was obvious he was a homebody.

Speaking of. They were both sitting up in bed in the little apartment they'd rented while the show filmed near Queenstown, and he was reading another fantasy epic—a giant hardback version. It was one of his rare days off, and they were having a lie-in, as he called it. He wasn't even going to do his usual workout until ten. Gasp. He certainly lived on the edge.

Piper was pretending to read on her tablet, but the book she was reading wasn't stopping her mind from wandering —or her gaze from wandering to Grant.

He must have sensed her watching him, because he looked up from his book, then smiled, exposing those minusculely longer canines along with the rest of his pearly whites. "What?"

"Nothing. Just thinking about stuff."

One of his dark brows lifted. "Such as?"

"The usual. What to do with the rest of my life. That sort of thing."

"Ah. Nothing heavy, then."

She smiled. "Nope. I'm thinking I'll be like Audrey Hepburn and just be known for my philanthropy."

"Just don't be annoying about it."

She knew what he meant: do it for the altruism, not for the publicity.

He leaned toward her and kissed her, his fingers combing lightly through the hair at the nape of her neck and his thumb caressing her jaw.

Her skin tightened with the pleasure of it.

When they parted and he was leaning back against the headboard again, he said, "Perhaps I'll be like Audrey, too. Or Jane Goodall or whichever one it was who lived with the gorillas. But not the one who was murdered."

"You don't have time to live with gorillas. You barely have time to sleep."

"Hmm. I've been thinking about that, actually."

"Thinking about your lack of sleep?"

"Yes. Well, more to the point, the cause of it—*Battle*. I'm bored of playing the same rotten character who never grows or changes. It's not about the money anymore—and ha. Wouldn't the tabloids love that irony."

He was referring to when he'd once been quoted as saying he was only an actor because the money was good.

His eyebrows came together in a pensive expression.

"I've grown and matured as an actor—and, I'd like to think, as a person—but I keep playing the same bloody villain. My contract is up after this season wraps in a few weeks. I'm not going to renew. In fact, I'm done, too. I'm fed up with all the rubbish in this industry. I'm fed up with not having a *life*. I want to have a pint when I feel like it and eat enchiladas every day of the week if I bloody well want."

She gaped at him, speechless for a moment. Finally, she said, "Are you sure about that? That's pretty drastic."

"Absolutely. You won't mind if I develop a Guinness gut, will you? And you *do* have your gran's enchilada recipe memorized, yeh?" His expression was hopeful. He'd discovered Abuelita's Tex-Mex cheese enchiladas with her special chili gravy, and it had been true love ever since.

Piper was amused at his deliberate avoidance of talking about his career. She wasn't going to let it slide, though. And she couldn't even picture him with a beer gut. It defied the imagination. "For the record, if you did get a beer gut, I would still love you. And yes, I have Abuelita's recipe memorized." It was about the only thing she could cook well, although not in New Zealand. It was hard to get the right ingredients here.

He truly did look relieved, though. He'd almost coaxed the Tres Leches recipe from Abuelita the last time they'd seen her. Almost. And everyone knew it was just a matter of time before she caved and gave it to him.

Piper set her tablet down on her lap. "Back to what you said about ending your career. If you're serious, that's a very big deal, Grant. Maybe you should think about it a little more before throwing it all away? I mean, I totally get what you're saying, but I can speak from experience. I told myself getting fired from my sitcom was maybe a blessing in disguise, that I would have a chance to broaden my horizons and get new, more challenging roles. Instead, all I've gotten is an offer to plug hair products on HSN. And now that's not even on the table," she added glumly. "I think I'm about to be dropped by William and Cynthia both."

He reached over and took her hand, giving it a squeeze. "Don't be ridiculous. You're an Emmy Award–winning actress, not to mention the fact that they both love you. They'll rep you till the end of time."

She shook her head. "My point is, not having any prospects sucks. But maybe being an actor just isn't my path anymore."

"Then we'll find a new path together."

God, the things he said to her sometimes slayed her. She tossed her tablet out of the way, took the thick book from his lap and got rid of it too, then straddled him. "You, Mr. Cammish, are one of the most romantic, sweetest guys I've ever met. How did everyone get it so wrong?"

His mouth twisted wryly. "In their defense, tact has never been my strong suit."

She grinned. "I love you."

He answered her with a steamy kiss that said in no uncertain terms that he loved her too. "Perhaps we should console one another over the impending demise of our careers."

"Console?"

"Yes. I'm taking it quite hard." He said it with a straight face, even as the boner she could feel through his boxers told her just what kind of "hard" he meant.

She giggled. "Does this lift your spirits?" she asked with innuendo, rocking forward and back over his cock.

"Quite. I appreciate your...vigor," he said in a strained voice, closing his eyes in pleasure. He said "vigor" like *vig-ah*.

She would never, ever get tired of his accent. This time she initiated the kiss. He quickly took control, though, and his tongue did magical things as it stroked and twirled with hers, things she felt deep and tight in her rapidly heating center—and lower.

Still, even though their actions were escalating to the point where her brain cells would be useless—especially when she felt his hot mouth on her nipple through her thin pajama T-shirt—she couldn't help but be disturbed at the thought of Grant completely bailing on his career.

But, as Scarlett O. was famous for saying at the end of *Gone with the Wind*...

Never mind. Grant was about to give Piper an O of her own, and she couldn't finish the thought.

---

GRANT ENTERED EZRA'S caravan without knocking and sat across from his desk. "I want to be written off the show."

Ezra raised a bushy gray brow, but otherwise he wore his usual unreadable expression. "Oh?"

"Yes. My character is going nowhere. There's no challenge for me as an actor anymore, and frankly I'm tired of being the resident arsehole and man-whore."

"What a shame. Just as I was going to offer the part of Heledd to Piper."

Grant stilled, letting that soak in a moment before saying, "Don't offer her the role just to get me to stay. She would hate that."

Ezra's smile was wry. "You overestimate your value to me, and you underestimate hers. She had the role the moment she doggedly guarded you while you were in the hospital."

Frowning, Grant said, "What are you on about?"

Ezra gave a nod. "She guarded you like a—well, a fierce warrior princess that day. And she was adamant you get two weeks off to heal." Ezra held up his hands in mock surrender. "She had me quaking in my Italian loafers. I knew in that moment she would be the perfect Heledd."

Outrage brewed inside Grant. "Why in bloody hell have you not told her? It's been almost half a year. She thinks her career is over, for fuck's sake. She's contemplating becoming Audrey bloody Hepburn—the philanthropic version—or some such twaddle."

Ezra shrugged. "It got put on the back burner with the crazy shooting schedule we've had. I've been meaning to have Harriet contact her agent."

"Have you not noticed Piper's been on set every fucking day for the last four months? Could you not have tossed her a bone?"

"Sorry. It slipped my mind."

That was bollocks and both he and Grant knew it. "You're a right bastard, you know that, Ezra? You withheld it to punish her, didn't you? For standing up to you. Because no one defies the great Ezra Vidmar."

This didn't seem to perturb Ezra. If anything, his expression confirmed it. Piper had to be taught a lesson.

"What if she'd got another offer while you were sat on your arse?"

Ezra tilted his head, derision in his next words. "I think we both know that wasn't going to happen."

Grant itched to punch the pompous douchebag. "If you think she'll kiss your arse like the others, you'll be disappointed."

"I look forward to sparring with her."

Grant ran a hand over his face in frustration, but not

because he feared Ezra would sexually harass Piper or anything like that. No innuendo had been in Ezra's statement. Ezra was a lot of things, but he wasn't one of the creepy director ilk. No, Grant knew Ezra had meant exactly what he'd said. He would look forward to sparring with Piper. As much as he loved his sycophants, Ezra also grudgingly admired someone who would be honest with him and not completely bow down to him—if that person were a hard worker and gave every scene his, her, or their all. Which, Grant knew in his bones, Piper would do.

"So go ahead," said Ezra smugly. "Do the angsty-actor-tired-of-selling-out thing. It would be a shame, though, since the role of Heledd is being created to, partly, reform your character. She was going to be your love interest. You two would certainly have the chemistry for it."

Despite his extreme annoyance with Ezra, Grant couldn't help but be a bit intrigued.

"Still want out?" asked Ezra, the glint in his gaze saying that he already knew Grant was having second thoughts.

"If I stay, I've stipulations."

Now Ezra was wary. "Like what?"

"No nude scenes."

"*Pfft.*"

"I'm quite serious."

Ezra sighed as if Grant were now supremely trying his patience. He steepled his fingers over his desk. "Don't make idiotic demands, Grant. It doesn't become you."

"Then I'm out."

"Be reasonable. It wouldn't make sense for Rolf to finally fall in love and then not have sex with the poor woman, especially a warrior princess with a lusty appetite."

"Sex can be implied. My bum does not have to be on-screen mid-shag for people to figure out what's going on. No more porn."

Ezra waved a hand in dismissal. "Let's not haggle over this point. The agents can iron out all these details."

"True, but I'm making it clear to Jessica what my terms are. There won't be much room for negotiation." Even as he was taking a hard line, the thought of getting to work with Piper lit a spark within him he'd not felt for his job in a long time.

Fingers still steepled, Ezra nodded. "Duly noted."

"And all this goes for Piper, too. I don't want her shown starkers." He knew that might be a deal-breaker. It was unheard-of in today's industry, but Grant didn't want people ogling her body.

Ezra's bushy brows came together. "Starkers?"

"Naked."

Ezra rolled his eyes as if Grant truly were an idiot. "And what if she doesn't agree to that?"

Grant wanted to say that she would, but the truth was he didn't know how she would feel about it. And perhaps his protectiveness of her *was* a bit unreasonable. Nude scenes were part of acting, however unpleasant they were to film. It was the nature of the beast. He sat back in his chair. "I suppose that is ultimately up to her."

Ezra nodded. "As I said, let's let the agents do the quibbling."

Grant took in a deep breath and exhaled. "I'll think about it. I need to speak to Piper first."

"Everyone loves a good villain who's reformed, Grant. It would showcase your range as an actor, and you'd be the good guy for once. It would be an epic love story."

Given how he felt about Piper, Grant couldn't help but laugh. "It already is."

## 32

---

Grant's house—correction, their house—had a six-car garage. Three of the bays actually held cars: her Prius, his beloved Stingray, and the new Tesla he'd bought to offset the fact that his Stingray had never met a gas station it didn't like. The other three bays Grant used for his various hobbies. It wasn't exactly a man cave, more like a man cavern.

That's where she found him now, messing around with a bunch of electronic parts on a folding table. His brow was knitted in concentration, and a curly lock of black hair had fallen onto his forehead.

She leaned against the doorjamb that led from the house into the garage, content to watch him for a minute, savoring this simple moment in time before their lives were changed forever. Chewie sat on standby next to her feet.

They'd worked together on *Battle* for the last two seasons. Fans had loved their contentious love affair, especially in this last season, where ruthless, battle-hardened, womanizer Rolf had finally redeemed himself and admitted his love for Heledd. She'd admitted hers for him too, then promptly shoved her sword through his belly after a passionate wedding night. After all, Heledd liked being the supreme ruler of her kingdom, and she wasn't about to share it with a man who might usurp her, even one she loved.

Fans had been shocked and outraged, although most said it fit Heledd's badass character. She had been Rolf's equal in every way—and ultimately his downfall.

In real life, Grant had wanted to be written off the show. He'd been offered the lead role in a new feature film based on his favorite fantasy novel series called *The War King Chronicles*, which was loosely based on the ancient Assyrian king Ashurbanipal. Yes, it was similar in some ways to his role on *Battle*, except this time he would be the hero. And it would be kid-friendly—hardly any bare chest scenes and no "arse" ones. The buzz around town was that it would be the next *Lord of the Rings*, Mesopotamian style. It was right up Grant's alley, and if the first movie was a success, it would turn into a franchise. The film studio would, of course, milk it to the last penny.

For her own self, Piper didn't mind becoming *Battle's* new resident villain. It was certainly a far cry from her role on *Nine's a Crowd*. She hadn't been called America's sweetheart in a long time, and that was just fine with her. She was starting to get offers for side projects that could be filmed in the off-season of *Battle*. She was interested in several of them, but she would have to see how she could fit it all in and still find time to keep her marriage strong. She and Grant had been married for a year and a half, and she didn't want to do anything to put their relationship in jeopardy—like being separated from him for months and months at a time. She was not going to be another Hollywood divorce statistic, especially now that she'd confirmed her suspicion: the pregnancy test had finally been positive.

Neither she nor Grant had wanted to wait to start a family. She'd just turned thirty-one and was feeling her biological clock start to tick, and Grant was more than ready for kids—lots of them, apparently. They'd been trying for what seemed like forever, almost since their wedding day.

She'd taken this last test on a whim. She'd thought it was really too early to detect anything, but she'd felt different the last couple of days, just had a niggling feeling, so she'd decided to take yet another one. She should have included Grant, but she really hadn't thought it would be positive. She'd only hoped, and they'd been disappointed so many times before. She'd wanted to save him the frustration.

Holding a copy of the *Glitz Report*'s most recent issue, she came up behind him, resting her chin on his muscular shoulder and wrapping her arms around him. Chewie had followed closely at her heels.

Grant's junipery, pepperminty, wintry, all-things-Granty scent mingled with the faint smells of cars, tires, and other man stuff. "What are you doing?"

He turned to meet her lips for a quick kiss, then replied, "Having a go at building my own gaming computer."

"That's adorkable."

His body vibrated with a chuckle, and his beautiful grin caused a surge of love to bubble within her.

He noticed the tabloid she held against his chest. "What's this?"

"Oh. I want to show you something." Still standing behind him, she tossed the issue onto the table and leaned over him to turn to the third page, then grinned in anticipation. He couldn't see her face because his attention was on a slightly grainy photo in the top right of the page. It was of her leaving a coffee shop and had actually been taken several weeks ago. In the photo, her lower belly was circled, and underneath was a small blurb: "Is Piper Torres gaining weight again? According to the latest rumors, no. This time, it's a baby bump. Sources say she and hubby Grant Cammish are expecting."

It was, of course, ridiculous that the magazine had printed this. First of all, it was an old photo, *so* last month. Second, she was in the best shape of her life. She didn't have a choice. She was on a physically demanding Netflix series, plus her husband was a health nut. Yeah, it did kind of look like she had a small belly in the photo, but she'd been wearing a baggy shirt over yoga pants. It also looked like the photo had been taken from a weird angle. In short, she looked a bit chunky in the photo, but it was just a trick of the camera. She hadn't been preggo at the time. It was typical, though, that the tabloid was making an announcement like this with zero evidence to back it up. Unnamed "sources" didn't count.

"Those fucking wankers."

Piper raised her brows, surprised at his vehemence.

"I'll sue them again for this," he hissed.

Although he'd won his case against Jason Nagel and the *Glitz Report*, this hardly justified a court battle. Still, she was touched he was so riled up on her behalf. Thinking she'd better soothe him quickly, she said, "It's really not that big of a deal. In fact—"

"It bloody well is," he said, expression thunderous. "Why is your weight so important to them? They just keep dwelling on it, even after all this time. It's preposterous. And to imply you might be pregnant. Whether you are or are not is none of their business." His jaw clenched, but after a second his face softened to concern and he took her hand, pulling her onto his lap. "I'm sorry if this hurt you. Especially the baby bit."

Holding in a grin, she said, "Actually, it doesn't bother me at all. I'm totally okay with it."

He watched her closely, a tiny crease between his brows. "You are?"

"Yeah." She couldn't hold in the grin any longer, and she knew the elation she felt had to be obvious. "Because the wankers finally got something right."

The crease remained for a moment as what she'd said sank in. Then he swallowed hard. "Good God. We're to have a baby?"

"Yep."

"Bloody hell." It was a good "bloody hell," though: he tilted his head back and laughed with a jubilant abandon that made her laugh with him. Then they kissed.

Desperate not to be left out, Chewie barked at them, wagging his little tail furiously.

Grant scooped him up and set him on Piper's lap. "Don't worry, mate. You'll always be part of the family."

And nine months later, Francisco Geraint Gerard Nigel Cammish made his debut into the world—with a black thatch of very, *very* curly hair.

# ACKNOWLEDGMENTS

Thank you to:

My parents, as always. I know I can always turn to you when I'm doubting myself, and you guys will lift me up. I love you.

Randy. Thanks for not complaining when my books lose more money than they make. Someday, honey, maybe I'll be in the black.

My two girls, one of which has recently flown the coop. *looks away with chin trembling* I love you chickadees to the edge of the galaxy and beyond.

My in-laws, for treating me as one of their own. Yes, it's true. I actually love and get along with my in-laws. They are the best in the world!

The fabulous Storm Navarro for the sensitivity read and the uber-cool (and funny) Maria Meagher for the beta read. Hopefully I got the Latina aspects of Piper correct, thanks to your input. If I didn't, the fault is my own.

My awesome, hilarious friend from London, Dallal, for answering all my "Do British people say..." questions.

Damojackson at fiverr.com for also making sure I got the British stuff right.

Christi Stanforth, the best editor in the world, especially for this book because her hubs is British.

Annabelle Costa. Thank you for being my critique partner and all your brilliant plotting suggestions. Not sure what you get out of this relationship, but I'm not looking a gift horse in the mouth.

My sisters from another mister, Ramona and Heather. Just because I can tell you girls anything.

The three anonymous betas from Hidden Gems. Your honest feedback was excellent and INVALUABLE.

# ABOUT THE AUTHOR

Molly Mirren loves being a writer. She also loves witty company, exotic food, creative cocktails, and obscure music. When not writing, she is doing laundry. She is also a firm believer in the Oxford comma and defends it fiercely. Long live the Oxford!

Molly also loves to read and will read almost anything if it holds her attention. However, the stories that pop into her head, so far, have all been romances. See the "Also by" page at the beginning of this book if you're interested in her other works.

Curious what Molly has on the back burner? Join her VIP list here: https://www.subscribepage.com/mollymirren

She will NEVER bombard you with useless info or sell your email to a third party. In fact, you may never hear from her because she's kinda lazy when it comes to writing newsletters

Molly would love to hear from you via social media, her website, email, or—last but certainly not least—a review at your favorite retailer.

You can find Molly:

On her website at https://mollymirren.com

Or email her at molly@mollymirren.com

Or on social media:

- facebook.com/mollymirrenauthor
- twitter.com/MollyMirren
- instagram.com/mollymirren
- bookbub.com/authors/molly-mirren